THE
GERMAN BRIDE

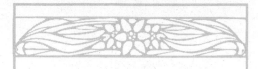

THE
GERMAN
BRIDE

a novel

JOANNA
HERSHON

BALLANTINE BOOKS

NEW YORK

Copyright © 2008 by Joanna Hershon

Published in the United States by Ballantine Books, an imprint of The Random House Publishing Group, a division of Random House, Inc., New York.

BALLANTINE and colophon are registered trademarks of Random House, Inc.

LIBRARY OF CONGRESS CATALOGING-IN-PUBLICATION DATA

Hershon, Joanna.
The German bride : a novel / Joanna Hershon.
p.   cm.
ISBN 978-0-345-46845-1 (hardcover : alk. paper)
1. Germans—United States—Fiction. 2. Family secrets—Fiction. 3. Domestic fiction. 4. Jews— Fiction. 5. Jewish fiction. I. Title.
PS3558.E788G47 2007
813'.54—dc22   2007032842

Printed in the United States of America

www.ballantinebooks.com

2 4 6 8 9 7 5 3 1

FIRST EDITION

Book design by Jessica Shatan Heslin/Studio Shatan, Inc.

For Derek, Wyatt, and Noah

The self forms at the edge of desire. . . .

—ANNE CARSON

PART I

BERLIN

HOLIDAY, 1861

FATHER HELD THE CHICKEN FEATHER IN ONE HAND AND the candle in the other. By the light of the small candle's flame, Henriette and Eva followed him through the house now that the day was done. They searched for bread or anything resembling it—cookies, cakes, biscuits, noodles, Eva's favorite things. Father dusted corners with the feather, while holding light to the darkest places to make sure each crumb was caught and placed inside the sack. As they gathered crumbs, Mother practiced the piano.

During the winter months Mother remained at home, but she more or less constantly played music, or else she withdrew to her rooms. When the season began at Karlsbad (where Mother took endless baths meant to have restorative healing powers), she brightened briefly before packing her things and leaving. And, as Mother's exodus was fast approaching, Father—made plainly cross by her eminent departure—became impassioned with religious fervor, which, no matter how often it was asserted, always seemed sudden. During the weeks leading up to the Passover holiday, he roamed the hallways after his workday and vigorously recalled his own dear departed parents with increasing devotion and righteousness. Father came from devout people and Mother did not and Passover was always the year's turning point, a time when Father and Mother displayed themselves just as they did now: Father focusing on the ritual task while Mother played a Mozart sonata. The music floated gently (if a bit unsteadily) through the house. Mother had already shared her love of the healing waters—the *Kur*—with her daughters and despite enjoying the pine-needle baths and the climbing tours (which ended with a delicious cherry tart), Eva could not imagine what could possibly be in Karlsbad that reassured Mother so deeply.

Father must have wondered, too. Eva knew, if nothing else, he longed for a more orderly home. The chaos of the kitchen usually sent him into a furious state (it wasn't unusual for Father to inspect the kitchen and find something amiss: a milk plate mixed in with the meat plates, a box of chocolates that Mother claimed she hadn't realized was there), but Eva preferred the fury to what increasingly looked like hopelessness. It was too much to bear Father's bald head in his broad hands; Father asking Mother—gently at first and then not so gently—why it was so difficult for her to organize the help who were for heaven's sake hired *because they were Galician Jews and weren't they meant to know a thing or two about keeping a kitchen?*

Eva imagined the servants' downstairs quarters, where she knew they'd be taking their supper now, probably too exhausted to converse. This morning Eva had helped Rahel and the others hang Passover linens out to dry with special wooden pins kept exclusively for the day. She thought of them now, all finishing their supper, and she couldn't help but wonder—if they weren't too tired—what they might have to say. A few years before, Father had insisted on hiring extra servants for Passover but Mother had refused, claiming she could only trust Rahel. But when Father prevailed and Mother compromised (agreeing to hire extra servants but *only Rahel's relations*), unflappable Rahel—having already told Eva that she had only brothers—produced several sisters, one after the other, all of whom looked nothing like her. Mother didn't seem to like Rahel very much but she always wanted her nearby, always called out for Rahel from the depths of her bedroom, where the curtains were usually drawn.

And—after years of refusing to eat in the Frank home because they didn't trust the kitchen—Father's devout relations were coming to the seder. Father had evidently said something quite miraculous to convince them. "Promise me that you girls will do your duty this year," he asked them solemnly over a month ago. "Your mother . . ." he said, shaking his head, and while Eva simply stared at him with nothing useful to say, Henriette took his hand and said: "Dear Father, of course." Henriette was four years older than Eva, and sometimes Henriette taught Eva fine needlework, discussing at length her favorite colors, which were subject to change any day, and when Eva didn't pay her proper attention, Henriette would accidentally poke Eva with a sewing needle.

Father didn't stop Mother from making her preparations for Karlsbad and Mother didn't argue about the kitchen. She said, "I'm sorry darling," to Father in the very same way she said it to Eva and Henriette when they questioned if she might not like to stay home. Mother gave dry kisses to her daughters—kisses that landed more on the air and less on their expectant cheeks—and Henriette had taken on the household responsibilities as if she'd only been waiting to be asked all these years. Eva was amazed to see how she didn't seem daunted at all. Her older sister actually seemed far more comfortable being in charge than Mother ever had been—discussing a schedule with Rahel and the "sisters," choosing not only her own elaborate Passover ensemble in advance but Eva's new clothing as well. And Mother hardly seemed to mind this loss of authority; her mood actually improved as Henriette ordered the appropriate crates out from the storeroom, dispatched servants to purchase *matzot* from the special bakery, the meat from the special butcher, the scalding cream for the pots and pans, and the kindling—stacks of it—for hearth fires as well as for this night's ritual burning of the *chometz*.

Father's footfalls were hypnotic in their placement on the stone steps, the wood floors. Eva had always enjoyed this ritual—the hunting, the quiet, the crumbs—but this year she realized her mind was wandering and the wandering came from boredom. Her sister was wearing a corset and her cheeks were flushed; she looked as energized as she had when, last month, her first suitor came to call. Eva wasn't sure why but she felt herself on the precipice of absurd laughter (her very favorite kind) and she was gratified to see that her smile was still contagious; Eva could see that, even in her most officious state, Henriette was smiling, too.

"Evie!" her sister whispered. "Why are you smiling?"

"Why are *you*?"

"Because you are!"

"I'll stop then," Eva promised. But it was too late.

"Please," insisted Henriette, but Eva could tell she too was about to break into laughter, and Henriette's was the best in the world; her sister went from perfectly proper to literally snorting with giggles. "Please, please, please," Henriette mouthed, as Father turned around and Henriette pinched Eva's arm.

"Girls," said Father, before turning down the guest wing hallway, continuing with the search.

"Evie," Henriette hissed.

When she saw that Henriette was truly upset, she vowed to pay closer attention; she swore that when the small sack was close to full of all of the remnants of bread in the household, she would be the one who volunteered to fetch the matches and Mother. "I'll be helpful tomorrow," Eva promised. She took her sister's hand.

"I know you will."

"You have such faith in me, Monsieur." Eva fluttered her lashes. Her sister had promised—she had sworn on the Torah—that Eva had nice eyes.

"Mademoiselle," said her sister, "I have no choice."

THE FAMILY STOOD OUTSIDE IN THE GARDEN. THE SEDER TABLE HAD been laid for the following evening, and Eva missed the linens hanging on the clotheslines like sails against the sky. Father struck a match, the kindling caught fire, and he poured on the bag of *chometz*. The crumbs and bits of cookie, the starchy odds and ends—they all burned away, and soon the Franks were faced with an extravagant flame.

• • •

WHEN HENRIETTE FOUND EVA IN THE MIDDLE OF THE NIGHT, SITTING at the piano in the music room, she gave an elaborate sigh before sitting down beside her.

"I can't sleep," said Eva.

Henriette nodded and patted Eva's back. "Neither can I."

Eva suddenly realized how lonely she'd felt, sitting in the dark by herself. It was often that way with her; the loneliness arrived only after she settled comfortably into another person's presence.

Her sister rambled on and it was a cadence as familiar as wind through the trees. ". . . I imagine it's because of the holiday, you know. I want everything to be perfect."

"It won't be," said Eva, and Henriette didn't bother responding. "Nothing ever is," Eva insisted, more or less cheerfully.

"You're a funny girl," her sister said.

"So you've said, Monsieur, oh so many times."

Henriette didn't smile and held out her hand. "What are you hiding?"

"What am I . . . ? Nothing," said Eva. "Nothing."

"What is in your mouth?"

Eva shook her head. She swallowed.

"Show me."

Eva produced the half-eaten cookie from her pocket. She had hidden it, over a week ago, in a box of sheet music and had taken it from the box only minutes ago. It had been her plan to savor it slowly.

"Why?" asked Henriette, and Eva couldn't tell if her sister was more curious or appalled.

"I'm not sure," said Eva, and it was true. When she hid the cookie, she'd been filled with a kind of glee, as if by breaking these sacred laws in secret she might have her own kind of revelry. Suddenly the taste of illicit cookie in her mouth was not moist with brown sugar and almond paste as she had so keenly anticipated, but instead it was chalky and bitter.

"Come," said Henriette. "We'll go outside in the garden and throw it onto the fire."

"It's too late," said Eva, but Henriette shook her head.

·

"Listen to me," she said, and Eva could imagine her years from now, presiding over a busy household. Her sister would have her own little monsters soon enough—a cluster of naughty boys and girls, all with romantic names. "Those embers are still burning outside," Henriette explained. "Don't you see? We have time." And they walked out into the garden to watch Eva's cookie burn away to an inconsequential mistake.

PORTRAITS

HENRIETTE INSISTED THAT EVA SHOULD SIT FOR THE
painter first. Such deference had become unusual, and Eva
was suspicious; her older sister liked to make a strong impression, having gone so far as to faint in the doorway if a
gentleman caller seemed worthy. A book was hidden under
Henriette's featherbed detailing how a lady might faint
without trouble, without any damage to her dress or deport-
ment. The book explained how drinking coffee made a
young lady's complexion sallow and that a very good anti-
dote was buttermilk mixed with lavender slathered over the
neck and face. Perhaps this was why Henriette also claimed
to be too delicate for sunlight and seldom ventured out of
doors so that when she did venture forth—to the Tiergarten, to Wannsee Lake—it was always something of an
event. Henriette had plenty of suitors now, the most handsome of whom had been a Catholic, who was politely informed by Father that his elder daughter had long since
been claimed by a distant cousin, a jeweler who lived in
Prague. Eva thought it was both wrong and amusing of Father to create such an elaborate lie, and she'd assumed her
sister would be outraged, but to Eva's surprise, Henriette
didn't seem too bothered. Despite all her dramatics, she

didn't seem to be in any great hurry to find a match. When the suitors came to call, they usually found her in the parlor, laid out swanlike on the divan, just the way she sat then, watching the painter prepare his messy tins of paint for the very first time.

The painter was not a suitor. His name was Heinrich, like the great poet whom Uncle Alfred so admired, and his fine features invited further comparisons. But as Henriette pointed out before the painter arrived, the painter was not a Jew.

"Did you know that we are Jews?" Henriette asked rather archly, while Eva blushed, trying her best not to move her head.

"Yes of course I know you are Jewish."

"How did you know?"

The painter did not smile. He continued painting. "It is merely an instinct." Eva noticed how his mouth twisted then, how his amber eyebrows raised. Eva noticed how, though he was thin with bony hands and wrists, his broad shoulders made a straight T. "Tell me," he asked, "have you any brothers? The house smells like flowers."

"We have no brothers," said Eva eagerly, "but we have an uncle. He used to live here."

"You see," explained Henriette, "Mother's brother is a revolutionary. He lives in Paris now." She sighed wearily, before peeling herself from the divan. "He is in exile."

"Poor fellow," said the painter. As he worked, Eva noticed how his mouth was not quite closed, as if he was concentrating too hard on his paint and canvas to notice anything as trivial as his own expression.

"Not at all," said Henriette, striking a new pose on the divan, as if it were she and not Eva who was currently being painted. "He goes to all the best salons. He has a big, full beard and a wealthy wife. They used to meet in secret before they were married—in the forest—"

"They did no such thing," said Eva.

"Please," the painter said softly, "please continue to look at me."

"In a *mill*," Henriette continued. "An abandoned mill. He told me in confidence in a letter."

"He did not," said Eva.

"And now they live in Paris," Henriette continued, undeterred. "They met Heine, you know."

For a moment, the painter's cool expression looked genuinely surprised. "Heine? And what do you know of Heinrich Heine?"

"I know plenty," said Henriette. "We both do."

The painter shook his head. "Forgive me," he said, smiling, "but no."

" 'I don't know what it may signify that I am so sad,' " Eva softly began. " 'There's an ancient tale that I can't get out of my mind. The air is cool and the twilight is falling and the Rhine is flowing quietly by . . .' " The painter was watching her and not painting anymore. "Uncle Alfred sends us letters. Letters written expressly for us. Father used to read them of course, but now he just passes them along. And so you see . . ."

His eyes met hers for a prolonged moment, but she was instantly sure she'd imagined it. "Do you admire Heine?" he asked Eva.

"I do."

"Uncle Alfred said that before Heine died, he was paralyzed and apparently in wretched pain but brilliant, just brilliant. Very wry, you know. Full of double entendres," said Henriette. "I long to be in exile."

"Oh hush," said Eva, but she understood Henriette. Their Uncle Alfred's letters were greatly anticipated, even more than Mother's from Karlsbad. When, many years earlier, Uncle Alfred had gone to join the battles in the countryside (battles that amounted to what Father disdainfully described as "less than folly"), Mother cut the strings of the parlor piano and that was when Father first took a summerhouse in Karlsbad, with the hopes of Mother getting some rest. Among Father's beliefs was the notion that Mother had doted too heavily on her younger brother and had not enough energy left to create her own home. When Mother cut the piano strings, she had screamed afterwards and it had sounded— according to Father—as if the front door was coming down, as if the soldiers had come looking for the entire family, eager for their blood. The revolution had moved from France to Germany, sweeping up young men, and like a summer storm it came and went and nothing looked particularly different in Germany except that Alfred was no longer there and Mother shifted her attention from her younger brother to playing the piano and taking the *Kur*.

Sometimes she welcomed visitors. There was a dairy farm near the house where they were permitted to help milk cows, and though Eva had always been afraid of the rubbery teat and made Henriette pull it for her, she'd known what she was doing all the same; she preferred to watch. She watched the painter now and he was closing his eyes, as if he was resting or even praying. She watched him; she sat very still, but her mind raced in circles like the ivy growing in Mother's garden where a noontime lunch was served, where trays were dropped and men brought ice and after lunch and dinner, guests stayed the night in the guesthouse; one was an Italian (Eva remembered him suddenly— he wore a jade green silk cravat) with a shy daughter called Lulu. Eva watched the painter's long fingers and thought of how she and Henriette had explained to the girl how, in their language, "lulu" meant urinating.

"Don't look so nervous, Evie," Henriette said. "He doesn't want to see your nervous face."

"I'm not," Eva hissed, "truly."

The painter lifted his brush for a moment and smiled for the first time. His sullen mouth turned upward and his teeth peeked through as if he'd been trying to hide them. Although these teeth were not straight and were stained (Eva imagined his fingers rolling small cigarettes, the smoke curling up toward an equally discolored ceiling), this smile brightened his whole pale face, even his very light eyes. "What a fetching frock," he told Eva, as if although he'd been painting her for over an hour, he had not noticed her until that moment.

"No," Eva said, shaking her head, smoothing the pale gray fabric. "It's ordinary."

"She's modest," muttered Henriette, arranging a pillow on the divan.

But the painter continued to smile at Eva and her heart raced and somehow forced her to twirl her red hair ribbons around her stubby fingers until she could barely feel her fingertips. "Do *you* admire Heine?" she asked quietly.

"Yes, very much," he said. "I admire how he answered to no one."

"Oh so do I," said Henriette. "I admire him deeply."

Eva laughed and quickly covered her mouth, as she saw how serious Henriette's face looked just then, as if she had no other concerns but those of the mind.

"Fingers," the painter said sternly, forcing Eva's hands to fly down to her lap, folding quickly one on top of the other. A breeze came through the door, lifting the fine hairs at the back of her neck. She found it nearly impossible to look straight ahead at the painter. His eyes were blue and not blue and they sat below a high forehead with paper-pale skin, which would have looked feminine but for the expanse of strong bone beneath it. His wrinkled coat looked as if it might never have been laundered. The ends of his hair were matted. He had already tracked soot on the Oriental—a black mark that she knew she'd look at in weeks to come and thrill at the memory of sitting so appallingly still. He became the very definition of afternoon, the center of the first dying light.

"Henriette, why don't you play us something," she said, or meant to say. She wasn't sure her voice had gathered in her throat. She wasn't entirely certain she had spoken until her sister answered coyly:

"Well, I don't know . . ."

"If you do not mind," the painter said, "I'd prefer the quiet. I generally do."

"You don't care for music?" Henriette said, sitting up with uncommon haste.

"No," he said calmly, continuing to paint with his mouth slightly parted. "It is only that sometimes, when there is a breeze and I'm in a pleasant room, a feeling comes over me—it is difficult to explain—and I prefer the quiet." He stopped painting for a moment and lowered his voice. "I become calm, very calm, and without it feeling forced. It is as if people are spirits—benevolent spirits—created for me to regard."

"I understand," said Eva, surprising no one more than herself.

"I don't much feel like playing anyway," said Henriette.

Eva did not even notice her sister's pout. All she saw was how his hands carved the air as he'd attempted to make himself clear. "I understand exactly."

Henriette sat up on the divan and gave a little cough. "If my sister prefers quiet sometimes, it is because she is simply too lazy to talk."

"This I doubt," the painter said, with a beguiling smile.

Eva returned the smile, before becoming flustered. "It must be nice," she blurted, "to be paid for what you love to do."

"How do you know I am being paid?"

"Well," Eva said, "I only meant—"

"Must everything be about money?" he said flatly, returning to his canvas, his brushstrokes firm and deliberate.

"Whatever are you talking about?" Henriette laughed, reclining again. "Father is paying you. He commissioned you to do our portraits."

He stopped painting once more and gripped his brush tightly with both hands. "How do you know that I didn't see you, both of you, in the Tiergarten and decide: I'd like to paint those young ladies? Tell me that? How do you know it has anything whatever to do with money?"

"I," Eva stammered, "I don't know—not for certain, anyway."

"That is correct."

"You saw us?" Henriette questioned skeptically, but she reclined again, slowly.

"Maybe," he said. "And maybe I do not take money from bankers unless I find the subject matter extremely worthwhile. Which is it, do you think?"

"You're insulting our father," said Eva.

"I am merely being honest," he whispered, while looking Eva straight—too straight—on. She had never been looked at in such a way. She felt as if she were turning a kid glove inside out—the tight snug fingers one by one. "Now please," he said softly, "your hands. Please keep them where they are."

EGGS

AT NIGHT THE HOUSE WAS FULL OF COMPETING SMELLS that kept Eva up. The sour scent of pickled herring and pickled meat was overwhelmed by the smell of goose fat (from special geese with tremendous livers—truly delicious), which was in turn replaced by stewed winter fruit, which sweetened and lightened the air. Eggs didn't smell but they were comforting to think of, each one snug in the long wooden board with perfect egg-sized holes. Everything was hidden away in the cold room, biding time in storage.

"Henriette, are you awake? Are you?" Eva closed her eyes and kept very still and imagined the painter—the soot smudged on the carpet, the mixed paint under his fingernails so dark it may as well have been dirt. "Are you eager to sit for your portrait?"

"Shh," she said drowsily.

"What will you wear?"

Henriette didn't answer and Eva assumed she was sleeping until finally she said, "The painter . . ."

"Yes? What about him?"

"I'm afraid he is terribly in love with me."

She imagined that instead of a girl, a particularly small girl of sixteen, she was that long wooden board in the cold room, keeping smooth, tan eggs in place. She didn't respond, her heart was beating too fast for that, and before long, Henriette was unquestionably asleep, her heavy breath punctuated now and again with an unladylike wheeze of a whistle.

Eva let herself think of her favorite time of year, just before the holy days when everyone prepared to eat apples and honey, to pray for inclusion in the book of life, and also to sit for the shoemaker, for a new year meant new shoes. Each September the two girls sat atop the window cabinets in height order and stood up when it was time to get their feet measured. In memories sometimes Uncle Alfred was there, although that would have been unlikely; but there he was: not yet a revolutionary, just a towering young man who would not take his socks off. The shoemaker's hands shook like two brown leaves as he held paper measures up to each of their six feet. Henriette's feet were narrow and long, yellowish white like lye, and *That hurts,* said Henriette, and Uncle Alfred told her it didn't hurt, but the shoemaker still apologized; then he laughed very loudly at nothing funny. He was a short man who smelled like rye and he positioned himself at the inkstand before making careful notes. Moments later he looked up at the girls quite blankly, before Uncle Alfred finally spoke: "The *Streusand,*" he explained, "it's for drying the ink, do you remember?" And daring to instruct an elder, he stood up and gently picked up the pale piece of china on the inkstand with both of his hands. "Look," said Alfred, and everyone always did. Dark sand poured slowly, fixing all of their shoe sizes in ink.

But before the holy days there was also a great deal of laundry to be done and Rahel was there to do it. Rahel, whose eyes were dark as pitch and who looked frightened even when she wasn't, even when she was laughing amidst her constant cloak of soapy, vaporous perfume. Even after spending an hour hanging clothes under oak trees, even when the wind had pulled many strands from her tight, black bun, she smelled like soap and water. She never seemed fully dry. Eva stood at her heels and said, "Rahel, you are old."

Rahel shrugged, finished folding one of Mother's undergarments. "You must hang yourself when you are young," she said, "if you don't ever want to grow old."

Before the holy days Eva treaded lightly on the tile floor while following Rahel to the servants' quarters in secret. In the servants' quarters
lived The Giant, who was actually a machine filled with heavy stones.
He pressed table linens and made them smell even fresher and cleaner
than they already were; The Giant was hot—hot to the touch and busy.
Eva hid under the freshly laundered linens and watched Rahel feed The
Giant. She heard the familiar sound of Rahel singing in a high, scratchy
voice, songs that were really just sounds. It was difficult to see from under the linens, but because Rahel had stopped singing, Eva knew someone was coming.

"Rahel," said Eva's mother.

"Yes, *Madame.*"

"You will stop what you are doing, please." Mother's voice sounded as
if all of her teeth had come loose at once, the way they had in Eva's
dreams.

"*Madame.*"

"Will you please look at this?"

Eva poked her head out from under the pile of linens and was surprised to see her mother in nothing but a dressing gown. Mother held a
sheet out to Rahel as if it were a wailing baby. "Look," she said. "Are you
looking?"

"*Madame?*"

"Do you see it?"

Rahel didn't respond.

"Do you not?"

Rahel shook her head as if she'd been asked this question many times
before. "*Madame,*" she insisted, "there is nothing."

"There is . . ."—Mother paused in a choked whisper, clutching the
white fabric with both hands—"there is a stain."

Taking the sheet from her, Rahel nodded and nodded, wholly uncon-
vinced, and placed it atop the mound of dirty linens. But Mother did not
leave. She did not move.

"I do not want to see that stain."

"Yes, *Madame,* I understand."

"I don't want to see it anymore."

In Eva's dreams Mother still cried softly *My teeth my teeth,* and when Eva said *Mama let me see,* Mother opened her mouth and out came her teeth, smaller than real teeth and far too many, like pebbles or *spätzle* or rain.

But Eva wasn't dreaming, not yet. She lay awake and thought of eggs in the cold room, the clean sloping shape, the round wood holes. She tried not to think of the stained sheets or Rahel's wet skin or what Henriette had said about the painter's affections. She pictured the soot on the Oriental; she knew it would never fade.

WEDDINGS

HENRIETTE TURNED DOWN HER FOURTEENTH SUITOR. She had received all of them with such grace and attentiveness that the prospect of yet another rejection exhausted everyone but Henriette, who claimed she was only doing what any young lady would do when a man came to call. She poured tea with perfect posture, laughed at any humorous attempt, and at the end of each visit, played the piano passionately, sometimes even closing her eyes for moments at a time. She had always been very fashionable and each time a new suitor requested a walk in the Tiergarten—usually a prelude to a proposal—Henriette seemed to require a little something extra: a hairpiece, new gloves, an improved lace collar. Each time she stood at Father's library door and made the request, he demanded to know if the current suitor was making a favorable impression.

"Oh very favorable. He speaks French. Did you know?"

"So you will agree to marry?"

"Father," she said, suddenly coy, "he is coming to call this Sunday, and I do not see how I can wear the organdy dress again."

"Henriette, my dear," said Father, sighing, "I must admit I

am curious what you imagine will be left of my modest fortune when the time comes to fashion you with a proper trousseau."

She took a well-timed breath, and after looking up at the ornately framed portraits of her and her sister hanging in their now-established places on the wall—Henriette in a flattering blue silk dress of which she'd never tire—she said, "I fear that I look like a spinster."

As soon as she said the word that agitated everyone except for Henriette, Father began to open his desk drawer. "You admire the man?"

"I do, Father, I told you I do. I only want to make a good impression."

So Henriette's wardrobe grew and she acquired a signature style of refusing her suitors—always with an expression of profound regret. When they were gone, her voice would return to its customary cheer, and she would ask Eva to brush her hair, which Eva was happy to do. "Evie," she said. She sighed, deliciously. "I would like to meet a flawless creature. Is that really too much to require? Or at least a man whose flaws I might excuse or understand."

"Henriette, take your time," she said. "You are very beautiful and still young and Mother is not here to help you decide."

What Eva didn't say was that she loved the paintings hanging on Father's library wall nearly as much as she loved any living, breathing member of her family. What Eva didn't say was how these paintings portrayed not only two sisters during a moment in time but also the specific experience of being alive at precisely such a moment. Eva didn't mention to Henriette how she made excuses to go into Father's library all throughout the day so that she might look at the paintings again and again and that the more she viewed them, the more confident she felt that these paintings were special and were no less important than if they had been painted by a master. What Eva didn't say was that she was grateful for Henriette's ambivalence about the suitors. She was grateful not to have the attention and the worry passed along to her.

AFTER SITTING FOR HEINRICH NEARLY ONE YEAR AGO, THE SISTERS had bid the painter farewell, but he'd whispered to Eva where to meet him the following week, and she had simply nodded as if she had no choice, as if her head were simply fastened to a string. When their driver had left her at the Center for Welfare (where she sewed with other young Jewish ladies, fulfilling her charitable obligations), and after she had been inside the door and she was certain the driver had gone, Eva wrapped a scarf around her head and hired another carriage at a stable across the way, and she felt as if her heart might burst right out of her chest, as if she might fly off the ground. As she approached a part of the Tiergarten where she had never been, she couldn't help thinking that on seeing her, he would say he was sorry but that it was Henriette for whom the invitation had been intended. Instead he offered her his arm under a low hanging tree. Instead he smoked opulently and talked of Goethe and attempted to identify the particular brown of Eva's eyes. He speculated how, in due time, the Italians, the French, and the Dutch would all journey to Berlin expressly to see the eyes of Eva Frank. She thanked him and looked into the distance, where the faint sound of dogs barking made her feel sad. Though before and throughout most of their meeting she had been terrified that someone would stroll by and recognize her, she soon realized that he had chosen this area carefully. The grass was slightly unkempt; besides a few men who looked as if they were waiting for something or someone, there was no one else in sight. With this late revelation came a shudder of horror and also of deep relief. He invited her to meet him again and again. She told no one. The very air seemed changed when she was near him, as if they were racing together down a steep hill. Her breath was shallow; she shed weight from her already too-slight frame.

"I often think I want to die when I am happiest," he said, while eating a green apple. They had enjoyed an early supper by the river. It was nearly time for her to go. "I feel so lucky to have this." He gestured vaguely to the patchy grass, to Eva, reclining before him.

She saw how his long fingers lingered on blades of grass and she wished she were those blades of grass; she wished that he might touch her every moment of every day, instead of only when they said goodbye. He usually touched her neck, her back. Twice he'd touched her waist. Once he kissed her as if he were going off on a long journey and might never see not only her but also any woman ever again. *I feel luckier,* she wanted to say, but by the time she opened her mouth to speak, the feeling took her by the throat and speaking seemed irrelevant.

Heinrich lay on his back and looked up at the sky. "Happiness is so fleeting compared to so much suffering in life. Most people suffer so deeply. They lead tedious lives at best and still they don't ever want to die." He finished his apple and instead of tossing it into the bushes or the river, he sat up and placed the core on the grass. "I don't understand this."

She loved the sudden pattern of lines in his forehead, the way he raised his brow, perplexed. She loved the way he spoke as if he were speaking only to himself, as if she lived not in a mansion in Charlottenburg but right inside his mind. "Don't you, though?" she asked. "As soon as I have just a little bit of joy, I forget all the sadness in life."

"I shall remember that," he said, and he leaned forward and touched her cheek. "I shall try to be more like you."

AND SO SHE WANTED NO ATTENTION FROM FATHER, NO QUESTIONS about her own match—not when she was visiting the far reaches of the Tiergarten and off the twisting paths near Charlottenburg Palace, not far from her home and yet worlds away, not when she was with Heinrich the painter one day a week, on the day that she was supposed to be making crafts for those less fortunate, for those living in reduced circumstances, two words that never failed to incite in her a mix of pity and shame.

She was grateful for Henriette's string of proposals when, one afternoon, she was ducking into a pine grove, alone and about to change out of her own clothes and into a crimson dress with a thick, black silk sash. Heinrich had explained rather urgently how he wanted to paint her in this specific costume, a dress which he'd claimed belonged to his sister, but Eva only knew that it smelled like a woman, a stranger, and that it was also far too big and so she slipped it over her own plain dress, and when she emerged he said, *My god, you are so small.* He said, *When you have your face tilted down, you resemble Jenny von Westphalen.* She lay in the fields, the green-violet fields, and let Heinrich paint her and paint her. She imagined she had a *von* in her name. The dress smelled faintly vinegary and also like smoke. They barely talked. She did not move. She did not know where he lived. She thought of a room, a single room, up a narrow flight of stairs. When, without warning, a dark cloud passed overhead and a storm threatened with a change in light so sudden that it seemed to blur her vision, they ran toward a small shelter behind a stand of overgrown weeds. The crimson hem trailed in puddles and mud, and by the time they stood surrounded by rotted wood reeking of elderberries, the dress was ruined. They stood there for a spell, waiting for the storm to come. There was the sound of wind, the slap of leaves, but not the sound of water. There was, unmistakably, the sound of their breath. She could smell herself suddenly: smoke and vinegar, cheap, unfamiliar perfume. Inside the closed cabin it was nearly dark, but even if she hadn't been able to make out his shadow, she would have known that he was coming closer by the dank heat—heat that was rising and somehow insistent as the rain refused to come. And as much as she knew she should scream, or run out into the storm that threatened to strike at any moment, she could not still her own body. His hands pulled her toward him and his legs held her up, and she felt as though she was rising up, up, up until she felt him poking there, pushing inside and the pain spiked right through her. It never rained. He found her lips and touched them and left a trace of paint, a light cloud blue so minuscule that she didn't see it until the next day, when she looked into the hand mirror at her bedside—she'd come down with a fever—and finally began to cry.

Henriette stood outside her barely open bedroom door, asking a silent question.

"I miss Mother," Eva said, before slipping into sleep.

Ivy GREW IN RAPID CIRCLES ON THE CEILING FOR DAYS, CREEPING UP the walls, through the windows and under her pillows, brushing the tips of her burning ears. Rahel sat on the edge of the bed, wrapped in white sheets, and The Giant stood in the corner of the room, taking the sheets from her body. Rahel stood naked next to The Giant, and Eva could tell she was angry. Heinrich was there the whole time. He took Eva's fingers from her mouth, telling her not to move. He lit cigarettes furiously, one after another, filling up the room with smoke so dense she could barely see him for all the plumes and haze, but she did see him, and she also finally saw the reason for Rahel's anger: The sheets had been terribly stained. She must have been cleaning for days.

Her family was not present. She did not recall how Father stood in the doorway, how he grabbed onto Henriette's shoulder as he watched Eva twist and turn. She did not have any memory of Henriette breathless at her bedside, begging Dr. Lowenherz for help. She did not even remember Father reading her letters from Mother (detailing the latest effects of the *Kur*), followed by a new one from Uncle Alfred. Eva heard nothing of Alfred's fine sentences, peppered with references to his political heroes—his Bamberger, his Jacoby—names brought up more frequently than those of his two young children. He was convinced that a more expansive amnesty would be granted, that he would not only return to his homeland and see them all again soon, but also—more important!—he would resume the fight for a unified and democratic Germany. Eva did not hear the way he signed his letter: *I do realize, dear Ernst, your views on my enthusiasms and I, in fact, have lived long enough to be aware that this has been a time of extended flowering, which is often more fulfilling than the flower itself, perfect and plucked from the ground.*

She remembered nothing of this when she woke drenched in cold sweat one midsummer day, and her sister said, "Good morning."

"Oh," said Eva, looking around the room and up at the ceiling, which was free of crawling vines. "I didn't die."

"Of course not, darling. You cannot die."

Oh, she thought, *but I should.*

"Well, you cannot die *now,* anyway. Not when I am to be married." Henriette smiled, and there were those long bottom teeth that always reminded Eva of piano keys. "Oh, Evie, I'm so glad you are all right. I'm sorry," she cried, suddenly tearful.

"Sorry? But why?"

"I have not always been the kindest sister to you, have I?"

As Henriette stroked Eva's damp forehead, Eva closed her eyes again and it felt as if she could go back to being the Eva of not so long ago: a small girl with nice eyes, curious, uncorrupted. "Don't be silly," said Eva, though she couldn't deny she took a certain guilty pleasure in all this sudden attention. "You are a wonderful sister. You'll be the most beautiful bride in all of Europe." *Even if I don't live to see it.*

She could swear—if only for a moment—that Henriette was reading her thoughts.

"Don't be foolish," her sister said plainly. "You wouldn't dare miss my nuptials."

"No," said Eva. "Of course not." She touched her older sister's long loose hair; she drew the ends close and inhaled.

DELIVERY

HEINRICH FOUND HER IN THE FALL, WALKING WITH FRIENDS in the Tiergarten.

"Walk with me," he said.

"I mustn't."

"Please," he said, "I know you have received my letters."

As they walked, he stared at her impolitely, never averting his eyes. He said: "I must see you again."

"Here I am," said Eva, "and there you stand. It seems we have met. What a pleasant day."

"Stop," he said.

"There is a breeze but it is not so strong. You enjoy a breeze, don't you? Isn't this what you said? Before you insulted my father?"

"I never—"

"Why did you pretend he wasn't paying you for the portraits? Why did you invent that story about seeing us?"

"I *did* see you," he insisted.

"But why did you pretend it was your idea? That you were loath to accept my father's money?"

Heinrich looked uncomfortable, biting his lip, and then he looked away.

"You will never speak ill of my father again."

"No."

"My father is a good man," she said.

"I know it."

"One summer in Karlsbad when I was a child, our Mademoiselle Dautrey brought us to the train station to watch the trains passing through, and when the train chugged toward the platform and Mademoiselle cried, *Regard,* we looked up and saw our father sticking his head out the window. He must have been heading somewhere to do some business and planned this surprise. He waved and we screamed and he threw silver packages covered with colored paper birds and flowers and they fell softly and they were full of candy and none of it spilled. It was thrilling."

"What a lovely story," he said. He took a step closer.

She smelled smoke in his hair, strong soap she didn't recognize. She thought of her father's bald and shiny head, and how, when she was younger, she'd liked to pat it in the evenings as he smoked one pipe and prepared another for the very next morning. He played billiards on Wednesdays; he ate too many tortes; he could not pass a sea of blossoms without picking one for his buttonhole.

And on the subject of Jews becoming Christians he was very clear: One did not flee from a besieged fortress; it was the act of cowards, of slaves. It wasn't necessarily a question of religion so much as a question of integrity. He might have rejected the Orthodoxy of his youth, but he could never reject his people, his culture, his God. There is no shame in being Jewish, he told his children; there is only shame from passing through life taking on origins at will.

Eva shook her head. "Mademoiselle had told us that the train would not stop, not in such a small station, but I hadn't believed her. Candies weren't enough for me. I wanted him to get off that train. I was a stupid child. Just as I am stupid today."

"Please," he said, "I apologize. You must believe I am truly sorry."

She looked at him, straight into his eyes, and instantly regretted it. He had her then, right there in his starry irises, in their promise of another kind of world. He was not Jewish, nor wealthy, nor titled. But he was exceptional. He made her feel exceptional. She could barely hide this but she tried to hide this as she made her face a stone.

"I'm sorry," he repeated.

"Why?" she whispered, hard. "Why are you sorry?"

He cleared his throat. "The crimson dress," he muttered. "That day."

"I don't know what you are talking about," she said, and she turned from him, shaking, taking care to walk and not run toward her friends who would be so full of questions, who she could see up ahead and moving forward, arms linked in a chain.

HENRIETTE WAS MARRIED AT THE HAUPTSYNAGOGUE TO A COMPACT man with a booming laugh and gray, bushy eyebrows. Julius Greilsheimer, some twenty years older with a rare professorship and a home in Heidelberg, overlooking rolling green hills and the river Neckar, had—for reasons unexplained—never married. Mother had met his mother at the baths, and they'd discussed their unmarried children. Father had not trusted any part of the match. For one thing, why would Henriette—his sophisticated daughter, a true Berliner—make her life in a small town such as Heidelberg? Father questioned every aspect of the arrangement until Mr. Greilsheimer had, with great affability, produced the following documents:

1. Certificate of good character signed by the mayor

2. Certificate of good character signed by the rabbi

3. Birth certificate

4. Proof of employment at the university

5. Bank records

Evidently Mother's wits were not entirely missing, or so she said in an arch, frail voice, along with giving Henriette her blessing, after she'd stepped slowly off the train, finally home again. The doctors had advised that she was well enough to travel, but she'd return to Karlsbad immediately following the festivities. The reception was a lavish feast in a fine hotel with Henriette looking unsurprisingly exquisite in ivory silk and French lace—her dark lashes impossibly long, her chestnut hair up-swept grandly—and aside from sitting for the wedding portraits, during which she appeared serious and ethereal, the bride could barely refrain from laughing along with her new husband. He was not whom one would have anticipated as Henriette's choice (he was far less pompous than her usual taste), nor was he what one might expect from a distin-guished professor of law. He was a red-faced practical joker whose deep voice broke very quickly into fits of boyish giggles. They drank fine wines throughout the evening, sharing the same silver cup long after they did so as a symbol of their joined future. When Henriette took a small sip, Julius urged her to please have another.

That Julius had made a successful life in Heidelberg was particularly significant in light not only of Heidelberg's small size but also its lofty status as a famous university town. Everyone at the wedding reception had said so. What was not said at their wedding celebration or what was whispered but not announced: *He must be exceptionally respected, mustn't he? Because, after all, Heidelberg—it is not exactly cosmopolitan.* The idea of a Jew succeeding at the university there seemed fantastic, even heroic. But Julius seemed oddly immune to the renowned discrimina-tion. He was friendly with a count who'd sent him a barrel of wine along with compliments on a recent lecture, and when the count's estate was rumored to have a sign at the entrance prohibiting Jews and dogs, Julius confronted the count and the count claimed that he knew nothing about it, that he would look into the matter and have the sign promptly re-moved; in the meanwhile, he sent more wine barrels.

FOR MONTHS HEINRICH APPEARED BEHIND TREES—TREES FAR TOO skinny to provide adequate coverage. Once she passed by a produce stand and he was standing behind stacked crates of turnips and pota-toes.

"You are killing me."

And then behind the skating park, at the mouth of the woods. She was waiting for her new friend Marta, who excelled at the waltz. It was snowing and the tips of Eva's braids were frozen. His black hat was capped with a perfect layer of white. She turned and began walking into the woods, the snow soft and pliant underfoot.

"I would marry you," he said softly.

She stopped walking and turned around, inhaling wind and snow.

"I would. I want to."

She pulled in her breath so hard it hurt. "It would be for my money," she said plainly. And once she said it, she knew that it was true. And not true.

"I love you," he said.

She believed he thought he loved her or loved what she represented— a cosmopolitan, a girl of whom he would likely never tire, if only because he would never understand her—but she also knew that despite all of his posturing toward purity, he was covetous. She could tell that right away from how he moved through their home. He not only noticed but also wanted. And though he was hardly upper class, he would consider it a small sacrifice to marry a Jew, a sacrifice deserving of finer things. *I would marry you.* "You would never marry me if I didn't have money," she finally said, in what was not an accusatory tone, but an honest one.

"That isn't true," he said, failing to mask his frustration.

And her tears came as a relief; once they started they would not stop, and enough time passed during his second of hesitation for her to see the full scope of what such a future with Heinrich would look like. There would be low whispers in the park, in the corners of gilded rooms—*How long do you think her parents wept? Did they tear their clothing? Did they cut off all her funds?*—Nothing would silence the talk in Jewish houses. And the Christian houses? She was not stunning enough to be immune to speculation; prettiness and correctness would never be enough for the years of Christian rooms that she would enter and exit over the course of a lifetime. And she could feel, in Heinrich's hesitation, how he would deny such talk existed, deny it until he resented her for forcing him to admit he heard such ugly things, until he hated her and her Jewish birth, the fact of which no baptism would ever wipe away.

"I would like to marry you," he said again, this time with more volume.

"My father hates the portraits, did you know that?"

"Eva."

"He says they look like the very worst of German ideals—drunk with self-love, sick with acquiescence."

"Is this what your uncle writes in his letters? Your beloved revolutionary?"

"You know nothing about my uncle. My uncle loves his country. He only wants to live in a democratic nation; I should think that you do too."

"It is not your fault that you are a Jewess; you were born into this curse as one is born into poverty or riches. But now you can choose your future. With baptism—such a simple ceremony—you can wash it all away."

She shook her head. "I will not change my faith." Up until she said it out loud, she hadn't been entirely sure. But she knew right then that, although she often perceived her religion to be exceedingly dark and sad, and although the only time she felt devout was when mournful music played, she would not choose to be excluded from her own people only to become an intruder elsewhere.

"But why?" he asked, his voice still full of patience. "Why not leave it behind and convert, as so many others do?"

She took a few steps toward him. Her boots made a crunching sound. "Like that?" she asked, nodding back toward her small and seemingly insignificant footprints in the snow.

He reached for her, his arm wrapping tightly around her waist as if he could not hold her close enough. His breath was warm and smelled like cloves. She fought him for a moment before stopping short, nearly out of air. Eva looked up at the sky that was white on white: The skeleton branches shrouded under snow pointed every which way. She could swear she heard them crying out, desperate to be seen. "Let me," he said, and he kissed her gently, eliminating the image, obliterating all the words.

• • •

AT JUST OVER SEVEN MONTHS PREGNANT, JULIUS ALLOWED HENRI-
ette to accompany him on a much-anticipated lecture tour. He would
give a talk in Berlin before continuing to Breslau, and Henriette would
have the chance to visit with her family, whom she was missing terribly.
Upon her arrival she was showered with attention. Eva played the
Chopin Minute Waltz, Father recited Goethe's "Die Braut von Korinth"
but forgot the last lines, and Henriette finished it for him—with high
color in her now plump cheeks—before detailing her many nauseated
months with equally impressive dramatic flair.

Eva was happy to see her sister but, as it was with her lately, when she
closed the door to the washroom, she was that much happier to finally be
alone. Rahel had drawn a bath, and Eva could not have been more grateful. After unpinning her hair, she lay in the bathtub and wept. She wept
until the water grew tepid, until she could no longer distinguish tears from
bathwater. She thought of how a few days earlier, she had told her friends
Marta and Ilse that if she was allowed to come skating with Marta's Aunt
Lotte, she would be downstairs, ready to be collected at a quarter to five.
She thought of how, in a true attempt to be a normal girl with respectable
social appointments, she had asked her father for permission, and how
(she was sure he'd grown vaguely suspicious) he'd claimed it was too cold
and wouldn't grant it. She thought of how she'd stood by the window and
watched the girls and Marta's Aunt Lotte—how they'd all barely stopped
to wait for her but had instead dashed off to the skating park, laughing all
the while. Although they had looked for her just as they'd promised, it had
been so clear they did not and would not miss her; it was somehow terribly obvious that no one would miss her but Heinrich. That afternoon
she'd wept at the unbearable weight of secrets, just as she wept now, until
the sun no longer slanted through the picture window, until Henriette
knocked on the door and called her out for dinner.

"DARLING." HENRIETTE LAUGHED, AS EVA SAT ACROSS FROM HER,
chewing a modest piece of lamb. "Just because I am a pregnant woman,
big and ugly and frightening, you needn't look so serious!"

"My dear," said Father, raising his index finger into the air, "please don't be foolish. Your sister always looks this way."

"I'm sorry." Eva smiled a shaky smile, her heart beginning to race. "I didn't intend—"

"My wife is a vision of excellent health, is she not?" Julius asked proudly, helping himself to more lamb. "Just look at her big, rosy cheeks."

"But are you well?" Henriette asked Eva, suddenly concerned. "Father?"

"We're all just splendid," Father said. "Everyone here is in perfectly good health, Henriette. Even Mother writes of returning home. Her headaches have subsided."

"How marvelous," Henriette said, her eyes welling with tears.

"Don't cry," said Eva. "Please. Everyone is fine."

"I am only so happy to see you," she said. "This is why I'm acting like a fool."

"Nobody is a fool," said Father. "At least not in my house. Go on my dear—take some more potatoes. Make sure she takes more potatoes, Julius."

"Tell us, Eva," said Henriette, after daintily taking a bite and swallowing her tears, "how many marriage proposals have you had?"

JULIUS CONTINUED TO BRESLAU TO GIVE HIS LECTURE, BUT ONLY AFTER embracing Henriette so many times and so tightly that Eva grew concerned for the baby. He would be back at the end of the week to escort her back to their home, where (Henriette had confided in Eva) the maid and the cook had received her politely enough before ignoring any requests to do things a bit differently. Father was busy each day in the city, and each morning of Henriette's visit the sisters woke late and sat by the fire, discussing Henriette's new life: Julius, she explained, was popular and generous. He wasn't handsome but he was kind, which was far more important, more so with each passing day. He enjoyed playing billiards like father and often hid gifts for her in unexpected places, after he'd been cross. After so many cheerful testimonies of domestic habits and preferences, Henriette inevitably lowered her voice.

"Evie," she said, leaning in close, "there is no need to be afraid of having a husband—of lying with a husband—it is not frightening after all."

As Henriette blushed, Eva nodded and tried to be the sister to whom Henriette imagined she was speaking, someone worthy of such precious and now irrelevant advice. She knew that Henriette sometimes felt that in order to have a conversation, she usually had to start, otherwise the girls would just sit in silence, and so Eva made a concentrated effort at being amusing. She told the famous story of Mr. Blumenthal, a guest of Father's, who, during one winter's evening, drank seven glasses of wine, ate ten toasts with goose liver, and twelve buttered potatoes. She made Henriette shed tears of laughter at her fine imitation of the jolly but hapless maid at Karlsbad, who—over the course of just one day—dropped a tart at breakfast, a whole fish at lunch, and a bottle of wine during dinner. The sisters drank milky coffee and nibbled on rolls and butter and cheese, and sometimes Henriette felt queasy and Eva brushed her hair, and sometimes she insisted on a walk. They donned furs and walked through the Tiergarten. The grass was still covered in patches of snow, but it was easy to imagine the push of springtime, the dark and fertile soil. Sometimes Eva closed her eyes for moments at a time, and when she saw Heinrich in a dark wood, so serious in a snowcapped black cap, she opened her eyes instantly, somewhat surprised that he wasn't standing in the distance, calling her name, the sound carried by a sudden wind.

"Berlin is so much lovelier with sunlight," lamented Henriette. "The stones turn a whole different color—they look almost blue! And—"

"Henriette," Eva said, her gaze fixed on the ashen sky. A black crow glided overhead; Eva followed its flight until it landed on the poor choice of a spindly branch and was forced to take flight again. "It couldn't be more perfect than right now."

Her sister abruptly stopped walking, her large frame looking suddenly weak, as if the weight of the baby might pull her straight down to the frozen ground.

"Henriette?" Eva said, panic rising—panic like none she had anticipated. Her sister would need to become an animal in order to do this, she realized, an animal that pushed through peerless pain. Eva also realized—with an odd absence of surprise—that she could not imagine her surviving.

"I am perfectly fine," she said, looking at Eva strangely.

"What is it then?" asked Eva, shaking.

"You're changed," Henriette said.

"Am I?"

"And you are not going to tell me why."

"There is nothing to tell," Eva said. She wriggled her still child-sized hands through the brass buttons on Henriette's coat and found the warm solid globe taking up space between them. She looked into Henriette's glossy hazel eyes, at her rosy complexion, and she lied.

HENRIETTE WAS ANXIOUS TO HEAR MUSIC. IN THE PURPLE BERLIN twilight, she held Eva's arm as they approached the concert hall. They had done this for years—this stroll toward the palace, this walk and talk in anticipation of music, but usually it was alongside Mother, who liked to point out ladies she knew and comment on their fashionable or un-fashionable furs, their rumored arguments and affairs. Henriette and Eva strolled by the queue leading up to the doors—a queue comprised of those who weren't fortunate enough to possess tickets ahead of time. Eva couldn't help but notice how these women's furs were not done in the current fashion, how the men's suits were inevitably too short or too long. This evening, during the long intermission, Mother would not be there to offer Eva and Henriette apple cake. She would not be there to offer sparkling hellos to fellow piano pupils and to parade the girls before her beloved teacher, Mrs. Shein, who would usually be seated at the bar, enjoying a glass of champagne.

"How was it," Henriette asked, "that Mother attended all of those con-certs? Why did Father never insist that she remain at home and get her rest?"

Eva shrugged. "She once said that being home too often was what in fact made her nervous, and that hearing her beloved music played was just the thing that made her well. I heard them quarrel in the drawing room."

"Did you?"

Eva nodded, remembering how she had smelled Father's pipe outside the heavy pine doors. Only the occasional glass being dropped or match being struck had interrupted their familiar coarse voices.

"Do you remember Mother's skin?" Henriette asked suddenly. "How beautiful she was. Now she is . . . well, her hair has turned white! She barely brushes it!"

"She always said—she still says—that when one listens to someone play the piano, one can always recognize a person's nature, in so far as whether the person is temperamental or not. But I have always wanted to say: Mother, since one can only deduce this through music and most everyone knows that musical people are temperamental to begin with, please tell me, what is the use?" Henriette laughed and Eva saw the fine lines feathering her sister's hazel eyes and felt proud to be with her, to make her laugh again. "Look," Eva said, nodding toward the doors. "Look at those people who are first in the queue." Her gaze lingered on one man among them. A man with a dirty coat. A man with long, pale hair. "Do you see them?" she asked, her pulse quickening, as she could not help but try to catch a glimpse of his face. "They have all been standing here for hours. I've heard that some attend an evening performance and simply queue up for the following evening right then. They have a party throughout the night . . ." The man took something from his pocket and passed it between his hands. "They stand together on this queue all that time."

"Such endless standing for nothing but a closer view," Henriette said. "Can you imagine?"

"Yes," said Eva, picturing dull silver flasks of brandy, fingers linked to keep warm. "I believe I can."

The sun set in glowing embers over the stony city. A buxom lady laughed, a dark silk glove covered a delicate rouged mouth. Henriette stifled a yawn.

"Are you certain you're well?"

"Perfectly," said Henriette. "I don't even feel the cold."

"Uncle Alfred was never cold," Eva said. "This is what Mother always said. Do you remember? On winter walks we would all blow into our hands and she would speak of how Alfred only looked straight ahead when it was cold, as if he were standing by the sea."

"You don't remember that."

"I do."

"She said that only once. You were too young to remember."

"I remember," Eva insisted. "When he was fighting, when he was in hiding, I remember thinking: I hope he isn't cold. 'Things are going to improve'—he wrote that over and over in his letters—'not only for Jews but for all of Germany.' He is still writing that."

They passed by the man in the dirty coat on their way toward their entrance; he ran his hand over his own pale hair, and when he turned to the side and squinted, Eva saw a particularly thick mustache, a crooked pair of spectacles. They walked past the man who wasn't Heinrich at all, past the buxom lady who was no longer laughing. Inside, the anteroom was done in ochre brocade. A silk upholstered chair was immediately brought forth.

"Look," Henriette said, sitting herself down. She didn't bother to hide how she was out of breath as she pointed to the concert entrance. Eva had forgotten her sister's impatience, how charmingly it combined itself with hope. "The doors are opening."

"It only seems that way," said Eva, her heart still beating rapidly at the sudden possibility of seeing Heinrich. "Be prepared for a nice long wait."

AFTER THE PERFORMANCE, HENRIETTE INSISTED ON BUYING THEM not only apple cakes but also sweet rolls before hiring a carriage. Many people passed them by, as Henriette's legs couldn't easily support her present weight, but she was in no hurry. Her sister missed Berlin; Eva could see this plainly and realized that she could not imagine ever going too far from home herself. But then a child walked by, holding a mother's hand tightly, and Eva noticed her sister's expression, how she could not suppress her joy. Henriette's choice of husband, her uncomplicated happiness—it was as foreign to Eva as the idea of meeting Heinrich's family—provided, of course, that he had one. It was as foreign as looking into his parents' eyes on the threshold of his home and seeing only kindness.

One year when she was a little girl, during *Taschlich* after Rosh Hashanah, the whole family went to the Spree River to empty their pockets of sins. They had curiously joined Father's relations—the very religious family of twelve—all of whom wore scratchy, bad-smelling clothing. It was the clothes she remembered most—heavy wool in a dark color that, not unlike the familial bond, was a cousin to navy, a cousin to black, but somehow exactly neither. Aunt Esther, a stutterer, (they'd met again at Henriette's wedding) instructed the girls to cast stale breadcrumbs into the water below. Eva listened carefully and knew she was to name her sins inside her mind in order to cast them off, and yet she had searched in vain, coming up with not much more than pestering Henriette or eating too many pastries. As she now walked the crowded streets of Berlin between winter and spring, with her sister holding her arm, Eva remembered when sins were a novelty, no more familiar than the taste of sausage, which she now saw through a foggy window, darkly steaming on a platter.

"Do you remember what Father used to say about sausage?"

"Let the good Lord eat sausage," said Henriette immediately, "only He knows what's in it."

They rounded a corner, laughing, and when they saw Heinrich, they were each taken aback and—for different reasons—could not help but smile. He bowed his head, asked after Henriette's health, offering quiet congratulations, and as Eva watched her sister's sparkling manner, she knew the carriage ride home would be filled with guileless babble about the mysterious painter who would really be quite handsome if he bathed and stood up straighter, if he didn't do that funny thing with his hands as if he needed something—a paintbrush, a cigarette—to hold.

"Let's go," said Eva, but her eyes were fixed on Heinrich's hands, convinced that she'd actually conjured him forth by the sheer force of her longing. "You must be tired," she said to Henriette, but Henriette shook her head.

"It is so good to be here in my city," Henriette said. "And how lucky to see you again, Heinrich. Have you been very busy with your painting?"

"I have been preoccupied as of late," he said, and though Eva would not lift her eyes, she knew that he was watching her. "I can be found too often at the café across from the academy. Many students and instructors gather there."

"It sounds like a lively time," said Henriette.

"I suppose it is lively. But not for me. I can be found there every night," he said pointedly, "well into the night. I must admit I have been melancholy."

"Well then," said Henriette, teasingly, as if she were not seven months pregnant but rather virginal and lounging on the sitting room divan. "Perhaps you should paint us again. Perhaps you simply miss us terribly."

"Henriette!"

"I am only teasing, Eva. He knows I am teasing."

"It is nice to see you again," Eva said to Heinrich, finally looking into his eyes. "But we really must be going."

"Of course," he said, and then softer, "only if you must," before turning around and becoming part of the passing crowd.

AFTER BIDDING GOODNIGHT TO HER SISTER, EVA FRANK FOUND HERself wanting to take some air. At the time she couldn't admit why she fetched a wool wrap, why she stood outside for at least one hour in the garden. She looked around at the familiar rose bushes, beaten limp by the cold, and up above at the patterns of stars, as if they alone might absolve her of what she was about to do. And then, very much in spite of her better self, she hid her hair with her wrap and prayed that the servants wouldn't see.

She began to walk. She walked and breathed the air—the air that was not enough somehow—past stone and tree and gate and thorn and, as a fine mist gathered into light rain, she picked up momentum; she could not articulate the destination, only the bottomless need. Underneath a

stable master's roof—a stable far enough away from her father's house—
as if she had been preparing for this inconceivable behavior all throughout her girlhood, she hired a horse and driver. The driver balked when he
saw her, as no sane young woman hired a carriage unchaperoned (not to
mention the late hour) but she'd provided for this reaction. He accepted
the extra coins from her tightly clutched purse and, without a word,
helped Eva into the anonymous coach and out into the night.

THERE WAS, AS HEINRICH HAD SAID, A COFFEEHOUSE NEAR THE
academy where he often lingered with a few instructors. She knew this
already for she occasionally had found an excuse to visit that street during the daytime and had looked through the glass where, through the
floating vines of smoke, through the burnished amber light, she had seen
him. She had memorized the blue eyes in turmoil, the smooth, high forehead, the thick, fair brows drawn in concentration, as if he himself had
drawn them—charcoal in his tapered pale fingers, charcoal pushing into
thick, cream paper the distinct shape of a V.

This time she didn't stop at the window, but went straight for the door.
There was a talkative set that carried an air of expectancy as they rushed
inside, and she trailed them—hoping to blend in—a bit of flotsam
caught in their buoyant wake. She was standing alone for what felt like
hours, but it was no more than a moment before she found him reading
a folded newspaper, sipping from a full glass of beer. There was an empty
seat beside him, and sitting down felt like landing, like a paper bird
coasting through the air.

He reacted so quickly, she was sure he'd turned over the glass, but
there it stood, a glass of brown beer on a small café table between them.
She stared at the beer until her lips, if not her fingers, stopped trembling.

"My sister," she said, her eyes downcast, tears becoming trapped in
the table's knots and grooves.

He took her hand and leaned in close, as if he were making a point.

"She doesn't know I am here," she somehow managed to say. "If she
knew . . . if my father—"

"My darling," he said, "my sweet girl."

"I came alone. My family—"

"Come closer," he whispered.

As if she had no choice at all, Eva did as he told her and leaned across the table, close enough that she could smell light wool mixed with the malt and grass scent of beer. His shoe touched the top of her boot, and doing so, sent tiny colored lights colliding through her vision like a swarm on a summer's eve.

"Heinrich!" cried a young man, approaching. "Great artist of our time!" The man had long, wavy hair, a broad grin, and a beery bass voice that echoed like a drum.

Eva pulled away and sat stiffly in her chair, hands locked in her lap. At first she thought she was mistaken when she heard him say, before breaking into laughter, "Heinrich, great sponger of the rich!"

She braced herself for Heinrich's fierce rebuttal, but he only shook his head with a stiff smile. "Go on, go away now."

"You will not introduce me to your friend?"

"No, I don't think so," said Heinrich.

"I apologize," he said, with a sobering expression. "Merely having some fun."

"I must go," Eva said, and stood, gathering up her skirt.

"Don't leave," he called out. "We like to tease him. I am only jealous— he's such a skilled guest of the Jews. We all need such commissions but—alas—my talented friend will not make the necessary introductions."

"Shut up, Fritz," Heinrich said, but curiously, he was still smiling.

"He is apparently the most fashionable fellow to paint all their portraits. And—make no mistake—he is well compensated. Or at least that's what I'm told." He clapped Heinrich warmly on the back.

"Is that right?" Eva asked, as Heinrich stood up too, and the café passed in swatches of brown tables and white candles, in coffee poured and wine spilled, and outside the street was empty, misty, barely lit by streetlights. She had never been alone at nighttime on any kind of street, let alone one as strange as this one. Heinrich appeared within seconds, but she walked away, ignoring him, until the narrow street came to an end. There was stone in all directions.

"I came to see if you still wish to marry me," she finally said, through infuriating tears. "But I do not wish to know anymore."

"He is drunk," he said, taking her hands. "He likes to tease me—do you understand?" His touch was soft, grateful. He moved one hand to rest on her cheek. "I mean to say, though he is a fine artist, there is jealousy among painters and—"

"He does not have your charm—is this it? Your way with Jewish daughters? Is this why he says hateful things?"

"But he did not think for a moment that you are a Jewess."

Eva shook her head and his warm hand fell to his side. "No," she said, "probably not." Aside from understanding its irrelevance, she knew she took some small pleasure in this fact and it shamed her. A strange grin twisted across her face.

"What?" asked Heinrich. He had stopped touching her. "Why do you look this way?"

"How many daughters?" She asked—although she knew that whatever truth she was after was never going to be revealed. "Please, do tell me— how many have you loved?"

He shook his head as though nothing could be of less consequence. "We could be free," he whispered, as if he truly believed.

"But I cannot be. I cannot be free as a German without also being free as a Jew." She gave a little shrug. "I'm not even quite sure why."

"If you are not sure why, then you cannot possibly be certain. It is something else," he said defiantly, as his expression turned bitter. "I wonder—would it be different if I were a baron? If I were a professor of law like your beloved sister's match? Could you then *be free*?"

She realized that it was nighttime, and that she'd come quite a long way here.

"My sister . . ." she said, but this time it was in recognition, as there— impossibly—was Henriette. Henriette approaching in the darkness. A Bengal tiger could not have shocked or frightened her more. "Henriette!" she cried. "But what are you doing here?"

"I was worried," she said plainly, in a voice Eva did not recognize. "I knew," she said, as Eva rushed to her side. "I woke up and I knew. Or maybe I knew all along and was afraid to admit it could be true."

"Henriette," Eva said, but Henriette was breathing heavily, leaning now against a closed butcher's stall. Eva swore she could see the faintest bloodstain in the grain of the well-worn wood, a brown scratch that could have been anything, but it was old blood, she was certain.

"Are you mad? You should not be here!" Heinrich cried.

"Oh dear God," Henriette said softly, even calmly, as a puddle of water began spreading in a pool beneath her skirt.

"Help us," Eva screamed, and Heinrich responded with the promise of help, calling out as his worn shoe soles smacked the stones and echoed into silence, into the smell of a side street at night—smoke, gravy, beer—a smell with no trace of a woman.

"Help us," Eva called again, in case he had merely run away. Then: "Isn't it too early?" She worked her small hands under Henriette's arms, doing her best to hold her sister up and off the ground, and then she saw three men from inside the café come running out to assist them. She didn't know whether to be frightened or relieved. "Henriette, what will you name him?" Eva whispered, as if the existence of her second question could serve to counteract the answer to her first.

"You believe it is a boy?" Henriette strained, wincing with obvious terror.

"I do," Eva said. "I do." Her voice shook, as she saw how her sister's round face had already drained of color.

ONLY WHEN HEINRICH HIRED THEM A DRIVER DID EVA REALIZE THAT he too was terrified—not only of what was happening to Henriette but also of being somehow implicated and punished. He seemed no stranger to punishment, but also—even as he directed the driver in a suitably forceful voice—he seemed suddenly and considerably younger. Eva wondered, as she gripped her sister's hand and smoothed her hair, as the carriage sped uphill and back toward the world she'd been unhappily fleeing, if she would ever see him again.

She would look on that moment as the last one of its kind, for the idea that she would—that she *could*—ever see him again: It would become a dark and ridiculous joke.

As the driver approached their street, Henriette insisted on getting out a short distance from the house, so that no one would wake and catch them in this inconceivable position.

"No!" cried Eva, and she could hear how her voice was trembling. "We'll go straight to the door and send this carriage for the midwife. I will live with my consequences. My punishment means nothing compared to your safety."

Henriette yelled to the driver to let them out right there. She yelled with the certainty of a true mother. Eva hollered back but the driver must have been frightened of what would greet him at their destination, for he listened to Henriette and stopped exactly where she'd requested. "Keep driving!" cried Eva. "For God's sake, can't you see her? She is having—"

"Hush," cried Henriette, as she made her way out of the carriage, imbued with sudden energy. "Come!" she hissed, and Eva saw that she had no choice, that to argue would mean endangering her sister that much further. "You listen to me," her sister said, as she walked at a fearsome clip. The night was pale and humid and they were part of it, part of the air and mist and the minutes ticking onward into an impossible morning. They looked up at the grand houses of Charlottenburg—houses they had known their whole lives—which were now looming above them like great kings at rest, ignorant of sedition. Her sister said, "I will never speak of this night to anyone."

"Thank you," Eva managed to whisper, as their family home came into view.

"You think this is only for you?" Henriette cried. "This would ruin all of us, don't you understand?" She shook her head gravely before stopping for a moment and clutching Eva's shoulders. "Are you really so ignorant?" she demanded, her voice stern but disappearing into a severe embrace. Eva could smell Henriette's perspiration, the terrible water soaking her skirts. "Oh Eva," Henriette whispered, seconds from weep-

ing, but instead drew a sharp breath. "Promise me you'll never speak of
what you have done."

"I promise," Eva said, as tears poured down her face, tears so plentiful
they ceased to matter.

They passed through the back entrance without incident. They hurried up the stairs before silently changing into dressing gowns and Eva
ran toward their father's bedroom door, crying out for his help. The servants were woken. Water was boiled. The midwife was called and finally
arrived.

THAT NIGHT, HENRIETTE—DRENCHED IN SWEAT, LANK HAIR STICK-
ing to her back—became the very animal that Eva could never have
imagined. This—Eva thought, while grasping her sister's hand—was a
fierceness that must only be possible once in a person's life, at the very
moment of discovering that such strength in fact exists. Here was power
undiluted by effort, with a face hollowed out to the very bones working
to scream out in pain. The engorged breasts were shocking, swinging beneath a sweat-soaked nightgown that Eva took small comfort envisioning
being bleached and hung to dry. She was shocked at Henriette's voice,
how it lowered and growled with fury as much as with anything else. She
was shocked at the way her hips moved under the sheet, thrusting in violent motions as her knees stabbed up and out to the side like wings of a
monstrous insect.

She was so shocked that it took the midwife shaking her shoulders in
order to make Eva *come back, come back* to the peach-colored room of
their childhood, where she had been standing for nearly twenty hours.
She was shocked to recognize how silent the room had grown, a silence
that she could barely distinguish from the baby's piercing cry. She heard
the baby, the baby boy! She swore she heard him crying and screaming
to the ceiling and out beyond the roof—sound spilling madly into the
dark and starry night. But the baby's mouth was closed. He was beautiful
and tiny and perfect and he was not crying. He was not making a sound.

She held him in her arms until she realized that Henriette should be holding him, that it should not yet be Eva's turn. By the time Eva turned to see her sister—mouth slack and arms splayed, drenched in the unknown yet instantly certain fatal hush—the midwife was forced to utter the words about her sister and the child, words Eva refused to repeat in this country, in this language, and later, in another country in other languages that she would come to know. She would write them, sometimes over and over, for many years to come, but the exact words would never cross her lips. And though logic played no part in her conviction and she believed very deeply in logic, Eva knew that she alone was responsible.

She had been with Heinrich. She had stood there and loved him even as she knew he hated her. Maybe it was only a small part of him that hated only a small part of her, but it was hate just the same and she had loved him. This was her doing: this moment, this fatal birth, and Eva lay on the bed with her long-lashed, willful, frivolous, sweet, sweet sister—clutching the still baby to both of their breasts. And then the silence came to an end and she realized the violent banging was not in fact inside her mind but outside herself, outside the door, where Father pounded fist to wood over and over again.

AFTER

AFTER THE MIRRORS WERE COVERED AND CLOTHES WERE torn, after Father took out his grandfather's ancient prayer book and began to pray relentlessly, after Mother had been carted off the train from Karlsbad and inserted back in her old feather bed as if for all those seasons of taking the waters she had merely been taking a nap, after Father stopped praying and drained six bottles of wine before sending word to Julius in Breslau and Alfred in France, Eva finally rose from the corner of Father's study where she had been sewing and sewing—if only for an excuse to prick herself with a needle—and excused herself, making her way toward Henriette's bedroom, Henriette's bed. She lay down beneath her sister's sheets, inhaled the orange-water, sourbread, violet smell, and understood the fact that she would maintain this shame for the rest of her life. This shame wasn't going anywhere and if she was to keep breathing day in and day out, she would need to make some room. It would be living undiluted inside her now, inside her heart and bones.

They knew nothing. They all knew nothing but Eva became convinced that somehow, in some way, they did. She could not speak for two full days, but on the third day she looked into her sister's gilt-painted vanity mirror and said, "I am sorry." She smeared the glass with her fingers and said it again. "I'm sorry I'm sorry I'm sorry I'm sorry I'm sorry I'm sorry." Her hands pawed at her appalling reflection as the words *I am sorry* were like knives on the tongue. She wished she could say it to the rooms full of mourners; she wished for that sharp pain again and again, but she knew that to articulate her guilt would be, beyond anything, selfish. Her parents stood at risk of losing not one child but two, and only she possessed the power to contain their loss.

And she knew there was no end to *I am sorry,* to this small, incessant sentence. There was nowhere it could possibly go.

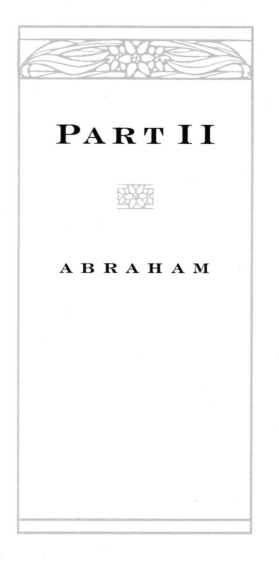

PART II

ABRAHAM

FORTUNE, 1865

He was an imposing man, a man who liked to take chances. At sixteen he had begged his father and brother to invest the better part of the family fortune in a certain kind of sewing machine, invented by an eccentric American. According to a family connection in New York City, the American was an actor—though supposedly very clever—and, through this family connection, the opportunity for investment had presented itself. Abraham had assured his father and Meyer of the eccentric American's bright future, his inevitable and phenomenal success, but his father and brother had considered the risk too great—too many people were making advances with sewing, the man was an actor—and because Abraham had listened to them, because he hadn't enough experience yet to make substantial decisions, other men of industry prospered while there was no Singer sewing machine fortune added to the Shein family name. In addition to this criminally bad decision, the product that his father and his brother had deemed a sensible investment was a new-fangled confection of chocolate-covered bananas and the whole damn shipment, widely anticipated, melted on the journey from a West Indian island whose name he'd decided to forget. Abraham could barely look at a sewing machine or a goddamn banana without spitting on the ground.

He was a man who liked to take chances. He was shocked and thrilled when his timid brother alighted for America in lieu of military service, and he had not only followed Meyer soon after but he was the first to make the long trip not only farther west to California, but back home to Berlin for a visit. He was a man so swollen with pride that, in his early days of doing business, if a customer questioned a quoted price—even perfunctorily, even if the customer didn't hear so well—he refused to sell him the goods. Dry goods. Everything from a pin to a piano. He kicked the customer out into the street—out into the hot dust and dirt and burro shit of Santa Fe, refusing to accept money from such a man. He was a proud man, proud of many things, chief among them his ability, while traveling, to keep up not only his own spirits but those of his traveling companions, and he was also proud of his thick hair, his height. He was a tall man, tall for a Jew or a gentile and he liked the outdoor life. By now he had crossed those Great Plains on horse or mule or ox and buggy many times; he'd shot antelope, buffalo—butchering the meat and cooking it himself.

Upon his return to Berlin, he was ready to describe these trips; he was ready to be feted. He was primed to toast the Shein Brothers' American success and was almost eager for all kinds of questions about the exotic frontier. But when he walked into the handsome apartment, where he had not been in over ten years, it was nothing but darkness and gloom. Someone had died—one of his mother's former piano pupils—a young woman. This was tragic of course, but he had not known her, and there was his own mother, despondent on the day of his arrival! She had also grown old. With each of his mother's letters that had miraculously arrived in Santa Fe, she had begged her sons to make a European trip, and yet now that he was present—offering his arm while walking, giving detailed reports about their profits—she seemed to find little consolation.

He went to the *shivah* of his mother's former pupil. Why did he attend? Perhaps he wanted to pay his respects to the family—he had something of a formal urge to represent his father whenever possible—

or maybe, in addition, he remembered the pupil's sister, a young girl with whom he had walked nearly twelve years ago, and he was curious how she had grown. It had been in Karlsbad, that dreadful spa town, and his mother had been talking with the most pale-skinned woman he had ever seen. There was a clingy daughter who could not have been more than five years old, who kept climbing on her mother's lap, who'd insisted on holding her hand, and it was clear the two ladies wished to speak without the child's interruption. It was a hazy plum sky, the end of summer. His brother had already sent for him, and his only ideas of America were perfectly dripping with gold. In the spirit of generosity he took the little girl's hand and she had wept bitterly. *What is it?* the pale woman had exclaimed. *He is so ugly,* the girl had cried.

Would his mother have reminded him of that amusing story? If she had done so, it would have been an impressive form of persuasion, as Abraham liked nothing better than to prove himself, if only to a formerly petulant child. Or would his mother have said nothing of the sort—or at least not until much later—when such tales would be briefly inflated with retrospective meaning? Most likely, Abraham Shein attended the *shivah* in order to get out of the dark rooms of his ancestral home, full of familiar smells and old reminders of his beloved father, a smart man with a simpleton's death—he died soon after Abe left for America from a sour stomach; it was said he died from eating too much fruit.

If his mother *had* told him the story about the little girl in Karlsbad, he would immediately have recognized the woman sitting by the window as being that very same girl, for she still looked like a child—her delicate black boots barely grazed the Oriental and she clasped some bits of string, which she passed back and forth between her hands. Her childlike quality was no doubt exaggerated by the contrast of her severe mourning attire; her impish face was hollowed by shadows. She appeared as if she had been crying for days, and yet he liked the look of her.

It was hopeless to imagine the possibility of her smile, as her eyes seemed to take up the whole of her face, eyes so deep and seemingly imploring, as she turned from the window to face him.

"Oh," said Eva Frank, as if she had been woken from a dream.

"Abraham Shein," he said too loudly, followed by an important nod. "My condolences."

"Mr. Shein," she said, "thank you." She played with the string, and he thought of the alley cats outside of his home across the world, how they kept him up at night with their hungry mews, scratching fenceposts outside his window.

"I have just arrived from America," he said. He could not fathom ever tiring of those words.

"Yes," she said. "I know about you."

"Is that so?"

She turned back to the window, and he too looked outside: bare spotted birches and a wrought iron gate. Nothing. It occurred to him that perhaps she was simple, and the thought did not displease him.

"What is it like," she asked softly, "to live so far from home?"

Though she kept her gaze out the window, he smiled expansively and took hold of his suit lapels; he waited for her to turn around. He noted the slender slope of her neck, how one lone hairpin had sprung loose from the pile of curls atop her head.

More than black peignoirs and painted lips, more than breasts moving in shadow behind muslin, more than breasts—tawny and utterly available—presented in the flesh, more than the hungriest whore in the most lawless of American territories—this one lone hairpin in a dour setting suggested such possibilities. There were other young ladies of marriageable age—ladies who were richer and fairer, on whom he had intended to call; there were other families waiting to receive him, but they would be waiting in vain. "It is another world," he said, pleased with his decision.

She looked in his eyes and began to cry—her narrow shoulders rose and fell, a stilted movement under starched, pressed black—but he assumed these tears had nothing to do with him. The girl had lost her sister, there was no way around it, and he expected she would mourn for a suitable period of time.

BODIES

SHE DIDN'T BLEED. HE DIDN'T NOTICE. HIS BREATH WAS heavy with wine. He breathed audibly and strangely sweetly, while his hands were rough and hardly shy. He grabbed her more tightly than seemed absolutely necessary, because *where exactly,* she wondered (and not without a hint of surprising amusement) *did he think she intended to go?* But he made her breathe like she'd been for a swim, and beneath the covers, beneath the shadows on the high ceiling, she was dizzy, and nothing like the swooning and nearly sick sensation she'd had with Heinrich. It was something else, something new—closer to a bite of stinging sugar after a gnawing hunger. The ivory sheets at the Hotel Fürstenhof were scalloped with lace, and Eva studied the lace, examining its elaborate patterns as her new husband lay beside her. She imagined the French women who had likely done the stitching, the refined scalloped hems—how they'd labored over lace for generations, damaged their backs and necks and nails, shredded their fingertips, lost their vision. Eva pictured a village of blind women with scars on their hands, serving their husbands supper. Abraham rose to open the window. He stood immodestly—leaning slightly on the sill—and there he was, naked and strange. He lit a Mexican cigar.

"Look," he said. "Come look at the view."

"I'm tired."

"Of course you are." He was a big man, nearly twice her size, and the sheer force of him was something; when he'd stepped on the glass at the ceremony's close, it had shattered into nothing but glitter.

"You must look for both of us," she said. "Tell me, what do you see?"

"I see a German sky."

"How can you tell the sky is German?"

She watched as he yawned, taking his time. Muscles moved along his back like ropes being pulled. Mother had blushed when, after the ceremony (there had been no reception), he'd scooped her up and off the ground. "How can I tell?" He laughed. "Because it is small."

"How can a sky be small?"

"Just wait until you see how these stars—they are nothing but shadows of stars."

"And this moon?"

"A ghost of a moon."

They left Bremen on an American ocean steamer. Though they rode in first class, during one particularly sudden storm Eva mistakenly ran beneath the third-class deck, and was too frightened by the sound of thunder to move away from the foul-smelling crowds. She listened to the creaking of the boards as the ocean tossed and swelled and observed sights of which her mind would not let go: a loaf of black bread that on closer inspection was white bread covered with cockroaches, feet covered with bloody rags in place of proper shoes, a mother nursing her baby without covering herself—even when the child refused the milk—her nipple hanging dark and enormous. Eva had tried to close her eyes, but this too was disquieting, for nocturnal scenes instantly began in distracting carnal flashes. Every night Abraham came to her, doing things she could not think of in the midst of any type of crowd, because— even with her eyes wide open—if she thought of her own nipples, her own troublesome body, she flushed such a deep and lasting crimson, it

sent those around her into unnecessary panic, assuming she'd contracted
a fever.

On pleasant days Eva tried to walk as much and as often as possible.
She tried to keep alert by donning a blouse of Henriette's (hardly filling
the bosom), fixing her sister's cameo at her neck, her sister's bone hairpins in her hair, and dabbing her wrists with what was left of her sister's
violet perfume. (The rest of Henriette's things—poor Julius had wanted
only her dressing gowns—lay hidden in Eva's trousseau, pressed between Mother's Passover linens, stitched rather morbidly and fancifully
with symbols for the ten deadly plagues.) Boosted by Henriette's clothing and scent, encouraged by the reminder of why she was here in her
secret and self-imposed exile, Eva walked the deck.

Abraham—who'd been asked to join a high-stakes poker game in the
quarters of a crippled industrialist—had the notion she was attending a
sewing circle, and Eva did not discourage it. She walked alone, grinning
at Abraham's childlike excitement at having been asked to join this particular card game, and she removed her bonnet, allowing the sun on her
face. Twice she was approached by a well-meaning matron, who mistook
her for a lost child. On these calm, clear days, the first-class deck was a
fine place to be—gentlemen read old newspapers and discussed political
affairs, while ladies sewed and even sang, accompanied by a skilled
quartet.

But after days at sea, she was drawn again to steerage, where—
perhaps because of the unfamiliar diversions—time passed more
quickly. She had her palm read by an Oriental, whose hands were even
smaller than her own. She watched four men juggle milk bottles while
two women danced together, their fleshy arms touching then pulling
apart, turning in circles so fast that Eva thought they would surely faint.
One day she saw a cockfight. Russet birds were set free from cages and
Eva drew closer to see them, nearer and nearer until she was in the
midst of strangers hollering for blood. She sensed nothing of the crowd's
heightening stench. She could have sworn there was a swarm of bees
hovering above, but when she squinted and looked up, there was noth-

ing but a filthy ceiling. The crowd chanted, the cocks squawked and screamed; they clutched and pecked until the floor was stained with guts and strewn with bloody feathers. Men raised their voices and exchanged coins with such lightning speed that in moments it was as if the spectacle had never taken place. Eva tasted salt on the air—salt and blood—not unlike outside that horrid butcher's stall. And, just as it had in the city she'd once sworn she would never leave, the heavy air reeked of carnage and blocked out every last trace of Henriette's violet perfume. The very idea of perfume was suddenly gone. Nothing existed but feathers and blood, birds and men. She half-expected to turn and find Heinrich, smoking a rolled cigarette.

"*Bonjour,* Mademoiselle," slurred a stranger right beside her. "*Baisez-moi.*" He leaned down, his breath hot on her neck. It was as if he could tell that she had been ruined, that her wedding night was a lie. "*Venezici,*" she heard him cry as she fled—tripping twice before the din of the foul crowd drowned his voice, before she found the stairs and the din itself was siphoned away by wind and green, dark sea. She vomited overboard—as did another stout woman at the railing—and ran back to the cabin, where she rinsed her face with the brownish water, which had nearly become familiar. She was less and less shocked when faced with her reflection in the glass. Her face was pink, her eyes flat, and there were more curls loose than fixed atop her head. Mother would have been horrified at the freckles imprinted on her forehead and nose, like cities spread haphazardly across an American map. From the moment Heinrich painted her, she had been marked. Her life had begun to show.

Her parents were not pleased with her match. They had made this perfectly clear. Though Abraham was from a good enough family, it provided nothing in the way of social advancement, and though Abraham had provided Father with documents evidently displaying the future promise of the Shein Brothers' business, Father was reluctant to hand over his daughter's dowry to a man whose immediate plans were to take his only living child across the sea. Father had in fact nearly put his foot down against the marriage, but after Eva had begged for his blessing (shedding tears that her father assumed—incorrectly—to be the symptoms of a love match), after Abraham convinced him of the riches and freedom in America and the fine house that lay across the sea—Father had relented and parted with both Eva's dowry and trousseau, but the goodbye was bitter and disappointed. It was her own urge to confess that she feared, and thus she had no choice but to flee, but she knew that despite her overwhelming motivation to protect her parents, she had managed to break their hearts. She could not think of it; she would not allow herself to think of it. Instead she thought of her husband. She supposed she would have been grateful to anyone who offered her a way out of betraying Henriette (*promise me you'll never speak of what you have done*) and preserving her parents' precious memories, her father's good name, but of all the people it could have been, she supposed she was pleased it was Mr. Shein.

In New York they passed through Castle Garden, where all kinds of music persisted amid a dazed, exhausted throng. There was a five-story emporium on Broadway that extended for what seemed like acres; it was grander than any cathedral, with plate-glass display windows and a cast-iron façade, and as they rode up and down in the elevators, she felt that she could stay all day. They took a suite at the Fifth Avenue Hotel. She drew a bath and soaked until Abraham was forced to knock on the door.

"There is no bathtub—none at all—in your new home."

"How then will I bathe?"

He laughed as if she'd been joking. She thought of how much her mother loved baths and was surprised she had never really thought about how they were similar that way, how her mother too must have, all these years, enjoyed the sense of privacy, the heat. Eva held her breath and heard Abraham light a fresh cigar. Smoke seeped through the closed doorway and into the bathwater, where she plunged her head under and began to count. Water filled her ears, her mouth, and lungs. Ivy snarled through the milky mass. Henriette's face was just out of focus; Heinrich's paint-stained fingers turned the water red. When she came up for air, she flailed about, wetting the spotless tiles. "I fell," she explained, when he demanded an explanation for her soaking wet hair, her pallor.

The berries at the hotel were the sweetest she had ever tasted. All she wanted was berries and cream. He suggested she eat more beef. His portmanteau overflowed with new white shirts. He bought her a square Steinway piano.

"Is this not better than a bathtub?"

She smiled and said no.

From New York to Saint Louis they traveled by railroad with a bathtub (purchased finally from Abraham's mysterious friend, Big Bo, who lived down by the docks), the piano, and their trunks of clothes. They shared a car with two other men—men with unkempt mustaches and mud-encrusted fingernails, who stared at her unwaveringly as she gazed out the window.

"Been a long time since we seen a lady," one of them said. "And you sure are a little one, arncha?"

"She's short as a tall hold on a bear, is what she is."

"Don't go walkin' snakes now, Hiram. You don't mind if we feast our eyes, now do ya, Abe?"

Abraham didn't translate but Eva understood more than he thought. She knew now for instance, from listening carefully, that before Abraham had returned to Germany, he'd traveled to San Francisco. He had gone to buy cheap dry goods—some poor bastard had gone bankrupt— and he'd been with a Spanish woman. They'd had some fun; her skin was brown as caramels.

She looked out the window and saw depressing little houses. Dust-covered storefronts. A bank. The men smoked up the car and instructed Eva slowly and excitedly about the unpredictability of the Indian race. "They got faces inexpressive as a hotel platter, but goddamn if they won't steal the hair from your head if you're not careful." Abraham unrolled a greasy cloth and started dealing cards. The sun beat down on the heavy leather curtains until it was finally sundown. Clouds threatened them as they chased toward nightfall, lumbering overhead like giant bandaged fists, which shook until the dressing unraveled. Then, before her eyes, the sky was strewn with pillows—a giant bed of feather down against a slate-blue floor. She pictured the Spanish woman lying on the pillows:

dark mantilla, jasmine air, thick black hair. One of the men—the one with the skinny long neck—was asking her a question.

Abe said, "Eva, Mr. Jameson would like to know: What did your father's home look like?"

She looked at Mr. Jameson. His eyes were round and unpromising as two small coins. "Tell him . . ." She started, and she could see it all before her: the crumpled bills scattered on Father's walnut secretary, the nicks and scratches on the dining room chairs, every speck of flour on the ceramic kitchen tiles.

"Eva?"

She couldn't arrange it into memory just yet. "There was a special closet for a grandfather clock."

"It was the loveliest home a girl could have," she heard Abraham translate instead. "My father is quite a wealthy man."

Mr. Jameson gave Abraham an affectionate slap. "Well look who's grinnin' like a possum eatin' a yellow jacket!"

She would eventually acknowledge how well she understood English words (if not the mysterious nuances—Snakes? Possums? Why all this talk of dreadful creatures?) and it would seem as if she had not learned the strange tongue from her sister, who had been a natural linguist, and from the girls in her sewing group, but all at once and only since meeting Abraham. This would please him. She did, after all, want to please him. But for now she enjoyed this, her perceived incomprehension; it allowed her a particular privacy. *"Como estás, mi amor?"* He had insisted on teaching her Spanish so she could greet her future Mexican friends and neighbors in their native tongue.

"Bien, gracias," she articulated. She felt like a lapdog. The men congratulated Abraham for finding such a fine wife, and Eva again returned her gaze out the window, to where the pillows of clouds had wafted away, leaving nothing but a starless Ohio sky.

In Saint Louis they took a veranda cabin on a small riverboat whose flag was at half-mast. The United States leader—it was suddenly all anyone could talk about—had been shot in a theater during a performance, which sounded to Eva like the ultimate proof of this country's reputed barbarism. She looked down at the churning, muddy waters, the foamy trail of the steady wake, and yearned to report the calamity to her Uncle Alfred, whom she knew would be interested. The very idea of writing to him and reporting this piece of information filled her with childish excitement, but before she could take pen to paper, the day slipped into evening and she found herself asking her new husband how something like this could happen, as she turned down the bedcovers that night.

"This Booth," Abraham muttered, "this fiend in human shape—he will go down for posterity as the cursed of the accursed!" He whipped off his shirt roughly as if he was preparing to go and string up the devil himself. "I served President Lincoln in the Civil War. I was a captain—have I told you?"

She nodded. "You have."

"We might have all been ruled by a pack of Texans by now."

"It's astonishing."

"I beat those bloody Texans down the Rio Grande. We beat them straight out of New Mexico! And now this maniac—this coward in a theater!"

"My dear," she said, "please."

"Please . . . ?" He began, before stopping himself and pulling on his sleeping attire. "You mustn't . . . ." And he looked ready to state yet another strange rule of life here that had, until now, gone unexplained. Instead he said, "Show me your hair."

Eva turned away and began extracting hairpins. She could feel him waiting, his breath was eager; it made her take more time and she enjoyed taking her time. She even enjoyed the strangeness that breathed between them like an uncouth companion, ready to turn savage at any moment. Beneath their two bodies marooned in dim candlelight— beneath the floorboards and second class, third class, the cooks still cleaning the kitchen, beneath the stockroom full of dank supplies threatened by flooding and mosquitoes and the engine with its grimy environs, which she could barely conjure at all—the Missouri River surged and she felt as if she were a part of it. *Missouri:* It felt so exotic on the tongue. She carved the word with her mouth. She tried to recall the streets of Berlin (she was sure she'd never see them again) and how the stones had looked more green than gray, more purple hued than blue. Her thought—accompanied by an awareness oddly tranquil—was how on that night in the alley, when Henriette's water broke, it was not only her sister's fate that was sealed. It was not only her sister and the baby who died, but also the Eva who would grow old in the city of her youth, the Eva who could take for granted having friends and family surrounding her. Abraham suddenly grabbed for her across the bed—her hair half undone, the bedside candle still burning. Despite all his planning that encompassed two continents and three languages, he was impulsive, impatient; she'd learned that much already. He was instinctively rough and not afraid to hurt her. It was better this way. "Missouri," she whispered into Abraham's knot of a shoulder as it thrust urgently toward her.

When he was finished, his voice grew hoarse. "In one year's time, I will build your new house." She blew out the candle; smoke curled in listless patterns.

His voice, his inflections—they seemed to dictate the very shadows on the wall.

"But," she said, turning on her side to face him, "I understood there was already a house."

"Yes, of course there is," he said drowsily. "There is a house. Of course."

"Of course," she said. She could barely make out his shape. The room was dark and silent. He fell asleep so easily. Sometimes he talked through his dreams.

"Too much blood," he exclaimed. And then: "You, Señor, are at the wrong window."

She knew he was asleep but even so, it felt odd—even discourteous—not to reply.

"I am sorry for the President," she whispered. It was all she could think of to say.

• • •

KANSAS CITY, A WINDY AFTERNOON. THEY DISEMBARKED ONTO THE riverbank, her cloth shoes sunk into the mud, and soon she had seen too many family reunions to count and was finally finished with crying. Abraham was furious. He was looking for port officials, but the offices were closed, hung with the official black drapery of mourning. "Goddamn Lincoln," he finally said, plainly finished with his last night's sentimental show of patriotism. "Where the devil are the escorts?" Available to the newlyweds were only two buggies—one large and one small—a team of spotted horses and a well-built young servant named Tranquilo. Eva was so happy to have a servant that she curtsied to the boy. *"Buenos dias,"* she remembered, and the Mexican stared before offering an animal skin, which she accepted from his dark-brown hands. She later understood that he was sent by Abraham's brother Meyer as a precautionary reinforcement—a decision not only wise but evidently necessary. Where were the freight wagons? Tranquilo had no idea. Where were the company caravans, dispatched to welcome his bride? To protect against the Indians, thick as hops along the trail? Abraham addressed the boy in rapid Spanish, obviously displeased, and Tranquilo, after a brief explanation that clearly did not satisfy, began to search for a team—among the many skinny youths anxious for work—who might be of some assistance with the transfer of the bathtub and square Steinway.

"This will do," Abraham declared, after a hearty blowing of his nose. "This will do just fine. The fewer in our party, the fewer chances of contracting cholera." He gestured to the burning tar barrels surrounding the depot, which she knew were to ward off the dreaded disease.

"You don't mean to say?" Eva began, coughing from the smoke and overwhelmed by the surrounding throngs anxiously searching for family, the young boys calling out, offering transport, shoe shine, baskets of apples, newspapers, and accommodations that promised not only to comfort but also to shock and delight. "But this cannot be our only transport."

Abraham did not answer. Two mules swatted flies with their tails. She draped the skin across her shoulders. It smelled like manure but she drew it close. The wind was picking up.

THE SANTA FE TRAIL; WHERE TREES CAST OFF IVORY BELL BLOSSOMS and long-tailed birds walked faster than the mules. Where lizards transformed from sinister to bejeweled as they darted reliably under a molten midday sun. There were buffalo so numerous that after a short while these beasts became a sight barely more unusual than pigeons clustered on cobblestones. The first time she saw one dead, she had the desire to touch it; the hair on its neck stretched from her fingertip to the top of her head. She knew that some Jews of her homeland were so wealthy and so dedicated that they brought a ritual slaughterer on hunting expeditions in order to ensure that the animals trapped or caught would be no less than ritually slaughtered, and she tried to picture what one of them would make of these buffalo. That very night she ate that same creature's pickled tongue; it was so delicious she could not afford to be disgusted.

When Abraham said *look,* she looked; when he told her not to fret, she was somewhat soothed. She could imagine him leading troops into battle. He pointed out sights with authority and not a small dose of wonder: a hairy tarantula crawling from an innocuous-looking hole in the ground; smoke from Indian lodges atop a mesa in the distance; rounds of water, strung across the earth like beads on a string. "Buffalo fight toward a purpose," he said approvingly. "They go head to head and walk slowly in a circle. Just watch them! Look how they create depressions in the ground in order to catch the rain . . . If you are ever dying of thirst," he said gravely, "these muddy, insect-ridden puddles will save your life—"

"Abraham!"

"You will slurp it down like nectar, make no mistake about it!" He raised his voice, and then smiled when he saw her disturbed expression. "I am only being clear that in such a situation—"

"Heaven forbid!"

"Well yes all right then—*heaven forbid*—but here is the truth: You shall have only the buffalo to thank."

They traveled through days and nights—the pitted trail driving spikes up her spine despite the hay-filled cushions. Tranquilo led the way with the larger wagon, while Abraham followed with the trunks of clothes and his nervous bride. At night she desired nothing more than daybreak, but as the sun rose and she stared into the distance, there was nothing to see in front of them but grasslands, and when she turned in the opposite direction, there was nothing but two wheel-born lines, those same two lines, which were as comforting in their infinite nature as they were deceiving, for they led exactly to where she sat, which was precisely nowhere.

And the maddening images, reliable and fixed as a deck of cards whenever she closed her eyes: Eva Frank sat by a window. Abraham Shein walked into a room. She followed these pictures through the inroads of her mind's eye as they shifted and changed until Abraham opened the window wide, leaving her just enough space. In her mind she saw an invitation in his heavy, dark eyes and in that one moment she knew that she could jump through the window and that by doing so, Heinrich would marry a Christian, grow drunk and bitter or proud and content and either way she wouldn't know. Distance meant something and what she'd thought it could mean was a more efficient and perhaps gentler delivery from memory. But she was still falling out that window, and instead of being caught by a husband, he was falling with her into land and sky so fluid they ceased to have a surface.

The buggy pressed on, but it hardly seemed possible that it was moving forward because direction itself had disappeared. Where they came from, where they were going—it was quickly losing authority. Shadows emerged not as shadows but caverns. As the buggy drew closer to the striking shade, it seemed they'd be swallowed whole. Forked lightning sent thunder rolling and she heard her own scream as the darkness turned to a sheet of falling water. She managed to stop screaming only when Abraham grabbed her wrist so tightly she could picture the bruise, as a fine, white mist came through the tightened canvas and pearls glistened—so incongruously pretty—throughout Abraham's dirty hair. She closed her eyes as the horses drove ahead, as their hooves thundered into darkness and her wrist throbbed from his thick grip, but she didn't exactly want him to let go. When they emerged in a patch of sun shining through scattered clouds, she was so shocked she began to laugh. She would track storms over weeks to come, as if by seeing them she might just stop their fury—those ragged, noisy beggars limping off in the distance, shaking their cups of coins.

THE SOUND OF SPANISH, THE SMELL OF FLESH. SHE WOKE FROM A bottomless nap atop a pile of table linens and cotton undergarments, their lavender scent both a source of disorientation and comfort. But it was no more than a moment before she remembered where she was, how she had crawled underneath the canopy of the wagon and pried open one of the trunks, desperate for a familiar touch as much as for sleep, and, as if she were hiding during a favorite children's game, she'd fallen asleep inside the trunk as the men continued to drive the horses clear across the plains. She woke (breathing in the scent of a lavender sachet) to find that the wagon had finally stopped and evening had once again begun its slow and frightening finale. The sky still held the sun's fiery impression, and Tranquilo stood outside the wagon, holding a rifle. If he noticed her watching, it didn't register on his somber face. She felt smaller than the cigarette in the Mexican's hand, more insubstantial than the blue smoke rising in the air. Abraham, having already skinned the hide of an enormous beast, was butchering the meat and hanging the last of it to dry from the top of the buggy. The red-brown strips took the final glint of daylight—glistening with blood and ribbons of fat, a long way from being cured.

"I shot a buffalo," he said. His eyes darted from Eva to the horizon, then back to the task at hand.

"I can cook," she said, surprising herself. "I can cook something delicious."

Only then did she notice the sound of barking dogs—faint enough that it took a moment to distinguish from the wind. Abraham shook his head and gestured to Tranquilo, who began taking down the meat. "We'll leave at once. No campfires. Comanches. Do you understand?"

"I do," she said, her stomach turning from not only the reality of what he was suggesting but from the meat so close and drawing flies, her fierce incongruous hunger.

The sound of dogs grew more distinct, even as the wind blew stronger, even as they continued on. They had lost their way. It happened all too frequently—or so Abraham defensively explained. Those barking dogs were Indian dogs—Indian dogs at an Indian camp. Legendary Rebekah took shape in her mind, Rebekah en route to her fiancé—captured by Indians and killed. Rebekah the human sacrifice. Rebekah the Jewish bride. Poor Isaac searching the Indian camps, searching for her until he died.

At her husband's suggestion Eva ate a bit of partially dried meat with thick tortillas, but she instantly retched into a pail, and the wagon didn't stop. They raced across the plains, only stopping when, finally, the horses needed water. The moon was a sliver and the stars were shrouded. She could make out neither trees nor the land beyond where Tranquilo spread blankets on the hard, cold earth and the men lay down. She climbed into the bigger wagon, unlaced her boots, placed them under her head, and reclined in the porcelain bathtub, where she then began to pray. She prayed for the first time since Henriette cried out in pain. She prayed ambiguously—not so much for her survival, but as a way to speak her own language to someone who knew her well. In a place so wholly unfamiliar, she took small comfort from fundamentals: a blanket—no matter how coarse or rudimentary—drawn close was still a blanket, and no matter what Abraham had said, the moon was still the moon, the same one she'd always known. Most of all—in a manner neither spiritual nor profound—she took comfort from herself: her stubby hands, her unwashed yogurt scent. These things she knew. She pictured the portraits above her father's desk. Eva in gray, before drawn curtains. Henriette in blue, on the divan. Why hadn't he chosen her sister? Had Heinrich set his sights on Henriette, the portraits would have by now taken on a different meaning, as Henriette would have ultimately discouraged him. In Eva's mind the two events were absolutely aligned: Had Heinrich set his sights on Henriette, by now Eva would not be risking her life in a shoddy wagon on the open frontier, but instead in her father's comfortable home enjoying afternoon coffee and cakes, perhaps recalling that brief period of time when the painter came daily—the painter who was so very serious, so keen on Henriette. Eva somehow did not question that had she not been with Heinrich, her sister and her nephew would be alive. She took comfort right then, if only very briefly, from her own secrets. If there was little rectitude at her core, then there was certainly familiarity. Never had she so recognized its virtue.

In what seemed like only moments, the sun shone brightly. She could feel the heat coming through the floorboards, how the dust that wasn't in her throat was spinning like tinsel through shards of light. Eva emerged from the cool tub, drew the heavy leather aside, and at first only noticed that Abraham still slept. It was strange to see him on his back, on the ground, exposed. For a moment she felt as if she were dreaming when she saw what lay beside Tranquilo, barely a horse's length away. She didn't scream when she saw the wreckage of oxen and wagon, petrified as ruins against the morning light. She didn't wail when she saw what she realized were hundreds of envelopes scattered about like remnants of muddied snow: all those letters—she would think of them later—all of those sentiments left unexpressed, aborted on the trail. She couldn't find breath to gather sound in her throat when she saw two bodies splayed like kindling. Two men, scalped. She knew the word but until now she hadn't fully understood the meaning. She turned away but in the other direction were the ashes of another man. He had been tied to a tree and burned. He was naked. She needed water. She called out but the only sound she heard was Tranquilo's low moan. These men would need to be buried. She felt the earth closing in over their heads, filling up her own dry mouth.

They had, unknowingly, slept on the site of a massacre.

Abraham sprung up, clutching his gun, and pointing it in her direction. His eyes were wild and when they met hers, there was no trace of recognition.

SMALL EXQUISITE THING

APPROACHING SANTA FE AT DAWN, EVA COULD BARELY hold up her head. These nights had both kept her on perpetual watch and instilled the unfulfilled desire for a few drops of laudanum or at least a glass of beer. She had become immune to beauty, to the view along the way: sky vast and blank as a bare opera stage, strange red soil sprouting silver shrubs. She was finished with craning her neck to see the muddy Sangre de Christo unfailingly poking the stars. She was finished with the stars, which had looked sharp before but now just looked far away.

"It's so cold," she nearly hissed as they approached a narrow river where three half-naked children stood bathing, so unashamed that they waved; she could not bring herself to wave back. Now that they were close to their destination, her constitution was beginning to fray. Dogs howled, emerging from stainlike shadows, but thankfully kept their distance, and as the howls diminished when they'd safely forded the river, Abraham reached once more for Eva's wrist, but this time he did it gently. With his calloused thumb, he caressed the underside. When she drew a breath, her chest smarted; the air was brisk, laced with pine smoke.

"Pine," she said hazily.

"*Piñon*," he corrected. "Smells sweeter in Spanish, don't you think?"

From a distance, the city—so long awaited—looked like no more than a pile of bricks laid out to bake in a yard. Church towers rose out of the rubble, as if struggling to make good on a far-fetched architectural promise. The wagon drew closer to the sound of ringing bells and the sound was surprisingly moving. The bells chimed on for longer than any that she had ever heard, as if wanting to make perfectly clear to everyone within earshot that morning had broken. More big-eyed brown children played in an alley before a cluster of what appeared to be oversized pigsties; the children sat perched atop shaggy goats and attempted to lasso a chicken. She was torn between trying to envision her own children playing in this dust and dirt, and feeling relief upon seeing a chicken. She had anticipated endless meals of nothing but beans and corn cakes, and seeing the chicken darting this way and that made her feverish with dinner possibilities, immediately wondering if there was a cook she might teach to make a blackberry sauce, perhaps some pickled cabbage. She pictured her phantom children growing fat and being content to play in dirt, but then she wondered at how—even for a second—she had the impudence to imagine she might actually survive the births. It was an Indian—plaited hair hanging long on both sides—that saved her from imagining further. "Good Lord!" Eva cried, on seeing a savage so close, his skin not red but bronze, lit darkly by the sun.

"No no," said Abraham, laughing. "He's a Pueblo—different from the Comanches. Fine fellow."

He was clad all in white, draped with blankets, driving a herd of burros. The burros were everywhere; most hauled bundles of wood, but some seemed to roam without destination, hungry dogs weaving between their legs.

"What do you think?" Abraham smiled and gestured vaguely to the unpaved alley and the shacks that looked plastered with mud, to shelters with iron-barred windows if any at all and nothing in the way of adornment besides red chilies hanging on strings.

"We've only—I've yet to see very much," she answered, fighting the corners of her mouth from turning downward.

Abraham then instructed Tranquilo, pointing around a corner.

"We'll go straight to the store," said Abraham abruptly.

"But where is our home?"

He shook his head, not meeting her gaze. "First, my brother. He'll be anxious to see you."

"I am anxious to change out of my traveling dress."

He chuckled but did not change his mind.

"I look frightful," she implored.

"You look good to me," he said with a shrug. "You look like mine."

As the wagon proceeded, she did her best to collect her curls in a knot, to pinch her cheeks, which were as dry as dust. When they came upon the plaza of which he had so often spoken, she was surprised to discover that although it possessed a few small paths and a modest gazebo at its center, it was no more than a rectangle formed by white-washed buildings. "There's a store!" she cried out absurdly at seeing trinkets for sale, nearly giggling with relief at the sight of men in suits, men walking and talking as if they were not in any danger or any rush but rather out for a stroll.

"There are quite a few stores," he said. "Did you think ours would be the only one? Competition is good."

The plaza was indeed lined with a few stores—Sheinker's, Spiegelman's, Isinfeld's. German names, Jewish names—as amusing in these incongruous surroundings as they were reassuring. Of course Abraham had told her that she could expect other Germans, other Jews (he'd named a few good families doing business), but she realized she had not believed him. She realized she was entirely surprised to see the names right there in print, on carefully painted signs—signs far more elegant than the stores themselves, which looked better suited to animal feed than "imported quality goods." Not until that moment in the plaza did she realize she had married a man whose word she had not trusted.

Of all these stores—she couldn't help but be a little proud—Shein Brothers' was the largest. Two dark salesrooms overflowing with the most

confused stock, the store looked like the attic of a treasured—if a bit
touched—relative that had been opened to the public. Groceries plain
and imported (Tinned herring! Tinned salmon!), vats of flour next to
bolts of muslin, burgundy velvet, a cast-iron stove. The fanfare of their
arrival coincided with the daily unbolting and unchaining of the doors,
and some hundred cowboys apparently returning from a round-up. The
cowboys, though darker and shorter, looked as though they'd stepped
right out of a picture book that Mother had showed her, which Uncle Alfred had loved as a child. As she made tentative steps on the pliant mud
floor, they turned to her in unison and doffed their sombreros, as if they
had been choreographed.

Clerks who patted Abraham on the back were introduced as cousins
from Wiesbaden, a few Mexican employees bowed their heads in congratulations, and—she was delighted to notice—called Abraham *El
Guapo*. They went off to help customers—who, in addition to the cowboys, were also a few señoras, a sallow nun, a weedy man in a cinnamon-
colored robe. Immediately she noticed the guns. Guns in holsters and on
countertops, rifles in straps slung across men's backs like children in *re-
bozos*. She found herself reaching for a pistol, but was afraid it would be
unseemly. Instead she took up a silver and ivory comb; it was cool to the
touch and surprisingly heavy.

"Expensive taste," said a man's voice behind her, and Eva put it back
on the shelf; its inlaid mother-of-pearl designs glinted in the shadows.
She turned toward a face that could have only belonged to her brother-
in-law, a face that was a somewhat squashed version of her husband's.
Their resemblance was unfortunately similar—unfortunate only for Meyer,
as the similarities between the brothers only enhanced the differences—
the combination of a hawk nose and Abraham's prominent jaw looked
rugged and headstrong, while the same hawk nose united with Meyer's
weak chin looked slightly feeble. Both sets of eyes were large and brown
and both had a hound's intensity, only Abraham's resembled a hunting
dog, while Meyer's resembled a stray.

"It came yesterday from New York," he said, reaching for the ivory
handle. "Arrived in the same caravan that was meant to stop in Kansas

City and collect something else quite small and exquisite there, something far more important than a comb." He smiled the same crooked smile as her husband, but his had a comic twist. "I fear your journey was terrible." He shook his head. "Please take this with you." He placed the comb in her hands.

"I couldn't."

"Please," he said. "Take." He kissed her hand shyly. He was older than she had anticipated.

"What is he offering?" Abraham asked, returning from the storeroom.

"Your brother has been most kind."

"Is that right?"

"Abe," Meyer said. "Please."

"What did you give her?"

Eva realized she was holding the comb behind her back.

"Show me."

"It is only a comb," said Meyer, strangely apologetic.

"I'll treasure it, Meyer," she said, presenting it to Abraham.

"A little welcome gift?" Abraham asked.

"It came in the last shipment."

"I should think my bride would have preferred the escort and supplies."

The brothers stepped outside and had words. She watched Abraham yell and Meyer shake his head before launching into a sober explanation. She could not tell who was ultimately in charge, for though Meyer was older and had started the business, Abraham was clearly *El Guapo,* the larger, formidable presence.

By the time they were back in the wagon, the sun was high in the sky. The brothers had parted with a handshake, leaving Eva with an idea of just how often they quarreled. After passing a saloon and rounding a narrow corner, Tranquilo soon came to a halt in the very same alley they had passed through on their way to the store: the unpaved strip of mud-cake huts where burros were now stationed in a tethered row, drinking water out of troughs. The cold air smelled of dust and sweating mules. She gripped the ivory comb tightly; each separate tooth dug into her hand.

When Abraham turned a key in a padlock and opened a barn-like door, she assumed that this was one more stop along the way before they reached home. She was just getting accustomed to the potentially irritating and even charming idea that her husband was someone whose daily trajectories rarely went from one place straight to another, but instead split off into never-predictable detours. She was ready for him to introduce a cobbler or the caretaker of their house, or even the maid. It had been this way with Big Bo, who'd sold the porcelain bathtub: Abraham had walked into a warehouse as if he'd owned the place; he'd made friendly, rough talk as he demanded to see more bathtubs. She'd watched and learned how, in Abraham's world, socializing and doing business were very much one and the same.

As she glanced around the interior of this hovel, at its dull mud floor and its whitewashed adobe walls, at its deep embrasures topped with potted geraniums, its low ceilings and highly depressing sense of dignity (evidenced in the oddly formal dining room table and unpolished but nonetheless silver candelabra) she wondered who would soon show their faces as the inhabitants. There was a tiny kitchen with no stove and no place to store anything cold. She imagined the black-edged fireplace giving off not only heat but also terrible smoke, when whoever lived here cooked anything from a pot of coffee to a side of beef. She could not begin to imagine the claustrophobia that would undoubtedly grow while enduring daily life in a place like this, and she noted with tremendous relief for whomever lived here that there was a separate bedroom with a closed door, behind which she could only imagine were the straw pallets and sad piles of scratchy blankets sitting on a mud floor.

"Who lives here?" she asked, as if, by now, she still did not know.

She hardly felt better on seeing that the bedroom had a bed, in fact a very beautiful bed—hand-carved oak and painted with flowers—the bed of an American princess, with plump feather pillows to boot. She scarcely registered the back garden (where the bathtub was fated to live), a weedy but peaceful outdoor space where the mountains rose in the distance like the promise of something bigger and better, in what felt like a private view. She kept her eyes on those mountains in dubious silence until Abraham finally broke the pretense that anything else was possible.

"Don't look so miserable," he said firmly. "It doesn't suit you." He ushered her inside and spots of angry pink and green dashed across her vision. Here was something she would never get used to—the frequent movement between such vivid, almost blinding, light and the darkness of indoors. "Misery doesn't suit you," he repeated, shaking his head, discouraged but oddly bright. "Not anymore."

GOOSE

As the push of nausea broke through her sleep, Eva ran to the chamber set, tripping on her nightclothes. She was pregnant—she was sure now—she knew it at the same moment she heard the unfamiliar squawking. She'd become accustomed to the accompaniment of roosters at this hour, the barking of dogs and thud of horse hooves making their way out of town, the gamblers cursing—their voices strained and desperate—having lost their very last coins, but here was a honking most unfamiliar and yet she swore she'd heard it long ago. As she rinsed her face with cold water that did nothing to stop her insides from turning, she had a shameful first impulse to abort the baby (was *she* to have a baby and not Henriette? Could God be just that insane?).

Then she realized the squawking belonged to a goose.

Under the *vigas,* with a shawl wrapped tightly around her shoulders, she stood sucking down the palliative of new dawn air. The squawking had stopped, there was no goose in sight and she laughed out loud then, knowing she'd only imagined a goose and it was because—despite or because of her nausea—her appetite was actually returning for the first time since arriving in Santa Fe over six months ago. There was no goose, only stinking burros swinging filthy tails and a lone drunk who staggered down the center of the alley, seemingly attracted to both sides of the street and fiercely unable to choose. She hid behind the door, so he wouldn't catch a glimpse of her, but she refused to close the door entirely. The early morning sky was one of the few truly glorious aspects of this undignified life in which she'd found herself and a deadly winter was fast approaching, so that to stand in an open doorway without badly shivering could only be counted as a blessing. A winter chill was on the air, but it was as if it were already in her bones: These mud-walled quarters would be that much closer when one could not let in the cold, and she envisioned spending her days waiting for a shipment of woolens—a shipment perpetually delayed or held-up by robbers, one band more frightening than the next. She could imagine being told how Billy the Kid and his men made off with a shipment of ladies' woolens, while the other shipments—the snuff, the razors, the Mexican cigars— were somehow left alone. She could already hear the conversation play out with Abraham—in a tone she was ever more accustomed to, somewhere between teasing and hostility—as he'd remind her how she had a fine education in needlework, conveniently not understanding that all the fancy embroidery of her youth was no preparation for a life of sewing woolen undergarments, that such an intention was hardly planned. Winter would be brutal indeed.

But after standing in the doorway—goose or no goose—after breathing this revelation of an October morning with a secret of a baby finally in her belly, she was suddenly full of what she slowly realized was pride. While what she'd told Abraham was true—she had done nothing to *prevent* being pregnant up until now—it was also true that she had not exactly welcomed it. How could she allow herself such a full life, a life that her sister would never have? "Henriette," she said, the way she did sometimes, as if the name had transformed itself into now what was only a changeable word—for *help* or *heavens* or even *hello*. Sometimes she said it when Abraham did not come home for dinner or when he raised his voice in answer to her question: *When will you build our house?* During those times she sometimes hissed it damningly—*Henriette*. And once she called another name right into her husband's pillow, a name that remained strange and beautiful because she never said it out loud, a name she still did not know whether to love or hate. She mouthed this name when she knew she had chosen this life in response to the possibility of another, when—on certain mornings—her husband's pillow smelled of lard oil and pretzels and she knew without asking that he'd been at the cheapest saloon that was also the closest, where a Mexican whore offered whiskey and women—brown-skinned, cigarette-smoking women—who moved slowly through the streets on their way to work, as if to say: *Have a look, we're not hiding, you should know.* But it was her sister's name that she whispered now and it was said with appreciation, as the rising sun cast the sky as sand sifting slowly into more sand; a wan sky nearly impossible to distinguish from the faded adobe buildings, from the earth itself.

When she looked away from the shifting layers of the horizon, she realized she hadn't imagined the squawking after all. The goose stood before her quietly—even somberly—his beady black eyes boring into Eva's as if he could see into her mind, at a daguerreotype of Henriette at twelve years old as she gathered blackberries for a sauce. The goose (whom, she quickly decided, did not belong to anyone) was stippled brown and gray with rumpled, white-edged feathers, and stood close enough to nip her ankle; it stared squarely as she remembered how blackberries had stained the thin cotton of her sister's skirt and how Henriette had been so upset about the ruined skirt that she'd lost her appetite for her favorite dish of nicely crisp roast goose.

"*Va!*" Eva cried, testing out her *español,* which she could rarely bring herself to do in front of live human beings, not since Chela had somehow made it clear that her voice sounded as though she had something lodged in her throat. She'd refrained from telling Chela that it was the entire German language that was stuck there, the language that she loved.

"*Va!*" she cried again, louder this time, but the fowl merely shifted its weight until it was she who retreated back inside the adobe hut that Abraham called their home. She stood in the center of the kitchen, and recalled how, only hours after her arrival, she'd set out to organize their separate sets of dishes—one for milk and one for meat—and Abraham had stood watching her briefly (she'd imagined he was pleased, even moved) before saying, "We're done with all that, puss. There's no need for it here." He'd smiled, almost beatifically, as if proclaiming the laws of *kashruth* quaint, and walked off to work on a Saturday. During those first weeks she had stubbornly looked to her *Kosher Gastronomy*—a parting gift from Father—as small as her hand and bound in brown leather, with mottled beige pages covered with proclamations regarding the compatibility between Jewish ritual and culinary refinement. She'd looked to this book to provide some kind of solace to those who were far away from home, but instead found a punitive set of directions written by one very self-righteous Jewess, whose primary focus was how ignorance in the kitchen lent itself to either "bountiful excessiveness" or "frugal tedium." There was a recipe for waffles, which of course required a waffle iron, which the author promised could be found at any fine ironmonger of the Hebrew persuasion. After reading that bit of nonsense (*a Hebrew iron-monger?*), Eva put down the book for days, before searching for a lard substitute and—after numerous tries at melting down beef suet with rosemary, after stirring in a few precious drops of flower water with a wooden fork—she shut the book and gave up entirely, dipping into Chela's lard and learning to enjoy the hiss it made when it hit the frying pan. She learned two things from that lard-rich meal: The roof did not fall in (as she half-expected it would), and (to her dismay) she truly loved the taste of it.

Abraham was not at all ashamed to have people to dinner in such tight quarters, between uneven whitewashed walls that looked cavelike in the dark and perpetually dirty by lamplight. He proclaimed their situation temporary with great confidence and a broad smile, as if naming it "temporary" landed the whole living arrangement squarely in the realm of great fun. If the topic of building more comfortable homes happened to come up in mixed company, Abraham tossed off the reassuring sentence that Eva had heard daily for the past few months: The plans for the house were being drawn. After that he could be counted on to boast how much he enjoyed *livin' like a real Santa Fean.*

He somehow painted a romantic picture of their spartan life, a charming fiction for various dinner guests, in which Eva was not the melancholy girl from Berlin whose idea of spartan life, until joining lives with Abraham, was a summerhouse in Karlsbad, but she was Eva the healthy *Fräulein,* who cared nothing for city comforts and who had jumped at the chance to marry a Man Who Takes Risks. It was almost amusing how completely he diverted the talk from houses, and heartily convinced others that he and his wife were not scraping along in squalor amid large insects, peculiar cooking smells, and refuse from frequently emptied chamber pots, but that they were rather great adventurers and this living arrangement was no different than taking a long trek in the mountains or sailing out to sea.

He was adamantly not ashamed of the kitchen in plain view where, as the starry-eyed guests finished their strudel (or her primitive approximations of a strudel with dried apples or meticulously pitted dried chokecherries), Chela soaked the first-course plates—the Frank family china!—in a slimy bucket full of scalding water boiled over an open fire. Abraham promised her a cast-iron stove each and every week, but somehow never delivered on that promise.

And so, while she heard whispers in the store and in the plaza of how her husband was *un rico Israelito,* he was strangely selective about how he spent his rumored wealth, for all she had to work with was a fireplace shaped like a horseshoe that left burn scars not only on Chela's and Eva's hands but also on the walls. While he either "forgot" to have a stove delivered, or claimed that he enjoyed the smell of *piñon* smoke, that nothing made a man feel so *right peart* as a home with a roaring fire, he also felt perfectly comfortable pointing out to his colleagues the square Steinway, or Eva's beautiful dresses (that had of course come with her trousseau), or that theirs was the first bathtub in Santa Fe—even if the pale porcelain sat on the ground out back, and was mostly used as a bird bath. When at first Eva had insisted the house was not fit for entertaining, Abraham merely laughed. "We live in the great American West—not a somber mansion in Charlottenburg."

She meant to ask: *What exactly is the matter with a mansion in Charlottenburg? And just where could possibly be a more pleasant place to dine?* But she said nothing—nothing about how her dowry was meant to set up a household, and if the dowry wasn't doing that, then what exactly was it doing?—and she gave Chela the fine serviettes for washing. If they were to receive guests, then the guests would—at the very least—always have fine linen in their laps. Her mother had offered the family linens only after Eva agreed that she would put them to use even if they were laid nowhere but across the desert floor, even if she was reduced to serving *traif* to naked savages, and though Abraham laughed when he repeated these conditions in order to illustrate both his mother-in-law's sense of humor and the absurdly formal ideals of their homeland, Eva thought this promise was as touching as the linens were beautiful. She'd repeatedly told Abraham, "I will use them until they are worn down to nothing but lovely dust."

"Of this I have no doubt," he'd responded, patting her gently on the head. "Now please go with Tranquilo to Fort Marcy and enlighten our guests as to what time we shall expect them."

One evening in June, as the sky went from orange-purple to ghostly pearly green, they'd sat outside with their Yankee guests and she'd served champagne and canned oysters from a recent Shein Brothers' shipment. When Abraham tilted his chair back, setting his feet up on the *portal* post, she was mortified until—much to her surprise—the other men followed suit. With his rakish hat, full whiskers, and a supply of evidently amusing Western expressions, Abraham held the Easterners in thrall with tales of the trail—tales that Eva had never once heard, and she wondered, almost in passing, if any of them were true. As she watched her husband, she was aware of sitting severely straight and yet she found herself reeling back and forth, perpetually adrift between skepticism and awe until the mosquitoes swarmed and the rains came, sending them all inside to light candles. Her hair was secured in a chignon adorned with eighteen hairpins—enough to not only hold her hair in place but to make her head ache miserably, but even in spite of her aching head, she couldn't deny it was a gay affair.

Among the guests was a phrenologist, a quiet man who'd held her aching head and insisted that her skull was unusually smooth, full of secrets, and that, in addition to protecting these secrets, she needed to consume more animal food. "Meat," said the phrenologist. "The answer for you is meat! It will act on your mind as manure does on flowers, forcing a degree of expansion and bloom not otherwise possible to attain." The other guests—a remarkably short officer and his flirtatious wife, a newspaperman, and a handsome engineer—were too high on champagne to notice how strongly she blushed as the strange man held her head, and Abraham was too busy enjoying the strange prognostications to give much thought to what his wife's secrets might be. Contrary to his expressly practical nature, Abraham adored the idea that life could be revealed, and that fortunes could be cast in shapes, in cards, or leaves. But she knew how fortunes were cast—and she didn't need any parlor scientist to tell her. Fortunes were cast by making decisions.

After months of insisting Chela sweep the portal at least twice a day, Eva now instructed her to discard all the apple peels and cores there to attract the elusive goose, in addition to tossing handfuls of cornmeal at the very suggestion of a squawk. The portal quickly grew filthy with meal and apple mush, and Chela grew so cross after one near-biting incident that Eva was terrified of losing her the way she'd already lost two other girls who'd cleaned and cooked before her (Luz fat and quiet, Juanita tearful and loud), but Chela stayed and the goose finally built a nest on the low, flat roof, and soon it began to guard the doorway with no less effect than a watchdog. It was a wonder that Abraham didn't shoot it immediately, considering the way it announced his frequent late-night entrances, but contrary to what a skilled shot Abraham had been on the plains, he didn't much care for doing away with anything at close range. He claimed it wasn't worth the effort, but Eva liked to think she had chosen a husband who—though unquestionably up to the task—did not have great enthusiasm for killing. For while she had initially attracted the goose for nothing other than their dining pleasure, she had become un-

deniably and irritatingly attached to the poor thing. When she told him
so late one night as he cast off his gravy-stained clothes, he balked and
took his pistol from where he'd cast it off on her carefully lace-cloaked
dresser. In nothing but his unmentionables he returned to the moonlit
street and fired a hasty shot, but the goose flapped its wings in a distracting riot, and when the bullet was swallowed by a slanted hitching post,
Abraham returned to the bedroom, cursing the son-of-a-bitch-no-
account-goddamn goose, and Eva was silently relieved.

SHE SHOULD HAVE BEEN AWAKE LONG BEFORE HIM IN ORDER TO
serve breakfast, but her limbs felt too heavy, and even as she registered
the slant of light through the small window, she pretended to be asleep.
She pictured herself from up above and saw her now-four-months-
pregnant body as a leech affixed to bed sheets, a leech gorging itself on
the lingering pleasures of sleep. And there was also the pleasure of
watching him—when he wasn't aware she was doing so—in the early
morning light. On especially chilly mornings, armed with the excuse of
being with child, she stayed under the covers and watched his breath
gather on the increasingly bluish air; she watched as he tried not to
shiver. At all other times of day he seemed so comfortable, so entirely at
home amid so much dirt, among such a motley population speaking
strange languages, but during cold mornings he looked alone and uncomfortable. There was—she was not unaware—a tinge of cruelty that
accompanied her enjoyment as she watched and felt a vicarious morning
chill.

After nearly nine months of marriage he'd remained in most ways a
stranger, and she was content to watch him move through his morning
routine. There was still novelty in the black hair curling on his barrel
chest, in his big, white feet and their heavy stomping, and the way he
raised a racket even when his task at hand required a far gentler touch.
She stared through half-closed eyes as he buttoned a button with so little grace, hurling his suit coat over his shoulders as if it were not a coat
but rather a beast he'd wrestled to its grizzly death only minutes before.
Somehow all of these rough measures produced a puzzlingly magnetic

effect. She could watch him—mysteriously compelled to do so—for a rather long time. When he disappeared toward the kitchen she sat up and reflexively looked into her hand mirror. Abraham did not like her to wear a nightcap—he claimed it made him think of hospitals; he spent a frightening month in one as a child with a nearly fatal bout of influenza—and so with each morning there came a hair-taming struggle, a rush to gather crude curls from their various directions and crush them into one presentable shape. She swung her feet out of the bedclothes and onto the floor and embarked upon the task of getting dressed.

Within minutes there came the scent of frying, a sizzling of butter and cornmeal and chilies that invariably made her long for a simple dry roll. *"Buenos dias,* Chela," Eva ventured. "My darling"—she approached Abraham in their language—"are you certain you wouldn't prefer plain potatoes?"

He looked at her as if she were suggesting he eat a hog.

"I only mean to say that Chela's *desayuno*—delicious as it may be—it is a touch . . . rich."

"This is a fine Mexican breakfast," he answered her in English. "Nothing wrong with that. On the contrary—we could use some fire in our blood." Then he rattled off something in Spanish to Chela, who stood at the stove laughing quietly, cracking eggs.

"What did you just say to her?"

"Nothing, nothing at all."

"Well you said something. Certainly you said something."

"Have you been practicing your Spanish?"

"You are perfectly aware I have been."

"And so you'll understand soon. You'll understand all the meaningless things I say to Chela." He laughed, and Chela—boldly now—laughed with him, as she presented his eggs and frijoles.

"Gracias, Chela," Eva said, as Abraham tucked a serviette beneath his collar and began to eat.

"My dear," Abraham said with his mouth full. He chewed and swallowed quickly, took a swig of coffee. "You look pale. You should stroll around the plaza. Take some exercise."

"I feel embarrassed," Eva said, in nearly a whisper, as she sat in the chair beside him. "To walk without a corset? Everyone will know."

"Oh balderdash," he offered, with his mouth full again.

"What does this mean? *Bald and Dash?*"

He waved his hand, impatiently. Sometimes it was as if he spoke not three but ten different languages.

"If you have respect for yourself you will have nothing but respect from others," he continued, indulging her with German, slicing charred green chilies into very small pieces and eating them one by one. "Are you not proud of your condition? And please, no false modesty, now—you know how I loathe this aspect of your sex."

"It feels . . . I feel as if it should be my secret—a sacred secret."

"Like a little fox, you and your secrets."

"Not a fox."

"Oh no? What then, a bird?"

She shook her head.

"A bear?"

"It's you who is a bear." She couldn't help smiling. "A big brown bear."

"Ferocious?" he asked, his face growing flushed from the chili.

"Fat," she said, feeling light. "A big fat bear." She sighed and gave him a weary smile. "I am only cautious."

"Well, my little fox, I am not. I am, as you know, a man who thinks large, and it is because of this thinking that I am able to tell you officially, and"—he stuck his finger in the air as if to check the wind's direction—"with great pride: The house—*your* house—is being framed."

"You mustn't tease me about this," she said reflexively, before allowing herself a pang of hope.

"Tease?" Then he shook his head with a smile only barely suppressed. "You must have faith, my fox, faith."

She nearly kissed him on the mouth right in the spill of morning light, right in front of Chela. "But this is wonderful news!"

He nodded, and she could tell he was trying to contain his pleasure and pride at seeing her so elated. "And so if you would like to see the truth of it, I suggest you take your newly plump and perfect little self out for a stroll." He took a final swig of coffee. "It's a fine day."

"I only think of my sister and . . ."

He shook his head.

"But I do."

He banged his hand on the table, but instead of shouting at her, instead of demanding more spicy food, he announced, "The bishop is coming to dinner."

"Oh?" she said, surprised but not displeased with this patent shift in subject. "So he does exist after all? I was beginning to think he was a cultivated character invented just for me."

She'd in fact heard not only from Abraham but from copies of newspapers as far and as widely read as *The New York Herald* how toward the end of his nearly yearlong absence, after having traveled to Rome in his tireless pursuit of more Jesuits, and to France and Lyon for more funds for the construction of the new cathedral of Santa Fe, the bishop and his new recruits had been not only killed somewhere near Fort Larnet, but scalped and horribly mutilated. Eva had witnessed grief manifest itself throughout the town as requiems had been sung, tears had been shed; Abraham, in addition to Mr. Isinfeld, Mr. Sheinker, and Mr. Spiegelman, had said a rip-roaring Kaddish in his name. So when Bishop Lagrande and his people came trotting into town, they were—despite heavy rains and thunder—greeted by joyous throngs and all the bells the town could ring. It had been, she gathered, the most excitement Santa Fe had ever seen.

"He is rested from his terrible travels and has decided to pay us a visit. He would especially like to meet you."

"I cannot imagine why."

He pushed his plate away and stood to leave, ignoring her modest comment. "You have an important job today."

"Why does he wish to meet me?"

"One of the meaningless things I was telling Chela was this: The bishop is a Frenchman."

"I am well aware."

"He narrowly escaped being murdered by savages. No doubt he would like some *pâté*."

BECAUSE OF HER CONDITION, SHE SAT IN THE BEDROOM UNTIL THE slaughter was over. Because of her condition, she wasn't to see how Chela snapped the strong neck and dunked it into scalding water. For Eva was weak—allegedly weaker than usual—and she was to exercise extreme care, which meant—in this new life—not lying on the divan and listening to her sister play the piano, but rather it meant sparing herself from participating in a goose's noisy death. But not the evisceration or the plucking. Not the plucking and plucking and endless plucking. And she'd made certain the blood was drained, for although she had quickly given up on adhering to any dietary laws, Abraham did like, when at all possible, to have the blood drained from the animal—a practice that she suspected he approved of due to the meat's superior taste and not because he possessed any lingering interest in preserving a kosher tradition. *Only remain firm,* he liked to call out in his play-acting version of a rabbi, whenever he brought home a chicken from Manuel the chicken man, *not to eat the blood, for the blood, it is the soul, and thou shalt not eat the soul with the flesh!* Abraham would then likely snack on a piece of ham and biscuit, declaring: "Deuteronomy." As if reciting a bit of Bible in the home could counterbalance the existence of the ham. Up until now she had grudgingly drained the blood herself, but today she'd attempted to show Chela how to tie the goose upside down over a pot, before realizing shortly into the instruction that poor Chela thought she meant to drink its blood, as if she and Abraham were a pair of *Nosfaratus*—pale-skinned, blood-sucking Jews. *"No,"* Eva repeated, with a horrified expression. "Not to drink! *No tomar! No, no."* And then, because she tended toward the dramatic when attempting other tongues: *"Dios mio! Chela, no!"*

But Chela merely made the sign of the cross and watched dark crimson drip and gather in the pot until it was time to proceed. They worked side by side in the windowless kitchen. Eva chopped walnuts and dried

apricots as Chela pounded spices between two heavy stones. Outside
the day exploded into sunlight. Outside there were cavalry parading
through the plaza, a hanged man swinging from a tree. There were Navajos filling skin bags with well water, Spanish women with wing-like *rebo-
zos* carrying black-haired babies, drunkards moving through rubbish as if
wading through algae in the ocean. Outside a house was being framed
against a startling sky. A group of men called out to one another as wood
beams were hauled from street to lot, as hammers struck down on each
dark nail, insistent on possibility. As long as she imagined and envisioned
instead of checking to see if it were true, then she could not—*she would
not*—be disappointed. And so there would be no taking a walk—at least
not for today.

Outside there was possibility. Outside there was chaos and contrast,
but inside this cocoon of endless tasks there was no room for such dis-
tinctions. There were no windows, there were two women, and the light
sparked not from the sun but from the open flame on which Chela
baked tortillas, doing delicate battle with the sneaky flames which flared
like tongues of desert snakes at any given moment. Two women with
dark hair wound in coils, with wound-tight constitutions. Four small
hands not playing a nocturne, but chopping and pounding and prodding
with, if not sisterly grace, if not the transcendental effect of time melting
class and skin color away, then with economy and a similarly pressured
style of working, a style which Eva—had she been able to look in on this
scene—would not have recognized as hers. She had been a drowsy girl, a
girl who dreamed frequently if not always pleasantly, and she was not a
girl anymore. She knew this: Long before she stepped foot on American
soil, she'd lost all claim to that word. But she was also not yet a mother.
It was as if the baby in her belly was a hard stone sunk to the bottom of
her sea—a solid reminder of all that was in betwixt and between and
most importantly irreversible. And it was a strange but not altogether unpleasant sensation to be so solidly between two states of being; it was
one of many strange sensations that accompanied living in a small mud
house with a forceful man, and working not on conversational French or
fine needlework, but preparing a goose with a Mexican girl in honor of a

Catholic bishop. The charred edge of tortilla caught fire once again—which, for Chela, did not merit a single utterance. She fanned the flame and then herself and then the flame once more.

When the goose was ready for roasting, Eva stuffed it full of apples and nuts, sugar and cinnamon, toasted strips of tortilla. Chela shook her head disparagingly and indicated the pot she'd prepared, full of onions and chilies and water, and Eva—very much to her own surprise—stared Chela down in exactly the way she'd seen Tranquilo stare down a burro. She had essentially, until now, deferred to Chela. Though she'd been raised with servants and knew no good could come from such obsequious behavior, she had been too nervous to suggest so much as a less munificent sprinkling of spices. But now she was staring into Chela's eyes—the unusual topaz color all but blocked out by huge pupils—and Eva felt afraid only of her own unfortunate tendency to blink, for she was sick with the thought of another stew, of everything boiled with chilies and onions as if whatever was being rendered—be it a cut of beef or this long-awaited delicacy of a goose—was nothing when compared with the true players of the meal, the stars of spice and heat.

And a Frenchman was coming to dinner. A Frenchman! Yes, he was a man of the cloth, but surely he was not entirely ascetic—he was a Catholic, after all, not a disciple of Luther. As she finally averted her eyes from Chela's and tied up the goose's cavity with a needle and thread, she saw Chela head outside to dump water from the pot, and Eva realized she had won. The goose would be roasted.

In challenging Chela, she had conquered one of her many fears. She had so many fears they were tiresome, even to her: the fear of dying (actually a specific *way* of dying that she would not dare to articulate, not even in the far recesses of her mind) and the fear of giving birth; the fear of cholera, madness, poverty; the fear of Indians, robbers, scorpions, and snakes; but mostly there was the fear of her past coming back to greet her. She was afraid of this: something her own conscience had no trouble identifying with absolute certainty—that she and no one and nothing else had caused her sister's death. But for now, in the hot kitchen, those fears kept their distance. The baby in her belly acted as a scepter, beating them back with an accumulating presence and bestowing Eva with a new sense of importance. The cult of motherhood! What could be more powerful? What else could trump religious affiliation and create a common ground? The bishop wanted to meet her? *Let him come,* she thought. *Let him step down onto our mud floor.* At the moment, she had nothing to hide. For Abraham was right: If she respected herself, then she would have the respect of others; she was a wife and an expectant mother. She would soon have a house. She was hungry.

Eva fried the liver and Chela sulked but learned quickly, chopping it up and mixing in onions, dashes of brandy and cream. By the time the *pâté* was covered and placed under their bed—the coolest spot in the house—it was late afternoon and the house was thick with the scent of rendered fat. If she were going to faint, she thought, it would be now and it would be lovely, falling not immediately to the dirty floor but slowly— surely it would be slowly—through a haze so intoxicating she felt as if she could crawl right up inside of the scent, that the scent alone would support her. She could instruct Chela, they could both take a rest, float- ing through the air like smoke or snow and nobody would recognize them. No one would know where they'd gone.

His face was square, with deep-set eyes, a thin, crooked nose, and a line of mouth that curved downward in the caricatured opposite of a smile. He was long-boned and not particularly handsome but certainly grave and important-looking enough that Eva could not help but think— as he bowed his head in greeting—of how many women might have loved him. She guessed he was fifty-plus in years, although his weathered skin suggested a higher number. He presented a small bottle of wine. "This is," he said slowly, softly, "made by me." He lowered his eyes. "From Auvergne. I cut the vines myself. We need wine for the sacrament here, and also," he said, with one side of his down-turned mouth twisting up, "we need for the table. Something decent, no?"

"*Merci beaucoup,*" said Eva, and his stern face came alive.

"*Parlez-vous français?*"

"*Mais oui, bien sûr,*" she said, as she encouraged their guest to sit down in the high-backed chair facing two large candles she had made herself from sheep's tallow. As she apologized for the modesty of their table, she felt simultaneous pride in how the melted tallow ran evenly down the candles onto polished tin, only to immediately feel foolish for not only her pride but her apology. This was a man whose face bore the ravages of sun and wind, having clearly toiled for many years outside the walls of any cloister. "Forgive me," she said, dropping the flirtatious tone she knew she donned reflexively whenever speaking French. "You must think me very spoiled."

"I think you are lovely," he said simply.

"My wife is also a very accomplished pianist," blurted Abraham in English.

"Nonsense. I am merely adequate."

"Adequate," scoffed Abraham. "How German of you."

"Yes, adequate." She was afraid her tone was peevish, but it was only the truth. *"Très bien?"* she said lightly. *"Non."* She would not inflate what little talent she possessed. "I was the worst player in my family. My sister—"

"Bishop," Abraham interrupted, slapping the bishop right on his back, as if he were a common faro dealer, "although you have lived without society for many years, you cannot have become immune to a proper roast goose and *pâté.*"

"No certainly not, certainly not." He had a full smile now and took in his surroundings, his eyes fixing once again on Eva. "Forgive me, Mr. Shein," he said without averting his gaze, "but your wife looks astonishingly like the village patroness from my boyhood. *Notre Dame de Bonne Nouvelle.* She was all-knowing, and all she knew was good. I would visit her each afternoon in the sanctuary. But, alas," he said gaily, "she was only ten inches tall. You are, if I may say so, far more formidable."

Abraham laughed too loudly and uncorked the bottle of wine.

"I stole away from the town I love so dearly," the bishop mused, in the manner of one who lives far from home and has—having been pressed for his personal story of flight far too many times—become a sporadic and often gratuitous raconteur. "I wore civilian clothes because I knew my family would disapprove if they knew I was to leave them."

"But why?" She couldn't help but ask, "Why did you want to go so terribly?"

He did not look taken aback by her question or the exposed intensity—perhaps even impatience—in her tone.

"I wanted, as I still want, to be of use."

"To change people?"

"Oh we can change little." He laughed a bit. "But perhaps one small corner of a soul . . . And what of your sister, *Madame*?" His voice was so kind; she imagined telling him everything.

"Do you know that my Uncle Alfred lives in Paris?" she said brightly, and she could feel Abraham's sigh of relief that she did not answer the bishop's question, steering the promising conversation in the dour direction of Henriette's death. During his brief tenure as her husband, Abraham had had numerous occasions to point out how nothing cursed an evening quite so efficiently as launching a meal with talk of mortality. He liked to remind his wife of how death was all around them, it was simply the way of the world, and as they sat together under solid roof, by fragrant *piñon* fire—there were poor, green pilgrims, at any given moment, receiving Indian haircuts.

The bishop unfolded his napkin slowly. He fingered the navy stitching; he touched the linen briefly to his cheek.

ABRAHAM'S AMERICA

On Abraham's very first night in Santa Fe, Meyer Shein's final words before retiring were: *Whatever you do, do not step foot in Doña Cuca's saloon*. Abraham knew better than to question his brother the first night in his home, but Meyer continued as if Abe had done just that, and he lowered his voice with a warning: *She has sent more than a few men down that primrose path that leads only to the hanging tree*. There were rumors. That Doña Cuca had extended credit to the man who was her lover and, when he failed to pay on time and after only two warnings, he was found not only dead from a hole in his head, but also naked in the center of the plaza. That Doña Cuca kept locks of hair from those who lost badly at her table; that she had her man Antonio hack off hairs closest to the neck, and it was said that Antonio was careless. *You'll stay here with us tonight, Abraham. Understood?* said Meyer. And then, as if he knew the likelihood of this instruction being followed: *At least for now*.

Abe then stole out of his brother's house and walked the dirty streets, searching for a sense of where it was that he had finally and miraculously arrived. How could he be expected to sleep alongside two half-Spanish nephews who (although they bore the face of their German grandfather) spoke a rapid-fire *español?* His brother had married a native and his children were little Spaniards; it was almost too much to sort out. But after nearly dying on a wagon train from Independence, Missouri, Abraham had sworn that if his fever broke he wouldn't waste a moment of his goddamn life, and so he promised (as he tried to imagine the inside of Doña Cuca's establishment) to give the matter no further reflection. The boys were well behaved, his brother was prospering; more incredibly: He, Abraham, was alive.

His teamsters had been about to leave him to die on the prairie; they believed he had cholera and weren't about to take the chance with such a deadly contagion. But as they propped him up on a bed of grass, a single wagon appeared and—with the uplifting affect of a chimera—it produced a tall, slender man. That tall man leaned forward like a bending birch and offered Abraham a place in his wagon. He spoke French-accented English in low, hoarse tones and promised Abe that he would not be left to die. That man had been the town's bishop, and as Abraham walked these unfamiliar streets, he looked into the distance at the crenellated towers of the town's adobe church, and thought of the bishop with a by-now-familiar shudder of gratitude. It was because of this bishop that he was not a pile of nineteen-year-old bones on the prairie, but twenty, healthy, a young man in Santa Fe. He stood straight and lifted his lucky hat, smoothed his esteemed thick head of hair, and when he saw the saloon glowing yellow in the distance, he walked on toward the light.

Inside, he was surprised at the sight of the dreaded dealer. She was younger than he'd expected, dressed in red-gold taffeta and an expression more blank than tough. She stood behind a gaming table, flanked by a man with a striking cleft chin, whom he supposed was Antonio. Men approached the gaming table time and again; some won and some lost, but no knives were drawn and he became convinced that his brother had been typically alarmist in his warnings. Meyer had been an old man by the age of ten, with skinny shoulders sloping with responsibility, with his repertoire of warnings already well-honed; in the spring, when they were boys in the Tiergarten, he'd instructed Abe as to how, under no circumstances, was he to dirty his trousers, talk to unknown shopkeepers, play rough.

Abraham ordered a whiskey and sat at a table closest to the door, making a half-baked promise to himself that in the case of a shootout (he'd thus far only imagined a shootout), at least he could get up and run. He drank and watched the action, took in the greasy fingers of men speaking too quickly for him to understand, accepted a cigarette when a little brown girl offered. He couldn't help but think that the whole scene was extremely diverting, a hell of a way to spend time. And back he came for the next six nights, drinking his fill of what a few sunburnt New England traders called *Oh-Be-Joyful* and stepped on the toes of more than a few languid *señoritas,* who did not act in the least bit angry. He noticed how Doña Cuca spoke only to a few men, how every so often she would whisper to Antonio (or the man he presumed to be Antonio—they had certainly not been introduced), and Antonio would approach a fellow and either proffer a drink, a few stern words or, in belligerent cases, escort him outside. Once he'd heard a terrible scream before Antonio came back through the door, but Abraham assumed the poor bastard had likely deserved whatever had come his way. One had to be a damn fool, he'd reasoned, to get that drunk and spiteful at the only decent saloon in town.

On the seventh night, when Abraham walked through the door, he noticed how Doña Cuca whispered to Antonio, how Antonio placed a whiskey on the bar and beckoned with his cleft chin that Abraham should sit. And Abraham realized that of course he'd been waiting for this very invitation. At the same time he reasoned that he could sit at the bar, a person could sit at anyone's bar without going in for a gamble.

More whiskey. A nod from Doña Cuca. Finally, a smile. It was as if he were being cajoled into standing—as if the feeling of liquor in his blood and on his breath, his coming to his feet and approaching the Monte table was all some kind of joke—a private joke—between Doña Cuca and him. He laid his piece out on the green and when she finally spoke, her voice was unexpectedly quiet. Abraham did not understand Doña

Cuca's Spanish, and she said deliberately in English (but no louder), "*Caballeros* do not get drunk."

"Ah," he said, releasing an expansive breath. "But I am not a *caballero*."

A husky laugh—a laugh that felt hard-won. "Your wife, she permit you to go so far from home?"

"No permission." He smiled. "No wife."

She nodded, looking suddenly bored. "So you play now?"

He knew nothing of gambling besides what he'd learned during his sea voyage in steerage and at grimy saloons near the docks of New York and the streets of Saint Louis, Missouri: The house always won. He looked around at the distinctly not-Jewish crowd, at the pearl-handled pistols on tables and in holsters. Monte was a game of cups and swords and suns; it was a game one mastered by losing. But he heard himself say, *"Si."* He repeated, *"si,"* louder this time, and he couldn't help but smile. He was in New Mexico. "I play."

That night twelve years ago he was a young man in debt to his careful brother for his passage from Germany, a man with no money besides the coin on the table and the coin in his pocket, and he was also a man who found himself gesturing toward a pile of silver. "How much?"

She looked at him more closely and leaned across the table, gaudy brilliants gleaming in her flame-colored hair. Her taffeta dress rustled with movement and it was some kind of goddamn exciting sound. "Perhaps five thousand." She didn't blink her copper lashes or lower her gaze, and he could tell what she saw when he looked at his European shirt, at his groomed moustache, in his eyes.

"I will do more than play. I will bet ten thousand on the king of swords against the bank."

"Señor," she scoffed.

He felt the *Oh-Be-Joyful* warm throughout his legs. In Berlin he was the son of parents who'd met in a cultural salon and were engaged in a concert hall. He was a Jew who was secretly tone deaf, who cared little for symphonies or study or his father's antiques business with its detailed aesthetic concerns. In Berlin he was a Jew who either fought with gentiles or became too friendly with gentiles and was too often forced into being reminded of his fixed social position. Here, in this room of Spanish officials, a few Yankees, a bombastic Portuguese, and a cluster of plump, brown beauties, he was a German merchant, a *rico,* even though he had yet to work a single day in this country.

"Please," he said, "let us begin." And he began to realize that the drink in his gut was brandy, only brandy, dressed up sweet and tart. He had tossed back a great deal of it with the Portuguese, who was now sitting in a red velvet chair with a girl in his lap, a girl who couldn't have been more than fifteen years old.

"You are very certain of yourself, Señor."

Doña Cuca was not pretty, he noticed, and he felt a mean kind of power in noticing. There was nothing pretty about her except her strange red hair. "Evidently, Señora, so are you."

"Señorita," she corrected, and lifted a brightly striped *rebozo* to reveal a pistol nestled between her silk sash and ample hip.

"I have placed my bet," maintained Abraham, and looks were exchanged between Doña Cuca and the silent Antonio, a man with hair so black it glinted purple in the lamplight. He stared her down and the cards began to turn. Doña Cuca dealt swiftly, her strong hands in motion, turning up a deuce and a seven on the table as Abraham became aware of the gathering crowd with its murmurs of *Jesucristo.* When the third card was turned, Abraham let go of a breath he had not been aware he was holding, and as Cuca revealed the fourth card, he let loose a whoop, a great, hearty cry he had never once heard from his own pale throat.

Antonio betrayed no emotion as he collected the coins and handed them over to Abraham.

"Bravo," said Doña Cuca, before wrapping tobacco in a corn husk and lighting its pointed tip. "Tell me your name."

"My name is Abraham Shein." And upon hearing his father's surname in what was, after all, an undisputable den of iniquity, he suddenly felt like a boy. He leaned in closely so that Antonio would not hear him. "I must admit something to you, Señorita"—he dramatically bowed his head—"I do not have much more than a fist full of dollars in my pocket. I'm afraid that if I'd lost, I would have owed you terribly. I would have had no choice but to become your slave." He collected his silver and dared to smile.

"Abraham Shein," she replied, and he met her hard, green gaze. "I know this deck of cards like I know you. You are young and stupid but you will help me one day. I dealt you those swords purposefully—make no mistake. I did not *wish* to take the chance of having to shoot you dead."

Doña Cuca was still working nights these many years later, overseeing the gambling, the bar, and the girls. She was still blank-faced and quiet, still a *señorita* who would not marry unless marriage moved her up in the world, and up a great deal further than she had already come with her very considerable skills. She was still notoriously danger- ous only to other people—only to suckers and saps—when Abraham stormed through the doors on a Friday night after dining at his brother's house. He had seen Eva home after dinner, but had not even stepped in- side. She never asked him where he was going, and it bothered him that she did not ask, for silence was worse than inquisition. Her dark eyes were galling in their accusation; what right had she to those eyes? They fixed on him even when he could not see them, even when she was sleeping soundly in the middle of the pitch-dark night.

As Abraham sat at the bar, Antonio handed him a brandy sour fol- lowed by a bowl of pretzels because Antonio was an excellent bartender and knew how he liked pretzels by the handful, especially when agi- tated. "Cuca," he called out to her, confident of her affection even as he was acutely aware of having recently lost more than a few times at this table without paying up. He was confident even as he knew (he was no green-horned dupe) that he had quietly slipped into the circle of Cuca's debtors, with whom he could hardly expect to be associated, be- cause, after all, Doña Cuca and Abraham Shein—they had a special rapport that transcended the dealer-gambler relationship with a certain understanding—an unspoken sensibility made perfectly clear in jokes and wordless exchanges. He was certain that Cuca knew it would only be a matter of days—maybe weeks—before he paid her back with interest, and she certainly didn't seem to be in any hurry as she made her way toward him, through the reliably thirsty crowd. When she approached, smirking, with her strange red hair and green eyes, he offered his customary welcome: "Some poor Irish bastard must have had quite a time with one of your many ancestors."

She too provided a ritual response: "God help the good Meyer Shein—going into business with a devil like you."

Sometimes, without warning, this joke galled him deeply, and this was one of those times. It was true Meyer established the business and conserved the money and that Abraham was not the most fiscally conservative man in town, but sometimes Abraham was sure his brother's fiscal responsibility was solely derived from the pleasure he received knowing jokes like this were tossed around, and that when Abraham took failed risks now and again, Meyer could freely impugn him.

He was a little bit broke. Though he was able to swig brandy and eat pretzels and receive credit without hindrance (in fact, Cuca usually put on a big show of being insulted, should he offer to pay drink-by-drink, night-by-night, like a stranger), and though he was able to delight officers' wives by sneaking silk shawls to Fort Marcy along with Mexican cigars and sugared plums and fine French wines for parties, he not only still remained in debt to his brother for his passage from Germany, but Meyer was losing patience with how these items disappeared in the name of generosity toward others. The slow damage Abe was doing, or so Meyer claimed, was not worth Abe's way with a customer, his admittedly curious powers of persuasion. The storeroom goods sold well enough with or without Abe's show. Unlike Abraham, Meyer had not come to America with any elaborate fantasies, but only as a way to avoid German military conscription; unlike Abraham, he had not enlisted in the American Civil War and he cared little about status and reputation, only work and family, family and work. Excitement for Meyer was riding horseback with his Spanish mouse toward the pueblo on a Sunday, where, as far as Abraham could tell, they did little besides eat supper on a blanket, staring off in the distance like sheep. Meyer did not gamble, not even at Wolf Spiegelman's weekly poker game, which would be starting soon.

"Tell me," he said, watching her worn face through a veil of scent and smoke. "Have I been helpful to you, as you predicted so long ago?"

"You know you have been a help—you have lost so often at my table!" She laughed her husky laugh, which usually made him feel comforted, but tonight it did no such thing. "Have you brought me what you owe?"

He coughed, the whiskey burning his throat, and he was ashamed at his surprise; he had not ever imagined being asked this question. "I haven't brought you anything," he answered, perhaps too quickly. "My apologies," he added, making sure to look straight into those mean, green eyes that never seemed to blink. "You needn't worry about all that," he said boldly, "not with me."

"Oh I do not worry," she said unaffectedly. "Worry is for fools."

Abraham laughed then, and he heard how his laugh was already different. It was the laugh of a man growing used to losing; he fought not to let disgust seep through his expression, which was no doubt an alarmingly broad smile.

"How is your princess?" she asked, as if inquiring about a termite problem, perhaps a case of gout.

"My princess?" He sighed. "Well, I suppose she is just fine," he said. He tried not to think of his wife's jewels, her precious heirlooms that comprised a significant portion of her dowry, which were never meant to be sold. The fact that he hadn't ever come close to pawning his wife's jewels was how he liked to measure his character. Still—he couldn't deny it—he liked knowing they were there. Sometimes he checked under their bed as many as ten times a day, where the jewels lived in a locked box, to which only he and Eva had the key. "My princess—she needs to rest."

"Don't we all," she said neutrally, having obviously not changed her opinion of the mercurial Mrs. Shein. Abraham had seen Eva smile warmly at Doña Cuca one day while strolling in the plaza, and then, not one week later, give her a look so frigid that Abraham was ashamed—not so much for his wife's snobbishness but because he knew its deeper source. He knew her watchful face in the middle of the night, when he came late to their bed smelling worlds apart from the man she'd seen early in the morning. He knew Eva assumed Doña Cuca was running a brothel, which of course she was, and that he was a regular patron, which in fact he was not. There was a girl with wavy black hair and an alluring gap between her teeth who sat on his lap now and then, but no matter how much liquor he swallowed, he'd always managed to walk away, declining all invitations. Cuca sucked smoke deep into her lungs and the sight did not repulse him. "I hear about the governor's ball," she finally said.

"Yes," he said, "good for Shein Brothers' business."

"Oh I think so. Supplying a Fort Marcy fiesta—*muy bien*." She stubbed out her cigarette in his near-empty drink, and he couldn't help but lament its last good sip, even as he realized what hostility lay in that stubbed out butt. "Shipments of oysters on ice—I hear about this—crates of French champagne? And what will Mrs. Shein wear?"

Her mouth was pursed impatiently, awaiting his reply, but he could only say, "You will have it." He said it so softly; he had no choice but to repeat himself.

She stuck out her bottom lip for a moment, before sighing. "Well this is good, Señor. This is very good." Then, decisively, she took the ruined drink away. "Antonio," she called with a furious smile. "Another for *El Guapo*. He looks thirsty, no?"

At the eldest Spiegelman's house, the game was underway, and when Abraham came through the door the men barely nodded, so high was the concentration. The dirt floors here were covered with *piñon* planks and as they creaked under his boot soles, he realized he could no longer step on a wood floor without feeling guilty. He recalled last month's very first official Yom Kippur in this town (which was said to have finally occurred because the arrival of one additional Jewish bride—*Mrs. Eva Shein!*—had successfully galvanized the population to

hurry up and finish acting like wayward children set free from their traditions), and how when his family and colleagues had gathered to observe
in this very room, what he'd felt most strongly was not religious nor community spirit, but panic and resentment at how Eva's face had struggled
with unholy envy. Her eyes had gone immediately to Spiegelman's silk-
covered walls crowded with portraits in oil, which, for his wife—more
than any convenience—seemed to embody a certain European sensibility that—much to her evident satisfaction—she was apparently not
alone in still desiring. Later that night, she'd reminded him of how Wolf
Spiegelman—his esteemed colleague and fierce competitor—seemed to
share her interest in wood floors, an interest he'd dismissed if not dis-
dained. She'd reminded him of how Theo, the younger Spiegelman,
would likely return soon from his trip to Germany with a new bride and
immediate plans for a proper house; the two usually went in tandem.
She whispered sharply while turning from him under their bedcovers,
her tight little body curled in on itself, reminding him of nothing so
much as a caterpillar. As he wrapped his legs around her, as he lifted her
nightgown (voluminous to the point of ridiculous), she insisted she was
not ashamed of such comfortable desires even if she did live far from
their homeland. Even if she lived here in what she had come to call,
quite bitterly, Abraham's America.

Accepting a bourbon from Don Romero, the former governor, he sat in
his usual spot between Spiegelman and Isinfeld, but Isinfeld sat across
the table and in his place was none other than the bishop, who, after
years of scrupulously declining social invitations if gambling was to take
place, had recently caved in after his most recent trip abroad. He was
starved, or so they all liked to rib him, for Europeans, *any* Europeans,
even Jews. So there he sat, sipping wine and looking glum, as he so often
did when he witnessed their games, as if he were a sickly child in a
school yard, not so dissimilar from Meyer, when all he really wanted to
do (or so Abraham imagined) was to place a bet, yet he never once
played a hand. It was the second game he had attended since his dramatic and long-awaited homecoming. Having survived not only Indian
raids (not to mention peril at sea, bouts of dreaded cholera) but death it-

self, death *in print,* Bishop Lagrande was a hero of no-less-than-mythical stature.

And yet here he sat, cutting a morose devout figure, eyes clouded over with gloom. Abe did not remove his jacket and did his best to ignore the bishop's demeanor, which he could only translate as bad luck. The circle finished the current hand, and he marveled at how Cuca had come right out and asked him for the money. He found himself dwelling *not* on how he was going to get that money to her straightaway, but on the galling fact of how her question—given the feeling of friendship between them, to say nothing of his standing in the community—was insulting, indecent, and an outrage. He raised his finger to the dealer, and as the cards landed softly before him, he couldn't help but note how he loved the near-inaudible sound of them, and how his lucky watch burned a hole in his pocket the way it did before a big win.

"Bishop, play a round, just this once," said Abraham, finally, feeling the satisfyingly crisp touch of cards in his hand. He studied his cards and, after arranging them, slugged a generous sip of bourbon. It was a shoddy hand, but, Abraham reminded himself, although it took more than good cards to win a hand, winning a crucial hand did not require good cards. He leaned back in his chair and stretched out his legs as if he couldn't be more comfortable.

Isinfeld peered nervously through wire-rimmed spectacles, Spiegelman tapped his too-long fingernails and bit his lower lip as Sheinker lit a fresh cigar. These were men with lifelong, nervous habits, men who were all obviously wondering whether Abraham planned on living up to his reputation and raising the stakes. It was never a surprise—whenever he walked through Spiegelman's door—to recognize how his arrival was dreaded as much as it was welcome; his presence was inseparable from his potential to take a game that much further than any of them were in the habit of expecting. At times he found this reticence endearing, but tonight he saw them through a lens of disgust: They too had made it across ocean and prairie; they too had made it through packs of savages, through patches of rough weather and brutal terrain, only to sit here and worry. They were all so timid, so afraid of loss.

He made a show of yawning before he reached into his breast pocket and took out the banknotes he had designated for tonight's crucial win. He laid them purposefully on the table—a silent answer to their silent question—making sure to meet each pair of eyes. Each man met his gaze with an obvious interest in whether Abe in fact had the kind of cards to support this type of wager. Sheinker put his money down, followed by Isinfeld, until the pile was nothing to joke about. "Bishop," Abraham persisted, "are you in?"

The bishop shook his head sadly and Abraham felt like punching him suddenly, giving him something far stronger to contend with than a glass of wine. He wanted to force him to laugh not the wistful excuse for laughing (which commonly emerged as a thin, Gallic sigh) but something more authentic, a laugh that would temporarily remind the good bishop just how much of a man he still was, even though he was a man of the cloth, and just how little the difference was between him and a room full of peddlers.

"What on earth is the matter?" cried Abraham, in a voice that did little to disguise his vague irritation. How was he to play any kind of successful hand with this disapproving shadow? *I do not believe in Jesus Christ*, he nearly hissed. *Do you really think you can judge me like some Mexican bastard on an isolated* rancho, *a maid servant begging for blessing?* Abraham was suddenly and utterly convinced that the bishop knew everything—not only his shabby hand but his secret debts and burdens, his empty promises—and was looking so bereft as a subtle means of censure.

Spiegelman grumbled, and Abraham pulled his chair out from the table. The wood made a scraping sound on the floor, a sound that was oddly satisfying. "I want to know," Abraham said. "I simply want to know what is troubling our friend the bishop. Does anyone not recognize a troubled man?" He put his hands on the bishop's shoulders and felt the surprise of knobby bones beneath the scratchy wool cassock.

The bishop half-smiled and waved him off like a woman denying her husband is drunk, a woman insisting with a wistful smile that she too is having fun. But Abraham was not drunk, not really; his was a hearty con-

stitution that had aged over time like strong, sharp cheese; it took a great
deal on any given night to send him into slurry forgetfulness. Why, he
wondered, had Cuca talked to him that way? His money lay in the center of the table, underneath the pile. For a moment, he saw no currency
but only dirty paper covered in elaborate script and ambitious illustra-
tions. He saw that someone had chosen the motif of women adorned
with Grecian garments, which were (ironically—he couldn't help but
think) meant to represent justice and honor. The pile of banknotes
looked childlike and flimsy and yet—all that paper: it seemed as vulnerable and regal as feathers of a dead rare bird. "Our good Catholic
friend"—he lowered his voice, suddenly feeling nothing besides the urgent need to know the bishop's mind—"you cannot fool me."

"Leave him be, Abe . . ."

Abraham's hands no longer touched the bishop's shoulders but hov-
ered just above, the palms outstretched. "What?" he asked, the way his
mother might have, when one of her boys made trouble. "He sits here
despondent after *surviving*! He should be reveling in his life. His life!"
He picked up his cards and kept them close to his chest, where his heart
beat a brutal march because his heart knew what was coming next even
if he wasn't so sure. He felt the same warmth throughout his legs as he
had the first time he'd ever placed a bet in this town; he felt the same
unstoppable momentum that he had come to respect. "Is this game so
important that we cannot talk as friends?"

"It is nothing," said the bishop succinctly. "I am only . . ." He stopped
himself, obviously aware of how Abraham had somehow succeeded in
forcing him to speak up. He made his voice clipped and quick, as if to
get through the sentence as soon as possible. "I beg your pardon, but I
cannot locate any more funds. My resources . . ." He shook his head. "I
have no further resources."

Spiegelman shifted in his seat, looking at the pile of money as if it
were yet another dodgy character. He glanced from his cards to the
money before giving his cards one final study and matching the bet
amount. "And the French Society?" Spiegelman asked the bishop, obviously distracted, annoyed by this turn in conversation.

The bishop stuck out his lower lip and slowly shook his head. "If I do not think of something, all of my planning—the very fine stonecutters in France, *n'est ce pas?*—this will all be for naught. The cathedral will exist only in my mind. This is—you see this—*C'est un désastre,"* he muttered finally.

Abraham sat down and looked at the bishop. He pictured the faces of his cards lined up like souls. As he took another sip of bourbon, the men's faces blurred, and he ceased to even see his cards. All he saw were oil flames glancing off Isinfeld's spectacles and Sheinker's glowing cigar tip and the queen and swords of the Monte game twelve years ago when he understood what it meant to win by bluffing, that bluffing was the greatest victory of all. He saw all of this and most of all he saw himself. He saw himself the way a hunter sees his prey—wild, vital—and it was from this vantage that he liked himself best. He saw how he placed the rest of the money—every last bill—on top of the pile and how the men's faces looked pale. He knew they were counting up the unusually high pile in their fastidious minds and wondering if Abraham had finally reached his limit. He pictured the brown silk lining of his left breast pocket, the empty space so recently filled with greenbacks taken little by little from the Shein Brothers' office, from a spot under a floorboard that Meyer didn't know he knew about. And as all the players besides Spiegelman took their turns and folded like the conservatives he knew them to be, as every man but Spiegelman refused to match Abe's bet— cutting their losses and forfeiting what they'd already laid down— Abraham Shein and Wolf Spiegelman were left facing each other, and the room was so fraught with tension that Abe was not surprised to see even the bishop knock back a full glass of wine in one shot. This moment was what he loved best, and he savored the way Wolf scratched his head as he weighed what to do; Abraham enjoyed this drawn-out question but he enjoyed the answer more: Wolf Spiegelman folded; he put his sweaty cards down with a scowl.

Abraham made sure he maintained a smile, a stubborn assertion that this was nothing but gentlemen's fun, and he reached to gather all the finger-smudged inky delicate beautiful beautiful money. His hands were

shaking because he knew the night's risk-taking was not quite con-
cluded, that this was no time to hold back. "I insist," he said, breathing
oddly heavily, smoothing his hair with one hand. "Bishop, I insist you
take this money I have won. You are a great friend to all God's creatures,
even the Jews . . ." He forced a smile, but not one man was laughing.
"My friends," he pleaded. Once again he tried to look them all in the eye,
but Spiegelman refused, tapping his long fingernails rapidly on the table
as if it were a military drum. "I cannot sit idle while this great man is in
need. Therefore I insist, I *absolutely insist* that you take this money right
now. The last impression we want to give our friend is that we have become part of some—how do they say?—some hard-hearted codfish aris-
tocracy. So please, Bishop—"

"Abraham—" the bishop interrupted.

"I will not hear a word until you accept."

Bishop Jean-Paul Lagrande looked sheepishly from one man to the
next and reached for the money before Abraham changed his mind. He
was obviously too relieved to say much more than thank you.

"Gentlemen," Abraham said, "please continue." Upon realizing he'd
successfully ingratiated himself to a far more respected (if more impov-
erished) member of the community than Doña Cuca, he took a cigar
from the ebony box on the table, and stifled a smile as genuine as it was
terrible. He had no business making grand gestures like this one; he was
aware of this. He was aware that his wife deserved a house and that
Doña Cuca deserved her money back, just as he was aware that it wasn't
right to have essentially stolen from his brother. He was also aware that
these were not stupid men; each one found Abe's benevolent motivation
quite suspect, and yet they had to respect the fact that Abe had won that
money fairly. He had also put them in an undeniable fix, for whoever
suggested continuing to gamble for personal profit tonight would certainly look less than civic-minded, and these three men thrived on reputation almost as much as on profits. On the other hand, none of them
would have wanted it to appear as if they were merely following Abraham's example. He was aware of their fury, but they couldn't say anything without looking miserly or like a follower, at least not tonight. One

only had to look around to understand why Abraham couldn't help himself: The bishop seemed to have shed ten years from his wizened complexion, and the men? The men looked trumped.

They stared at him—his co-religionists, co-gamblers, his cohorts—and as Abraham sucked on the tasty cigar, he knew each one was trying to decide how to proceed. Because no matter what had just transpired, he knew they all looked down on him as vaguely dissolute; after more than a decade in the territories—despite the fact that there were ladies in town now, despite how he'd gone to the considerable trouble of finding himself a German bride—not only did he still frequent all manner of drinking establishments no matter how low, but he insisted on speaking—almost exclusively—not regular English, but the English of American outlaws. He knew these men had shared with the bishop a subtle disdain for his booming voice, his often provocative statements, but he also knew that although they had silently scorned his sometimes crude ways, they had also been thankful for him—thankful for his being different and offering them a certain solidarity, a bond with each other and with the soft-spoken bishop that, with Abraham's sudden and unstinting offer, had just been palpably broken.

"Carry on," said Abraham amiably. "And count me out."

ABRAHAM AND THE BISHOP STEPPED OUT FROM UNDER SPIEGELMAN'S *vigas*. They stood together in the empty street under a spangled sky.

"I fear your generosity has spurred them toward higher stakes tonight," the bishop said after a silence. "Do you suppose they will finish before morning?"

"Oh I doubt this has anything to do with me. They like to win," he said almost defensively. Then he shrugged. "So do I."

"Yes," said the bishop, smoothing his clean-shaven face with his ringed hand—as if the thin layer of stubble of this late hour was an unfamiliar, perhaps unpleasant, sensation. "I am aware of this," he said. "And"—he cleared his throat, kept his eyes on the stars—"I will do everything in my power to make sure you do. Your benevolence will not go unrewarded."

Abraham shook his hand, and spontaneously drew him into an

embrace. There was the burnt and waxy smell of candles clinging to the bishop's cassock, but also a hint of richness—a scent he would later identify (while laying awake hours later as the sun began to rise) as butter. He clapped the Frenchman's bony back twice before finally letting him go. Wagon wheels turned a few blocks away; burros brayed at the moon.

They walked their separate ways, kicking up dirt in two directions.

"Abraham," the bishop called out from yards away. *"Bonne nuit."* Abe had never heard his voice so loud. It was unsettling, somehow.

When he could no longer see the bishop in the distance, he imagined the outline of his own body against the night sky, the wobbly delineation of a simple child, smudged roughly at the edges. His back and his shoulders ached all at once, and he wondered if he might not duck into Doña Cuca's for a final restorative bourbon; at this late hour, after a full night's profits, she was known to be a shade more reasonable. It was a windless night and he could hear everything, every rock underfoot, every coyote in the distance. He imagined that if he listened intently enough, he would hear beyond these thick adobe walls and discover matches being struck, arguments about money, vulgar scenes of love, but as he grew closer to the corner, he actually heard the real, if faint, sound of whimpering, like a dog about to die. He heard this whimpering over the saloon piano in the distance—speedy and out of tune—and the percussive slurs of drunkenness, crescendos of intermittent laughter. He heard this sound of whimpering and felt a punishing sadness but no curiosity. He walked faster toward the familiar noise and light, and was somehow desperate now for Cuca to understand that he was not a man to whom nothing was real besides his own personal fortune. He was moving so quickly by the time he rounded the corner that he almost missed the source of the whimpering. Down the alleyway where the trash was piled and had been piled for months now, where scrawny, hungry dogs had long exhausted their resources, there were two shadowy figures pummeling some poor bastard, and from the diminishing sound of the whimpering protests, they were doing one hell of a job. Abe didn't look, not even for a moment, because he knew their faces well—they had worked for Cuca for

years doing exactly this; this was no cause for surprise. When he opened
the door to the saloon, he felt his face cleave in two and he realized he
was smiling. He pictured those men in the alley—one pudgy Mexican,
one big Anglo from Denver—and at first he thought they must have quit
their blows because he couldn't hear the whimpering anymore—it had
been so damn insistent—but then he realized he had only to step
through this particular door for the room to draw him in and block everything else right out. The outside world, for a little while, remained somehow wholly in the dark.

BURRO ALLEY

SISTER BLANDINA CAME FROM AVIGNON, LEAVING FIVE unmarried brothers behind. Sister Theodosia dreamt of chocolates—she left a sister in Riom who made the best she'd ever tasted, covered in toasted almonds. When Sister Josephine left Lyon in tears, a rainbow spread over her father's house and then a day later he died. Sister Philomene didn't say much—her lips were pillowy, she often sang. They came to aid the bishop in his quest to civilize, to corral young misses on the path toward virtue in a land that was most untamed. They came to care for orphans and to teach orthography, reading, writing, grammar, arithmetic, geography, history, and—for the more intelligent—astronomy (with the use of globes), natural philosophy, and botany, also needlework, bordering, drawing, painting, piano and guitar, vocal music, and finally, French.

The nuns. They lived around the corner, frowning behind the adobe walls of the old bishop's palace, whacking little Spaniards on the hand. They said their novenas between cursing the laughter that floated through the all-too-open swinging doors of Doña Cuca's.

"*Bon soir,*" Eva Shein said through a strained, surprised smile, standing in her doorway. The afternoon air was a surprise—she hadn't felt it all day—and it carried clanging of bells; the heady scent of *piñon* smoke curled thinly skyward.

"The weather turned so soon this year," Sister Blandina responded in English, after an authoritative clearing of the throat. "It is frigid simply standing in this doorway."

"I'm sorry . . ." She could barely get the words out, she wanted to shut the door so badly, but she could hardly have them tell the bishop how she turned them away, refused them as they stood in the cold. Her third winter in Santa Fe promised to be a difficult one. The newspapers filled weekly with stories from the plains: five soldiers killed, six merchants scalped, rivers gone solid thick with ice. "Please do come in."

"We do not wish to disturb you," Sister Theodosia declared as they stepped down through the doorway. They trudged inside over the newly swept dirt floor. Chela had spent yesterday sweeping, looking up every so often at her strange mistress standing in the doorway, for Eva could not bear to be alone in her room any longer and she could not bear to go outside where the sky was too vivid, too open, and people always stared.

"Tea?" The word floated out of Eva's mouth. It sounded amazingly strange, as if she were hearing it right that moment for the very first time.

"Have you been outside yet today, dear?" Sister Theodosia said, sitting right down at the table.

"Chela, *por favor*—" She wanted so badly to beg Chela's help (*help please make them disappear*), but she realized with a start that Chela was not in the house. Chela was with her own family—a chili-farmer husband, a stout son, and a daughter. It was Christmas Eve, she remembered, and the smell of green garlands and roasting meats were also suddenly present on the winter air. *"Joyeux Noël,"* she managed to say instead. "How kind of you to visit, when this is such a special day. All those good Christian children—why, you needn't bother with me." She could do this in her sleep. She could be so gracious—she knew this is what anyone said in her defense, should someone make unfavorable mention of her moods. She was gracious but not expansive and she had yet to make a suitable friend. The nuns sat themselves at the dining room table. The swish of black fabric, if for one peaceful moment, was the only sound in the room. She looked at the nuns, their cow eyes and pie faces, how they waited for their tea, patient in all things. She smiled. She smiled. She could do this in her sleep. Perhaps she was asleep. Perhaps she had not woken in a house of mud, only to stand for hours alone, pacing and then standing, staring at a dirt floor long since swept of blood—the dirt floor hers, the blood hers—blood dark as aubergines mixed with soil—further proof of her fickle womb. What, after all, did she expect? At least she had lived.

"You know what Doctor Sam says about taking air," said Blandina.

"You do not want to grow melancholy," added Josephine in her high and nasal voice. "You must think of the next time."

The next time, thought Eva, *I will turn away. After that, I will insist on a shield—either animal skin or rubber—which I know is available at the store along with sexy pictures wrapped in brown butcher's paper from China and from France.* She could no more say this to the visiting nuns than she could actually manage to do it. Because the next time would be soon, and when he came to her she would simply close her eyes; she would breathe deeply and fall. She was a woman. She could not hide behind a holy costume and make love to a heavenly father. This was earth; it was time, and the first three had not held.

Dear Mother and Father, she had written not long after her arrival here in town, *Abraham says it will not be long now until the house is built. He is a German and he wishes very much for the house to reflect this. The house will be the first in Santa Fe built in any style besides Spanish, Mexican, or Indian. It will be a brick mansion with scroll saw woodwork and probably a cupola. Perhaps I may have my own grass garden after all with apple, plum, and cherry trees. Rest assured, Father, there is indeed grass here—it is hardly one big desert as you had feared. There will be a fountain in the garden and, best of all, a carriage house. So you see there shall be plenty of room, should you decide to brave the frontier! Abraham says it is only a matter of days until the foundation is laid. Isn't that exciting?*

Dear Uncle Alfred, she had written, *I have missed you all my life. I take it your family is in good health? I know you believe that America is the only truly free country, but this morning I looked outside at first light and saw not one but three men hanging from an oak tree. Some nights there are the sounds of gunfire. Oh, Uncle, what have I done?*

"Won't you play us something?" Theodosia asked, after two cups of tea.

"I don't really feel—"

"Your touch is unrivaled," she insisted. "It is Christmas." There were crumbs on her habit, on her chin.

"What would you like to hear?" The square Steinway sat in the corner, like a canary trapped in a mine. *Heinrich, pleasantly drunk, takes a walk with his girl through the wintry holiday streets;* here was her very own bird-of-thought trapped in her limited mind.

"Oh anything, dear. Play us anything. Or, perhaps Mendelssohn, if you'd like."

Eva made her way to the piano bench, as if slogging through a swamp, her skirts weighing her down. Despite—or perhaps because of—the profound absence of society in Santa Fe, she was expected to don corset and gown not only when walking about, but also while at home during appropriate hours, should anyone happen to call. When she'd arrived in town, the news had made the front page of *The New Mexican,* so it was her duty, or so she understood, to best reflect Abraham's significant stature. And she was proud of him, to be sure—proud of his courage and tenacity and of the manner in which all men—from the Yankee prospectors to the half-breeds—greeted him with tremendous respect when he passed by.

"Oh look at her lovely posture," whispered Josephine.

She adjusted the bench and the pedals, finally closing her eyes as she always did right before playing. Because she remembered she was facing the wall and that they could not see her face, she kept her eyes closed. Then she touched her fingers to the keys, merely grazing the cool ivory through the ubiquitous fine layer of dust. When the faint scent of violets released, when Henriette's carefree giggle filled her ears, she then began to play from Mendelssohn's *Songs Without Words,* starting with the most childlike piece and progressing toward the most difficult, the one she always thought of as Henriette's showpiece.

Playing the piano had become not unlike running: It was something she had done as a child—if not excellently then effortlessly—without much consideration, and it had now become an action to take when under peril. It wasn't that the piano no longer gave her pleasure, but it had become a refuge, the closest thing to a state of grace in which conversation was not necessary and expectations were easier to understand. Her back was straight, her fingers quick, and for a fluid span of moments she was lost somewhere in time, flying over rooftops in winter Berlin, picking blackberries during a Karlsbad summer, watching Mother powder her fine white skin. Finally she was listening to the piece her hands created, but it sounded far more stylish and strong, because it was Henriette who was playing and she was only watching. She really liked to watch. Instead of slightly tinny and out of tune, the sound was rich and unending—a sip of cool water, the first sip, after traversing the desert for days. She was no longer surrounded by well-meaning nuns but by something so much larger than she could ever name. She had not known what safety was before she had forsaken it.

She was floating on a minor key near the end of the piece when a sudden urge to stop became too strong—like the cramping right before the blood came, signaling an immutable end. She tried willing her hands to move, even stopped and started twice, before giving over to the silence, the disappointed silence in the room.

"Please excuse me."

She rushed by the black-cloaked figures sitting at her dining room table. Blandina, Theodosia, Josephine, Philomene—such exotic names, beautiful names—looming like the hills surrounding the city, a smudge of judgment, cloudlike, on the sky. They sat in their incomprehensible existence as women; they sat in a unity appealing as it was horrendous— like a pair of massive arms moving closer, closing in.

In the washroom she soaked a cotton cloth in the copper bowl of water and pressed the cloth against her forehead as Chela had done for her so gently while she was still permitted to rest in bed. Head against the splintery door, she closed her eyes and she listened.

"But we cannot," said Josephine. "It has not been even forty minutes."

"I, for one, have no attraction for entertaining wealthy ladies," hissed Blandina.

"The bishop says—"

"She is suffering . . ." The rare voice of Philomene—hazy, high.

"We all must suffer, mustn't we? It has been nearly two months. It was God's will. For heaven's sake, she isn't even baptized!"

"Her husband is a friend to the bishop."

"Her husband is a Jewish gambler!"

"Hush, Sister Blandina."

"Well he is."

"The bishop says . . ." continued Josephine. Lake Josephine, as Eva thought of her: flat and placid. Or was it fat and flaccid? "The bishop says we must stay one hour's time. I, for one, will honor his request. It is Christmas," she said virtuously.

When listening became too much to bear, Eva flung open the door in a sudden burst. "Of course my husband gambles!" she said. She might have screamed it, she wasn't sure.

"Whatever do you mean?" cried Blandina. Their pale faces tinted with sudden heat. They bowed their heads, all but Sister Philomene, whose eyes—almond both in color and shape—blinked furiously.

"Gambling is a sport," said Eva. "It is a game."

"Please forgive us," said Philomene.

"Do you hear me?" Eva's hands began to shake. Of course the nuns could not possibly have called on their own volition; she was entirely too unpleasant to stand. It was the bishop, her only true friend; he had sent them with the best of intentions, not able to understand how these nuns were merely a clique of ladies who loathed her. They loathed her weakness, her indolent ways. They disapproved of her reading habits, how she had no use for a Bible but instead retreated into German novels full of unquestionable wrongdoing. And they were especially suspicious of how she did not even have the moral foundation to know how to sew her own clothes.

But Philomene walked slowly toward her; she reached out and touched Eva's face.

"Philomene!" cried Sister Josephine.

But Philomene did not pull away. Her hand was warm. She smelled like the inside of a treasured book.

"Please," Eva whispered into her ear, small and pink as a shell.

"What is it?" Sister Philomene whispered in urgent reply; with her breath came mild garlic, a garden of wilted roses.

"Please . . ." It was all she could say. She choked on the other half-born words that rose up in her throat.

Philomene took Eva's trembling hands, and—as if she understood everything, or at least this one odd craving—slipped Eva's fingers under her own heavy veil, allowing her to touch the soft, clipped hair.

THAT EVENING, WHEN THE CANDLES WERE LIT, HER CORSET TIGHTened, and her face scrubbed and rouged, she waited for Abraham, but instead she found two visitors knocking at the door.

"Mrs. Shein," said the tall one in English. He was a hulking fellow in a good suit, toothless and jowly-pale.

"My husband is not at home," she replied, with one of the first sentences Abraham had insisted she perfect out loud. She felt uncharacteristically confident of its cadences, so she was surprised when the shorter Spanish man stepped forward and asked where her husband was.

"My husband is not at home," she said louder. And then, "Maybe you leave a card?"

"We ain't got no card," said the tall one. "No, ma'am."

The Spanish man laughed so she could see all his teeth, some of which were covered with gold.

SHORTLY AFTER THEY'D GONE, ABRAHAM RETURNED, SMELLING OF brandy and snow. "You look better," he said in German.

She tried to smile, but it came out as a sigh.

"I saw Mrs. Smithson at the party. She sends her very best. They all do." He handed her his coat and hat, and she went into the bedroom to put them away. "It was a jolly crowd," he called to her through the wall. "The room was full of hundreds of candles. You would have loved to see it."

"I'm glad you enjoyed yourself," she said, too softly, she knew, as she looked frankly at her gaunt reflection in the speckled looking glass. There were hollows in her face, dark and ghastly. Soon she would be nothing but a play of light and shadow, a study in contrasts to the bone. She pulled herself back into the dining room.

Abraham sat at the table, waiting to be served.

She brought the platters to the table and poured wine into crystal glasses. He took a bite of beef and chewed thoroughly. "You might think about beginning to call on the officers' wives."

She took a long sip of wine. "I cannot have them here, this is for certain."

"You might call on them"—he continued, as if she had not spoken—"before it gets too terribly cold, pay a visit to the government quarters."

"I might."

"You cannot stay inside and weep forever," he muttered, having switched over to English, which irritated her beyond measure. She would speak English to anyone; she didn't mind, she really did not. But he was her husband and this was her home. His insistence was maddening.

"I do more than weep," she said tersely in German.

"Oh?"

"I played the piano for the nuns. They paid a visit." Moth shadows flickered on the wall behind his head in globes of yellow candlelight. Flames cast shapes on the ceiling: dancing wraith, paper flower, bear. He looked up from his plate. Another thought occurred to her. "Or maybe *you* had the bishop send them?"

Abraham held his fork aloft as he laughed. "And why would I do such a thing?"

"To comfort or frighten me. I am not certain which."

"Why would I want to frighten you?"

"Tell me," she said in English, ignoring her heart beating faster than it should have, "who are the men?"

"Which men? You are not being clear, Eva. You must try to be clear when you speak."

"Here," she said slowly. "Here. At the door. They ask for you. Two men."

"Well how should I know? You know how many people want something from me and Meyer?"

"They did not ask for your brother."

"You cannot set store by any of these border ruffians. What did you tell them?"

"You do not wish to know what they looked like? What they said?"

"What did you tell them?"

"My husband is not at home."

"Good girl."

She nodded, took a good sip of wine. "How is business this week?"

"We are prospering. You know that."

She felt familiar pin pricks at the backs of her eyes. "Then . . ." she sputtered, as the sweet sandy resin slid down her throat. "Then—then— why has there been no work done on the house? Each day I walk by and it sits there—like rubble—abandoned. It is embarrassing. My dowry . . ." she began, but she was too ashamed to have to ask. *"Why are we living here?"*

"You are perfectly aware—"

"Your brother Meyer built a house. His wife has a stove and she is a native! Alma Lucia was *raised* to cook over flames!"

"Even in this modest home, you are coddled," he said, shaking his head. "You are—"

"This is not what you described. Nor is it what you promised my father."

"Still," he said softly, sitting back and watching her in the way he often did, with frank appraisal, "you would have come."

"There is refuse and burro droppings under our portal; if we had to live this way it would be a different matter. If we had no other choice, I would not say a word. But . . . Abraham . . ." she pleaded, hands gripping each other under the table so as not to gesticulate. "My darling, I don't understand . . ." She looked into his rich, brown eyes, his thick-combed hair which would never need a drop of bay rum. He was her husband. "Where does the money go?"

"You would have come no matter what I described. Am I wrong?"

"I wanted to go with you." She dabbed at the corners of her eyes.

"I sometimes wonder why."

"Why do you think?" she asked, and there was a part of her that was still flirting after all this time, flirting just like Henriette taught her to flirt, so very long ago. She thought that if he chose to smile at this moment, everything could turn around.

"It's funny," he said. "I had the distinct feeling that your father wanted me to take you to America."

She shook her head and nearly choked. "How can you say this?"

"I think he wanted you to go."

"You don't know anything," she said, and before she could stop her tongue, "They didn't think you were good enough."

There was never silence here in Santa Fe, not even in such a moment. Doña Cuca's saloon, the dogs, cats, and jacks, the bleating of cattle and hogs—he slammed his fist on the table. He picked up his glass and hurled it toward the shadowy wall. She couldn't help but gasp.

"Before Henriette was married," she said, her voice cracking through a glaze of pointless tears, as the red wine dripped down the mottled white-wash, filling the small room with its vinegary scent, "a painter came to make our portraits." She lowered her voice and whispered, "An artist." She stood and retrieved a broom. "He told me stories."

"Why would a father want his daughter to move across the ocean?"

"You are lying to me. My father wanted me to stay. He wanted me to stay but he let me go. Because I begged him! I begged him."

"And what did you say?"

"I said that I loved you, of course. I said 'Father, I love him,' and you"—she felt her face tighten, her temples begin to pulse—"you told him that you would treat me kindly. You told him there was great freedom and riches and—"

"And what about this painter?"

She looked at the shattered glass on the floor and thought of their wedding ceremony. "He painted our portraits," she said. "I told you." His eyes met hers and she continued. "He told me how while Martin Luther was translating the Bible, he threw an inkpot at the devil. The devil kept appearing to tempt him, you see . . ." She trailed off into coughing, as she bent with some difficulty and swept the glass.

"Why do you tell me this?" he asked, rising from his chair and placing his napkin on the table.

"In Wartburg Castle," she said quietly, "there is still a black spot on that wall."

"The devil does not exist," he said almost patiently. "There is only you and I."

"What about God?"

"This is not a question."

"Who is your devil?"

"Shh," he said. "Shh. I am sorry. I am sorry you lost the child."

"Tell me," she demanded. "Tell me where your devil takes you."

And, as he often did when questioned, he put on his hat and walked out into the night, closing the door behind him.

CONFESSION

CUCA'S SALOON, LATE NIGHT CHRISTMAS EVE: THE SAFEST place he could think to go. He certainly did not believe Doña Cuca could look into his eyes and order her men to harm him, especially not in front of a Christmas crowd, whose thirst may have been less than spiritual but was a great festive thirst nonetheless. The chaos of the saloon felt safer than his cramped home, where his unhappy wife looked as if she wanted to tear him apart with her strong little fingers.

He took comfort in the promise of the saloon's slatted doors and how, once he'd pushed through them, the girl could be counted on to shake off whatever body she was with and come to his side instead. She was sweet and fawning, he was happy and rich; these illusions worked well for both of them. She also never had to do much. He paid her and never once took a room, never left the safety of the table and the pretzels and the reassuringly drunken crowd.

Cuca ignored him as he came through the door and he didn't have the wherewithal to approach her. The girl took his coat and brought him a drink, and as a passing inner voice asked how long it would be before his credit was completely cut off, the girl sat on his lap. Her bottom was bony, her stale taffeta was ripped, and her face was marred by a welt of a birth-mark smack in the middle of her forehead, but she smelled like some-thing untried and untasted and after two bourbons tossed back in hasty shots, he buried his face in her warm neck and all but took a bite. The sound of her giggles was muffled by her heavy hair—about a quarter of it was pinned up, but the rest was endless. It fell darkly around him like a skinned hide, like the walls of a cave; it kept him confined before he fi-nally had to come up for air.

"Buenas noches, El Guapo." There was a gap between her two front teeth and whether or not this had something to do with the fact that she rarely spoke was unclear, but when she said something—even something as predictable as this greeting—he felt a foolish thrill. She was seven-teen or twenty, depending on when he asked, she had the tilted black eyes of a half-breed, and her name was Gregoria, which didn't suit her at all. The first night he asked her name (after she'd been bringing him drinks in the corner for hours), he gave her a few *centavos* and attempted not to slur his words. He said he'd be her friend, but he'd be calling her Lucia or Maria or Florita—anything he damn well felt like—but not her Christian name because whoever had named her had got it all wrong. *Who named you, girl?* he'd asked. But even though his Spanish was good and he could tell she understood every word, her only response was to smile and put the money in her red shoe. And even though he had stayed true to his intoxicated word and called her something different every time he came around, she always responded to whatever he invented; it came to feel like a game.

"Conchita," he whispered on Christmas Eve, after leaving his lovely wife to sweep shards of broken glass. She would leave him soon; she would find a way to do it, especially when she found out just how deeply in debt he was. Cuca's men would come for him and Meyer would dis-cover that he'd not only stolen a crate of silver shortly after he'd returned from fighting in the war, but that he'd also been the one taking the money from under the floorboard little by little all along. "Conchita, take me to a room."

Though this was the first time he'd made this request, she didn't seem at all surprised, and she rose from his lap and took his hand, as if he were a blind man. As he passed through the black doorway with its tacked up swath of pink silk (a not-so-subtle promise of what happened behind the door), he thought he heard a few whistles and jeers, but he was drunk now, drunk for real, and he couldn't be sure what he was hearing—this happened sometimes—whether it was gunshots or foot stamping, singing, or screaming; there was sudden potential menace in everything from horse hooves clomping along in the dirt to the silence down a dark hallway. For it *was* truly dark back here, and unfamiliar dark places were always that much darker.

The cramped hall seemed too small to lead anywhere, and as the girl lit a lamp and his eyes adjusted, he had the gradual sense that everything was contrived, that Doña Cuca would appear at any moment, trailing her fingers along the peeling wallpaper—fingers rife with sunspots despite all her time indoors—and detail exactly how he could expect to be punished. He could envision it happening and yet he still continued to follow the girl, as if by following her he could reject his intuition. His eyes trailed her hips, how they hardly swayed at all but rather moved straight ahead like a wagon in the night, racing west from state into territory. He wondered if this girl was not unlike the wagon train driver he questioned late one night on a dizzying flight across the plains, whose reasons for pressing on couldn't have been clearer when the driver answered brusquely—while maintaining an eerie focus—that he was frankly too terrified to stop.

The girl stood before him, taller than Eva—taller and so much more substantial. His wife's touch was initially always a little indistinct, as if it took his hands to wholly bring her down to earth with her feet in the dirt like everybody else. This girl stood before him with her poor posture and gaping smile, which seemed to dip and rise with boredom and expectancy. She seemed that much younger when she unbuttoned the top buttons of her blouse; the forward gesture seemed born less from a desire to seduce than a longing to be more comfortable in a constricting costume that someone else had chosen.

He reached out suddenly and touched her waist and when his hands crept upward, she opened the door to one of the three rooms. "Not yet," he snapped, retracting his hands like a child though he was in fact nearly desperate to rip through the fabric and clutch her skin, which he imagined to be exactly like the skin of a Spanish woman he had learned to dance for long ago, a woman he had loved in California—a landowner's ambitious daughter who'd made it clear she would never marry him and then proceeded to teach him dirty words in the secret rooms of her father's hacienda. He stood now watching *this* girl's slanted black eyes and imagined her skin to be just like his memory, though sometimes he doubted whether such a memory was authentic because if it was, if he really had made it to California, with its somehow more sophisticated freedom, he had a difficult time believing that he ever would have left. But he had left, and he knew why. He had wanted more and he had found it in a spoiled little woman from Berlin.

Those slanty black eyes flashed matter-of-factly, and he felt them travel from his shoulders to his belly, from his calves to his toes with a definite promise, but also as if he consisted of nothing but gold and she might like to hack off a piece of him. He came closer and put his hands on her full breasts, still constrained under crude whalebone and cheap fabric, and he felt hot breath from her thinnish lips as she mumbled words—either prayers or seductions—he couldn't understand. When he closed his eyes it was only Eva that he saw, and maybe it was the liquor, and maybe it was his father's dead spirit—so moral and infectious—but instead of withdrawing from the girl again, this time he lifted her up and pinned her to the wall and drove himself inside of her until he opened his eyes and saw nothing but a strange Mexican whore and he couldn't hear his father's voice anymore. And then he ran away. He ran scared through the dark, papered hallway and through the black door, until he was swallowed by the crowd's leather-bourbon sweat and spat back into the night.

He continued to run from Cuca's without a destination, until he heard no shaky piano or raucous laughter and he was doubled over, unable to catch his breath, as if Cuca's brutes had pummeled him after all. He sucked down cold air laced with *piñon* and the salt-smoky remnants of this feast night, and as he grew bitter cold, even while remaining very drunk, he realized he was right outside the church, listening to the echoes of the midnight mass. He didn't remember ever standing this close to the adobe church; he was used to seeing it at a distance, how the tawny structure appeared to grow straight from the red-ocher hills like a bigger, stronger tree. He saw, at that moment, no need for the bishop's elaborate plans for a new cathedral. The French architect from Toulouse, the *very fine* stonecutters—it all seemed pointless. This adobe church was noble and good; it stood up to its setting, which was, at turns, ruddy and gold in square daylight or livid with the violet of oncoming storms, or how it was just then on this winter's night with the sky first dark as a warning and then lighter as the snow began.

Instead of heading home as he knew he should, he took refuge from the weather by stepping inside the church, where he slipped right in without provoking even a shudder of commotion. He imagined doing this in Berlin, and was ashamed to feel his stomach flip with fear. To enter a midnight mass—it felt as provocative and illicit as having just bedded a whore. He looked around at so many people clustered together, their focus unwaveringly toward the painted altar, where Bishop Lagrande lead the service. It was as if the bishop were the moon itself—brighter and stronger than all of the candles illuminating the church. Abraham took comfort in crowds, which always came as a small surprise, and he couldn't deny being uplifted by the sense of a common purpose. Though the women looked like prostitutes in their heavy rouge and gaudy adornments, and the men looked strangely dull with their heads uniformly bowed, Abraham felt the strangest sense of amity. He allowed himself the rare acknowledgment that his wife might well be barren, and then he came as close as he could to prayer.

Just this evening—within the border of *luminarias* outlining the plaza—some of these same somber individuals wore masks and played out a ritual dance in which the young women held hollow eggshells filled with scented liquid and chased after men they fancied, smashing the eggs upon their heads with a mix of flattery and mockery. Though, while watching the spectacle, he'd laughed when an Eastern general took the occasion to quip: *What a perfect display of Catholicism in New Mexico,* Abraham had privately thought the general a puritan and had even regretted laughing.

He was not a religious man, it was no more or less than fact, but as he saw this sea of dark eyes trained on the bishop, when he saw what kind of power his Gallic friend possessed—he couldn't help but admit a sense of wonder. Here was Jesus, wooden on the cross, vermillion paint for blood. Here was an alien church, strange in every way but for its faint echo of taunting Catholic schoolmates and distant relations who, much to his father's horror, had chosen the way of conversions. His father had been so deeply against conversions at a time in Germany when it was commonly seen as a necessary step to truly move up in society, and because Abraham respected his father more than he could measure (or even, for that matter, justify), all he ever thought—all he ever *permitted* himself to think on the matter of conversions—was what his father had repeated again and again, up until his death: *Nothing good will come of this.* But now here he stood in a new world, where society was measured not by titles but by greenbacks, and he had already polluted the possibilities.

Snow blew through the crack in the doorway, and he imagined the vaulted roof blowing straight through the stars, and this room, this flock, blanketed with snow until nothing was left of this particular rite but the silence between prayers.

WHEN THE SISTERS FIRST ARRIVED IN SANTA FE, THE BISHOP GAVE them his own substantial quarters so that they might have convenient access to the cathedral, but he'd kept two rooms there for himself until he'd found other arrangements. His new home ended up being a ways out of town, and though it sat on many hectares of fertile soil (the bishop counted extensive gardens among his many aspirations), it was not only Abraham who wryly speculated that its generous distance from the good Sisters must have figured into his final decision. In any case, the temporary rooms had not been altered and he made use of them on nights such as these when it was too late and unsafe to ride. This was where Abraham followed Bishop Lagrande after the penitent crowds had dispersed, and as he trailed the skinny man in the long, dark cassock through the heavy falling snow, he felt the absurdity of his behavior, the inappropriate hour, but still he didn't question why he was drunk and heedlessly freezing, instead of warm (if guilty) and in bed with his wife. As the bishop let himself into the ground-floor room, Abraham hid behind an empty wagon, trying and failing to light a brittle cigar.

Minutes later he knocked at the door—he was sure he knocked—but he also couldn't have denied letting himself in. When he stepped inside, the bishop was already asleep. Abraham knew that he needed nothing so much as to leave, but all at once he was incredibly cold and suddenly exhausted. As the bishop breathed deeply from a single cot, Abraham noticed a square opening in the wall, which hosted a pile of kindling. Because he never went anywhere without matches in every pocket, the temptation was too great, and within seconds the *piñon* caught quickly.

"Why are you lighting a fire?" the bishop asked simply, in Spanish.

"I am not lighting a fire," Abraham heard himself say, and remarkably, the bishop continued to sleep. Abraham turned slowly from the flames, and as they warmed his back, he looked in the direction of the bishop, whose creased face was occasionally revealed by the orange-blue light. As his eyes adjusted, Abraham looked around the jail-like space and saw the long, dark cassock draped over a simple chair. He was tempted to put it on, for warmth as much as for the humor of it, but he resisted the temptation, only to do something far more stupid.

"Give me my goddamn money," Abraham said, but the bishop didn't even stir. Abraham felt for the revolver at his hip—an additional bit of cold, dark weight, heavy with reassurance. "I need my money," he repeated, with an unfamiliar and ugly lack of restraint. And still the bishop slept.

Abraham meant, he did, to beg. He meant to say that he was overextended, that he'd never had the right to hand over the money, that it wasn't really his to give. He meant to come clean and beg the bishop's forgiveness and ask for his money back. He needed to do this but what he did instead was what he had been doing all night. He ran.

In *The New Mexican* there were headlines: *Attempted Murder, Narrow Escape, Gracias a Dios*. The articles explained how, on Christmas Eve, Bishop Lagrande had smelled smoke and woke in the middle of the night, just in time to see an unidentified man racing out of the room; he'd also seen the glint of a gun. In these articles the bishop expressed only concern for the mystery vagrant. *What a wretched soul,* the bishop said. *He must have been very desperate.*

CURRENCY

THERE WERE NO BANKS. THOUGH PROMINENT MERCHANTS had safes—which had come to be used by Indian representatives to make substantial deposits—it was a cash-scarce economy, one with an unfavorable balance of trade. Meyer Shein had installed a safe in the back room during the Civil War when (as his younger brother took every opportunity to point out) Abraham was off fighting for their new country, but not even the safe was large enough to store all the silver that had arrived in need of protection. Meyer had quietly improvised, storing the silver in nothing more than shipping crates previously containing axes. When the war was over and one of the crates went missing, Meyer regarded Abraham with constant suspicion, and regardless of how many times Abraham protested his innocence, Meyer was never fully convinced—a suspicion that only intensified with Abraham's growing love for the gambling table.

Meyer feared corruption and betrayal more than anything, but Abraham did not fear it because he accepted it; he believed it was to be expected. He trusted only in his gut and gave Meyer rather inspired speeches outlining reasons to trust *him*, because only Meyer had the key to the safe, but despite his protests—ranging from rueful to irate—

Meyer would not make him a copy before he cleared his chronic, unpaid debts (debts of which Meyer, as it happened, didn't even know the full extent). It was because Abraham didn't possess this key that he had not insisted on storing Eva's jewels there. Surely the jewels would have been safer in a *safe,* but Abraham couldn't stand the thought of not having access to them whenever he wanted. He liked to look at the diamond and sapphire necklaces, the ruby ring and emerald brooch; he liked to finger them all and close the box, knowing he was not that desperate.

Meyer couldn't have had any clear idea how much Abe owed other people, but if the debt he'd accrued to the company was any indication, there was little hope of Meyer ever freely giving Abraham anything again, let alone a copy of that key. Even when the debt had been less than outrageous, if Meyer saw him going into Cuca's saloon, or heard about an audacious bet placed at Spiegelman's, he'd berated Abraham and often stopped speaking to him for days at a time.

Still, they were brothers.

And Meyer was shy.

When they were boys, Meyer had been teased mercilessly by gentiles, beaten on a sometimes daily basis. It had taken his younger brother to put a stop to it, and Meyer was ever indebted and also resentful of these memories. Only so much time could pass in their current life before he eventually capitulated and issued his younger brother a reticent invitation—obviously craving his company.

They drove to the pueblo to trade. They never spoke of why they each valued these visits to the point of sentimentality. While they were both raised with the conviction that being surrounded by beautiful things could elevate the mind, only one of them happened to believe it, but in this case it didn't matter. Because if Meyer felt allied with their parents' collecting ethos and the way in which their Berlin parlor was full of unusual objects, and if Abraham felt no such alliance, Abraham also happened to harbor an increasing interest in the Indians, an interest bordering on fascination (which could just as quickly turn to hatred if the topic was murder on the trail—a hypocrisy of passions that he refused to see as such), and so they shared an equal enthusiasm for stocking the store with Indian pottery and curios; their intrinsic appeal was one rare thing the brothers agreed upon. When these items did not turn a quick profit, neither brother mentioned it. Abraham simply changed the displays in the store, and, using his personal gift of conviction, guided French and Yankee traders in the appropriate direction.

The Shein brothers' rapport was never better than when they'd finished trading on the pueblo. Abraham, smelling of leafy smoke, wore beads and hides, while Meyer wore a quiet smile, pleased with the acquisitions.

ON ONE SUCH EVENING, NOT LONG AFTER CHRISTMAS, THEY DROVE a wagon full of pottery, sitting side by side, warding off winter's chill. Like most conversations of the day, theirs was focused on the vagrant who had nearly ended the bishop's life. Abraham, in particular, had much to say. He was insistent that the plaza be better lit, that men of honor should keep watch over the nuns' sleeping quarters. Meyer couldn't help but give a small smile. "What"—Abraham wanted to know—"is so amusing?"

"And do you plan on standing guard?"

"I know you think I am sentimental about our bishop, but I tell you, Meyer, the man saved my life. I will do whatever he deems necessary."

"I must say, I don't understand why this vagrant didn't steal anything. Lagrande's jeweled rings must have been there. You must admit that it hardly makes sense."

"And you wonder at my concern! Murder, Meyer, murder; this is my chief concern. Just like the newspaper said. Or maybe he only panicked before he had the chance to pocket anything? Good Lord, Meyer, but what about those funds you said you couldn't account for—just the other day? You said it wasn't much but you couldn't account for it all the same? Where did you say the money went missing from?"

"I didn't."

"Well, don't be surprised if it isn't the very same vagrant."

"Maybe," Meyer said. "Who knows."

"I just don't understand why you are so goddamn worried over what *might* happen in almost every situation, and then when danger—real danger—is afoot, you are loath to believe it. Can you explain this to me?"

Even as he ranted, Abraham could not help but notice how dusk was a dazzling silver; twilight made him restless and thirsty. He felt a stabbing pain and realized it was nothing but guilt. That same pain came and went just like *he* came and went to and from his home or through the swinging doors of Doña Cuca's, which lately had not been an escape so much as a gauge of how much time he had left before Cuca would not only cut him off but have him truly dealt with. What he needed, above all, was to come up with money to pay her; he could tell he didn't have much time. Tightening his grip on the reins, he looked straight ahead to where the town began to emerge from the landscape in craggy relief. "Mother loved a nice sky."

Meyer nodded. "She would never allow an argument during a sunset. It made her too anxious. Ach!" he said. "Do you think she would have lived if we had stayed?"

Abraham looked at his brother, who was red-faced, sweaty, literally wringing his hands. It never ceased to amaze him how well Meyer made out in the world. "Don't be a damn fool now. 'We will never be free unless we make our own society.' Have you forgotten all your talk? Could we have been free in any rotten corner of Europe? Meyer, you made a small fortune; you could have skedaddled back home and found yourself a German bride, but you sent for me instead, *and you took up with a native!* Now you question whether we should be here at all?"

Meyer smiled wearily, which Abraham knew was a response to his American colloquialisms. His brother and his silent Spanish wife, they'd no doubt enjoyed laughing sprees at his expense. "I apologize," Meyer said, "I am being self-indulgent."

"You are the least self-indulgent man I know," Abraham replied quickly, surprised by the intensity of his reaction. "Look," he admitted, "she died alone." The silver sky went flat again; smoke rose in the distance. Indians favored sunset as the hour to attack and after all those trips along the trail, Abraham reflexively felt nervous when the sun dipped behind the hills, almost entirely hidden. "Do you know that when one of the Ute tribe members dies, the whole tribe moves camp? That sounds like a good idea somehow, doesn't it?"

"I suppose," Meyer said. "Awfully hectic time to be moving though, isn't it?"

"The Acoma pronounce death when the sick person has no further hopes of living; death to the Indian translates as having no heart."

"No pulse? Or no will?"

"I only hope Mother was not dead long before she died."

Abraham felt his brother regarding him strangely, and he did not ruminate further. He didn't tell him about one day last spring when he was visiting with the bishop, and how the chief appeared to tell the bishop his son, Yellow Feather, was dead. *Shall I throw him away like a dog?— The white men call us dogs!—Or,* the chief asked, *will you bury him?* He made the motion of pouring water, to let the bishop know his boy had been baptized. Abraham didn't tell Meyer how he had gone with the bishop to the pueblo to collect the body, and how the wind blew from all directions in an eerie, natural requiem. How when they'd found the chief's son he was certainly ill but alive and standing, if propped up by his father.

Did you not tell me that your son was dead? the bishop had asked, quite understandably confused.

But Bishop, he is dead. I show you, the chief insisted, nodding toward his vacant eyes. *My son, he has no heart.*

They rode ahead in silence, and as they grew closer to town, Abraham pictured how Eva's face would appear when he came through the door with no answer to her eternal question of when construction of the house would resume.

"Meyer, hear me out," he declared, giving a nervous tug at the reins, "Spiegelman has issued scrip since before the war, and I've got to thinking that we should do the same. Can't you picture the paper bills? 'Shein scrip,'" he attempted, "'Good as gold.' And, listen—with that maniac running around town now—"

Meyer slowly shook his head without even bothering to look at him. "I don't think so, Abraham," he nearly whispered.

Rattlesnakes wriggled up a steep, stony hill, and black crows tracked them from up above—not just the men but every living thing—fierce birds gliding back and forth against the darkening sky in clean silent sweeps. Everything was too quiet. He craved gunshots, howling coyotes, some noisy proof of life.

Meyer had rejected his idea so quickly that Abraham's principal reaction was not one of anger or resentment but embarrassment. It was never more clear how Meyer assumed that, at heart, he was truly no better than a common criminal, and that if Shein scrip were in circulation, he would sooner or later yield to the temptation of available capital (which of course he had already done) and—like an opium-addled train conductor—derail the company that Meyer had built into a bottomless, bankrupt pit. "What can I do, Meyer?"

Meyer didn't look at him. "You can entertain," he said.

"Entertain?" Abraham said, bitterly.

"We need cash, Abe. Do you understand? We need to invest hard cash in a New York bank. It's the only way we'll earn interest. And the military deals in *cash sales,* not corn and goddamn sheep. So you will entertain our connections at Fort Marcy and you will procure us a military contract."

"And if I do?"

"If you don't, then I'm afraid I need to change the name of the business back to Meyer Shein and only Meyer Shein," he said, with a barely suppressed smile. "With not even a measly 'and brother' for company."

The sky had dulled, and as they pulled into the plaza Abraham smelled snow. Clerks ran out of the store—tending to the burros, helping them unload—and as the brothers dismounted, Abraham regained his gumption. "Let me get something straight: You will not issue scrip simply because you are afraid I will steal from you. Well, Meyer, you know we both agree you are smart as a steel trap, but that is one shit decision."

"I don't think you understand," hissed his older brother, squinting as the snow began to fall. "You don't have the right to comment on my decisions. You forfeited that right long ago." He picked up a crateful of curios and ducked into the store.

Abe followed him into the back room, where variety ruled and dust was thick; the merchandise needed sorting. "Now you listen to me, Meyer," he said, after kicking an empty box at his feet. "How much more respect do we have since I loaned the bishop that money? How much better do folks regard you when you accompany your wife and boys to *church?*"

"*My sons are Jews!*" he exploded, while somehow keeping his voice down, "I have told you this and told you this. She likes to go to church all together now and then but—*Goddamnit, Abe!*"

"But, Meyer," Abe said, "she is not in fact Jewish. So your boys are not really Jewish either. Not really." He said it as if it were nothing but a gentle reminder, when in fact it was his one winning card. Even though it seemed to Abraham that intermarriage was in fact all throughout the Bible, that really it made not a whit of difference, he knew this fact was his brother's greatest weak spot, that Meyer, in making a love match, believed that his children were technically Catholic and that he truly had done something wrong in the eyes of God.

Meyer pressed his fingers into his eyes as if patience lurked directly behind them, and he needed to tap its source. He let his eyes open and they stared into Abraham's ruthlessly. "What does it matter?" he asked, with a little, thwarted smile, and now he could not help but raise his voice. "What does any of it matter?" He uncharacteristically kicked the empty box back toward Abraham. Then he said, "I know you steal from me." He said it calmly, as if he were giving something away.

"You—what are you talking about?"

"I know about the money—here and there—do you really think I don't notice every last coin that goes missing? Do you really think I built this business from being careless? From being stupid? And tell me: Does this respect from the bishop, this great standing of ours, does it import stained-glass windows for the new house you have promised your wife? Will it give her the best medical attention in Saint Louis?"

Snow fell wetly outside; it gathered into a storm. Abraham's hands and feet went cold. "What medical attention?"

Meyer waved him off, as if Abraham should know better than to ask.

"I don't steal from you, Meyer. It is an outrage that you should suggest this. And I demand to know: *What medical attention?*" He saw two clerks lurking with questions, and he shooed them fiercely away. "And tell me—how do you know what I have and have not promised?"

"Abraham. She has not brought you a child."

"How dare you!" he exploded.

"She is too thin and pale, Abe." Meyer looked terrified, but he managed to continue. "Or have you not noticed?"

Abraham felt his right arm pulse as it hadn't since the days of rescuing his brother from beer-fueled bullies in the back streets of Berlin. In that moment, as the snow came down on the roof and turned to slush, his mind shot back years before, to the cobbled lot behind the dancing school only minutes from his family home. He had been trying to kiss a girl—his first girl—a wide-eyed sylph with big feet, a popular Catholic who hated to dance, whose lips made dancing seem irrelevant. They'd stolen outside during a waltz and were hiding between two unattended carriages, and as the shaky piano filtered through the windows along with the scuffling sounds of missed steps and hollered instructions, he had taken her hands in his (they were sweatier and warmer than he'd expected and somehow this was exciting) and he had just leaned down to kiss her, when he'd heard his brother's muffled nasal voice—a sound as familiar as his own excited breath—shouting out for help. Had he pretended, even for one moment, that he had *not* heard his brother's cries? Had he leaned in for the kiss he so wanted, the kiss he so *deserved*?

As he imagined this scene now, as he—a married man in New Mexico—felt his right arm pulse in nothing less than violent anticipation, as he envisioned the flaxen schoolgirl who'd been instantly frightened away, he wished he *had* pretended not to have heard Meyer calling for him that day. As he stared now at his older brother's bitter, homely face, Abraham wished—he did—that he'd kissed that schoolgirl's marvelous lips and let those bastards take another punch. He wished that these many years later, in the backroom of a store, *their* store, Meyer would have no choice but to remember not only how his younger brother had once been his salvation, but that he had been saved not just from bitter humiliation but searing physical pain.

So he did it then. Pretending he was one of those Jew-haters, pretending he was one whom he could not possibly loathe more—an entitled, red-faced Berliner—Abraham struck his brother in a solid cross-punch, just as he had struck Meyer's tormentor that day behind the dancing school when, at two weeks shy of his *bar mitzvah,* he was already taller than everybody.

Meyer's expression, when he finally turned to face Abraham, was curiously more pitying than anything.

"I'm sorry," he said. "I'm sorry, Meyer." But he wasn't sorry, not yet. He was mostly amazed that he had done such a thing, that his brother's nose was bleeding and it was he who had drawn his blood. He knifed off a substantial piece of fabric from a bolt on the floor. "Hold it against your face," he said, handing it to Meyer. "Hold your head up."

"You won't speak of this to anyone," Meyer muttered.

"No."

"Go home," came muffled through the impromptu bandage of crumpled calico. "I do not want to look at you."

As he walked through the center aisle and out the front door, clerks eyed him with suspicion and perhaps more than a touch of fear. He bid them good evening with a practiced smile. He thanked them for a good day's work, as if at that moment he had a perfect right to commend or disapprove of their workday, as if he wasn't, in point of fact, simply one of them—a glorified indentured servant, smoldering with ambition.

SYMBOLS

IN BERLIN, THE PASSOVER SEDER WAS A TIME TO WEAR new patterns and brighter colors after the winter had passed. The men had worn top hats and the ladies gowns and everything smelled fresh and new. Each year the cook taught the girls to make *Mandelbrot* and honey cakes and each year they forgot how to do it. One year, surprisingly, Mother taught them how to dye hard boiled eggs a brilliantly pigmented red for the seder plate, which, unlike the sweet things, Eva never forgot, and in fact she looked forward to how the dye inevitably stained her fingers, taking days to fade away. One year Mother had already left for the baths, and Eva and Henriette and Rahel accompanied Father on the train to Karlsbad, and there they had the seder in a hotel suite, where Mother was dewy-eyed and wrapped at the neck with multiple silks to prevent the ever-dreaded chill.

But this was not Berlin, nor was it Karlsbad. This was Santa Fe where, despite Abraham's promises of an elusive New York shipment, there was no new clothing, and the cooks spoke Spanish faster than she knew a language could possibly be spoken and insisted on boiling every meat and vegetable to their deaths. This was Santa Fe, where a thief had had the impiety to steal into the bishop's room on Christmas Eve, and, because nobody had been able to catch him all throughout the winter, Abraham had become increasingly fixated on the thief and very concerned about his wife's comings and goings. She found this both a bit ridiculous (Wouldn't the thief have moved on to another town by now? Weren't there other dangers all around them all the time?) but also, she couldn't help but find his concern rather sweet; since that fateful Christmas Eve, he seemed, more than ever, genuinely concerned for her safety.

For the seder they were going to Wolf Spiegelman's house where the wood floors, cast-iron stove, and portrait gallery were sure to send her into a covetous state, the likes of which she hadn't experienced since the last gathering for Yom Kippur; this combination of religion and envy was distressing. She felt guilty and superstitious and she promised herself to focus on the story of the Exodus. Instead of comparing living conditions, she would try to hear her father's gravelly voice in her head, how he read aloud with a bashfulness that drew her in to the story and somehow broke her heart.

It was a brisk, clear day, right on the cusp of springtime. She'd decided to contribute not only one egg to the Spiegelman seder plate, but a whole festive batch of them, without any help from Chela, who, as it happened, hadn't made an appearance today at all. The eggs steeped in a stew of red and brown onionskins, and Eva checked her crude stove hourly, pleased with the simple progression of the eggshells deepening from brown to burgundy. She took a brief rest in the afternoon, and when she woke, the color resembled the soil of the blood-colored hills rising outside in the distance. Even if she was inside a windowless kitchen, she knew the exact color of those hills at every time of day; she had memorized their severe yet intangible quality, how they were always there and always out of reach.

As the hours collapsed and candlelighting began its gradual approach, she heard Abraham outside, talking sharply to the burros as he hitched them to their post, and as she scrubbed her hands pointlessly— she knew the red stains beneath her fingernails and spotting her palms would be there for days—she hoped, despite herself, that he would offer something in the way of news—perhaps a miraculous decision to build the house with a newly assembled crew.

"It smells like a son-of-a-bitch in here!" was what he offered instead, as he sat in the high-backed chair and immediately untied his shoes as if his feet were in danger of suffocating. "What the Sam Hill happened to your hands?"

"Eggs," she said in German, far more meekly than she'd intended.

He looked at her the way he did sometimes, as if she were either a guttersnipe or a princess and he was trying to decide. "Where's Chela?"

Eva shrugged—she was used to the occasional days without a servant by now. No matter that she woke each day wondering if Chela would come—she couldn't bear the thought of hiring another stranger. She was attached to Chela and the girl knew it; Eva almost couldn't blame her for taking advantage. "I made the eggs myself," she told him. "They're a perfect symbol of springtime."

"And fertility," he said meaningfully. "This is what we were taught in my family." Her heart sped up with a by-now-familiar dread and excitement. If he only knew that she had been to a *bruja*—Chela had taken her in secret to Doña Teresa, who had administered peculiar instructions: *Keep cats away—if even one cat hair gets inside of you, infertility and/or baby's death will strike. Also frogs, keep away from frogs, for they are actually dead bad* brujas. *Find a man named Juan and have him tie a ribbon around your neck—during daytime, any color will do, but after dark it must only be red.* Doña Teresa had broken an egg over Eva's forehead, forbidding her to wash the yolk from her scalp for at least five hours. If he only knew she had obeyed it all.

"Come here," said Abraham, and she imagined he was going to question when he could hope to expect his first child, or ask, as he did sometimes: *What's wrong with your insides?* But as she walked forward and stood before him, almost touching his long legs—first bent like a table, then outstretched—he slid himself down deeper in the chair while silently reaching to grab hold of her. "Thank you for making the eggs," he said, and he pulled her into his lap in a way that was sweet but felt funny somehow, as if he were somebody else and so was she, someone not about to ask him about their house. Neither one of them, really, wished to speak of the future, nor did they—for that moment, between day and candlelight, before having to dress for the seder together—have to. With Chela gone, the house seemed different, and Eva was suddenly reminded of those long-ago candlelights on the Santa Fe Trail; he would come to her while Tranquilo was hunting. She was always surprised until she wasn't anymore, and by then she'd realized she was waiting. She'd thought of it as disappearing, and that's what happened now—as he undid her corset with big careless fingers, as he carried her to bed before bedtime—she disappeared limb by limb, so that even her voice was gone.

As they walked down Burro Alley during sundown, Abraham held the basket of Eva's wine-red eggs, and Eva pulled her shawl around her. "Are you cold?" Abraham asked.

"I'll be fine," she said, approaching Wolf Spiegelman's house, "we're right here."

"Oh no—I'm sure I told you—it's at *Theo* Spiegelman's."

"But they've only just arrived from abroad; his bride can't be entertaining already."

Abraham shrugged. "It's just at the end here."

"I know where it is. It's the one with the beautiful front porch. What a lucky girl, don't you think?" she asked tautly. "Arriving at the end of the horrid journey to find a house like that?" She wasn't surprised when he didn't answer. She wondered about the new bride, who was, with tonight's seder, not only making her social debut but apparently playing hostess as well. Theo Spiegelman had made a good match during his past trip back to Nürnberg, (a tall redhead named Beatrice was all Eva had heard) and they had honeymooned all over the continent. Abraham liked to say that Theo's wife-hunting trip was instigated by the fact that when the Spiegelmans placed a mannequin in their store window, *The New Mexican* followed up not with an article admiring the exotic, new advertising method, but with a bolded headline: *Theo finally gets a girl!*

"Remember," muttered Abraham, as they approached Theo Spiegelman's door, "you are more experienced than she. You might offer some assurances."

Through the windows, the rooms glowed gold, and she longed simply to be inside a beautiful place. "*My* assurances? How can I bring any reassurance to someone who lives here?"

"The girl will probably still be frightened and nauseous from the new food and water and climate. Plus all this talk of the vagrant on the loose . . . you might help ease her transition."

"Why are you so concerned about Theo's new bride? Did you lose a bet at Spiegelman's card game?" She was teasing—or at least she was attempting to tease—but he didn't laugh; he didn't even smile.

When Beatrice came to the door, it was clear right away that she'd need no such assurances, for Eva could tell (in the way that only a woman can truly tell) that she'd already embraced absolutely everything Western. It was in the way that (not two weeks in town!) she was wearing her hair long, over the shoulder; it was also in the way she moved broadly. The room behind her was lively; Eva glimpsed Abraham's colleagues and their various wives—Wolf's shy Hannah who hailed from Westphalia, Meyer's Alma Lucia and their boys (a trio who spoke only to one another and only in Spanish), Fanny Sheinker (also from Westphalia) who talked solely about the weather—and she noticed two dachshunds trailing Beatrice Spiegelman's skirts, barking insufferably until Beatrice barked a command in German, which seemed promising, but then she abruptly switched to English, crying out: "I have heard so much about you," before embracing Eva and then Abraham as if they had spent every Passover together and this was one more year. "Please," she said, "do come in. Everyone is waiting."

"Oh are we late?" Eva asked in German.

"No, of course not," Beatrice replied in English, standing her ground, but then, as if she knew she was being stubborn, she relented and continued in German: "The men always just want to begin so that they may say *kiddush* and take a drink."

"On Passover it is a *mitzvah* to drink in excess," bellowed Abraham, shaking hands with Theo and Wolf as he stepped into the parlor.

"I don't know about the accuracy of that translation!" said Eva to Beatrice, who smiled a toothy smile and gave the dachshunds a pat before ushering Eva inside.

"Did you bring them over with you?" Eva asked incredulously, staring at their little pointed noses, their round coal eyes.

"We brought them the whole way. Can you imagine? My little warriors," she cooed. "And Schwefel, you too," she cried, addressing a yellow bird in a hanging bamboo cage. "We brought you too—if only from the streets of New York." Eva heard the sound of cooks in the kitchen (how did Beatrice already have a working household?), and when she smelled sage and meats wafting into the parlor, she was afraid she might suddenly be sick. "It was terribly impractical but—poor Theo"—Beatrice continued—"I insisted."

"Your house is beautiful," Eva said, and hoped it didn't sound as resigned as she expected it did.

"Why thank you. Theo prepared it marvelously, though I'm afraid I think it's rather too much. I prefer a simpler style."

"Do you?" Eva examined the gleaming floors, the stained-glass picture window—how the dying light filtered through the jewel tones, gracing the room with subtle fancy.

"Indeed I do. I adore the native adobe. If it were up to me to build a house, I would use adobe for certain. I hear it keeps cool in the summer and warm in the winter. I like a practical house; do you know what I mean? I bet your house is adobe. I bet your husband insisted upon it!"

The yellow bird squawked, as if agreeing with its mistress.

"We're actually building a new house in the European style. Brick and wood—it's currently under construction."

"Of course my practical nature disappears when it comes to animals. I'm mad about animals, I admit it. If we're to be friends, you should know this about me. Before long there will be more birds in addition to cats and lizards in this beautiful house. If I lived in the wilds of Africa I'd no doubt have more than a few monkeys."

"It feels like the wilds of Africa here sometimes," Eva said, watching Abraham lift his nephews up in the air. Oddly enough—unless she was imagining it—Meyer seemed to studiously avoid shaking Abraham's hand.

"Oh have you been to Africa?" Beatrice asked, and Eva couldn't even bring herself to laugh.

"No," said Eva, "no I haven't. I was speaking symbolically."

"Oh I'm very literal, I'm afraid. Would you like to go?"

"Go where?"

"To Africa."

"Not particularly," Eva replied. "Here are the eggs," she said, handing over the basket. "For the seder plate."

"How perfect," she said, taking the basket. "You are full of symbols, aren't you! Eggs are the symbol of springtime, am I right?"

"Or fertility," Eva muttered.

"I had another symbolic gift today. The bishop made me a present of a sapling—from his garden, you know his garden."

"The bishop?"

"An orange tree for a sweet marriage. Isn't that clever? I don't know if you noticed it when you came in."

"Of course"—Eva managed—"how thoughtful."

"Don't you think? He even planted it himself." Beatrice was the scrubbed clean picture of health. She was someone who never sighed. "Everyone has been so friendly," she said, as if she wasn't surprised but simply pleased, as if it had all been her idea. "Wolf and Hannah feel like family already and the Sheinkers and the Isinfelds, and, well, isn't it obvious what a good fellow your husband is? What a dear dear man."

This woman was perhaps the most optimistic individual Eva had ever encountered, but still she had a feeling Beatrice was referring to something specific and not just the way Abraham was standing in the corner, obviously impatient to sit. "Forgive me, but what have you heard about my husband?"

"Well only what a fine example he is for our community! Donating five thousand dollars to the construction of the cathedral? Too wonderful! And of course all of the others had no choice but to donate as well. They would have looked badly letting your husband be the only philanthropist, and you know, of course, that our men are too prideful for that. How proud you must be!"

Eva felt immediately claustrophobic, as if her organs were urgently pressing together, preventing her from sipping the abruptly stale air, replete with cooking smells and different perfumes, traces of men's cigars. She looked at Abraham until she caught his eye, and she hoped he sensed what she'd just heard. "Oh I am very proud," she said fiercely, fingering the scars on her hands—some old, some still fresh—from cooking over open flames. "You can't imagine."

"Please, friends," said Theo Spiegelman, who would always have the look of a boy, no matter how grand his house or capable his new wife, "to the table."

It was draped with fresh white linens, good family silver, and crystal glinting in the candlelight. Eva couldn't help but picture the perilous journey these fine objects had survived, in order to not only decorate this table but to maintain an entire culture. She also couldn't imagine ever seeing a beautiful object without picturing its journey, and how the people on the very same transport had been no doubt ashen with fear or doubled over with cramping from the monotony of beans (if they were lucky enough to have beans) or from hunger. By setting the table just so, by gathering together, each person in the room was making a promise to those they had left overseas that they were still deeply linked. She was momentarily overcome by the sheer loveliness of the scene and the lengths they all had traveled, only to take up their traditions— traditions which she had honestly never pondered too deeply—once again on the other side of the world. But then Theo Spiegelman made the *kiddush* and Wolf mumbled a blessing over the crisp tortillas being used as a stand-in for *matzot,* and as the story of Moses unfolded, Eva's heart was not with her people wandering in the desert (a scenario that now held unquestionably deeper meaning) but turned inward and aggravated as the seder went by, joining the other seders in what was becoming her increasingly blurred past.

Abraham had no business giving away money when she was reduced to begging him for a completed house, or at the very least, a stove. She couldn't bear to imagine what Father and Mother were doing on this holiday, and was immediately filled with anger while picturing her parents either at home alone or in a hotel suite in Karlsbad, Father having brought along Rahel or whoever had become the household cook. Or were they at the unfamiliar home of Father's very religious relatives, a place Eva couldn't imagine Mother ever agreeing to step foot? She tried and failed to picture Uncle Alfred too, with his wife and children she'd never know. Did they make seders in Paris? She couldn't imagine his life at all and this pained her; she could see only the superficial: yellow lights on the boulevard, Alfred inking drafts of speeches and talking late into the night with bearded men just like him.

As she dipped her pinky finger into the wine, shaking drops onto the clean white plate, she found herself mouthing the ten deadly plagues, finding Hebrew words without thinking. "Ten drops for ten plagues," Theo Spiegelman said, his voice cracking with seriousness. "Wine is a symbol of joy and freedom—"

"Amen," cried Mr. Isinfeld, and Eva was only relieved it wasn't Abraham.

"And thus diminishing our wine drop by drop symbolizes diminished joy and freedom. God did not want to kill the Egyptians, and it pained Him to do so," Theo Spiegelman continued, clearing his throat, sincere and utterly humorless, and yet this pained sincerity made her feel that she could love him, or, for that matter, that she could love anyone who was simply who he said he was, even if it was nothing more.

She ate the chicken soup and took pleasure in the way the children watched the *kiddush* cup, which had been set aside for the prophet Elijah, who—as Meyer quietly explained—never died, but went riding up to the sky in a chariot of flames. She could barely look at Abraham, even as she participated in the evening; she ushered in Elijah's ghost from outside, watching the boys shriek with pleasure as Wolf Spiegelman covertly shook the table and insisted that the wine was disappearing, that Elijah's ghost had truly come and boy was he thirsty. She couldn't hear the joy in the children's voices as they watched the *kiddush* cup intently, she couldn't smell the sweet wine, but she could see the prophet

Elijah. She couldn't *stop* seeing Elijah engulfed in flames and she wondered why, up until now, this had always seemed like a glorious image and not a frankly terrifying one.

It was clear by the way he engrossed himself in discussion with Theo Spiegelman after the final songs were sung that Abraham knew she was angry. After eating more than his fair share of Beatrice Spiegelman's dense Passover plum pudding, chewing heartily on the sticky sweet cake and knocking back glass after glass of wine, Abraham went on to impudently ask if Theo had purchased anything stronger on his recent European travels. Theo—though he'd known Abraham for years—seemed as if he was still unable to decide if Abraham was purely aggressive and rude or in fact more charismatic than anyone he'd hope to know, and the next thing Eva saw, from her seat in the parlor next to Hannah and Beatrice (who was holding forth on the difference between Navajos and Apaches) was Theo opening a bottle.

She'd wanted to suggest leaving several times, but hadn't had the energy to approach Abraham while he was in mid-conversation. She knew he would argue his case for one more drink with a particularly public charm, and she felt enervated by the thought of the potential spectacle. And so, just as she'd expected, they were the last guests to leave.

Outside, the night was startlingly clear; she savored the air and the endless, dark blue expanse, which, as Abraham had explained long ago, was indeed different from a German sky. Abraham dragged his feet in the dirt, and when he tried to take her arm, she pulled her shawl close so he had nothing to hold on to. "Are you in a pucker, pretty lady?"

She didn't answer because she knew that if she did, one of them would raise their voice, and though the houses were mostly built facing away from the street due to the Mexican love of privacy, she knew some neighbors would hear nonetheless and even if one person heard, that one set of ears would lead to a steady stream of talk.

"Are you feelin' glum?" He put on the accent of a gunslinger this time, willing to play the clown while the wine and spirits still held him aloft.

"Let's just get home," she said quietly.

"You must know by now that I really don't like to be ignored."

"You won't like my question any better." They were close enough to their front door, but all at once she felt her wall of silence burst and she raised her voice: "You could have *loaned* him the money!"

Abraham waved a hand in front of his face as if he'd encountered a summer swarm. "What are you talking about?"

"The gift to the bishop? The gift Beatrice Spiegelman seemed to think was very *civic-minded*?"

"Quiet!" he shouted, and they rounded the corner, only to meet with the familiar smell of fresh burro droppings, which overpowered any kind of response. She held her tongue until they were inside, where she lit candles as he threw off his coat and angrily started pacing. "You embarrassed me tonight," he said, as if he was some kind of puritan.

"*I* embarrassed *you*? You drank all of their liquor. You drank more than they offered."

"It's a holiday!"

"I want to know something," she said, sinking into the high-backed chair. "Forget about the fact that we are living here in this dreadful place, and that I am cooking over open flames—"

"That is not cooking over open flames. I wish you wouldn't exaggerate. Being on the Trail in the desert—*that* is open flames. This is a *type of stove*—"

"Forget about all of it. If you mysteriously had money to offer, why didn't you loan it to him?"

Abraham kicked his shoe across the room and it took a triangle of whitewash from the wall. "I did not come to America to become a money lender," he snarled. "I could have done that back in Germany. I could have done that in France. R-respect . . ." he stuttered. "Respect," he repeated, calming down.

She took in his unfocused gaze, and she whispered, "I know respect is important. Believe me."

"To give the bishop that money—to earn that kind of respect—this is an investment in our future. The house will come eventually. You must learn patience or you'll drive us both mad."

She began removing her bone hairpins, and her hair came loose in heavy sections as if it didn't belong to her.

"Look here," he said abruptly, "I have something to tell you. I wanted to announce it after the meal but my brother—*El Prudencio*—wouldn't let me."

She crossed her arms, preparing for the worst, even though he seemed awfully pleased.

"Well?" he asked brightly. "Don't you want to know what it is?"

She nodded. He was drunk, she realized. He was drunker than she'd thought.

"I have secured us a contract, a good, solid contract in the mountains."

She made her face into a smile.

"My brother was very pleased," he said. "I'd hoped that you would be too."

"Of course"—she nodded—"of course I'm pleased." She resisted asking what such a contract would mean, exactly.

"Well then, why do you still look so very goddamn suspicious of me?" he asked with a boy's impatience.

"Forgive me"—she began—"but if Meyer is so pleased, why did he seem to be avoiding you this evening? Why haven't we been invited to dinner lately?"

"I don't know what you're talking about. Everything is fine."

"It doesn't seem that way."

" 'It doesn't seem that way.' " He chortled. "You are so dramatic. If you had a baby to care for, if you had responsibilities, you might be less inclined to worry over nothing."

"Yes!" she shouted suddenly. "I know. I know, I know, I know." He took her firmly by the shoulders, as if he could stop her from speaking just by the touch of his hands.

LESSONS

BEATRICE SPIEGELMAN'S HORSE DIDN'T SPOOK WHEN Eva touched his sleek, brown flank. "Hello, friend," she said.

"He likes you," Beatrice observed, in a tone that managed to be both enthusiastic and faintly disapproving. "Now put your foot in the stirrup," she instructed. "And know that it is true that horses can smell your fear."

Eva jumped up and immediately wanted to gallop; she'd leave no trace, only red hot dust. "What fear?" she asked, sharply, before offering a conciliatory smile.

THE RIDING LESSONS TOOK PLACE EACH DAY AFTER BREAK-fast, when Eva was delighted to leave the cramped and dusty house, which reeked of Abraham's cigars and Chela's frijoles. Beatrice was a natural instructor and insisted Eva was making progress over the course of a month and so despite the fact that Beatrice sporadically insisted on speaking exclusively in English, and even though she asked incessant questions while her ability to listen to their answers was dubious at best, and despite how she seemed to enjoy swatting flies with a fervor that bordered on fanatic, Eva was intensely grateful for the new activity and came to crave the vantage of being on horseback—how it made her feel for moments at a time as if nothing could catch up with her, least of all her sense of propriety. How thrilling it was to feel that she and the horse might run off together at any moment like a pair of sweethearts.

When Beatrice, whom she'd started to call Bea, deemed her ready, they ventured beyond the town's perimeter. Before Bea suggested it, such an activity would have never occurred to Eva—not only because she assumed she lacked the required skill, but also because she was much too concerned with what others might think. Beatrice, however, was utterly *un*concerned, and yet instead of seeming rebellious, she somehow changed the standard. There was something about Beatrice Spiegelman that, quite maddeningly, seemed above reproach.

They galloped past desert and scrub brush to where the bishop lived and cultivated a kind of enchanted garden. There were grapes from cuttings of California vines, black cherries and peaches and rambling roses. A footbridge bisected a trout pond. While the horses cooled off under an enormous cottonwood tree, the two women stood on that charming bridge as if they were tourists in Florence or Paris, gazing not at the Duomo or at Notre Dame but at the bishop's modest adobe house, where his cook—ignoring their protestations, when they learned the bishop was not at home—prepared refreshments.

"How civilized it is here," said Eva, noticing thick bushes of rosemary and mint.

Beatrice nodded, her thoughts obviously elsewhere. "It is generally more civilized here than I'd imagined. Here in America, I mean."

"You seem almost disappointed!"

Her smile was uncharacteristically sheepish. "Do not misunderstand me, I was grateful to find some comfort after that harrowing stagecoach ride. But I suppose I'd had this . . . notion."

"What kind of notion?"

She shook her head. "I must learn to keep these things to myself."

Eva said nothing; she gazed in the distance at what she guessed were peacocks. They looked like turquoise beads against the silver sky.

"Listen"—Bea spoke up, as Eva knew she eventually would—"the fact of the matter is that I come from a very wealthy family. I hope you don't find me rude for saying so. And I don't know about you—but I resent the attitude that a wealthy girl needn't learn to *do* anything! That education hardly matters and that a wealthy girl, especially a wealthy good-looking girl, will never have trouble finding a husband no matter how poor her skills are, or even how rude she is. I find such cynicism hateful. Don't you?"

"Of course," said Eva mildly.

"I just—I only was hoping to feel . . . necessary, I suppose."

"Necessary? To whom? You traveled awfully far for such a notion, don't you think?"

"Never mind," she said.

Eva laughed a little cruelly. "How I wish I was more like you."

"You don't mean that. Why say it then?"

"Come," Eva said, "let's walk."

They strolled the raked aisles, taking fast and then slower steps under the elm trees, the maples, and the weeping willows bowing toward the pond's flowered edges. Bea pointed out enormous cabbages and beets, the pear trees and pale blossoms attracting bees. "Now the bishop— there is a man who enjoys refinement," said Eva.

"But his is of a higher nature. He primarily wishes to show how much can be done with so very little."

"Or perhaps he simply misses fine food and wine."

"Mmn," Bea said, fingering a dead leaf before plucking it from its stem. "When I was a child in Frankfurt, we had a French governess whom we all apparently adored so completely that our mother never questioned her authority. She made for us the most exquisite meals— crispy potatoes, chocolate pots—just delicious. It was only after my younger brother Siegfried gleefully told our mother that Mademoiselle Landau's breasts felt *heavy like challah dough* that our poor mother had any idea of what was going on when Mademoiselle put our little Siegfried to bed. After his beloved Mademoiselle's dismissal, our brother refused food for a week."

Eva barely suppressed a laugh.

"Needless to say," said Bea, "we had only German governesses after that."

"Needless to say!"

"And you, Eva Shein? Did you have a governess when you were living as a girl in Berlin?"

It was as if Beatrice could tell there was something wrong with her and was trying to locate what it was. "I did," Eva evenly replied. "I too had a French governess and a summer house and I thought I would never leave my parents' house, let alone my city."

"And what made you change your mind? Oh you needn't explain. That is how it was with my Theo. Love makes us fools. And now we're here."

"Fools," said Eva, "how true."

"Which isn't to say you were a fool for coming."

"Of course not."

"I don't think any of us were fools to come."

"I know," Eva said, standing still and breathing deeply, accepting the gift of dry, sweet air. "I know you don't."

Beatrice seemed to wait for Eva to finish her thought, to say something to the effect of *Neither do I.* But Eva had nothing to say and only stood so still that she reflexively thought of the afternoon when she had her portrait painted, with the breeze coming in through the window, and the clarity and the heady first time of feeling squarely in the center of things. *You're intoxicated?* She wished she could challenge her younger, simpler self. *Why not just leave it at that?*

Beatrice shaded her forehead and peered, without squinting, at the slate blue swath of Jemez Mountains. "Stunning," she said. As if such a view should settle the question.

BY TWILIGHT EVA WAS WEARY FROM SUN AND EXERCISE AND SINCE by now she knew better than to imagine that Abe would be home in time for supper, she sent Chela home early, and instead of preparing a meal, opened a tin of herring and sank into the sofa as if allowing herself—if only for a private moment—to declare that nothing was worth the effort.

She ate the herring quickly with her fingers, one piece after the other, until her blouse was stained. The breeze through the small window was surprisingly chilly and it carried the melancholy sounds of another day's end—crying children, tired ranchers, sisters fighting over one domestic struggle or another—so she rose to close the window and when she did, she was surprised to see Meyer watching the house.

"Yes?" Eva said, upon opening the door. She hated that she'd been interrupted, that her blouse was stained with oil, but she made sure not to be instantly rude; for a moment she was afraid, but she wasn't quite sure why. "Oh, Meyer," she said, "good afternoon. Abraham didn't mention you were coming."

"No," Meyer stepped up to the doorway, his hat between his hands. "No, I do not imagine he did."

"Oh dear"—Eva gasped—"has something happened to Abraham?"

Meyer began to shake his head.

"Meyer?"

"No, Eva dear," he said, as if the conversation was already going nothing like he'd planned. "Nothing has happened. Rather—nothing that I know about, which honestly might be quite useless knowledge. You see"—he looked down the alley in one direction and then the other, until she remembered she hadn't invited him inside and gestured him through the door—"I don't feel that I know enough lately," he mused. He gave her his coat, but kept his hat. *You see,*" he repeated carefully, "I don't know enough about my brother. I'm afraid I never have."

She laughed, or made an attempt to laugh. "Oh Meyer," she said, in a tone that, even to her own ears, seemed better suited to the stage. "Tea?" she continued; he didn't even bother with a response. "Why you know he looks up to you. He respects you." She realized she was being obdurate, but she also knew that it was true.

"Does he?" Meyer asked, with the smallest smile, one too small to belong to anyone but a cynic. He was conspicuously refusing to sit, no matter how many times Eva had indicated he should do so. "I wonder"—he began, and he was remarkably direct now, offering an expression that left little room for pleasantries—"Does he respect *you?*"

"I'm sorry?"

"You are a lovely girl, Eva. It has always struck me as awfully strange that you agreed to marry my brother."

"Meyer!"

"I would watch him," he said, with indisputable meaning. He put on his hat, though he was still standing inside. "And if you wouldn't mind . . . "

"Yes?" she asked; she tried not to sound afraid, but she was too stunned to sound anything but.

"Tell me."

"Tell you?"

He nodded. "You could tell me where he goes." He left without saying goodbye, letting his troublesome words linger on the air.

SHE SERVED HIM PLAIN POTATO SOUP, COLD BEEF, AND CABBAGE, and just as she knew that this was Abraham's least favorite meal, she also knew from how he poured more than enough whiskey in addition to three glasses of wine that this would be a night on which he would need to take a walk. She asked him nothing. He seemed relieved. Not five minutes into her washing the dishes did Abraham top his smart coat with a fine, dark hat, and she found herself both perversely proud that she could anticipate her husband's actions and, more saliently, alone again.

When she stepped up to the window and looked out into nothing but the darkness of an unlit alley and the faraway flicker of lamplight, she came up with an idea so ludicrous it was better suited for children's games—the sort she'd never been good at—but before she could give it too much thought (and before he had a chance to go very far) she drank the dregs of Abraham's whiskey, donned a dark shawl like a Spaniard, and before she could articulate any of the many reasons not to, she passed under the *vigas* and—although Meyer undoubtedly didn't mean for her to do exactly *this*—she took her brother-in-law's inappropriate suggestion and followed her husband.

Adobe at night looked strangely luminescent, as if not sun but moonlight had dried each muddy brick—the same brilliant moonlight that now illuminated the sleeping burros and horses in the street. She heard Abraham before she saw him, stroking the neck of a spotted mare. He was singing a song about the railroad, one he'd sung with nearly liturgical repetition on both the steamship and overland buggy to combat inevitable waves of nausea. According to Abraham (and this was a serious point of pride) he had never—not once in his life after his *bar mitzvah* year—allowed himself to vomit.

He gave the mare two strong pats before making his way past the *portales* strung with drying red peppers, and Eva followed in his shadow. She watched as he bid goodnight to a scrawny, ancient fellow in a Union soldier's uniform who leaned on a rifle while mumbling to himself and who—at least deep inside his troubled mind—seemed intent on safeguarding the plaza. She watched how her husband stopped in front of a boarding house run by a widow from Missouri who, remarkably, admitted guests only on the condition that their rooms remained unlocked throughout the duration of their stay. The widow sat under her *vigas*, knitting, and Abraham stopped and bid her goodnight too; her face alighted at the sight of him. Just as Eva was poised to become officially jealous, he kept walking toward the summons of off-key dancehall music, the glow of rose-colored lights, arriving predictably at Doña Cuca's, where he walked in not only confidently but as if he knew that whatever he was after she'd be giving it away for free.

He hadn't seen Eva when she was hiding behind doors and posts and horses, and he didn't see her now as she walked boldly up to the storefront window—its heavy curtains were raised—where Doña Cuca herself was surveying the narrow street. As their eyes met, Eva was surprised to discover that, on closer inspection, the flame-haired Mexican was not beautiful at all, and while Doña Cuca pressed her fingers to the glass as if she meant to touch Eva's shoulder, Eva felt strangely sorry for her.

Come inside. Eva could swear Doña Cuca had mouthed the words before greeting Abraham, unsmiling.

Once behind the saloon doors, the very first thing that Abraham did wasn't to order a drink or make eyes at a whore but hand over an envelope to Doña Cuca; by the way it was both offered and accepted, Eva could tell this envelope contained a fair amount of cash. Doña Cuca not only nodded, but also clapped him on the back as if he had done something noble—as if he had made her proud.

What would Eva have said if Abraham had caught her hiding in the shadows? Or in this improbable doorway? She'd never find out, for Abraham had never looked back—not once on his nighttime walk—not even for one curious or distrustful moment. And as Doña Cuca posed a barbed invitation to come in and see for herself just what her husband was doing, Eva retreated without so much as a shake of her head—past the same daft man and boarding house widow and the sleeping horses and burros.

She didn't want to know. She didn't want to know what he gambled and lost, just how far it went behind those doors. What, after all, would she do about it? What could she? Where could she possibly go besides home to Abraham—not only tonight but always? She had made this decision; she had chosen. She would tell Meyer this, when she next saw his basset-hound face; she would say: *You are right, you don't know,* and *Please, what business is it of yours?*

But by the time Eva arrived at their Burro Alley door, she knew she could no sooner go inside than return to Doña Cuca's saloon.

Before she could steel herself against it, she had walked back to the end of the alley and mounted Abraham's ugliest horse (named—unimaginatively—Thunder), and as the breeze gathered force and turned to wind, she knew exactly where she was headed. The horse's back was warm and broad, and he took the turns so naturally and quickly that it was difficult not to love him. It was difficult to resist his brute, insistent motion or to argue against the fact that this was what she knew she'd be doing tonight as soon as she had followed Beatrice back to town when the sun began to set. She had left the bishop's garden at the appropriate hour but not because she'd wanted to.

It was not a beautiful night. The sky was murky even as the moon was bright, but she was not surprised to find the bishop outside, standing by the water. He looked startled as she approached, and, as if the pond was his emotional mirror, the glassy surface went suddenly wild as if hail had come pelting down. "Forgive me," she said, sounding more panicked than she felt. "Please forgive me for coming."

Bishop Lagrande looked up at her, and from this vantage he looked old but hardly weak. "Mrs. Shein," he said, and then in French, "I didn't take you for a horse woman."

"I suppose you will tell my husband," she said, attempting a graceful dismount. She realized she'd sounded irritable of all things and once again apologized.

"It is late," he said, but then the bishop shrugged, tearing crumbs from a loaf of bread and casting them into the pond. Once again the water became agitated and she laughed too hard when she realized the disturbance was caused not by some spiritual communion between the bishop and the water but simply by the bread he had tossed to the fish. "Here," he said, handing her a torn piece of bread. "For the baby trout—spry little fellows." He demonstrated—not entirely gracefully—encouraging Eva to put all of her weight into the throw.

She tore the bread and tossed it, surprised at the comfort found in doing so. As her eyes adjusted, she began to see the brown and green swirls in the darkness swarming fast and close to the shore where they stood. She noticed the bishop mutter something and smile and she had the distinct sense that she was interrupting something. She whispered, "They bring you pleasure—the fish. I can tell."

"Oh they do, they truly do. All of this"—he gestured abstractly—"in a land called arid and barren—"

"You want to set an example of how much can be done with so little?"

He shrugged again and coughed, releasing the rich currant scent of what was likely a fine approximation of Burgundy. "We all need to eat."

Eva had the distinct sense that—despite his passionate desire to build the new cathedral—this was in fact the place he felt closest to God. "Won't you ask me why I am here, what it is I'm doing on horseback after dark?"

"I will ask you this: Has something happened?"

She looked up at the darkness, at the wild plum and peach and pear trees. "Not yet," she said, "no."

"I may be a man who believes in miracles, but I'm not a simple man, Mrs. Shein. My instincts are very good and I usually suspect the worst."

"Are you often pleasantly surprised?"

He shook his head, stuck out his lower lip. "No."

"Strange words coming from a man of God."

"Oh but God owes us nothing. We have to earn His grace. There's nothing more frustrating than an ungrateful heart."

Eva could imagine days of his foul temper—this scratchy voice like a droning door hinge stopping just short of complaining.

"I am not married," he said rather priggishly. "But, my dear," he insisted, "you are. And young marrieds must tolerate each other's strange particulars."

"Of course," Eva said, not remotely interested in the expected litany of wifely duties.

"If you were married—let's say—to me, you would see how I am—for example—not as ethereal as you might suspect—"

"Bishop," she interrupted, but he ignored her.

"You would see that though I, for instance, cultivate an orchard, I will not allow apples into my house because I cannot bear to hear the sound they make when a guest's teeth pierce their skin—"

"Please," she insisted, "I really don't see—"

"You *would* see. You would see how—though I love those trout like the children I will never have—I also fillet them with such unflinching precision that even my cook steps back to marvel." She looked for his smile but it was missing. "We all have our shortcomings, *n'est ce pas?* Living alone, Mrs. Shein, has its gifts and blessings, but I would offer that it might not be such a charmed situation for someone like you."

"Someone like me?" And she was surprised to find that she was not defensive. Having such an unusual conversation under this wide open sky rendered the parlors of her covetous dreams suddenly dark and oppressive—patterned fabrics and fussy collectibles, satin-covered spit-toons . . . Eva felt a smile creep onto her face with no clear notion of why.

"My dear." His voice acquired a biting tone that she was surprised (and curiously excited) to hear. "Please go home. I don't know what you think I can do for you. You are hardly a penitent."

"Are you my friend?" Eva asked, teasingly and stupidly, as if the late hour and vaguely illicit nature of the bishop's wine-soaked breath and commentary had given her license to take her own liberties.

When he didn't answer she asked again, beginning to panic at what she had done by leaving the house tonight. *Are you my friend?* She wished she had taken Meyer's strange instructions for his own paranoia, for brotherly jealousies that had nothing to do with her. She wished she hadn't seen Doña Cuca's challenging expression, or the way Abraham looked so utterly at ease as he sauntered through the nighttime streets as if he were a bachelor and had never sought her out with interest or even desire. She wished too that she were lying under the sheets and blankets of her princess bed, sleepless but righteous. "I'll leave," she said, producing a shiver. "I don't know why I thought to come." She mounted Thunder after two attempts and he kicked at the ground, producing clouds of dirt, but they were hardly enough to hide behind.

It didn't occur to Eva that Abraham would be home before her, that it would be he and not she who would be sitting alone in the dark. All along—as she tied Thunder to his post at the end of the alley, as she touched his dust-smooth coat and felt such massive lungs expand and contract with hot hay breath—Eva had no idea that Abraham had been waiting.

"Where have you been?" he asked, with a drunkard's novel notion of his own moral authority. "Goddamn it," he said, and as she felt immediately and infuriatingly guilty, he rose to his feet, only to kick the chair aside. "Where were you?"

"Every time I walk by the lot—the wooden frame and piles of stone, I think: *Our house is already a relic.* It's as if we'd already lived and died."

"You are aware there is a dangerous vagrant who has still not been caught, are you not? You are aware that even without this specific terror you should never *never* go out alone at night? Do you hear me? *Do you?*"

"Abraham, we are going to need a proper house." She had said it before—dozens of times—but tonight it sounded different. Tonight it had some weight. She struck a match and, before burning her hand, found a candle just in time. She wanted to make sure that he could see her when she said what was suddenly the only thing left to say. He grabbed her wrist but she didn't even flinch. "It's happened," she said. "Just as I told you it would."

"What kind of nonsense are you talking now?"

"I'm pregnant," she admitted, giving away the secret she had squired away and held deep inside, somewhere more unfathomable and essential than her marrow.

His grip loosened and his face changed so drastically; at first she thought it was the candlelight playing a trick—he looked so maddeningly relieved.

She had dared this secret as she'd jumped on and off horses, as she'd thrown herself into speed and the wind with a force she'd so desperately needed in order to stave off crushing hope.

"How long?" he asked. He had, Eva knew, stopped looking at her body sometime in the past few weeks; he had continued to touch her but only in the middle of the night, and he hadn't taken a good look in some time. She could tell he was shocked now as his eyes settled on her belly, which was really quite shockingly expanded.

"Five," she said flatly. "A bit more." She had, up until that point, refused to behave as if it were true. It was only now that she allowed herself to let out her corset and place his hands on her, defining the fraught and mysterious space.

He gave a hearty whoop, but his joyful cry echoed in strained silence.

She knew that he would lie about his whereabouts tonight, and she did not have the confidence to argue. She would lie also. For even if she had nothing to hide anymore, she absolutely felt as though she did.

S H A M E

BOTH THE SHEINS AND SPIEGELMANS HAD CONTRACTS in a remote mountain village. In the interests of safe travel and sociability, the competing businessmen had joined forces and—perhaps recklessly—they had invited their families along. The caravan pressed on through the August heat, through rain-carved northbound paths. There seemed to be ever-present dangers of drop-offs, and now and then screams emitted from one of the wagons in the caravan. In the first wagon were Meyer, his wife Alma Lucia, and their two boys, while Abraham and the two Spiegelman brothers brought up the rear. In the middle carriage, Eva Shein nearly threw up for the fifth time that day. Three weeks ago she had given birth. Now all she wanted was beer. Three weeks ago she'd seen a creature come out of her now-numb body. There was no beer, none for her anyway, and she was forced to sit with insufferable Beatrice Spiegelman, who—perhaps in an attempt to distract Eva, perhaps to ignore her own traveling anxieties—expounded upon her plans to build a non-sectarian school for girls.

Not only was Beatrice excited at the prospect of the school, but she also had no shortage of other ideas. She was especially focused on the removal of garbage. Garbage, she

said, stirred her soul as a woman—it was woman's duty to scour a society, to take care that the heart of a city did not become a barnyard.

"Only then," said Bea Spiegelman, "will the way be cleared for great-
ness."

As the carriage wheels sputtered through a series of ruts and Tranquilo lashed the burros, Eva could feel the wagon wheels turning underfoot, under boots that were laced too tightly. Her feet were still swollen,
as were her breasts, which—though filling out her dear sister's oft-worn
blouse—were useless.

"Rule Three," said Bea, a touch wistfully—her oration no doubt reminding her of a long-ago school pageant. "If any animal should die
within the limits of the city of Santa Fe, the person or persons to whom
such beast or beasts belong shall be required, within twenty-four hours
after the death of said animal or animals, to remove the carcass or car-
casses out of said city to a . . . to a distant place, where they cannot in-
commode by their appearance and offensive smell." She coughed primly.
"That's an important one."

Three weeks ago they took her baby girl. Abe took care of it. She had
wanted to hold her for just a little longer—her perfect baby, her pretty
corpse—but Abe had insisted with tears in his eyes and she hadn't any
will left to argue. Just like her sister, in what seemed like an undeniably pointed turn of events, she had given birth early. And not only was
the blue-faced, blood-smeared creature born that night—only to die by
daybreak—but also Eva's guilt, born and reborn, as if the guilt was wholly
new. There was no question this was punishment, and though she
couldn't deny she deserved it, she wanted to know when it might stop.
There was also no more question of God's existence. He was proved to
her with this definitive horror, with this putrid silence that would not let
her rest no matter how tired she felt. She wanted her baby alive. And if
not alive, then nowhere—God couldn't have her down deep in the earth
as if she'd been allowed to live and breathe, as if she was one of His own.

"Are you not feeling well?" Bea asked suddenly. She had a tendency,
Eva noticed, to spurt out questions in a hardened rush, so that well-
intentioned inquiries took on the grave, even hysterical, cast of criticism.

"Not particularly."

"Poor dear. This will do you good."

Bea was younger than Eva, younger by over two years, but she did not seem to know it. And since Eva, on making Abraham's acquaintance, had decided to heed her mother's advice (advice that much more potent for being rarely given) and never reveal her birthday, she was content to serve out her life as a surrogate younger sister to all who were willing, for as long as she possibly could. "What will do me good?"

"Why, they are having a great party in our honor! A *fandango*—the bishop says the people are precious—simple and precious."

"The bishop?" Eva asked, and felt as if tears might be leaking down her face. "Have you visited with him often?"

"I've continued riding out to his garden. Theo and I also took a meal with him inside his home, and do you know he insisted we all eat with umbrellas over our heads so no dust would fall into the oysters?" Beatrice laughed, before nervously asking, "Do you remember what a lovely day we had? When you and I rode there together?"

Eva nodded. It wouldn't have occurred to her that she could have ever done such a thing had it not been for Beatrice. "I was so grateful to you," she said. She *had* been grateful then, and though she had carried the baby long after that ride and had felt, for weeks afterward, the baby's elbows and feet writhing healthily away inside of her—she now saw riding with Beatrice as part of an irresponsible chain of events; she could tell that Beatrice thought so too.

Hannah Spiegelman—Bea's shy sister-in-law—sat on a rickety bench across from them and attempted to nurse her baby, but the baby was crying and had been crying for what seemed like the entire two hours of the journey thus far. The cries had started as whimpers and had progressed to a crazed wail, with alternating sobs in and out; it was driving Eva mad. She wanted to shut that baby up—shut it up efficiently, like swatting a fly; she could nearly taste the silence. If the baby stopped crying and Bea Spiegelman stopped talking, she might be left to watch the passing sky—an event in itself, watery blue, obscured by voluptuous clouds. Or she could close her eyes and envision the walls of the new house, which

Abraham had finally *finally* begun, after not only securing this mountain contract months ago, but having also bet against a notoriously lucky diamond hunter during a game of high-stakes poker, whose luck (as Abraham put it) had just plum ran out. She tried to shut out the heat and the wailing baby by imagining the winter parties she would have as a new woman in a new house—a snow queen mother presiding not only over fat-cheeked children, but also ice sculptures and candied oranges— a happy woman stringing Bengal lights through tall acacia trees. In the snow of her mind it was silent as a January sky, but in the stifling carriage the little monster kept wailing.

"Can we do anything?" Bea demanded of Hannah, who immediately looked up and shook her head; she had the stunned, black eyes of a rodent.

When Eva started to sing, the baby cried harder. The harder it cried, the louder she sang. It was Offenbach, a light aria—one she'd long since thought she'd forgotten. Not only could she not recall the last time she'd played a single note, she realized she hadn't even thought of music—not the pleasure it brought her, not the warmth it could send to a stranger's face, softening into nothing less than gratitude.

Bea Spiegelman looked uncomfortable for Eva, as if Eva had offered up a breast for the wailing child and spurted curdled milk instead of song.

PASSING THROUGH THE DOORS OF THE SMALL VILLAGE HALL IN THE late afternoon were mostly Mexican men (a few sunburnt Anglos were sprinkled in the mix) with bowed legs and wily grins, all in need of a washing. There were men without women and women without children, harried-looking families whose husbands, on arrival, immediately hit the whiskey. Sometimes Eva felt like laughing for no good reason and this was one of those times: high-stepping on her swollen feet, parading through a dark, musty hall as if it was the Sofia Luisa ballroom, watching men line up not for a Française or a turn at the waltz, but to get their fill from a gallon of whiskey. Some men looked like burros tied to hitching posts, drinking from a trough. When one woman, with an unconcealed bruise on her cheek, caught Eva staring, Eva couldn't quite look away until she noticed another—young and plump and sulky—contemplating one barrel among many in the corner.

"Are you well?" asked Abraham, who had approached unnoticed.

She was startled, but—as had become her habit—she swallowed her first response and out came another in a calm almost lifeless tone. This affectation—it was palpable as the pink dust kicked up by burros on any given trail, and it had become as familiar as the mist that had surrounded Rahel (*you must hang yourself when you are young . . .*) or that of a Berlin spring. "You smell like whiskey already," she said. She tried to make her eyes teasing and bright, the way she was convinced she had once known just how to do, so that censure could pass as charm. "How I wish we had some for that baby. It screamed so dreadfully—"

"Listen," he said, his gaze diffused, "the fiddler." And when she followed his gaze toward the corner of the room, Eva saw he was watching the girl beside the barrel, who inspected its contents before plunging her hand in. Between Eva's damp fingers, she could vicariously feel the masses and masses of bullets in the barrel, harder and cooler than any tablets from Doctor Sam. But what the girl clutched was neither bullets nor screws but what looked, in fact, to be raisins. Eva and Abraham both watched in stilted silence as she devoured them with crooked little teeth, quickly, one at a time.

Screechy strings filled the crowded room, and the fiddler stood on a long, thin table, dancing like a poorly handled puppet. From behind skirts and under tables came the children—fingers raisin-sticky, faces smeared with dirt, lucky little urchin feet moving in a pack. The fiddler's tune sped up as a stout man in buckskins made whoops and cries, urging the couples lolling by the whiskey to take a spin around the darkening room—*Ladies and Gentlemen! Señores y Señoritas!* When a man scooped Eva up—a man nearly as small as she, a farmer so drunk she could smell the stench of moonshine through the pores of his hide-brown skin— Abraham did nothing to claim her. She protested as the man's stiff calloused hands led her forth, but after it was clear he was not about to release her, she tried to relax and let him carry her along. She took in as much as she could as she spun around the room; she looked for other respectable ladies who'd been forced to take a turn, but the figures moving around her were not only unrecognizable, but moving strangely slowly. In stark contrast with the fiddler's building tempo, they appeared as smudged sketches of real people. When Heinrich flashed into her mind, or *came over her,* as she had come to think of it—a sort of premonition— she had to briefly close her eyes. The room spun and she could feel his narrow fingers in between her shoulder blades and knew what she felt was the reverse of a premonition—it was the keen recognition of something that would never happen. She would never dance with him in the Sofia Luisa ballroom. They would never take tea along the Kurfürstendamm. She would never see him again. The dancers all around looked as clumsy and ill at ease as turkey gobblers fighting. *"Gracias, Señorita,"* said the man when the music ended, as if he was suddenly bashful.

"Señora," she corrected, before walking out through the swinging slatted doors, into the mountain air.

Everywhere she looked there were children. In the dying ginger light, they ran in a line like a dragon's tail—chubby fingers grabbing each others' pliant waists, some without shirts; they played at being Indians— howling, dancing, and spitting, rolling on the rocky ground. She walked a ways into a clearing with a stand of broken corrals and saw four older boys who took turns diving against what looked to be a dead ox, competing to see who could jump harder onto the poor beast's sun-bloated stomach and who could bounce off, landing furthest away. Gruff men stood over small fires, doing nothing to stop this game. They roasted slabs of meat and strips of chilies, and they pointed not to this revolting spectacle but to Eva—a strange, pale lady leaning on a gnarled, dead tree, hypnotized by children, their dangerous game. She saw the men pointing before she saw Abraham approach, grabbing her arm and steering her to where they were hidden in the tree's dank hollow. When he slapped her, she had the strange feeling of letting go—it had been a long time coming. He had never once hit her but had raised his fist often—stopping in midair—that it was nearly a relief to feel the follow-through. His hand tore through the atmosphere like a scythe cutting grain, and she went from being a respectable anomaly in a remote mountain outpost to a sin-gle stalk of wheat—thin and reedy, useless on its own. She smarted from the sting but didn't say a word.

"Have you no shame?" he demanded.

"He would not let me go!"

A spiky branch, which persisted in growing from the rotten trunk, nicked the back of his head. He spat at the ground instead of her. "You looked festive," he said—red face, red eyes. "You looked bright." She couldn't help thinking he was exercising control and that should an ani-mal have emerged suddenly, crossing his path—surely he would have shot it dead.

"Meyer still seems worried about you," she said. "You must tell me. You must tell me what is between you and your brother."

"There is nothing," Abraham said, still biting back his anger. "He asked me to secure this contract and here we are. He asked me . . ." He shook his head—silencing himself—before taking hold of his lapels and smoothing his coat. "I should not have hit you."

"No," Eva said. "It isn't right."

"Before God, I know it." He coughed a hearty, stalling cough. "You won't be worrying over Meyer and me anymore."

"And why is that?"

"Not only have I secured us this contract, here in this town, but an-other one is on the way. A big contract," he said, unable not to boast. "Military," he said, smiling.

"*Felicidades,*" she said with a tight smile.

"I swear," he said. "I do."

The hollow of this tree smelled of loam, and there was a barely audi-ble hiss, as if snakes were surrounding them in unseen slivers. She wanted to grab his hands. "I did not wish to dance with him," she blurted. "I wanted you to claim me. You should have claimed me."

He picked up a few sticks and handled them briefly, as if deciding which one was best. Then he stepped out of the hollow, backing away, throwing the sticks as far as he could. He didn't check to see where they happened to land, and it was unexpected that he didn't bother, as he was always in competition, if only with himself. Abraham believed very strongly that there were winners and losers in every aspect of life, and he did not become an American for his fate to be cast as the latter.

"Maybe you do not wish to claim me," she ventured. "Maybe you think I have brought you nothing but death."

"But after so much death you still look like a child." He was still angry but there was also something else. He looked the way he did sometimes before bed, when he was so utterly drunk that he asked her, without bashfulness, to please help him undress. "How is this possible?"

"But I am not a child. I feel one hundred years old."

He shook his head and cut the tip of a cigar. "God willing you should live so long."

Plum clouds faded to mauve and finally to gray. He lit a match, took a meaty puff, and as the dark closed in, the children's cries in the distance finally ceased. The boys had not plunged face first into the belly of the ox, coating their beautiful innocent bodies with dun-colored rotten guts. They had not cried out in disgust and regret. They had only grown bored and simply left the bloated ox to its naturally gruesome decay. The little ones were being taken now to their mothers' breasts, to share meager straw beds with other faceless children on sloping, muddy floors. She imagined that her babies—the three who never saw the light and the one who died soon after birth—were there with them, those nameless children, poor and dirty but alive. She wasn't sure how long she'd stood in the dank tree hollow, but the campfires had died down to smoldering orange embers. At a distance they looked pleasing—poppies on black silk—but she knew that as she grew closer she'd see the refuse of merry-making in a not-so-merry place.

Abraham was gone. She ought to have followed him inside, but instead had chosen to remain here, alone with his lingering impression. At times she wondered whether she preferred memories and spirits to living, breathing people. At this very moment there stood half-wits and half-breeds who—along with Abraham in his fine suit and combed moustache—jockeyed for the spigot on the five-gallon jug, wanting and wanting more. This, she thought, is America.

She heard her name being called, and, ignoring her impulse to retreat farther into the hollow, she emerged to see Beatrice Spiegelman holding a candle. "Eva," she implored, vaguely horrified, "you are standing in the darkness."

"I know it is dark, Beatrice. I've seen the same sun come and go."

"Well, for goodness' sake—"

"Here I am." She imitated a soldier on the march—which took considerable effort lifting knees up and down under a heavy skirt—but Beatrice did not laugh. Inside the hall, a roar broke out like sloppy battle cries.

"These people," said Bea, shaking her head and Eva followed her into the fray.

Low burning candles cast flickering shadows on the muslin-covered wall. Eva hadn't noticed the muslin earlier, but it was now quite apparent how the dingy cloth had been tacked up in an effort toward festivity. But just then festivity was being perverted: A circle had formed (around what was initially unclear), but as she and Bea drew closer, there was hardly a doubt as to whether sin was at its center. Through slivers in the crowd she could just glimpse torn dresses in motion, flailing arms, and swishing hair. At first she thought her eyes must have been deceiving her, but she could soon make out what appeared to be nothing other than two grown women fighting—clutching and striking each other like beasts. The chanting of the crowd rose in a chorus as the dark woman tore a chunk of the tall one's stringy hair. Eva strained to find Abraham, but she could barely see beyond the people just in front of her, shouting in sick excitement. Boots pounded in rhythm and a group of young men beat sticks together as if these women were no more deserving of dignity than those russet cocks on the massive ship she had boarded in Bremen. Then, as if this were only a nightmare and not her waking life, the women were each given knives by men who inflamed their anger even further—all for what was clearly a blood sport for spectators, a plea for sadistic laughter. There was a flash of brown skin—a calf? An arm?—and she had a flash of certainty that this fighter might have been the sulky girl she had seen before—the childlike raisin-eater—but then she saw a hard jaw line, a heavy bosom, and knew she'd been mistaken. And what did it matter anyway? These were all strangers, all poor mountain people whose fates were essentially the same: to marry their kin, go blind, go mad. The raisin-eater was probably working right about now—working in a back room reeking of whiskey-sweat and hoping to make a night's wage before the men grew too drunk to function, too mean to pay.

The tall woman slashed at the air with a theatrical flourish—chin held high, balance steady—and the dark one yelled as if she'd actually been stabbed, as if her blood were spurting from a punctured heart. Was this in fact, a show? Would the women later fall into each other's arms—gleeful at the bets placed in haste, the passions so inflamed?

She turned to Beatrice Spiegelman, and though she expected to see her flushed with outrage or even galvanized by such an absence of morality, primed for hours of indignant conversation—Bea was actually gawking, utterly dazed. As the tall woman took a stab and missed and missed again, Eva imagined Abraham was in the arms of that girl, the raisin-eater—the whore who looked most like her. For that is probably where he was; her defenses were too stripped away today for her to pretend she believed otherwise. Eva pictured how he crushed her into a sagging bed or sloping floor, how her small, sticky hands grabbed his lank, thick hair as he moved like the knife in the tall woman's hand, as that knife finally struck at the dark woman's breast . . .

"It's shameful," said Bea, not looking away.

"Yes," said Eva, "it is."

SHE'D BEEN JOLTED AWAKE BY THE NEED TO TEND TO THE BABY, A need met only with the harrowing fact that there was no baby fussing; there was not even the mysterious promise of a baby, snug inside her body. She had waited all night long for Abraham before, but never in a place like this. What, Eva wondered (and she couldn't imagine she was the only one wondering), had the men been thinking when they brought their families here today? Outside on the mountain, coyotes howled and the party continued with a never-ending stream of vulgar cries, while inside the ramshackle accommodations only burlap and hides divided the dilapidated space. To her right, Meyer and Alma Lucia muttered in Spanish, while Theo and Beatrice giggled on her left, until all was silent except an erratic snore and the threatening sounds of reveling— shouting and gunshots that grew louder and softer at times, but continued uninterrupted.

When he arrived in bed, Abraham smelled so foul that all she could do was cry. In the grim, gray light, he lay down on top of the scratchy blanket in his boots. "I'm a lucky son of a bitch," he said.

"Why is that?" she asked, her eyelids slowly closing.

"Look at you, puss."

"Look at me?"

"You're a huckleberry above anybody's persimmon."

She turned her head away. "Why do you insist on speaking this way?"

"I don't know what you mean. I speak English. We live in America."

"You are not a cowboy, Abraham. I am not a whore."

He unbuttoned his shirt while lying flat on his back. A button popped and rolled onto the floor. "You love Germany so much?" he growled low. "You are more German here than anywhere. Here, puss, you can be as German as you think you are, not as German as Germany will allow."

"What nonsense you are speaking."

"They sacked my uncle's tailor shop," he said in a drunken slur.

"Who did?"

"They beat him, too—beat him good . . . down on his bloody knees in the street . . . he did nothing but hobble away . . . went to work down the block in the same goddamn city."

"Why was he beaten?" she asked stubbornly.

He'd shifted onto his side and watched her lucidly, almost tenderly. She looked past him toward the rips in the burlap, the water stains on the ceiling. As he rolled on top of her, her heart raced sickly; there was ringing in her ears. She gagged from his bitter flesh and whiskey smell as he reached for her breasts, but he lay his head down and instantly fell asleep.

· · ·

BY NIGHTFALL THEY APPROACHED SANTA FE AND SHE NEVER THOUGHT she'd be so pleased to see its low mud-cake hovels, its paltry town square. Her throat was parched from a night of no sleep, not to mention a coating of dust from the trip, so she could barely respond when Beatrice pointed at the Shein store and exclaimed, "Well who on earth is that?"

A young man was under the portal. Abraham stepped down from the wagon and approached the stranger cautiously with a gun and lantern in hand. When the lantern cast light on the young man's face, Eva could see how he was badly beaten, with blood caked on his face and chest and one eye swollen shut. Abraham helped the boy to his feet, and when Eva heard the poor soul mutter thanks in a muffled, desperate voice, it took her a moment to realize that not only was he a stranger here but that he was speaking German.

LEVI

THE ROOM WHERE THE YOUNG MAN RESTED HAD ONCE been the bishop's wine storage. It still reeked dark and sweet—a pulpy marriage of fermented grape and cool, wet stone. It was so dark that only after spending minutes within its walls could one distinguish its faint gradations and sense whether time had truly passed at all. After the bishop had moved to his lodge in the countryside to make room for the Sisters and before the young man's sudden arrival, the wine room had become a place where willful pupils were sent to pray whenever they misbehaved. It had been a storage room, a discipline room, and, after Levi Ehrenberg appeared broken and beaten at Shein Brothers' door, the room became a sickroom, a dark and nearly neutral place lodged between life and death.

A week after they had found him in a heap, Sister Blandina announced that young Mr. Ehrenberg might benefit from visitors, and after some prodding from Abraham to bring the boy some biscuits for God's sake—*An embroidered handkerchief! Peppermints! Whatever it is that ladies bring when tending to the sick!*—Eva decided to pay her respects.

Those days she woke early each morning; it was still wickedly hot. Her sleep was consistently disturbed if not first by mosquitoes then by the significant portion of the population who weren't blessed with adobe walls and chose to sleep in the streets, preferring the open air (insect-ridden as it was) to their close and flame-hot quarters. There was inevitably a skirmish come daybreak, if not before, and so the first sounds she heard upon waking were furious outbursts— frustrated sounds, childlike in their heightened confusion, rendering not only the cause of the outburst but its very *language* unclear. The whole town was irritable, exhausted; there was a rising tide of impatience, but people went about their business, and Eva too rose to meet the day. She was childless but not ill, she reminded herself; and her house was actually being built. She was childless but not broken and bloodied like the poor German boy who was (according to Beatrice) not only the sole survivor of a brutal Indian raid, but who had made it to Santa Fe *on foot* through miles of rocky desert. Eva sat by the small bedroom window as she pinned her hair up, peering across the street at the convent, the school, and the chapel, while waiting all the while for an elusive breeze to graze the nape of her damp neck. *Poor fellow,* she whispered, as she imagined Sister Blandina's dry hands, Sister Theodosia's disagreeable voice. The nuns' collective, unflappable calm was doubtlessly hard-earned, but it was also severely discouraging; Eva could not shake the feeling that these sisters relished suffering, or maybe they didn't *relish* suffering, but in some indefinable and undeniable way, it was what they lived for.

No hint of a breeze arrived, and so she began the arduous task of putting on her clothes. After cinching, tying, and smoothing herself, she truly felt faint from the exertions but finally stepped out the back door and approached the apricot tree. It grew from a meager patch of earth, cordoned off by coyote fencing. She watered the tree and it flourished, drooping over the empty, scratched porcelain bathtub, dipping in one branch, then two, as if to convey that despite its undeniably lush looks, it was still thirsty. Eva picked the fruit for Mr. Ehrenberg but decided against baking the intended strudel and instead set out across the street with a sack of overripe apricots; her fingers, even after rinsing, were sticky from the juice.

She wove through swinging tails of hitched up burros with their attending drones of flies, felt the squint-eyed stares from men filling water troughs, and as the morning sun inched up through the vast metallic sky, the common sight of Mexican women wrapped in black shawls struck her—as it usually did—as unnecessarily oppressive in this heat, but then all at once the dark figures went from oppressed to strangely magnificent, appearing for one extended moment like dark bronze sculptures set against ocher palazzo walls. She had certainly never seen an Italian palazzo and couldn't imagine when she ever would, but the vision felt as authentic as the dried burro dung underfoot (which she noticed just in time to avoid) and the smell of moss and camphor coming from the nuns' quarters. She stepped inside one of the buildings, and there she relished the instantly cooler temperature.

The entryway was quiet and dark. There was neither knocker nor bell to announce a new arrival, and Eva inched down the dark corridor, peeked through a partially closed door. Grubby little girls leaned up against one long table without chairs. They chatted quickly but fell silent when they noticed Eva, their spoons poised at the ready, as if the lady herself was the feast. *"Buenos dias,"* Eva said; the two words permeating in the room until their polite, in-unison response erased the echo.

"Good morning," said Eva, as she saw Sister Josephine emerge from an undersized door on the opposite side of the room.

"Mrs. Shein!" cried the sister, short of breath. She looked almost whimsical, carrying a large tray of cups, but there was no whimsy in the way she set down a cup in front of each girl, accompanied only by a dark reminder to say grace; as far as Eva could see there was no other component of this meal. The girls slurped bitter-smelling coffee in concentration. A feast of mortifications, Eva noted, certainly was not wanting.

"Thought you'd pay the charity girls a visit?" chirped the sister.

"Yes." Eva blushed. "Yes, indeed."

One girl's mouth hung dangerously open; two were bald as infants, their heads scattered with scabs. "I brought apricots!" she said impulsively. "Picked for the girls just minutes ago."

Sister Josephine eyed her suspiciously. "Well," she said. "We thank you."

Eva handed over the basket. She waited for a moment, but the nun did not distribute the fruit and Eva realized Sister Josephine did not want to share the moment. She cleared her throat and said, "I've also come to see Mr. Ehrenberg."

"I see."

"I heard he was fit to see friends?"

"You are in the wrong building. This is the refectory. And that young man is hardly in any kind of sociable state."

"Yes, but it was my understanding that Sister Blandina said—"

"Are you his friend?"

"Well no, we've never met, but—well . . ." she stammered. "He is from Germany, you see."

She nodded, pointing toward the next building. "Well I suppose you are all related," she said, obliquely, before adding: "How nice."

Eva exited into the garden courtyard and among the acacia trees she saw a small, muslin tent. Before she could go and see what was inside, Sister Blandina appeared and took her arm, leading her to the other building, where a narrow hallway ended at another low doorway. Blandina turned the knob and stooped, making sure not to bump her head as it poked into the room, but she immediately shut the door again, before Eva could catch a glimpse of him.

"I'm afraid he is asleep," Sister Blandina reported with downcast eyes. She sighed as if Eva should have known better.

She pictured Abraham's frustration with her story, her excuse of why she did not pay her proper respects. "I could wait," Eva suggested. "Or I—"

"*Sister!*" a familiar voice hollered in the distance. Eva looked toward the courtyard where Josephine waved her arms about. "The Rodriguez girl!" she cried witlessly. "The wicked . . . *wicked* child!"

"Go," Eva assured Sister Blandina, "I'll see myself out."

"You may return some other time," she curtly replied before shuffling off, leaving Eva alone in the hallway.

She could hear nothing of the crisis in the refectory (where she imagined one of those coarse-haired, hungry, miserable girls was being
whipped and whipped and whipped), nothing of the mid-morning
crowded street with its ongoing negotiations between burro and driver,
or the bellowing stream of men's greetings, trading lewd jokes and com-
plaints about the heat. As she stood empty-handed in this unfamiliar
place, as she did not walk away, she could hear nothing except what
sounded like the very faint drip of water hitting stone, or maybe it was
not a drip at all but the rare hollow tone of silence.

The door handle was heavy and creaked when it turned. How easy it
was to slip inside.

In addition to the one candle flickering at his bedside, there were a
host of candles and matches on a stand near the door. Eva lit one and
carried it with her as she approached the sleeping patient. He was a thin
man with a full, dark-blond beard. He was more boy than man. He
might have been as young as sixteen, as old as twenty plus. Even though
one eye was hidden with a bandage and the other eye was closed, even
though his cheekbones were crowned with purple welts and his expression (if such a deeply sleeping man could have one) was nothing if not
slack, she had the distinct impression that when he was alert and on his
feet, he would have been described as quick. And despite the fact that
his bottom lip was swollen and his top lip was cut and stitched with
black thread, she could—though she had no grounds to do so—instantly
picture him laughing. He slept on his back with one arm slack and the
other in a muslin sling. Someone (*who?*) had cleaned and dressed him in
this approximation of a hospital gown, a garment that had obviously been
bled through, scoured, and bleached, leaving worn and faded patches in
the fabric. The graying bed sheets were cast off and hanging to the floor
in a snarl. His fingers—the ones at his side—began to twitch, and his
lips too twitched briefly. Her heart sped up, but slowed again, when she
realized he was only dreaming.

(There was a brindled mutt in Karlsbad on a blistering summer day;
he had appeared, hungry and dry-nosed, beneath a cluster of elms. They

had sat hushed—two sisters—watching the dog who was sound asleep but who also moved his paws frantically, whimpering as if he were chasing something always out of reach.)

She slowly walked toward the red chair at his bedside and tightly gripped the painted wood. She noticed—she could swear—that the young man was not breathing, and she was seized with such a bone-chilling fear that all she could see in her mind's eye were those charred dead strangers on the Santa Fe Trail, scalped and left for vultures, and she immediately wanted to flee. But she closed her eyes and forced herself to remain exactly where she was. She gripped the candle tightly and promised herself that if she opened her eyes and he was truly dead, she would run to the Sisters and tell them what she'd found, even though the act of entering his room would arguably be more troubling to them than the young man's death. She could already taste the particular guilt that haunts those who discover the dead and live to tell about it.

When she opened her eyes, not only was the young man breathing after all but he was looking right at her, startled and very much alive. He grabbed for the twisted sheet with his one good arm.

"It's all right," she said in German. "You are all right."

"Who sent you?"

"Nobody sent me. I have come to say hello."

"I told you I do not want it."

"You do not want . . . ?" Eva sat on the low chair. "But I'm not certain—"

"I hate you," he said. His face was pale, his lips red, and his good eye was glassy and narrowly set, like the eye of a fish or a doll.

"Mr. Ehrenberg," she said gently. "You have been ill."

"The snow," he said. "We'll be lost."

She rose from the chair and backed up against the wall. He stared intently as she smoothed her skirt, as if she was doing something altogether more compelling. "Mr. Ehrenberg?"

"Oh," he said, "oh, it's you," but this time he spoke gently, as if he'd been woken by a great noise and had found her there, nothing but a skinny cat outside his front door.

THE NEXT DAY SHE RETURNED WITH MORE APRICOTS FOR THE GIRLS and a strudel for Mr. Ehrenberg. "May I give the girls the fruit myself?" asked Eva, but Sister Josephine ignored her question and led her to the sickroom, where Sister Blandina attempted to hold a cloth to his fore-head as he raved madly in German—a German that not even Eva could understand—while Sister Philomene stood in the corner, nibbling on her thumbnail.

"Why is it snowing?" he shouted with sudden clarity.

"This is no place for you, Mrs. Shein," Sister Blandina cautioned, as she saw a spoiled German bride standing in the doorway, the wife of a merchant, a *rico*.

But heat rose up in Eva's chest with unexpected force. "Mr. Ehren-berg, it is not snowing," she told him plainly in German. "The Sisters are trying to help you," she nearly shouted, as if speaking to a foreigner when he was anything but a foreigner. They were from the same place, they spoke a common language; they were probably the very same age.

"Please see Mrs. Shein out," Blandina raised her voice to Sister Josephine.

"German?" he cried, tears pooling in his uncovered eye.

"Yes, yes," she answered, "you are safe here."

"Jewish?" he whispered.

"Yes."

"Me too," he said, sounding relieved, "me too."

She knew that no one had heard of his people, but who pretended to be Jewish in a Catholic land? He would become the responsibility of all German Jews—like any other distant cousin—or so Abraham had told her, rather proudly, as if it had been his idea.

"But what have they done to my brother?" the young man demanded. "Where is he?"

"Tell him to calm himself," said Blandina, unmistakably addressing Eva, and in doing so, recognizing that she was—if not exactly welcome—then not altogether expendable either, at least not at that moment.

Eva came forward, registering the murky smell of alcohol, the rheumy fever-sweat. She sat in the low, red chair. "Mr. Ehrenberg, you are in Santa Fe."

"I'm so cold, Julie."

"What is he saying?" whispered Josephine. "This is terribly frustrating."

"Levi," she said familiarly, as if she was play-acting, but she felt perfectly genuine, if suddenly very queer. "You are safe, dear."

"You smell so good," he whispered.

"Tell us what he is saying, Mrs. Shein," said Josephine. "For heaven's sake!"

Eva reached for the sheets and scratchy blanket he had cast to the floor and drew them up to his shoulders, pausing for a moment as he searched her face. She smelled unguent on skin, drying blood, but she did not recoil.

Blandina cried, "To touch those sheets—*mon Dieu*—you must wear gloves!"

"I am not afraid," Eva said, much to her surprise.

"Yes," she retorted, "and the disease is not afraid of you."

"What he said was—"

The young man stared at Eva, tears streaming out of his one good eye. "Touch me . . ."

"What does he want?" whispered Philomene.

"He—"

"Please, Julie . . ."

"My name is Eva Frank," she told him. "Eva Shein," she added, correcting herself. A moment or two passed before she looked away from his confused and pained expression, returning her attention to the nuns. "He says that he is very cold—"

"Philomene, fetch another blanket," said Sister Blandina. "What else, Mrs. Shein?"

She looked at Levi Ehrenberg and then up at the ceiling. "He says that he would like for me to come back tomorrow."

"Well," said Blandina. "I don't see how—"

"I shall return this afternoon," Eva said. She stood and smoothed her skirt in two swift movements, which somehow put an end to the discussion. Then she handed the strudel to Sister Philomene, and bid the nuns good morning.

HAD EVA, WONDERED BEATRICE SPIEGELMAN, HEARD OF MR. EHRENberg previously?

"Do you mean in Germany?" asked Eva, fanning herself with a folded *New Mexican,* the front page of which entreated drivers to stop testing the speed of their rigs in the public plaza.

"Mmn," said Bea, not looking up from her sampler.

"No," said Eva, who had not once considered it. She thought of how, when she visited the previous day—her fifth—the nuns finally finished behaving as if they were surprised to see her. After handing over her sack of apricots, she couldn't help but notice they had brought in an extra chair. "At least I do not think so."

"Well," said Bea, whose posture fluctuated from straight to stooped as often as five times in one minute. "I should think you would remember if you had."

"I have a terrible memory," she felt mysteriously compelled to say. It wasn't true, she remembered everything. "But I never met him." She took a long sip of strong tea, gone tepid with conversation. "Have you been to see the poor boy?"

"Mmn," said Bea. "You also, I gather."

Eva nodded, continuing to fan herself. "He is so sickly," she said, "and yet . . ."

"Yes?"

"He reminds me of someone. That's all."

"Who?" said Bea, hardly containing her urge to gossip, and though Eva found this side of Bea more appealing than her usually virtuous self, Eva refrained from telling any stories. She held back from relating even the very first memory—the one that somehow remained untouched by all that so dreadfully followed. *We sat for our portraits,* she did not say. *A painter came to the house.*

THE FOLLOWING MORNING EVA WOKE TO THE USUAL ANGRY VOICES and assumed it was just after dawn, but when she looked out the tiny window, she saw that the voices belonged to men who were saddled and on the go. She had slept late, it was mid-morning; the sun was high in the sky but the plaguing heat had finally broken. There were no apricots left. In one week's time, the ones remaining had fallen either into the porcelain bathtub or onto the parched ground, their mealy golden flesh crawling with bugs.

SITTING AS IF THEY HADN'T ANY OTHER RESPONSIBILITIES BESIDES tending to Mr. Ehrenberg were Sisters Theodosia and Philomene, laughing downright bawdily. When Eva came through the doorway, their laughter came to a halt, but Mr. Ehrenberg remained cross-eyed—his bandaged eye now liberated—making a clownish face.

"Feeling better?" she asked brightly in their language.

"Oh!" he said, his eyes shining. "I am feeling so much better, thank you!" His voice sounded younger, having escaped from beneath the many veils of bewildering fever-dreams. "You speak German?"

"Of course, Mr. Ehrenberg. We've been speaking for days."

He looked confused for a moment and then relieved. "It's you," he said, and then laughed at something in his head, guided by some personal logic only he could understand.

"Please tell him he is very lucky," said Theodosia. "Tell him we prayed for his life."

"You almost died," Eva whispered.

He nodded, and with his face downcast he could have passed for a twelve-year-old—his hair an untrimmed mess, his shoulders not particularly wide—even despite his beard. When he lifted his chin to face her, his eyes (the same bright eyes he'd been crossing for comic effect) clouded over with truth—the truth he'd attempted to stave off as long as he possibly could. His attempts at humor, his hopeful voice, nearly brought Eva to her knees. "Everyone is dead," he said. "Isn't that right?" And the whole of his frank and suntanned face darkened, became confused.

I am alive, she almost said.

Spending

A French carpenter who'd lived in Kentucky for a decade came west for opportunity; he had the bishop's every assurance that Abraham was a man of his word, and so he continued work on the Shein house, taking up where the old crew had left off. Miraculously, Abraham's promises (which had begun to amount to nothing in other, less visible circles) brought forth tremendous labor; within weeks the Frenchman had instructed a local crew in the ways of a wood beam structure and up went the walls, the windows were framed, and now the roof was forthcoming. Abe had promised the Frenchman payment at the end of the month, which would be easy to deliver even with Cuca to appease, because—as he'd been telling his wife almost nightly since they'd gone to the mountains—the last time he'd dined at Fort Marcy he'd plied General Tierney with filched (*borrowed!*) Swiss chocolate and Mexican cigars, and before midnight he had secured Shein Brothers' an enormous military contract, supplying the soldiers with an array of supplies from corn to paper to whiskey.

Between seeing some of the mountain contract income (almost all had gone to Meyer, toward a portion of Abraham's secret and endless debt) and the lucky game against the unfortunate diamond hunter, he had paid Cuca just enough so that she'd let him grace her precious table without making snide remarks. He knew, above all, that his presence was tolerated because she knew (everyone did!) that—due to Abraham's considerable skills—an unprecedented military contract now belonged to no one else but the Sheins. Meyer was finally pleased, and Eva was smiling instead of lying in bed. Abraham had to admit that lately she'd been less focused on him and his prospects and more focused on making herself useful. The hard cash he'd get from the contract would be significant. He'd be able to pay the industrious French carpenter, Meyer, and, most notably, he'd be able to pay Doña Cuca. Furthermore, by the time his name meant something real again to each and every citizen of Santa Fe, he'd have a house to match his reputation. There was nothing to do but oversee the construction and ultimately purchase the furnishings. He posted letters overseas to auction houses that his father had known, making introductions and special requests. He contacted some of Shein Brothers' dealers in New York, securing two Persian rugs and a crystal chandelier by using the company name.

It might have been the German they found outside their store that ultimately set him in motion. That night he felt as if he was looking at his own future, at his swollen-shut eyes and black-blood-caked face, his inability to walk on his own. The young man had been so physically reduced that it was impossible to imagine that he'd not only survived a heinous Indian raid, but that he'd had the strength to make it as far as Santa Fe without horse or burro, without—as far as they could gather—any supplies besides a leaky goatskin canteen, long since drained of any liquid. Why he had collapsed before the Shein Brothers' storefront was most likely nothing but chance, but Abraham secretly chose to believe it was a sign, and he vowed to pay the boy attention.

Although when he *had* paid the young man a visit, he'd been disappointed somehow. There was something about him, something he couldn't articulate better than this: The boy had given him the heebie-jeebies. There was a difficulty there, he thought—something cunning and almost feminine. Besides, he simply couldn't afford to get bogged

down by a needy, sick fellow who obviously wanted Abraham's connections (however tenuous they happened to be). He had walked away from
the sickroom door, determined to have the rest of the community figure
out what to do with him, but as he saw a group of nuns shuffle past, he
reckoned that the boy *was* needy and sick, and as much as he tried to
talk himself out of it, he also felt the boy's arrival had been some kind of
omen, and (certainly more than out of any do-gooder instinct) he wanted
to ensure that such an omen was not a bad one.

So it was that he said: "Good Sisters, please wait," and he asked where
he might find whoever was in charge. He did not think of the last time
he'd been to this church, or how he had walked by these very rooms under falling snow with a gun cold and heavy in his hand. He did not realize he'd been drunk and crazy enough to shoot someone, only that he
hadn't done so, and now he was here in blameless daylight with a perfectly good request. He knocked on the appropriate door and waited,
and when nobody came, he whistled what he hoped was a solemn tune.
He didn't look into any rooms, nor did he call out to make his presence
known. His tune faded out as he heard children's voices behind a closed
door.

"May I help you?" asked a clipped voice behind him.

Abraham cleared his throat and turned to face the Sister, who looked
suspicious—as if he was about to ask for money (Had his debtor's reputation crawled as far as inside a convent?) instead of about to offer it. "I
have come about the German," he said, rather loudly, as if volume might
serve to make his presence official rather than suspect.

"You'd like to pay a visit?"

"I already have," he said gruffly. "I haven't any more time. I've come
about his care."

"We are doing all we can, Mr. Shein. We are very *busy*, sir," she said
punitively, as if he did not know the first thing about working hard, as if
he were on some kind of goddamn holiday.

"You cannot doubt for a moment that I—that we all—appreciate you
are doing a fine job of caring for the poor fellow," he responded, with a
determined smile that his wife could always read as an instant prelude to

trouble. If she were here, she would have seen it and lured him out before he could make his request. But she was not here, and he pressed on with a set of eyes in the back of his head, hoping she wasn't about to turn up at any moment, as she'd been surprisingly eager lately to make herself useful here.

"I won't waste your time, Sister," Abraham said, taking off his hat.

"Sister Blandina," she announced. "Please, Mr. Shein, sit." She gestured him into a room and toward one of two small and monastic-looking chairs, and he shook his head as politely as he knew how.

"I'd like you to allow my wife to help tend to the young German fellow on a more permanent basis."

"Well," she said with impressive bluster, "I don't know what you have in mind, but this is not—"

"Now don't get huffy, please. My wife tends toward the melancholy. She gets downright depressed and she needs a purpose. I am very happy to compensate you."

"*Compensate?* You people have some idea of the religious life! This is not some kind of betting hall, nor is it your store, Mr. Shein." She pronounced *store* with as much, or more, distaste than *betting hall*.

"Why don't you tell me what you might need here, Sister."

"Why don't you take a look around this place, *sir*. Go on! Go look inside the schoolroom across the hall. Why don't *you* tell me what we need?"

Abraham did as he was told. He opened the door a crack, apprehensive at the notion of orphans gathered in a pitiful herd, at the idea of being seen, but no heads actually turned. There was nothing to establish the room as a schoolroom—no blackboards, no charts, no maps, no books except one in the teacher's hands and one for all of the pupils, who gathered around a small, skinny girl who held it very proudly. He closed the door and walked back to Sister Blandina.

"Why do you look angry, Mr. Shein?"

"They have no books!"

"Well no, Mr. Shein, they do not."

He took the bills out of his jacket pocket—bills he'd taken from un-

derneath the floorboard with the unfamiliar knowledge that he would re-
place the money very soon. He was well aware of the tenuous and ridiculous system that existed between his brother and himself—the system of
Abe taking money and Meyer choosing to ignore the missing bills
(though keeping a tally for certain), and Abe wondering how much
longer could he keep pushing until Meyer gathered enough courage and
alliances and had him run right out of town. Abraham now counted out
the stolen bills with a flourish no different from how he might in front of
any customer or any gambling man. "I'd like my fellow countryman to be
cared for, I'd like my wife to feel useful. *And*"—he smiled—"I'd like
these children to have books."

Sister Blandina looked disgusted, but she took the money immediately. She went back to her papers, and Abraham—somewhere between
respectfully and irreverently—found himself offering a military salute—
the very one he'd given his superiors in this country's civil and bloodiest
war.

HE CONTINUED TO RUN UP HIS BILLS AT DOÑA CUCA'S. THE PROMISE
of a military contract was more than enough to keep his tab wide open.
It never occurred to Abraham that Doña Cuca might have been actually
encouraging him to go further into debt; he was too arrogant and will-
fully ignorant to see himself as what he was: someone who had little to
no ability to recognize the truth. He was sure he had what it took to be
someone extraordinary, someone who didn't let life's possibilities begin
and end according to regulation. He looked in the mirror above Cuca's
bar and he saw *El Guapo.* He saw a thick head of hair and a survivor's
stature and he went about his days and nights. He brought home good
cuts of meat from *Dos Hermanos,* who always had the freshest kill, along
with tins of oysters and samples of fabric and finally, a cast-iron stove.
When she came home from tending to the sickly German and found the
cast-iron warrior sitting in the kitchen, Eva wept. She thanked him and
thanked him and so did Chela; he wondered why he had waited so long
to do this thing that she'd wanted so badly. Meals tasted the same if he
closed his eyes, but with his eyes open they tasted twice as good, be-

cause Eva was no longer slouched from exhaustion, flushed from the heat of the open flame. She had begun to leave the house during most of the day, making herself useful to the nuns in the sickroom. It had been more than two weeks now, and though she usually did no more than shrug when questioned how she liked the patient, he did not mind her lack of sentiment. *He is lucky to be alive,* was all she had to say on the matter. *Lucky indeed,* Abraham agreed.

He didn't give voice to how he found the young man rather insolent and maybe in possession of some kind of curse that, honestly, he hoped she might undo. He was aware—yes he was—that he'd passed into thinking like some kind of goddamn pagan, but he needed all the luck he could get. What was important, he told himself, was that he'd encouraged her to perform a duty; she had gone to the sickroom every day with a keen desire to serve. Every woman—or so his father used to say—had a nurse alive inside of her, and Eva's nurse had certainly emerged, after having identified for so many months as one who was not well. Lately, he had to admit, he was proud of her; she was, by the bishop's account, truly dedicated.

THE SICKROOM

THE BISHOP WAS RIDING OUTSIDE OF TOWN WHEN HE encountered a strange-looking animal. Determined to capture it, he pursued the animal until both man and beast were exhausted, and when he backed it up against a tree, it bared its sharp teeth, scratching and fighting as the bishop came closer and finally, after a struggle, he wrapped his cloak around it. When he was able to get a closer look, he was shocked to discover it was not an animal at all but instead a little girl, albeit a wild one, without doubt a half-breed, who could only grunt and growl. He brought the poor child to the nuns, who successfully subdued her, and cut her long tangled hair.

By the time *The New Mexican* printed a version of this story, it was already common knowledge. People had already been coming in a steady stream from as far off as Las Cruces to see the wild girl, and to commend the nuns on their good work in making her look just like the others. Needless to say, the nuns were very busy, and so, by the middle of the third week of Mr. Ehrenberg's convalescence, they were apparently content to pass their nursing duties along to Eva. Despite their strict claims that a nurse needed training and a particular set of skills, their severe restrictions quickly devolved into a set of perfunctory reminders.

Eva had a routine. Each day she visited the orphan girls, distributing pencils or candies or tablets or bits of colored ribbon, before heading off down the narrow hallway to tend to Mr. Ehrenberg. The wild girl (christened Maria) always examined Eva's neatly pinned hair so thoroughly that it had inevitably spilled from her topknot and onto her shoulders by the time she entered the sickroom.

Today, even before first light, she knew the day would be an exceptionally hot one, in spite of autumn having finally arrived. Her greatest concern went unmentioned and was reserved for the patient across the street, who, while definitely much recovered, still hadn't ventured out of bed. After Abraham left for the store, she did not go back to sleep, but rather dressed and doused herself with a liberal amount of violet perfume. She had used up all of Henriette's (the frosted bottle sat on the vanity like an artifact, refracting light through its empty glass) but she'd procured another bottle from a French trader who had been through town months ago. She told herself she wore the costly perfume in the charitable hope of bringing freshness to the dark and moldy space, which, befitting a sickroom, was stripped of adornment but was also utterly, depressingly empty of everything but Jesus on his cross—on the wall above the bed—who was of course near death and who (she couldn't help but imagine the nuns discussing this) bore an uncanny resemblance to the Jewish patient below—frail and bearded and full of fresh wounds.

"Mr. Ehrenberg, where is your pain?" asked Eva, as she entered the room after knocking. She often felt her entrance struck the wrong tone; she was either too gloomy or too gay.

"My pain," he replied, and then he paused a moment, considering. "My pain today is in my entire torso, my right shoulder, left foot, head, mouth, and behind the eyes. Also, it has crept into my stomach."

"Well that is a great deal of pain," Eva replied, and poured him a glass of water from the pitcher on the nightstand. "That is one more location than yesterday." One of her favorite qualities in Mr. Ehrenberg was his tendency toward trivial honesty. Standing in direct contrast to tales of his bravery—tales she'd heard from Bea Spiegelman and the nuns—was his lack of anxiety about appearing frail or ungrateful; these disclosures of weakness—instead of being off-putting, as she might have expected—were exciting somehow.

"And where is yours?" he asked in his scratchy voice, his matter-of-fact pitch and tone. "Where is your pain, Mrs. Shein?"

Eva handed him the glass of tepid water and lowered her eyes as he drank. The cuts around his mouth had yet to fully heal, and water trickled down his whiskered chin. "Don't be foolish," she muttered.

"Sit," he urged. "Complain."

She sat in the red chair and folded her hands, touched a handkerchief to the back of her neck. "And what makes you imagine I am in any kind of pain?"

"Maybe I have a morbid nature. Or maybe I just cannot imagine, at this point . . ."—he trailed off, gesturing vaguely to the bleak surroundings—"how anyone could possibly *not* be in some kind of pain."

"Maybe you wish for me to suffer?"

"No, that's not it," he said, taking his time, as if—at any rate—he had been willing to consider the possibility.

"Any pain I have," she said simply, "is of my own doing."

"That is the second mysterious comment you've made today."

"What was the first?"

He shook his head, as if perhaps he hadn't meant what he'd said, or else that it didn't matter.

"I mean to be anything but mysterious," she insisted, flushing deeply and looking away. She could feel him staring and she finally offered: "Sometimes I have pain in my chest."

"Mmn," he intoned, as if he were not a badly-beaten young man but instead a confident physician, set to take her pulse. His face was changeable; it went from vulnerable to mysteriously handsome with one ambiguous expression. Though he didn't have particularly striking features, his eyebrows arched in a way that lent him a certain distinction, and she half-expected him to say something wise. But he only coughed weakly while struggling to sit up, and she leaned over to assist him. She smelled his sickness—its insistent, dark acidity—and unexpectedly, inappropriately, she began to laugh. She sensed his thin arms shaking as she smoothed the blanket around him, before sitting down once again.

His reaction was curious; he looked neither offended nor amused.

"You'd like to know what kind of pain?" she asked, still unable to maintain a sober face. "As if I'm being stepped on," she said, frankly. "As if I'm being crushed." He was watching her, and she wondered if he could distinguish how her abrupt broad smiles were less a spontaneous expression of pleasantness and more like struggles within herself—quick, hostile clashes between inside and out, which always took her by surprise. "That is the kind of pain I have sometimes." She fought against her instinct to bite down on her lip. "It comes out of nowhere and I have never told a soul."

"Why not?"

"I suppose . . . I suppose I am afraid to find out that there is something terribly wrong with me."

He tried to lean forward and his wince turned into a tentative smile. "Mrs. Shein," he whispered, "I don't think there is anything wrong with you." He shook his head. "Not a thing."

And she issued a silent promise—starting right then—that she would attempt to provide strength and serenity or, at the very least, a sense of capability, the way a good nurse ought to. "Sometimes," she continued, with a complete disregard for her own instructions, "I am afraid of being buried alive."

He nodded, excessively. "I am afraid of the very same thing," he said. "I submit that I too am afraid of being buried alive."

She inched the chair a hair closer to the bed, hating the scraping of wood against stone, announcing her every movement. "Sometimes when I lie awake at night, I can feel the inside of the pine coffin; I can hear the dirt and pebbles hitting the wood. I can even smell the soil." She closed her eyes and realized that in her nightmare vision the earth smelled not unlike this room, with its crudity of illness and stone. Whether it was here—where Levi Ehrenberg's blood and sweat mixed with fermented air—or in her imaginary underground (which felt equally as real, if far more lonesome), there was, aside from death, a palpable sense of what she could only imagine as some kind of distorted fertility. There was not only the sensation of dying in both of these miserable places, but also, inexplicably, of *thriving*. When she imagined being buried alive, it was the fear of that final moment in the dark that kept her so afraid. More than the sense of disorientation, she feared the inevitable knowledge that not only would she never be as fertile as the surrounding soil, but also that death would come for her simply because no one in the world was listening hard enough.

"Tell me," he said, not fiddling with a button or the bed sheets, not looking at anything, indeed, aside from her, "why have you not told your husband such things?"

She felt her face flush as she heard his question—so unsuitable—come tumbling through the air. "Mr. Ehrenberg, that is hardly of your concern."

He shrugged, and she saw what he was doing, how—such provocation!—he was goading her into discussion. Still, she couldn't help responding. "And just what do you mean by that shrug of your shoulders? Don't you think you're being awfully smug?"

"He paid me a visit, your husband."

"Did he? He is very busy."

"Oh I can see that. I can see just how busy he is."

"What—tell me—what do you mean by this remark?"

"As I said—I can see that he is busy."

"Mr. Ehrenberg?"

"I tell you I don't mean anything other than this: I don't see how you can be content with such a man."

"Mr. Ehrenberg—" Eva gasped, but not exactly in anger. She was ashamed to admit it, but in that first moment, she felt nothing besides a kind of outrageous relief. But then she was faced with a second thought. She sat up straighter. "How dare you say this?"

"I said it once and I will not say it again. I won't ever say it again."

"No," she said. "No you won't. We'll pretend that you never said it."

"That's right," he said. "We'll pretend."

She wanted to get up, to go to the door, but she didn't want his eyes following her just then, and so she stayed right beside him in the red-painted chair, looking at the bed frame, the floor.

"Do you know why I chose to rest at the Shein Brothers' door?" he asked.

"I don't want to hear you talk about him."

"I only want to say one more thing."

"And then you'll stop?"

He nodded. "Do you know why I collapsed at Shein Brothers'?"

"Mr. Ehrenberg," she said, "you were surely delirious at the time; I doubt anyone would believe you were in any state to make a choice."

"But I did choose. I remember."

"You probably liked the way it looked."

She looked up and he was grinning briefly, until his cuts obviously stung. "That's just what your husband said."

"And what else did my husband say?"

"Why not ask him?"

"Maybe I will," she said. And then, against all her better judgment—judgment for which she'd worked hard—Eva smiled.

Not much could be heard of the outside world, as the walls were so thick and without windows, but Eva could make out some shouting and the particular bark of a dog she always noticed, a mutt who slept in the shade under whichever buggy was closest to the convent. He was a black, scruffy dog, a small one; he looked old and sick but he'd looked old and sick when she'd first arrived in Santa Fe. She had given him the name *El Maestro,* and his bark was infrequent but unmistakable.

"Do you hear that barking?" she asked.

He nodded.

"He is my favorite of all the dogs in this town."

"There are so many, no?"

She nodded. "But this one . . . his bark is one of complete indignation. It's as if he is saying, *This is a total outrage! Don't you see I am meant for more than these dusty streets?"* She never spoke these childish thoughts aloud and as she did so, she felt not embarrassment but a piece of unexpected joy. "It's as if he isn't a dog at all."

Levi Ehrenberg cocked his head as if he was trying to understand exactly what she meant. " 'She is an ailing pussycat,' " he began. " 'And he is sick as a dog. In their heads, I think, they neither are altogether right.' " This he delivered with what seemed like an apologetic air, as if he were sorry he'd taken so many liberties but also as if he would have liked to take a great many more. "Heinrich Heine," he said.

"I know," she said, nodding.

"You know?" he asked, and he looked troubled—his eyes radiant, his temples glinting with sweat.

"Yes," Eva assured him, suddenly concerned that amid all this conversation, his fever had begun to soar.

He shook his head, puzzled by, it seemed, something far greater than her intimate acquaintance with the poetry of Heinrich Heine, and Eva abruptly felt as if she were seated beside an awkward dinner guest and it was up to her to lead the conversation back on track. "Did your family send you to make good here? I bet they sent you off on that terrible ship, waving and waving until their arms were sore."

He shook his head and played with a button between his chest and belly; soon it would come loose and would have to be mended. "No," he said. His fingertips were square and wider than the fingers themselves. "I came to America to escape my family."

"Oh," she hesitated, "I see."

"Nobody says that, do they? Surely nobody likes to hear that."

She thought of her family's parlor: the Kaddish prayer of mourning, the pairs of wet and sunken eyes. She thought of the voices steeped in sadness; she could not meet a single sympathetic gaze and she felt certain that at any moment, she would cry out in confession and it would all be revealed just how deeply she was at fault. She thought of her father's library, how he sat behind his desk alone or sometimes across from a friend. All that week, she had stood behind the door, listening: *Our*

Henriette? her dear father had faltered, repeating himself again and again; he'd never sounded so confused. *It seems as if she is in the next room, as if her hair is still in braids.*

"I'd heard there were Germans who were thriving here," said Levi Ehrenberg. "I'd heard of your husband. I admired him, you see. I had heard that he'd traveled to California, that he'd fought in the Civil War. And I suppose I expected a more generous soul. I was naïve. Everyone is after his own personal fortune in the end. I am guilty of the same." He cracked his knobby knuckles one at a time. The sound was both crass and satisfying. "I needed—I need—help."

Eva instinctively looked away, as if to look out a window, which this dark room was conspicuously without. He wasn't feverish, she realized; he was smart. He'd known more than he'd let on about the town and its inhabitants but he had not wanted to come across as an opportunist. She thought of Heinrich, so averse to admitting he was painting their portraits for money; his pride had been too strong and at the same time—although she had seen through it—she had also admired him. "And so what happened?" Her gaze traveled the length of the wall; she realized she sounded perturbed. And interested. "What happened with your family?"

He took a few labored breaths. "My family was—they are—in the business of smelting."

"Smelting," she repeated. She could hear the faint sounds of footsteps outside the door; the heat was flat, hard. He was truly unwell; the nuns said he cried and sometimes screamed in his sleep. Nearly all of his ribs were broken.

He looked up from his loose button and let out a sneeze, followed by a scowl. She realized, that with all those broken ribs, the sneeze must have been excruciating.

"Gesundheit."

"Thank you," he said, and wiped his nose with his sleeve. "I'm sorry."

"Please," she persisted. "Your family. Smelting."

"Yes," he said. "It was profitable. We're eight sons and I am the youngest. I had a younger sister Sophy but she was thrown by a horse—"

"How terrible."

Mr. Ehrenberg looked almost happy for a moment, thinking of his sister. "She was twelve," he said, and then stopped himself with a shake of his head, redirecting his story. "Each of us worked for my father. I saw my brothers every day and we ate dinner together every evening and my mother forbid us to speak of business but we did. We always did. I liked to talk of business. I liked to sort out problems; even invented problems, solving them before they arose. As if life would not serve up enough problems, I had to go invent some in advance. One night I argued with my eldest brother over a small matter; who knows what it was. *'Hear me out!'* I hollered. *'What does it matter if he hears you, Levi?'* was the second eldest's response. I demanded to know what he meant by that and he laughed." Levi squinted and shrugged, cocked his head as if he couldn't quite see straight. "He had taken too much wine."

"Why did he laugh?" asked Eva, immediately aware that she had asked a stupid question.

"That laugh might have decided it," he mused, before dropping back into his story. " 'You are the youngest,' my drunken brother said clearly. 'You will never be a partner in this business.' And I looked to my father to contradict them, but he did not even look up from his plate."

"Awful," Eva said, but she wasn't suitably surprised or appalled. She'd learned a great deal more about men and trade since arriving in this town years ago.

"I rose from the table that evening," Levi continued, "I put on my coat and I walked out the door."

"But where did you go?" She realized she was clutching her hands, and had she been able to see the expression on her face, she would have been ashamed to admit it was one of plain delight.

He inhaled and this set off a round of coughing while Eva waited, and with dignity and with no small measure of patience, he waited until the coughing entirely stopped before he resumed speaking. "I went to work for our greatest competitor. He was a slave driver—brutal but honest; I saved money. I also lived in a cellar like a dog, abandoning the laws of *kashruth,* abandoning all my prayers."

"I would not have thought you were a religious man."

"I was," he said. "And I am not anymore." He'd never sounded more certain, and it was this certainty that brought her close to tears; it was as if he'd revealed in great detail the various reasons one could not count on God.

"You never saw your family again?"

"I knew that nothing would ever change." He shook his head. "I couldn't get far enough away."

"And now everything has changed," said Eva.

"And now everything has changed."

ONE LATE AFTERNOON EVA RELAYED HOW, ON THE CROSSING, SHE had her fortune told.

"And what was it?" asked Mr. Ehrenberg. "What did the fortune-teller say?"

Eva blushed and then blushed harder at the thought of her red cheeks. "She predicted I would have many children."

"You're not telling me the truth, are you?"

"What a thing to say. Of course I am." The palm-reader *had* actually said this. But she had also said, *You keep secrets.* "In any case, I don't believe in palm reading. My husband does. He welcomes prognostications of any sort. Isn't that funny? He never would have struck me as the superstitious sort."

"Do you mean before you knew him?"

"I suppose. Even now, it surprises me."

"How did you meet?"

"Mr. Ehrenberg," Eva said, "you don't exactly sound as if you want to know."

"It's true," he admitted. "I was being polite."

"You're not very good at *politesse,* are you?"

He shook his head slowly. "Give me your hand," he said.

Eva laughed. "Do you mean to tell my fortune?"

"No," he said. She was sure he would explain further, but moments passed and Eva realized he had no intention of doing so.

They sat in silence; she kept both hands in her lap. Even without a view outside, she could sense the sun was setting; the temperature slightly dropped. At first the silence was uncomfortable, but after a while Eva found she was sitting lower in her chair and that her breath was growing deeper, almost sleepy. Her gaze remained mostly on the floor and the walls, but when she heard church bells, she finally looked at Levi Ehrenberg and she sensed his focus had not wavered. He grinned as best he could—some of the swelling had gone down—as if to reassure her that despite whatever the palm-reader had told her, the future was unknown.

"WHO IS JULIE?" SHE ASKED, DAYS LATER. SHE WAS STANDING WHERE a window should have been. He was slurping from a bowl of broth.

"Julie?"

"While you were gripped with fever."

"Oh," he said, putting the bowl down on its tray.

"Yes?"

He began fiddling with his button.

"I should not have asked," said Eva hastily. But she felt inexplicably betrayed.

"You know."

"I beg your pardon?"

He looked at her queerly. "But don't you?"

"Well of course I don't."

"Very well," he said evenly, "who might you *guess* she is?"

Eva felt her face go maddeningly red, before blurting, "Well, I should think she was a girl you loved."

"So you did know."

"I know nothing. This isn't a game." She sounded angry but she wasn't; with him, she never was.

"I'm sorry. But it's an unhappy story. Of course most love stories are."

"How dramatic," she said, somewhat embarrassed and somewhat amused at just how much she sounded like her husband.

He looked at the ceiling as if he were about to ask her something grave, but instead he said, "I think I would like to take a walk."

"But you mustn't. Not yet."

"Will you help me out of this bed?" he asked.

"Will I—?"

"Or should I call for Sister Blandina to assist me."

"That isn't necessary. I only think you should wait for Doctor Sam to come and examine you again. You do not want to do more damage."

"Come here," he said. "Please."

She touched his shoulder, which was burning hot through crude cotton. "Did you really sleep through the night last night, the way the nuns described?"

"I did," he said. His lower lip was fuller than his top lip; it was this small imbalance, she realized, that gave him his strikingly youthful expression. "I have hardly any fever, if any at all."

She examined him for a moment longer than absolutely necessary. "Can you manage to move your legs this way?"

He looked away and seemed to use all of his concentration to get his bare feet to the floor. His feet were pale and wide, with high arches and tufts of reddish hair on his toes. For a moment she saw his feet as separate from him; they may as well have been prehistoric creatures, jarred samples for men of science, swimming in viscous liquid.

"Ready now?" she asked him.

"I am only injured, Mrs. Shein, I am not a child."

"Are you ready to stand, Mr. Ehrenberg?" She pulled him to his feet before he could answer, surprised by her own strength. "Well," she said, as he stood beside her, winded but upright, "I thought you were taller."

"It's possible I might have shrunk," he said, "prostrate in that bed for so long." His hands gripped her arm; he was shaking but he tried to hide it.

"There is no use in pretending you are stoic now. You mustn't forget that I know too well how much you love to complain."

He attempted a smile, but it was a twisted one, an acknowledgment that he was far more embarrassed than he would ever admit to be hanging onto her, to be rooted to the middle of this cell of a room, for fear that if he took a step he would fall. "The nuns say there is a ghost in this room." He looked around, as if adjusting to the shift in perspective, and then he took a step.

She led him toward the door. "You believe in ghosts?"

"Of course. I have seen far too many to ignore them."

"I don't believe that people are either alive or dead. My sister is far more real to me than anyone."

"Even me?" he asked, taking another step. "Even as I smell wretched and I lean on you like this?" He briefly exaggerated his dependency, and she felt the surprising weight of him, the heat of his exertions. He felt so alive, so utterly real and she thought: This simple touch, this flesh—isn't this what ghosts dream of?

"Even you," she said stubbornly. She could smell his unwashed hair. It smelled like a stable, like the dairy farm she knew as a girl, but she might have been projecting this earth-sweet scent because his hair was tawny. It reminded her of hay. "And this ghost who lives here? Have you seen him?"

"The ghost is a woman," he said, gaining more strength in his footing. "An unhappy Sister."

"Is there any other kind?"

"Oh I think so. They do enjoy a good meal now and then. Sometimes their breath smells of wine."

"Have you ever seen a male ghost?"

He shook his head and they stepped into the dark hallway, neither of them mentioning the fact that he was actually walking and doing so quite well.

"Ghosts are usually female," she decided. "Why is this, do you think?"

"Women are more romantic."

"Are you saying that ghosts are romantic?"

"I am saying that women are."

Were they to have mentioned the fact of his sudden vitality, they would have had to look at each other—he in his badly sewn patient's at-tire, and she in her closest approximation of the latest in *Godey's Lady's Book*—and neither one would have been comfortable taking the other in. She looked down the hallway and listened for footsteps, almost hoping for a reason to deposit him back into the sickroom, but there were none.

"Are you getting tired?" she inquired, and he answered that he felt better now than he had at any moment since leaving his family's home. She nodded and realized she was ashamed to admit that she had not actually pictured him getting well, that she imagined coming here and speaking to Levi Ehrenberg indefinitely, as if he would exist solely in these lost hours when only a ghost could possibly serve as proof that these conversations took place. Without realizing it, they had stopped walking and were now standing side by side in the hallway. She was acutely aware of her arm brushing against his and when she felt him turn to look at her, she did not face him until she was yielding through her arms and legs, soft at the knees as if she needed to sit down. She finally turned to him and when she did, it was as if she'd never seen him before. He was so close she could feel his shallow breath.

"Oh God," he said miserably. "I am in love with you."

"Don't say that," she responded, "please don't."

"I won't."

"You must lie down now."

But he refused to move.

"I'm sorry I said it," he replied.

"You should be," she said. "So am I."

"But I'm *not* sorry. I know it will do no good to say those words but I said them all the same, and I meant it. So now you know."

She tried to guide him back to his sickbed but he was sluggish. She wanted to run before something happened, before she allowed something to happen; a kiss or his stumbling to the hard, stone floor—she could imagine both too clearly and either way she was responsible. "Please," she whispered, her face hot, "I know you can walk." She nearly pushed him back to his bed. *"Now I know?"* she asked, frustrated and out of breath from the strange, bitter struggle of helping and fighting him.

• • •

AFTERWARDS SHE LINGERED UNDER THE ACACIA TREES IN THE COURT-yard, staring at the muslin tent, while her eyes adjusted to the vividness of the outside world that was slowly inching toward autumn. The last living rose of this terrible hot summer drooped so low to the ground that Eva almost took it upon herself to chop off its withering head. The heat stood its ground even as haze began to obscure a sky so blue it was bullying. There were no nuns in sight. Their silence felt conspiratorial. No herd of pale faces set off by black and white, no cluster of both the slouched and the straight, announcing their uniform presence with the same sounds as different types of women in dresses all over the world: the fanfare of fabric, the bursts of unanticipated laughter. Eva imagined them competing to explain the story of the wild girl. How she had been Mexican or a Pueblo Indian or most likely both, how her fingernails had been as long and soiled and curled as tree roots, how she had tried to eat a shoe.

When the rain came with barely a breeze of forewarning, it was as if she'd been biding time in the sun while waiting for rain all along, so that she might finally have reason to duck under the muslin tent. She didn't know what she was expecting there, but what she discovered was an abundance of strawberry bushes. She had not seen a strawberry since her time in New York, when she had eaten so many that she'd been forced to spend pitifully long stretches in the hotel suite's WC. As the rain beat down on the fortified muslin, she sat, lightheaded, in what she realized was a makeshift hothouse; the bushes were green and the strawberries large as plums. Suspecting strange and extreme cultivation methods, she greedily picked two handfuls and ran back through the storm.

"Look what I have for you," she cried, carrying the sour-sweet scent of berries into the sickroom, the breath of running through rain.

He did not react with as much spirit as she might have hoped. His expression barely changed. She knew then that nothing would make him happy now besides the one thing, and that she could never return.

"Why have you come back?" Outside, the wind whistled through soaked jade leaves; she could hear the faint groaning of wagons being stopped, mules being calmed and tethered. Levi did not smile. He blew his nose almost defiantly, vulgar as a daft old man.

She could feel her face go florid and she pulled out the few remaining hairpins that had held her hair in place. "You don't want these?" she asked, releasing the berries onto the bed tray. "They're sweet."

"No," he said, almost bitterly. "Just—please—please go."

She headed for the door without turning her back and so she saw how, in his silence, he never looked away. The rain hit the building in a steady wash; a stream of weather passing time, creating travel obstacles, rich earth, a mood.

SHE DID NOT RETURN THE FOLLOWING DAY. SHE TOLD HER HUSBAND that she was satisfied in knowing she had done her sickroom duties to the best of her ability and that she had been guilty of neglecting her household. After making an elaborate production of what Chela should cook for dinner for the next five evenings, as well as issuing an invitation to the Spiegelmans (reciprocating at long last, after Abraham had nearly given up on asking her to do so), she took a luncheon of coffee and a piece of cheese, while embroidering a handkerchief for her husband, stitching his initials in gold along with a scarlet heart hidden inside, where no one but he could take notice. She opened a trunk, which sat beneath her vanity, and removed a dusty box. Then she arranged herself out back at a rickety table and chair, opened the box to find her commonplace book, and immediately made her first drawing since before Henriette had died. It was only afterwards, while pressing a particularly bright strawberry leaf and an iridescent moth between the book's thin back pages, that she realized her new drawing was of a Bible, and it was not a Bible born of her imagination—the kind she used to draw as a girl, adorned with cherubs and scrolls—but the very one that had sat on Levi Ehrenberg's bed tray, a simple Bible encased in worn leather and cracked at the spine, beside untidy piles of the orphan girls' drawings and a seemingly unused comb.

Her commonplace book (she'd had it since her fourteenth year) was full of drawings of flowers from *Flora's Dictionary* whose names she'd entirely forgotten, brightly colored tropical birds with lacquer-black beaks, and plants so exotic they looked like insects (copied from a book in Father's library entitled *Wild Curaçao*). Further along there was a carefully pasted section of feverish notes in meticulous order from girlfriends she had long since lost—not to her marriage, not to her moving worlds away, but to her own withdrawal, to her secretive nature and broken dates and promises due to her time with Heinrich, to what she now realized she had never been able to so much as hint at in the confines of these pensive girlhood pages, so afraid she was of being caught. As she glanced back even further, toward the beginning of her inscriptions, as she ran her fingers over enthusiastic calligraphic lists of girls' names and boys' names, the names of German provinces, French cities, potential and unusual pets, she wondered at what point in Levi Ehrenberg's reading had he cracked the Bible's leather spine and set it down. She wondered if, instead of the Bible, he would have preferred Balzac or Goethe or even a picture book for children. And since he only had the Bible (obviously borrowed, as it was written in French), she also wondered if he'd attempted to read the stories he'd known as a boy, even though he didn't, as far as she could gather, understand French. She wondered if he enjoyed reading, and she thought it was odd that in all of their conversations, such a question had never arisen. They had spoken in peculiar fits and starts, in a language at once familiar and distant. She never asked what she wondered now: If, when undertaking the supremely private act of reading, he searched for comfort or instruction or if—like she did—he searched for escape.

GUILT

IT WAS LATE IN THE NIGHT AND THE MOON WAS BLOATED
from heat. No matter how much water it drank, it could not
shed itself. This fleshy orb, this predatory heat—it had in-
fected Abraham's dreams, and in them he was big and white
as the moon, suffocating from his own unbearable skin,
which he wore like woolens and could not escape, no matter how many layers he peeled away. When one layer was
discarded, another one grew, until he began to wonder if he
would soon disappear into his excess self.

When he woke—not thin, not fat—that blown-up moon
threw its light around, right through the open window
where a white sheet glowed beside him, where the empty
space churned like cream, and Eva was not sleeping; she
wasn't in the room.

Earlier this evening he had bedded not one but two
whores: one before his drinking and one before his game.
He wondered if his wife could smell the specific scents of
the others but even as he wondered, he imagined how, if
she were to ask, he'd sniff his own nightshirt for Eva's benefit, proclaiming with irritation how his sweat was nothing
other than the stuff of a long day's work. He also wondered,
with uncharacteristic detachment, if he might be able to

change his ways. Then he thought of something his brother had said years ago, soon after Abraham arrived in town. What had they been discussing? He didn't remember. He only remembered drinking whiskey late into the night and how Meyer had seemed to crave his company. *Change?* Meyer had said, sucking on a stale cigar. *We change only when we die.*

He opened his eyes to the familiar low ceiling, the bold outlines of wood beams in the darkness. Once he'd seen a spider hanging by its slight thread, impossibly constructing a web by the silvery light of the moon. Once a vagrant by the small window (a real vagrant, not one of his own dismal invention) shamelessly looked inside, even when Abraham sat up and looked him in the eye. As if spurred on by the memory, he reached for his wife as if to protect her, even as he realized she hadn't come back to bed.

He rose, and with his mind and limbs gummy with sleep, found himself seated at Eva's vanity. Though the room was too dark to see into the mirror, he sat before it—staring—as if, despite the darkness, his reflection might appear. He felt for a small bottle and inhaled its concentrated scent, but it wasn't what he was looking for; he was used to something more diffuse—made soft by her delicate skin—and, unsatisfied, he put down the perfume and picked up a powder box, fingering the puff until his hands were covered with powder, which felt like flour, and there he was—a boy—suddenly there in his family's kitchen with the air sharp like lemons; he was a young boy helping his beloved cook. He realized how he'd forgotten it all: the mixing bowls aligned mysteriously on a countertop, clouds of flour dissolving on the air, and the yeasty smell of bread rising while female skin perspired. It came back in an instant, but even still, he could not conjure the cook's face or name. *How fickle,* he thought, with real disappointment, *what a goddamn fickle mind.*

Abraham did not go in search of his wife but instead pulled strands of hair from her hairbrush, until there was no trace of the springy dark curls woven between the bristles. Instead of releasing the soft nest of hair through the window, he closed his fist around it, as a conjurer might do with a seed, accompanied by a promise that when he opened his fist, the seed would be something different. Perhaps thousands of freshly minted goddamn dollar bills.

And what then? Would he stop going to Cuca's then?

Eva was not in the washroom, nor seated at the piano striking silent chords. She was not in the kitchen nor under the bed, and, if only because there was nowhere else to look, he opened the back door. There, under an ornate sky, accompanied by an uncanny lack of wind, was his bride. There she was, white as bone, glorious and indecent. There she was, in the open air, soaking in the bathtub that had been so neglected, left to hold only leaves and insects and cloudy puddles of rain. In New York she had desperately pleaded for that bathtub, and yet she'd never mentioned using it once they'd arrived in Santa Fe. He allowed that she might have been waiting for him to do something—to at least suggest moving it inside near the fire—but she had said nothing about it. And so, whenever he'd looked out his back door and took in the generally substandard view—the withering roses, the piles of rocks, the dusty mountainous horizon—he'd learned to see the bathtub without really seeing it. If he thought of it at all, it was like an old dead tree, too heavy and bothersome to uproot. What he saw was something useless with delusions of grandeur. No other object could have more perfectly represented her chronic discontent.

Look, he thought, *look here; she has been here all along.*

He watched her now, moonlit, as she floated to the surface and sank down low, over and over again. He wondered if the first time she'd done this was tonight or if she had previously stolen outside and undressed without care like a whore or a child, if this had become no less than routine. But the sight of her distracted him from too much further speculation. Her hair was wet, her eyes were closed, and her lips pursed impishly. It was as if the derelict bathtub and the strange late hour put her not in the mind of something shoddy and uncomfortable, but instead, it was as if—with the floating and sinking, the rise and the fall—what she felt was some kind of relief. And for that moment it was all he wanted: to join her, to feel the jolt of water too, water that—no matter how dirty—still contained her.

Before he could stop himself, he was kneeling beside her, pleading for her skin. Instead of being shocked to see him, or ashamed to be outside, she silently watched him undress and ushered him into the water. She looked so forgiving and he was excited by this forgiveness. She climbed on top and they fit there together, breathing until something had to be spoken. He wanted to say *I'm sorry,* but all he said was, "Don't move."

"What do you promise me?" She seemed so tired, so young with her wet skin and hair.

"A home." And he meant it. He did. "Just look how far I've already come."

She nodded but it was an absent nod, as if suddenly the house didn't actually matter, as if all along it was only a symbol of something, a test; maybe she was even in a dream state, perhaps with someone else. His hands were greedy, ahead of himself, pinching and biting her pink and red; she was right there on top of him in the small, wet space, moving with him gently, in time. They were violent and considerate, quiet under the sky they shared with the rest of the world. They were stealing something from each other, taking their sweet time.

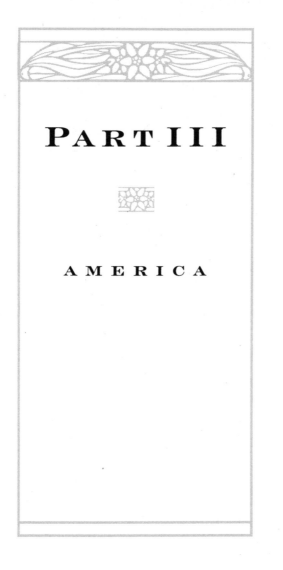

PART III

AMERICA

THE HOUSE, 1869

DURING KARLSBAD SUMMERS, THERE WAS AN ITINERANT daguerreotypist who carried his equipment from house to house. It was a good place for him to practice his trade because, during the season, the town was full of ladies with the time and the funds and perhaps the morbid nature to think this visit might be their last. Eva remembered how the daguerreotypist posed Mother in the garden, with her face alarmingly close to an orange blossom buzzing with one fat bee. Unlike Heinrich's portraits (painted just a few years later) these daguerreotypes were done for the purpose of a *carte-de-visite,* a surprise gift from Father, who obviously hoped that—armed with an appropriate visiting card—Mother might be more inclined to leave the baths and join city life more frequently. He obviously longed for her to call on someone in Berlin other than her piano teacher, to visit homes at which she might have use for something so novel and elegant.

Eva remembered watching her mother's pale face as she'd posed (subtly turning left and then right, offering her regal profile) and being aware—although she'd firmly believed that no one's pale skin or dark eyes could be more deserving of a daguerreotype—that her mother did not enjoy the prospect of having her image captured. Eva hadn't understood why her mother looked so uncomfortable in front of the camera, why she had been so curt with the jovial photographer, but now, on this very happy occasion of Abraham finally delivering on his promise, as she was finally standing on the hardwood floors of this, *her house* (even if the carpenter was currently hammering away at the beginnings of a banister for the staircase), Eva stood in the best possible afternoon light in the most spacious of all American parlors, and while she tried to be more outwardly agreeable than her mother had been years ago, while she smiled between turning left and right and tried to follow instructions, she realized, reluctantly, that she carried a similar air of reticence.

"Mrs. Shein, if you would, please ignore the hammering and face toward me." This photographer was young and from Swedish farm people. He'd left his family in Minnesota to pursue his dream of making photographs and hoped to eventually have his own atelier in California. In what she had come to recognize as an American characteristic, he'd been very forthcoming about all of his dreams within the first half hour of making Eva's acquaintance. He also had the easy manner of a salesman, which she supposed was an attribute because, in the end, he had to sell people on themselves and the idea that someone's image—no matter how ordinary—was worth capturing and preserving.

She faced out the window and looked over the photographer's shoulder at the flurry of activity that still surrounded the house, despite the fact that they'd officially changed residence over a week ago. After a few frigid days, during which nothing much could be done, the weather had suddenly turned mild and now she was reassured to see Bishop Lagrande planting the sapling of an unfamiliar tree with his own gnarled hands. He had promised he would make this thoughtful gesture and here he was, making good on his word even though it was cold enough that she could still see the bishop's breath gathering on the air. She was always a little uncomfortable around the good man, always felt as if he could not only read her mind but that—after that night when she'd rode to his garden—his presence carried an air of chastisement, as if she ought to know better than she evidently did. She was thrilled to see

Tranquilo approach the house with his signature sense of purpose, trans-
porting another buggy full of recently imported items that Abraham must
have sent from the store. Going back and forth from the buggy to the
front door, braving the makeshift platform from the low dirt lot to the
high front door, he brought crates into the kitchen and up the stairs but
he stayed away from the parlor, no matter how often she called out *"Gracias,* Tranquilo!" It occurred to her that Tranquilo could dislike her, even
loathe her, and she would never know. She shifted her weight and
shifted her thoughts, wondering what had come in this shipment, and
hoped against all hopes that it was the bronze wall sconces. She went
over the import list (long since memorized) that Abraham had provided
for her. In offering the list he had effectively issued an apology for so
many nights he'd gone missing. If such a list didn't erase such sleepless
nights, it was true he had spared no expense. Already the parlor boasted
a silk-upholstered wedding sofa in pine with birch veneer, and a walnut
tilt-top table with a matching corner cabinet. The first time they'd slept
in this house, she had stayed up all night, wandering through the rooms
before finally unpacking the perfectly starched and silk-embroidered
tablecloths from her trousseau. They were still in their German packing
crate, and she unwrapped the layers of thinnest tissue, making sure to
store them as they were meant to be stored—in a cabinet, protected.

"Mrs. Shein," said the bland-faced photographer, "think of something
pleasant, please."

"I am thinking of something pleasant."

"Well," he said unimpressed, "think of something else."

The circumstances were lurid: that their child was conceived in a bathtub amid dirty water and leaves; that it happened outside in the middle of the night when Abraham behaved so unlike himself—someone
with humility as well as strength, someone she wished she knew. But
still, there was a baby, another impossible promise growing yet again
inside of her. And she was living in a house now, a house that would be
perfect when it was painted and papered, when the front steps were
added on.

"Isn't this a lovely house?" she asked the photographer and he nodded with appropriate enthusiasm before sticking his head beneath the camera's black fabric. "I don't mean to boast; it's only that I am proud of my husband, his fortitude."

"As you should be."

There were no doors in any doorways yet, and she'd strung up sheets in their place so that at times—especially in the dark—the house looked haunted; when those pale sheets billowed between the rooms it was a strangely beckoning sight. And because there was no banister on the inside staircase, ascending and descending the unsanded stairs was a task that required true concentration, especially in her state. "I know I have asked you this many times but you are *only* capturing my face, aren't you? Nothing so much as below my collar?"

"Of course, Mrs. Shein. What kind of amateur do you take me for?"

"I apologize for asking so frequently. I am simply embarrassed. It was upon my husband's insistence that I agreed to be photographed in this condition. He was rather anxious to mark the occasion of our move, you see."

The photographer stood up straight and took an audible breath. He looked around the parlor and nodded. "This is a mighty fine house, Mrs. Shein. Mighty fine indeed. And though this is our first meeting, Mrs. Shein, and I have no comparison, I would hasten to say—and I hope you don't mind my saying so—that your eyes are, I am quite sure, lovely as they ever were. Your eyes sure don't look pregnant. Those eyes are meant to be painted by a great artist."

Eva felt herself flush and, without thinking, she sat down on the window seat. "I apologize. I'm afraid I am being foolish."

"And *I'm* afraid I'm no great artist, but since I'm the only fella up to the task—why not relax and look directly at me?"

"I'm sorry," she said, "but I don't think I'd like my portrait made after all."

The photographer looked puzzled but not insulted. He shrugged and took his leave as she'd requested.

When he was gone, she was hardly alone, as the carpenter continued to work, and she sat still and listened to the hammering, somewhere between irritated at the noise and relieved that the banister was being built at all. It was certainly possible to imagine Abraham trying to convince her how people don't really need such trappings as a banister; she could picture years going by with nothing to hold on to. Abraham, as it happened, had already fallen down the stairs once, jolting her awake in the middle of the night. He still disappeared regularly after dinner; in fact he did so now with more frequency, as if by finally moving them into an actual house, he had stronger license to behave like a profligate. She'd heard him lumber up those stairs frequently enough in such a short span of time that it had already become part of her dream life. She dreamed of great storms, approaching beasts coming in from the rain.

She listened to the hammering until the bishop—standing before her with soil on his clothes and hands—interrupted her thoughts.

"The Eastern mail has been making excellent time these days, especially in light of the inclement weather," he said, and he held out an envelope. "I accepted it on your behalf."

"It's for me?"

He nodded, handing it over. "It is. Oh I can tell this letter brings you joy. For that I am lucky to be the messenger. One never knows."

"One never does. This is from my Uncle Alfred—I mentioned him previously; he lives in Paris." She gripped the letter loosely so as not to smudge the ink with her hands, which perspired more than usual these days. "I will try not to rip it open this very second." She laughed.

"To prolong this feeling of joy, no?"

"And to maintain manners," she admitted. "After all, you are an important guest. Speaking of which, would you like some tea?"

"I am here to plant your tree, my dear," he said. "And look"—he pointed to the window—"I have done it."

The sapling leaned to one side as the wind blew; it looked vulnerable and thin. "It is completely beautiful," she said, taking his hands in a burst of gratitude.

"We'll have tea some other time. Please," he said, backing out of the room, "read your letter. It has journeyed a long road to find you."

She remembered the letters scattered like entrails on the Santa Fe

Trail, all those letters lost on the way. She almost told him the story but by the time she found the words to begin, the bishop was already gone. And when he was, she sliced the envelope open—not, as she previously had, in the perpetual near-darkness of the Burro Alley rooms, but under substantial windows in a space which—with the additions of rugs and settees, proper sconces and soft light—would be a perfect place to entertain. Never mind how she had little desire to actually see anyone; she imagined such a desire might come, now that the room existed.

As she read her uncle's letter, she appreciated how the afternoon light cast shadows on the wood floors and how her uncle's voice remained at age twenty in her mind, even as Alfred deliberated (as he did with each letter) moving his family from France, where life had an unquestionable ease, back to Germany, now that the amnesty laws were secure. The Alfred in her mind was a full-bearded fellow—brown laced with russet patches—with endless ways to talk about freedom. The young voice she imagined was particularly jarring when, at the end of his letter, he included advice for his niece. He insisted that his wife Auguste took daily walks during each of her pregnancies and that this was why they'd been blessed with such robust children. *Walk,* he wrote, in his hasty hand. *Walk until you have some color in your cheeks. And if you are foolish enough to be wearing a corset, for G-d's sake take it off!* Alfred never mentioned Henriette in his letters. Even if Eva wrote a remembrance, Uncle Alfred ignored the opportunity to respond. It was as if he'd decided the only way they could begin a correspondence was choosing never to dwell on the past.

They were both—in a fashion—exiled, and there was plenty to relay about their respective outposts, which could not differ more. Alfred also never inquired why, if she was truly unhappy, she simply didn't go home. She would have liked to imagine he refrained from asking because he thought America exciting and the only place to truly live out his own visions of freedom and democracy, but she knew it was because he feared Father and Mother's reaction if she returned after all this time. With Eva gone, both girls were out of sight and, if certainly not out of mind, then at least in a place of gilded memory, where their parents could eventually select remembrances during their final years. Her father wrote to her on behalf of both Mother and himself, but his letters were brief and unexpressive, dulled by what she expected was a deadly combination of sorrow and formality. He described the weather in great detail. Henriette was never mentioned.

Eva had not lived with her uncle since she was a baby and was aware that she'd inflated his erratic letters (some of which were frankly tediously written, obsessive in their political detail) with emotional significance. But when she saw his pointy script it was like walking into her childhood home without the mess that followed her childhood. She relished the fact that her feelings for Alfred were uncomplicated; she loved him for taking the time to write to her, and she never thought to question his authority. And so although she'd been afraid to do more than walk up and down her new stairs (the fear of losing another baby, after all, far outweighed the fear of crushing boredom), she decided to take her uncle's advice and, wearing her loosest bodice and a fox fur, set out to face the day.

The sky was vacant, a chalky expanse that matched the remnants of old, stubborn snow on the uneven roofs. She looked from the government quarters to the church across the way, the expanse of the plaza divided by a dirty and faded American flag, its colors issuing respectability, if not brightness, against the pallid clouds. She nodded politely when men doffed sombreros and bowlers, and when she saw a handsome buggy led by two white ponies that clearly belonged to a government official, she imagined it was the very same official who granted Shein Brothers' the Fort Marcy contract, and it was all she could do not to stop the buggy and thank the gentleman personally.

There was enough of a true chill that the plaza wasn't crowded, and for a moment she was struck with panic that Alfred was wrong, that he'd gone mad with French liberalism and that, if she wanted to give birth to a healthy baby, she should be doing as little as possible. She'd read every article in every ladies' journal she could get from the storeroom; the letters in these journals made her frantic with worry but still she could not stop from reading. She'd heard tale of simple taboos before—*salt and eggs are good luck, a baby should be carried upstairs before being carried down*—but seeing others in print brought her nothing but the need to read more, as if one day she would find the definitive answer that she, in her more intelligent hours, knew would never come.

There were letters written from homesteaders, ladies blessed with far less society than she, poor girls cooped up on the terrible plains, often left by their no-good husbands. *Dear Friends,* one letter stated, *I am pregnant six months now and I have a constant longing for plums. I think of them before rising, and I think of them while I'm dressing, and one day I was very tired and I wiped the corners of my eyes with my fingers and I thought, Well I don't suppose it matters, but then I asked my neighbor and she told me I was sure to have marked the baby, that if you have an appetite for something and you don't eat that something, and if you put your hand on your face or anywhere, or if you so much as scratch an itch, you'll mark the baby sure; your innocent lamb will be marked by your selfish longings. But I don't sleep for all the things I think of eating. And what are you supposed to do if you can't stop thinking of mush melon and it is well out of season? Or chocolate creams? I can't get those things now! Can these thoughts harm my baby? Oh please tell me what to do!*

Eva pitied this woman and knew such a fear was baseless, yet in spite of her reasoning, she found herself avoiding touching her face and feeling panic at the onset of her daily craving for *Brot*—the rich but sour taste of grain so conspicuously missing from this land. The more desperate and ill-informed the letters, the more she began to have serious doubts that she really knew anything at all. Beatrice Spiegelman had all kinds of theories—that with enough purpose (and with a little help from the Almighty) one could determine the child's gender: Conceiving two days after menstruation would produce a boy; indulging in intercourse as late as the eighth month of pregnancy at the moon's waning would produce a girl. And for discerning the baby's gender during pregnancy: *Girls steal your beauty,* Beatrice solemnly explained; *if your hips and your nose spread far and wide, you can bet a daughter is on the way.*

Eva had suspicions that Bea Spiegelman was also in the family way, although she knew Bea would be awfully good at keeping it secret until the appropriate time. When Eva had told Bea that she was with child again, she couldn't help but notice a certain disapproval that Eva had mentioned it before she'd felt any "quickening." It was bad luck (she knew it was!) to speak of it, but she had allowed herself one admission, her reasoning being that wretched luck had courted her four times before even though she hadn't said a word to anyone. Besides, she'd been unable to stop the words from coming from her mouth, so shocked was she to realize she was wrong, that pregnancy *could* happen again, even if—while she was ecstatic about it happening—she was petrified and felt as if it was the last thing she wanted because she knew that, realistically, she was also preparing to die.

She didn't necessarily believe in a heaven, but she didn't imagine she would be going there anyway, and so there wasn't even the comfort of joining Henriette, who was surely in heaven if it existed. Henriette died in a sophisticated city, where midwives suffered through considerable training; what chances did she stand *here,* where there was so little in the way of medicine? She'd heard tale of Indian remedies, steeped roots and brewed syrups, but the truth of the matter was that this was a country made for neither the sick nor the delicate; there was very little room here for that tenuous place between life and death. It was always shocking when someone was sick and actually recovered, which made his survival—Mr. Levi Ehrenberg's—ever the more stunning.

SHE BEGAN WALKING EACH AFTERNOON, THE SAME WALK EACH DAY, and though she hadn't seen him since summer, when she'd offered him the strawberries (strawberries, she'd since learned—to her intense embarrassment—that were not meant to be savored by the nuns but rather sold in order to support the orphanage), she always expected to see him here in the plaza, no matter what the weather, sitting under a low-hanging tree with that worn leather Bible in hand. She had in fact returned to the sickroom days later, but the nuns had told her how, against their strictest advice, he'd walked out of the convent, leaving no word of where he was going.

But she knew where he was now. She'd heard news of his recovery.

She knew that he would always have a limp and that after a mysterious disappearance (there was speculation he'd gone to Taos and Las Cruces and was somehow working for the railroad) he was in fact back in Santa Fe. And, more incredibly, he was now evidently employed by Shein Brothers'. When Abraham mentioned they had hired the "gimp German," she'd continued with her embroidery as if he'd made mention of a minor sale, offering an appropriate smile. "Where is the boy living?" she asked, and when Abraham told her that he was on the other side of the river, where she had never been, she nodded again until Abraham said, "Well don't look like that! What do you want me to do—invite him to live *here*?" She'd bit down on her lip to avoid asking another question about it, and she was also cautious about when she went into the Shein store. She only went when she was desperate for something that Abraham forgot to bring home, which, unfortunately, was not such a rare occurrence. She assured herself that she had not done anything improper with regards to Mr. Ehrenberg, but if she'd learned anything since she was a girl, it was this: One could never be too careful, especially if one's name was Eva Frank, and that would always be her name, even if no one knew it, not for thousands of miles. She had yet to see Levi Ehrenberg limping about, not even from her window, but she often thought that if and when she did see him, he would seem like a stranger, that whatever friendship had passed between them in that sickroom was undoubtedly a product of his illness and its accompanying delirium, which was, she was convinced, contagious.

AND YET, WHEN SHE SAW HIM—EVEN THOUGH IT WAS FROM AFAR, even though she was staring into the sun and he was nothing but a shadow—she knew him right away.

All day long it had been mellow light, more pink than yellow, more opal than gold, but now, as if challenging evening's approach, the sun turned on the full force of its authority, as if it wasn't quite done for the day. As Eva Shein hurried home after her daily walk around the plaza, her thoughts were preoccupied with instructions not to rush, even as she tripped on a rock and nearly took a fall. She stopped short in the middle of the street and briefly closed her eyes; there was no need to race, she realized, there was nothing to fear from the weather, the sun was still shining brightly. All around her men were finishing up for the day— bidding each other good evening, tying up their burros, hauling logs of *piñon*—while poor dark women shrouded in colorless wool offered their last hoarse bits of stories as she stood dumbly before them, wishing she had something to put in their parched hands, even if she couldn't decipher a word of their plights. She felt useless (she hadn't a single coin in her purse, only a calling card and two embroidered handkerchiefs which she briefly considered offering) and she felt foolish under their desperate gaze, knowing that sometimes she grew panicky over nothing but getting home on time; she wondered how she managed to leave her house at all.

She looked away from the women into the setting winter sun, immediately bringing her hand to her forehead. When her eyes landed on the figure only steps away, she realized, belatedly, that she was standing in shadow and that, unlike her perspective, which allowed for merely his inky outline against the blinding light, he must have been able to see her quite clearly.

"Mrs. Shein," he said in an unfamiliar, even tone, as he stepped forward to greet her.

His trousers were snug, reaching only above the ankle, his shirt was hardly boiled; his overcoat was oversized so that, with his clean-shaven face, he looked like a particularly dignified urchin. If she had seen him in Berlin, he might have passed for a student, but they were not in Berlin and if she had not known him she might have thought that he too— along with the wizened señoras—was begging for alms in order to endure the winter. "Mr. Ehrenberg"—she smiled, tensely at first, but eventually easing into something not only genuine but irrepressible—"you're looking very well." It wasn't a lie. There was color in his cheeks but his skin was no longer sunburnt. He leaned on a rough-hewn cane but made a somehow vital impression as he nodded and kept nodding—at a loss, it seemed, as to what else to do. "I hear you are working for my husband?"

Again he nodded, but this time, she realized he was staring at her in a different way than she recalled in those heady, strange sick days; now he was staring at her rounded middle, which suddenly felt like nothing more than evidence of her carnal desires. She pulled her coat closer and waited for him to speak. If she had felt self-conscious a moment ago, trapped by the true poverty of others, by poor wrinkled crones and their curses, she was suddenly unaware of anything else but this strange yet expected encounter.

"I went away," he said, rather dumbly. "To Taos."

"Yes," she said, "I heard. I must admit I was surprised that you were working for my husband. As I recall, you were not very fond of him."

She saw him grip the top of his cane. "I am working for Shein Brothers'," he said, his voice low. "It was Meyer Shein who hired me."

"Even so."

"I tried to find work in Taos; I swear I did what I could. There was nothing for me up north, which, of course, was the original attraction. Because here," he said meaningfully, "there seemed to be too much." He looked at the ground as she drew her coat so close and so tightly, she was afraid she might strain her arms. "There was no opportunity," he finally said. "A man needs opportunity."

"Of course."

"I returned out of necessity; you should know that."

"And you had no other choice than to work for Shein Brothers'?" She had vowed to refrain from pressing him—from asking anything at all—and she was startled at how upset she'd allowed herself to sound. "Please," she said, blushing, although she didn't suppose he could guess; her cheeks were already flushed from the fresh cold air. "Please, you needn't explain. Things are as they should be."

"Are they?"

She too found herself staring at the cold, cracked ground, fixed on the earth's many fissures. "It was wise of you to return, to take advantage of your opportunities."

He looked openly offended. Why did her voice seem so bitter?

"When last we met," he said, lowering his voice, "what I mean is that—what I said that day—"

"*Please,*" she said, sounding more fraught than she'd have thought pos-

sible; her life was set and there were no more choices. This was something from which she'd taken previous comfort. But she looked, for the
first time, straight into his eyes, which she remembered only as dark
eyes, and yet now here they were looking straight into hers, appearing to
be not black or brown but the steeliest of blues, like the very hottest part
of a flame. And she imagined his father and brothers, feeding ore into a
fiery furnace, shouting to be heard. She saw a scalded factory outside of
the city, a room full of Ehrenbergs, one more dogged than the next.
"Please don't," she said definitively.

"I only hope you're not angry."

"I'm sorry?"

"I hope you are not angry with me."

"Why would I be angry?"

"And," he said, "that you aren't disappointed."

"I disappointed myself," she said without thinking, even though she
didn't know quite what he meant. "But it was long ago."

He retreated little by little, his cane backing up before him. Before he
turned away completely, he broke into English; it was the first time she'd
heard him use it. "You look funny," he said, shockingly, nodding to her
rounded belly. He couldn't have described it better; it was just how she
felt when she saw her reflection, when she looked down on any given
day, but nobody ever said as much—so shrouded in seriousness was
motherhood and all of its rumored glory. Such an observation was entirely improper, and yet, she couldn't help but agree.

GAMBLING

The windows at Doña Cuca's saloon were draped from the inside with velvet curtains so that if, like Abraham Shein, a patron happened to come through the swinging doors earlier and earlier each day, by the time he'd had a whiskey or a lemon brandy he couldn't quite remember just how much daylight there was on the other side; by the time he finished placing his second bet he forgot there was any light besides the small, red lamps on each of the low tables. Sometimes, after enough losses and enough liquor, a man could even forget who he was. A mirror was hung above the bar as if to serve as a reminder; the glass was clear enough so that the reflection was unmistakable but cloudy enough to bring a soft focus to the remainder of the game. It also reflected the crowd around the bar. Brass-buttoned officers were a common sight but after a while they all blurred together in an arrogant echo of laughter.

There was Benoit, the sodden French Canadian, who spoke lyrically of fur, the luxurious beasts he had trapped and traded in order—or so it seemed—for him to gamble and drink in a far-off territory, miles away from home. And Don Perez, who herded twenty thousand sheep to California, sold the sheep, and returned just before the season's first snowfall with his life and his earnings intact. Perez had left Santa Fe a headstrong boy and returned as a man with dark shadows under his eyes, toughened and emboldened by his profits even as he'd begun to lose them to Cuca. Once every so often there was a mystery guest, and today's came in the form of a thin Southerner with a diamond stickpin in his black lapel. He drank an egg yolk, sugar, and soda before he began to bet, and as the hours passed and he accumulated more silver, whispers began to circulate even among those dulled souls whose interests lay solely in drinking: that the thin man was a professional, arrived from New Orleans, that he was seeking revenge on Doña Cuca for something that happened years ago—whether it was for a game lost or because he had been her lover, either way she had done him wrong.

Abraham was working on his third whiskey and, as he did during every other waking moment of his borrowed and questionable life, he was thinking about the letter. When the letter arrived, he hadn't lingered on the envelope for long; it was delivered by a low-level soldier, and there was no wax seal or return address to give the sender away. It was not even written on official military papers, nor was it graced with decent calligraphy or anything resembling an official stamp. Abraham pictured the flimsy thing—the tossed-off message, already memorized, was emblazoned in his mind. What galled him was the utter lack of respect. He was a war veteran of this country! While plenty of his fellow immigrants, including his brother, fled Germany to avoid military service, he had arrived in America and *enlisted* for a war whose significance he could only now begin to understand, giving all of his youth and strength and skill to a new language, new people, new bloodshed. He'd been a member of the United States Army before he was anything in this country— before he was a businessman or a husband or a debtor—and if that didn't cap the climax, it had been the general himself who had shook his hand and said, *Yessir, you tell that brother of yours that this year's contract belongs to Shein Brothers'!*

He thought of the letter when the gap-toothed girl approached him. Months ago, after he'd first secured the contract with Fort Marcy, he would have let himself be escorted by his favorite through the black, pink-swathed door like a cow being led to pasture, but because last month when his girl wasn't there and he was forced to go with another (a tall, proud one with a horsey jaw and surprisingly large, dark nipples) and he had taken her on the floor before ending a losing streak, since that day (or night—he wasn't sure) he had established a firm rule of going with a different girl each time before going to the gambling table. He always did it before the game—never after; it simultaneously relaxed him and goaded him on, reminding him of just how far he had fallen from any life of respectability, just how desperate he'd become.

"Buenos dias, Señor," said the gap-toothed girl. He had screwed this sloe-eyed cherry countless times; he had seen her bite down on her bottom lip as he drove too hard; she had seen him in the early morning twice, when he was piss proud and full of cursing, enraged that he had stayed until morning; he had done all of this and still she approached him as if they'd just been introduced, as if this were a picnic and he had come a-courting.

He grumbled something about his rule, how she knew they had been together last night, and when she looked as if she meant to slap him, he wasn't surprised; only he would be dumb enough to get this tied up with a whore. *"Donde está Carlota?"* he asked, sounding miserable even to his own exhausted ears.

The carpenter and his men had finished the house, and he and Eva had moved in. The house was enormous and full of imported luxury items, and this had all been possible because of the contract, because of the government funds that were forthcoming. If there had been trouble—if he had made trouble before—this was an altogether different shade of it; there was a physical foreboding, a sharp sense of vertigo that only grew worse when he closed his eyes. He hadn't had a moment of peace since he had read those words the previous day in unevenly spaced script: *The general regrets to inform you that due to an unfortunate report of your conduct as a gentleman, the contract has been awarded to another outfit.*

It would be hours, maybe even days, before Eva eventually found out the news, but he knew he would never tell her that the contract had been lost, and he wondered, not exactly sadly, what kind of lies he'd end up telling instead. His gap-toothed girl nodded with her chin toward the red door, where Carlota was waiting.

Later—it couldn't have been more than twenty minutes—as he approached the bar and asked for another drink, he felt not relaxed, not motivated, but disgusted and tired.

"You don't go home no more for supper?" There came the husky voice, the dampened tease. As Cuca sidled up beside him, he knew she had been there watching him since the diamond stickpin man had left, taking far too much of her silver (without having the decency to run up a reasonable bar tab) for her to be in any kind of neutral mood. He could also tell that she knew. She knew about the contract and she knew about its loss. And she had watched how Abraham spoke to her girls, whom he went with and whom he rejected, as if he had any right to reject a single one of them, as if he had any rights here at all. Those girls were busy all times of year but these winter months were the most fruitful. Men were cold, men were lonely, and whether they were married or not didn't seem to make much of a difference. As far as Doña Cuca was concerned, Abraham could see in her eyes that he was nothing but desperate, a desperate, marked man. He heard her disgust—implicit in the way she asked this simple question—*You don't go home no more?*—and he saw it in the very flick of her fingers as she rolled a thin cigarette.

"I'm here to play Monte."

"I thought you were here for a little something else—at least this is what my girls say—and these tough girls, they don't lie."

"No, not when they're being paid."

She laughed, surprisingly, but he had a feeling she would have just as easily shot him dead.

"Beautiful Cuca," he said slowly, "whose mind is sharp as a knife, and yet she is missing her heart."

"Believe me I am all heart. Why do you think you are in such good health?"

He smiled tightly without showing his teeth. "Are you dealing?"

"First you must pay what you owe," she replied, exhaling a deep cloud of smoke. "Your time has come. *Entiendes?*"

He turned to her, holding everything back, his long, boring tale of personal decline, his seemingly special excuses. *"Entiendo."*

They sat in silence for a moment and not for the first time that day did Abraham think of his wife with her swollen belly, the familiar and yet wholly unknowable fact of her. In his mind she was always alone, behind a closed door. "Let me play," he said quietly. "Give me one final chance. Because you know I will make it back. I will always find a way to get you your money."

"No," she said, "no good." She waved her hand dismissively, as if she were bargaining in the market for fancy soaps, baskets full of corn. "I'm afraid this is not so."

"You know what happened with the contract," he said, trying to cap his anger. "I know you know."

But she only gave him a look empty of everything including pity.

"It was definite," he said, even as he heard how insubstantial the words were. "It was as good as official. Those bastards did me in."

She turned away and only nodded and smoked, smoked and nodded, like some kind of goddamn seer. He suddenly realized that of course she'd played no small part in the loss of the contract. He felt deeply ashamed that it had taken him this long to understand this: She had worked with the Spiegelmans against him. "I want the house," she finally said, without even having the courtesy to look at his face while making such a request.

"You want my house?"

She nodded as if he'd asked if she might like something to drink. "And everything in it. Every last scrap of your wife's French lace."

"This I cannot do."

She stood up and smoothed her gaudy taffeta skirt. "No?" she asked unsurprised. *"Bueno,* you'll be hearing from my friends soon." She stumped out her cigarette until it was nothing but bits of ashy leaves. "Abe"—she leaned in closely; he could smell her: sour perfume and pungent tobacco, hints of charred onions—"you do not think of stepping through these doors again until you give me my money. *My* money. Whose money you think built that house? And *guapo*," she added, raising her ringed finger, "you don't have much time."

"You can have it," he muttered. He said it so softly, not even he could hear. She had already turned her back so that he was forced to say it again.

When she turned around, she seemed prepared to settle.

"You can have it; we'll make arrangements. Only let me play now. Give me one chance to earn it back."

"Earn it?" she said bitterly. "Is that what you think you can do? This is a game, *amigo*. It's a *game*." Then her face softened, and, "You want to play?" she asked him, sweetly, cruelly, as if he were an unappealing child.

WHAT HE REMEMBERED OF HIS FINAL GAME OF MONTE WAS THE queen of cups and how as soon as he placed his bet on that bitch, he knew he was doomed to failure.

He remembered using what felt like the very last dregs of his charm in order to recall old times, old favors. *Give me time,* he finally begged, because he finally understood he was begging for his life. *It costs you nothing. It's like asking for air.* But this request was met with nothing but scorn. He looked to see if the gap-toothed girl—if anyone—noticed he was leaving, but the room could have been any gambling hall anywhere. As he stepped out into the chilly evening, he was no more than a stranger who had lost everything and there was nothing special about that.

The sunset was eerily stunning, blinding one half of the plaza in a blazing white light. His pocket watch had stopped and he hadn't an idea of the time, only that time was now valuable and this day was nearly done. He watched his own storefront, how the handsome black sign bore his father's good name; a surname bestowed on his great-grandfather the goldsmith by a grateful patron, a baron who—after the *Code Napoléon* had taken effect—had announced that he would be honored to share his name with such a talented fellow, that surely such a

Jew deserved the dignity of a surname. Abraham gazed at this name next to a word that always filled him with a sense of incommunicable good-will: *Brothers.* He'd always liked being a brother, had always been proud—even with all its petty injustices—of the fact that Meyer was his, and now he was afraid to look at him; he couldn't recall the last time they had shared a meal. Their exchanges were limited to business hours, mostly consisting of Meyer reminding him (at first patiently and then not-so-patiently) about orders he'd forgotten to fill.

Just the day before, he had opened the letter in the back room of the store. He had read the letter and his very first instinct had been to find his brother. He had stumbled outside in a state of shock, finding not Meyer but young Levi Ehrenberg, who was engrossed in conversation with a cluster of Mexican workers. He couldn't imagine what they were discussing, or, for that matter, how the skinny German could possibly understand their talk. And he'd envied that frail young man just then, for his life was clean. He might have had nothing but the job Meyer had given him, but he had no responsibilities either. Still, there was some-thing so insouciant about the kid; his general expression was one of col-lusion, as if he knew Abraham's secrets and was pretending not to judge him. Even though he said nothing outright, it wasn't unusual for Abra-ham to feel subtly mocked by Ehrenberg and he could never decide if this suspicion was insightful or paranoid. And he still clung to the idea, his secret idea, that Levi Ehrenberg had brought with him to Santa Fe some kind of goddamn curse.

He realized that he'd stopped walking and he was standing dumbly in front of Spiegelman's store as if he might, at any minute, make a scene, or perhaps—more realistically—walk in and ask for a job. A laborer yelled at him to get out of the way, as he'd thoughtlessly stood right in their path as they hauled final crates of goods from carriage to store, and he hoarsely yelled right back for no sane reason, just as the cold sweat stench of worn-out burros propelled the whiskey he'd swallowed earlier spiraling up into his gullet. After somehow finding the will not to vomit, he looked out at the plaza and the church, up toward the mountains and the burning horizon—as if to gain some kind of broader perspective, as if he couldn't see far enough. And, as it happened, he saw something specific, something that indeed changed his point of view, even as he couldn't quite believe it.

His wife was in the plaza, his tiny, pregnant wife, and she was speaking with Levi Ehrenberg. Even though Abraham knew she was in the habit of taking walks, even though he had in fact encouraged her to do so, and even though he saw nothing but two people talking, he had never seen his wife out of doors unescorted like this, and the whole tableau unnerved him. There was a squirrel at their feet and the rodent didn't move; the very trees seemed to lose their sway. He came closer to where they stood and hid behind a large oak as if he were a goddamn assassin. She didn't see him, that was for certain, and it was the sight of her face—so unsuspecting and animated—that told him what he needed to know.

LONG AFTER NIGHTFALL ABRAHAM FINALLY WENT HOME. HE HAD wandered the borders of town and had finally headed into the hills, out toward the bishop's garden, when he realized he could no longer feel his feet and that there was no more light in the sky. He came home to the house he finally had built, a house he had described as *already* built when he'd asked Eva's father for her hand, and after nearly falling off the makeshift platform that was there in place of front steps, he silenced his cursing as he walked forward, deliberately. He had managed to find men generous with whiskey on his rambling walk and he was still drunk, he knew this, though he would have flatly denied it to Jehovah himself. As he walked through the door into the darkened house, he tried to focus on the solid nature of the hand-planed wood floors, but all he felt was instability, a viscous sensation in his limbs and eyes, as if he'd reached the end of his earthly limit and he might in fact dissolve. He didn't call out; he had no idea what time it was, but he saw small flickers of candlelight in the distance, listless patterns on the dining room walls.

The table was beautifully appointed. A ship of white linen on a murky sea, it beckoned with cooking smells of stewed meats and freshly baked bread, obviously long gone cold. There were bowls of soup and polished

silver and his wife was asleep in her new dark-green, silk-upholstered
chair with her head laid daintily on the edge of the table as if she'd
placed it there along with the serviettes, the salt and pepper crystal pots,
and the sharpened, gleaming knives. He sat down without removing his
coat or hat, as if he suspected he might still be outside, hallucinating,
having walked for so long that he was past the bishop's garden, standing
under newly falling snow.

When Eva opened her eyes, he almost didn't notice, he had been staring at her for so long. "Your hat and coat," she said finally, smoothing her
upswept hair. She was visibly shaken but this did nothing for him. He
didn't even stop to think of how he must have looked—cold-blasted and
filthy—and that he smelled like the women, the drink and filth of the
street; when he looked at his wife, he didn't think to wash a single part of
himself.

"My hat and coat?"

"May I take them? May I hang them on their pegs?"

Her hair was messed by such an awkward slumber; it curled tightly
around her reddened face, which bore the faint impression of the scalloped edge of the silver on which her cheek had rested. "I saw you," he
said. And he rested his hat (a hat that had fallen more than once today
into foul puddles of the backstreets) on the clean white tablecloth. He
wasn't surprised when she didn't react; this was her trick when she
thought he was drunk and she was very good at it. "I saw you," he repeated, and louder this time, skipping right to it.

She sat up straight and looked him in the eye, as if she didn't care
what he was going to say, as if this was nothing but a dare.

"I saw you in the plaza. I saw you talking to him."

She sighed elaborately, and that sigh was so simple, so condescending,
that before he'd given it a moment's thought, before he even believed it,
he cried out: *"Is that goddamn baby mine?"*

She stood and began clearing the china off the table—the bowls full
of soup were first—and he followed closely in her wake, not failing to
notice her rounded figure, which now looked strange and slovenly. She
brought the bowls into the newly tiled kitchen as if she were playing at

being an orderly wife. "You tell me right now—you speak to me!" But she didn't turn around until the bowls were set down on the sideboard, and even then she tried to pass by him, to continue clearing the untouched meal.

"Let me pass," she said. "Let me pass right now."

But he couldn't let her pass, he couldn't let her out of his sight, and he moved in closely, backing her up against one wall, then another, walls that were no longer his walls, not even in his mind. "I told Meyer not to trust him—"

"Abraham," she said, evidently using all of her self-control, "please step away from me. Darling, you don't know anything right now."

"I know everything," he said, leaning into her. He would leave tomorrow, he decided right then. He would take her jewelry box.

"All right," she said, blinking back the tears that he wanted to see— that he *craved* seeing—but she wasn't going to allow it. "All right then."

He suddenly backed away as if she'd kicked him, when all she'd done was lower her voice. "I know everything about it," he repeated, and his breath ricocheted like the beginnings of fire, those soundless vapors gathering force even as no one can see. She continued clearing useless possessions: china, crystal glasses, candlesticks, some brought from Germany but some purchased recently with money he did not have. And Abraham simply followed her back and forth without offering any help, hulking and silent like a lonely monster—the kind that only existed in children's tales. His every footfall, his every gesture echoed through this stolen house that suddenly seemed too big.

He tugged at her shoulder and she said nothing. She kept moving. He heard her silence and it was damning and as he pulled her around, he knew he would hit her before he did it. He knew it was the only way that he could leave. When he hit her (*such a small and soft cheek,* he found himself thinking), he was afraid of what he might do next. It wasn't that he'd overcome his anger, but he had become aware of his fear.

BIRD

EVA WOKE JUST BEFORE DAWN THE NEXT MORNING TO find Abraham stuffing a satchel full of clothing, a block of soap, bullets. Before she could form the words to ask what he was doing, he told her he was leaving town. "Don't tell anyone you know anything. You understand? If folks think I abandoned you, pregnant and all, so be it. Do you hear me? Do you, now?" He looked panicked and harried and she was amazed that she still possessed the troubling instinct to comfort him.

"Where are you going?" She winced, sitting up in bed.

"What is it?" he asked, and she was surprised he'd noticed her discomfort.

"I'm pregnant," she said with undisguised irritation. "There are many details that I spare you." She smoothed the blanket on top of her belly, as if to appease their unborn child. Then she said resignedly, "What is it you think you are doing?"

"I have a plan," he said predictably, tying his shoes. "There are mines."

"Gold?"

"Maybe," he said. "Maybe diamonds. Maybe better you don't know." He came closer to her bedside. "I'm leaving," he said.

"I see."

"Tell Meyer what you need." He continued to nod, as if he was waiting for his thoughts to catch up with his nodding. "It's better this way."

"Abraham. You are wrong about Mr. Ehrenberg."

"I don't want to hear it. I know what I know."

Her right cheek stung slightly. She wondered if there was even the slightest red mark and she hoped that there was. "And so do I."

She heard his lumbering footsteps on the hardwood floors, the sound of the door closing quietly, his mare making trouble. She was a new horse, and who knew how strong she was or how far he intended to take her.

As Eva registered the fact that he'd left, a slow burn of fear began creeping inside her, beginning at the base of her spine. She kept her hands on the baby as if she might hold it in place. She heard her own breath, the faint whistle of wind, but the rose-colored dawn was deceptively quiet. All the noise was inside of her, building and rising until she had no choice to let it escape. She'd screamed until her heart was a dull thud, and she was faced with the knowledge that no one could hear— not from this house set apart from her neighbors—no one could hear her scream. It was a quiet daybreak, a dawn so still that it was impossible to imagine the morning to come, when there was—eventually—a sudden and furious knocking at the door. The knocking propelled Eva out of bed and down the dangerous staircase, where she opened the door to find Meyer demanding: "Where is my brother?"

"I thought he was at the store," she said out of breath; she wasn't sure why she'd lied.

Meyer fixed her with a look she'd never seen from him—an expression of pity but of incredulity too, as if she were at fault for having married such a man, as if only she would be fool enough to be pregnant at a time like this.

She knew Meyer was a good man and it was this knowledge that made his fury so difficult to bear. She thought to follow him and tell him the truth, before realizing there was no going outside just then, not when she was so big and nearing the deadly time frame of poor Henriette's de-

livery and her own dead little girl. She had wanted a photograph of her
dead child but nobody had listened. It would have been easy enough—
the photographer had arrived in town by then—and she would have
looked at that picture every day for the rest of her life, or at least right
then, as Meyer's door slam echoed, emphasizing her brother-in-law's
frustration. It was the door slam that she remembered as the last sound
she heard before waking up in bed, confused and starving; Meyer was
looking down at her with an apologetic air. "You collapsed," he explained.
He was not exactly angry anymore.

SHE MUST HAVE LEFT BED BETWEEN THEN AND NOW; SHE MUST HAVE
eaten and bathed and spoken to Beatrice, whom she was certain had
come with wonderful biscuits and pickled peaches, or at the very least
she was sure Bea had brought her treasured yellow bird in its bamboo
cage who now lived by her bedside: Schwefel—little sulphur match—
who had survived all the way from New York. But she couldn't keep any
of it straight and it seemed to Eva that, after Meyer had left, she had
fallen asleep and woken to this: The nuns, like an infestation, had taken
control of her house.

Sister Blandina towered above and, smelling of lye, handed her a glass
of milk. Eva must have appeared as confused as she actually was. "You
drink milk now," Blandina informed her. "You've done so for almost a
week—three times a day. You've been very ill, coughing up blood, and
this is the way to build strength."

"But what is it? What is wrong with me?"

"Your fever is very high. Doctor Sam is at a loss. Are you certain you
didn't take something?"

"Take something?"

"Something you weren't supposed to take?"

"I don't know what you are suggesting. What is wrong with me?"

Sister Blandina shook her head in evident exasperation. "Drink, Mrs.
Shein. Drink your milk."

"There were babies on the trail," she heard herself saying before she
realized the memory. The parents had been from Rhode Island, a place

she had never heard of. "Twin babies who died because they drank milk; the cow had eaten a poisonous milkweed," she said. "I don't think I should drink it." But Sister Blandina didn't appear to have heard.

"Be grateful for this milk," the nun finally said, followed by an almost-smile.

"I am. I am grateful." She heard shuffling in the hallway, a sharp unexpected laugh. "I only wonder if I should allow myself to drink it." Schwefel had been moved across the room and in its place was a thick, blue Bible, topped by a book of prayers. She remembered years ago, how her fever had soared, how after Heinrich—after the silk sash and the mud puddles—she had gone to what had seemed like another world, where colors were brighter and unsettling. "I run high fevers," she said, in what she imagined was an accountable tone of voice. "Are you really here?" Eva asked. "I feel so strange."

"Well of course we're here. You listen to me, young lady—Mrs. Shein—the bishop, he likes you; he treats you—because he is so *good* and so *generous*—like one of his own kin. Now when the bishop pays a visit and asks how we've been taking care, you won't be saying that you *don't remember whether or not we were here.* Do you understand? Not when we've been cleaning this filthy house and Philomene has made so much soup. You do remember the soup, for heaven's sake?"

"It was delicious," she said, although all she remembered was the wet feeling on her chest when she spit it all up, the harsh wiping with a cold cloth that must have been held by Blandina. And all at once she had a pressing urge to urinate and she found herself throwing off the bed sheets in a clumsy attempt to go do so. But what she realized was that she was incredibly weak and that she couldn't get up on her own. She found herself held up by the black-winged nuns and escorted to the toilet. "How long has my husband been gone?" she asked, shivering, as soon as she lay back down again.

"Mrs. Shein, go to sleep now. The prayer books will protect you and your child from the devil. The devil, Lord knows, has visited this house far too many times."

"But where is Chela?" she cried.

"Who?"

"Chela," she repeated, suddenly convinced they were hiding her.

"There is no Chela here. A Mexican girl came by last week—"

"Yes, yes—that is Chela!"

"She said she has found employment elsewhere."

"Couldn't I see her?"

"You are speaking nonsense, Mrs. Shein. Really, you must rest."

THERE WERE NOODLES COOKED WITH MILK, CHICKEN IN A RUST-STREAKED pan, and Philomene's soup, which seemed more available than water; it was red and salty and yet it had no taste. When she asked what it was, they changed the subject just as they did when she asked about her husband.

In her dreams, however, the soup was plainly made from blood, but *whose blood?* They wouldn't tell her. Sister Blandina hollered, *Hold the knife up!* And, *Drink the blood soup!* In her dreams there was a knife slung low on her waist and it was an unusually pleasurable sensation. The knife, she somehow knew, had been placed there by the nuns and was solely for the purpose of fighting off the demons who wanted to eat her baby. And the blood soup? It was for strength.

This all had more logic than the silence in the room as no one answered her questions, and it made more sense than the seemingly intentionally terrible cooking that she refused until one day Sister Blandina pried her mouth open and Josephine stuffed it in. Then she vomited gristly chicken and crimson soup until there was nothing left inside of her.

Days upon days and nobody came to see her. Once she swore she heard Beatrice at the door but the nuns sent her away. Eva screamed that she was upstairs and that she needed to see Beatrice, to please let her in, but the next thing she heard was the closing of the door and footsteps on the stairwell, approaching. "What is it?" Sister Blandina asked gently.

"She is my friend. Why don't you let her see me?"

"I don't know what you're talking about."

"I heard her at the door."

"There is nobody downstairs, dear. Do I need to call on Doctor Sam again?"

Doctor Sam had cold hands that lingered too long. He talked about the possibilities of leeching her spine, but he'd left her some laudanum in a lovely brown bottle (which she'd managed to nearly finish, while hiding it from the nuns), and so her feelings about seeing him were decidedly mixed. As much as she longed for another brown bottle, she shook her head, contrite. "It has been so long since I've heard word of anyone," she said.

"Mrs. Shein," the nun said with a steely resolve that made Eva regret speaking at all, "this is not a holiday. You are very ill—"

"But what is wrong with me?"

"You are ill and you are with child. Do you take neither of these things seriously?"

"I only meant it might be nice to know of what is happening outside of this room." She forced her voice to be cheerful, as if a pleasant demeanor might make a difference. "For instance, the patient," she said lightly, "*our* patient. How is poor Mr. Ehrenberg?"

"Do you mean to provoke me, Mrs. Shein?"

"I only asked how—"

"If I understand you correctly, you are lying here in your husband's house, a house he built for you at considerable expense, and you are asking after Mr. Ehrenberg?"

"I do not see how the two are in any way related."

Sister Blandina walked to the window and drew closed the sheets, which on a day that seemed like years ago Eva had hung in place of curtains. The nun's back was turned, but Eva could tell her expression was grave. "Only God can judge for certain what constitutes a sin, but the rest of us are not stupid. Do you understand?"

Eva did her best to sit up, but without any assistance she found herself breathing heavily, exhausted from such a small effort. She felt the baby move—a knee or an elbow this time—and it startled her as it always did. She was never prepared. "No," she said, as she caught her breath, "I'm afraid I do not understand."

When Sister Blandina turned to face her, Eva was shocked to see color in her usually pallid cheeks. "I saw you in that hallway outside the sickroom." The nuns eyes were unblinking. "You were together—"

"No," Eva said, "you *gravely* misunderstood! I was helping him to walk. I was—"

"Only God can know for certain," said Sister Blandina, followed by the closest approximation to a shrug that this Sister was ever going to offer.

"I was helping him," Eva exclaimed before coughing so hard she couldn't stop.

As she coughed, the nun asked, "Do you have any doubt that God sees everything?" She asked as if she truly wondered what Eva's thoughts might be.

She looked up at the plaster ceiling. "Of course I have no doubt," she managed between coughs, and was surprised to find herself almost longing for the wood beams of their bedroom on Burro Alley, where she had never been remotely comfortable. "Of course not."

"Mrs. Shein, you are straining yourself. Please get some rest," she said not unkindly, and she was gone.

Schwefel's feet made scratching sounds. His cage was so far away. The drawn sheets at the window pulsed as if someone was behind them; the vanity in the corner hosted a silver brush and comb, bits of lace and sewing needles, her commonplace book. The mirror showed half of her reflection; it was blurred by the unpolished glass.

She had visited him and they had talked. They talked around subjects, never straight through them, and perhaps this had led to a feeling of flirtation, but surely it was harmless, is what she had believed—no more than a spark in a sick man's day. She visited him. She poured water, offered apricots, a taste of something sweet. She listened. She brought him strawberries. When he said he loved her she never came back. She didn't.

Did she?

She visited him. She loved him. She wore a dress that was too big, that smelled of sour flowers. She listened. The charcoal scratched the paper. Rain threatened. No, she realized hesitantly, that was before. But then she thought of the sickroom and there was ivy growing in circles, dangling low enough to touch Levi Ehrenberg's pale neck, his back. She thought of the sickroom and her sister was lying in the narrow bed, sweat-soaked and not breathing.

She choked on the image, forced her eyes open, only to realize they were already open, that the visions were more powerful than this room or this house—a house she'd thought would be solid enough to bind her life together. Her eyes were open—she touched her fingers to the whites to make sure—and there were four dead babies on the fine wood floors. There was Henriette's boy and her own blue-faced girl and the twins who died on the trail from the poisoned cow's milk. They were dead but their eyes were open and each of them was staring at her, asking a silent question she would never be able to answer.

She had not done anything improper, she reminded herself, but such a thought seemed insubstantial, even sinful, as she continued to see the poor babies, all unclothed and unnamed. She closed her eyes and there was only darkness and for a moment this was preferable, until she felt trapped and needed to draw open the curtains. She had no clear idea of whether the ground outside was tawny and rich or barren and covered with snow, and it suddenly seemed imperative that she know. And so she dragged herself across the floor, skinning her knees, closing her eyes to the babies strewn along the way, and when she reached the windows she grew tangled in the sheets; they smelled of air and she pulled them aside to see a glimpse of the world. It was late afternoon, almost springtime. She saw burros and wagons and men without coats, a lady with a black *rebozo*. She saw enormous clouds, filmy and whiter than the sheet drawn close around her, and then she saw Abraham.

He looked thin and tired and he was carrying sacks on his strong back; she knew the sacks had to be filled with diamonds or gold. He marched toward the house, ignoring people along the way. He marched toward the house and she began to wave, but not only did he not wave back, he made a sharp turn as he approached the house, and kept right on walking. "Abraham!" she cried out, as loudly as she could. She struggled ineffectively to open the window, screaming his name all the while. She called his name over and over, as if repetition could draw him in.

"*Mrs. Shein!*" Sister Blandina erupted, barging into the room.

Eva looked up from her place on the floor, tangled in the fallen sheets. "I saw my husband," she said.

Sister Blandina marched to the window and had a good look for herself. Then she turned to Eva and told her to look again.

"He came back," Eva muttered.

"Have another look Mrs. Shein. Go on."

She did as she was told and there he was, with his thick hair and his broad shoulders. "He's returned from his trip," she said, and began crawling toward the door.

But Sister Blandina lifted her from the floor and held Eva's head between her cold, dry hands. "*Look,*" she said, and Eva did. As if cast in a spell, this thin, tired Abraham—the Abraham carrying a sack of gold, the Abraham who would save her—became somebody who looked nothing like the man she married, and she realized, with a start, that Sister was correct. The man outside had a concave chest, a thin and pointy beard. He looked nothing like anyone she'd ever known.

"Oh," Eva heard herself say. "Oh my." And Blandina, with unsurprising strength, carried Eva back to the bed, Eva's face buried into her musty habit, which smelled of cooking grease and starch. Wordlessly, the nun lay Eva down, before tacking the window sheets back in their place, once again blocking out the light.

"You saw nothing but the devil," Sister Blandina said softly. "He is trying to get into this house. He wants the baby but we will not let him near you, will we?"

"I was sure I saw my husband." The child kicked so hard inside of her, she thought it must have left an impression. As she gasped, it felt as if her insides were being clawed apart.

"The devil takes many shapes." Blandina lifted the bedsheets and brought them down over Eva, producing a pleasant shiver. "He's preying on your weakness." She picked the blanket up from the floor and tucked it tightly around her, so that Eva could barely move, as the clawing inside her intensified. "I want you to look into my eyes this instant. This instant—do you hear me?"

It took a moment, but Eva did as she was told. The papery corners of Sister Blandina's eyes were webbed with wrinkles. Her eyes were a marbled gray, an oddly attractive set of eyes in a long-ago hardened expression. "I have closed those sheets at the window to keep the devil out. That is whom you saw. It was no husband of yours. Do you understand?"

Eva found herself nodding, hypnotized by the child's violent kicking, which had turned into a higher kind of pain. "But I have the knife," she muttered.

"What knife?"

"I have the prayer book by the bedside."

"What knife?"

Eva stayed focused on the nun's gray eyes; "You gave it to me."

Sister Blandina looked away, before fluffing a pillow behind Eva's head. "What is wrong with you?" she asked. She seemed suddenly very sad.

Eva touched her own face and it was wet with tears. "I don't know."

"The sheets will remain closed."

"But what about the prayer book?" Eva inquired sincerely, having begun to rely on the bedside protection, though she had yet to read a single page. She believed this much: She was in danger.

"A prayer book alone is not enough. To keep the devil at bay, we must let no light into this room."

"It would seem to me—"

"Do not leave this bed without one of us present." And with a swish of her skirt, she headed straight for the door.

"Wait," Eva cried, "please."

"What is it?"

"Do you think—do you think I deserve this? Do you think I am deserving of this?"

Sister Blandina did not make any attempt to hide her impatience at

being asked this question, but she did—after a moment's consideration—
sit down on Eva's mattress. "No," she said finally, if not exactly vehe-
mently. "You are not a bad woman." Then, shockingly, Sister Blandina
put her hand on Eva's wrist. "You are feeling wretched and I am sorry for
you. I want you to understand this. I was very sick as a girl, you know."

"I did not know," said Eva. "That must have been very hard."

"It was." Sister Blandina nodded. "You will find this difficult to imagine, but as a girl I was blessed with beautiful, golden hair. When it was
unpinned, my hair fell straight down my back like corn silk and when I
was sick, every single strand of that hair fell out."

"B-but," Eva stuttered, "but . . ." She was suddenly desperate to win
the nun's affection, to sound as sympathetic as she actually felt. Anything Eva knew about Sister Blandina—who had never once volunteered
so much as the name of her birthplace—she had learned from the other
nuns. The idea of Sister Blandina having been not only a young girl but a
sick young girl with long, lovely hair was enough to send Eva into a fresh
set of tears. "Surely it grew back?"

"No." She stuck out her lower lip in a way that Eva could not help but
think of as quintessentially French. "Not the same. It was never the
same. It was dull and coarse and ugly. But," she said, taking what
seemed like a rather energizing breath and standing once again, "I am
fortunate that my hair did not grow back, because that was the sign of
my calling. This was how I knew I was meant to devote my life to God."
Sister Blandina opened the bedroom door but paused at the threshold.
"Still," she said before leaving, "it was very beautiful hair."

"Wait," Eva gasped, as a vice wrapped tightly around her middle, bearing down on the core of her core. "Don't go."

THE SHEETS STAYED CLOSED. THERE WAS NO LIGHT IN THE ROOM
and so Eva could not tell how many hours or days had passed when she'd
stopped clawing her own arm from the pain. This labor (so improperly
named, as labor seemed like a fair proposal, another word for honest
work) was much more brutal than her previous experience, and she tried

to see this as a positive sign, that somehow this time her baby would survive, but she became certain blood was draining out of her and that these were her last moments. And what did she see? She saw Sister Philomene fiddling with Schwefel's cage, poking her fingers through the bamboo rails. She saw Sister Josephine come toward her with another cold cloth, though she had said (or she'd thought she'd said) *I'm so cold,* over and over through the hours. She heard Sister Philomene shriek and there was Schwefel the bird flying overhead, bumping into the walls.

She knew the baby was dead because where was the baby? She didn't see a baby anywhere. She wondered, as she saw the yellow bird and the black-cloaked nuns run amok trying to catch it, if there was ever any baby, if all along they had been torturing her, keeping her prisoner with their terrifying talk of the devil. She was screaming, she knew, when they called her name, when two separate hands grabbed her wrist. They countered her screaming with *Look! Look!,* but she was too afraid of what she'd see and that surely it would be her last sight. A pair of hands took her face—they were softer hands now, Philomene's—and when she finally opened her eyes, Sister Blandina placed a swaddled bundle in Eva's trembling arms.

She kept her gaze downcast. It was nothing like she'd expected. They had cleaned the child, who had a thatch of black hair. Eva touched the little head and was shocked by how thin the skin was, how she may as well have been touching finger to skull, the skin was so soft. It squirmed and Eva had never felt so astonished, so shy. "Thank you," she said, and said it again. The creature was light but certain, the most precise bit of weight in the world.

"And her name?" asked Sister Blandina.

"You're a girl?" she whispered into the tiny opal shell of an ear. The lips were full; the eyes shut but lightly, as if she was simply worn out from her long, impossible journey. Eva shook so terribly she was afraid she would drop the baby, but she was also afraid to let her daughter go for even a moment, now that the child was finally, *finally* in her arms.

"What is her name?" Sister Blandina repeated.

After forbidding herself to consider the possibility of names or that this child might actually live, she said, "Henriette," without thinking. "Henriette, of course."

"Why are you laughing, Mrs. Shein?"

"I'm not," Eva said, holding the child close. Kissing and kissing the top of her head.

The Top of the Stairs

From her spot at the top of the stairs (which was as far as she would venture outside of her bedroom these days), Eva heard Beatrice Spiegelman's loud, shocked voice as she sorted out the mess of the Shein house. She had been in Taos accompanying her husband on a trip for almost a month and was just now back in town. Accompanied by her maid, Luz, Beatrice had arrived at dawn, and though Eva had begged Bea to come back another time, Bea ignored her and instructed Luz to begin boiling water. They gave in to her demands that they bolt both front and back doors and shutter the parlor windows. They cleaned the parlor while Eva sat upstairs on the hard floor, leaning back against the wall, and as little Henriette suckled at her swollen breast, she gave into the sweet lull of milk that flowed and a baby who was hungry.

Eva's nipples were still sliced with small cuts from the first weeks of Henriette's frustrated attempts at feeding—those hours upon hours when such a tiny mouth could not open wide enough. Henriette gummed her poor mother's nipples with not so much a suck as a desperate bite, only to give up quickly, stick those tiny flailing hands inside her own mouth, and leave Eva's breasts pulsing. Recently though, Henriette had begun to actually draw the milk out in fast efficient comfort; they were, it seemed, both growing stronger.

She had waited for Meyer, but he hadn't been to see them since shortly after Henriette was born. After that initial visit he'd sent Alma Lucia a few times, who had blessedly cleaned the rooms, laundered the sheets, and left a basket of corn tamales, which—immediately following her departure—Eva ate in one sitting. She'd never been so ravenous.

But it had been over two weeks since she'd been down those stairs.

If the nuns paid a visit, Eva would ask them if they might be a dear and bring up a tray of food, and she'd lived on that food (until the next caller came), casting meager crumbs to Schwefel the bird, whose screeching had become a rare comfort. The bishop had come bearing a basket of fruit in addition to a plate of cold meat, and she'd feasted happily on that gift for days. For a flashing instant she was indulgent rather than broken as she tossed the bones and seeds out the window like some kind of mad queen. To these visitors she downplayed Abraham's departure, though she suspected she wasn't fooling anyone.

Two men watched the house. They were always there, looking bored and ready for violence, and whenever she looked out the window from behind the double-hung sheets and saw those men standing outside, she held her baby close and began to nurse, as much a comfort to herself as for her eager daughter.

One day over two weeks ago they came to the door and pounded and pounded, calling her name until she finally answered. She tried to keep her voice steady as she repeated her standard phrase through the closed and bolted door: *My husband is not at home.*

"Good goddamn woman, we know it," came a low, hoarse voice. "Now you open up this door."

"Please," she said, making her English worse than it actually was, "go to Shein Brothers' store."

"We don't need no supplies. If you don't open this door and give us our money, we'll get it however we have to." A cough, a murmur, followed by a single staccato slam of a meaty fist against wood. "We wouldn't want that baby of yours to get scared now. Babies scare easy."

Eva, after turning quietly as if responding to a common insult, went upstairs, and she hadn't been down the stairs since.

From then on they'd watched the house, sometimes pounding at the door, but they had yet to go any further. This morning they were absent, which made her that much more nervous, as it could only mean that they were planning something, and it seemed unlikely that these plans would include any kind of gracious retreat. Today they weren't under the cottonwood trees, poking holes in the ground, smoking and laughing the way they did so that all of their bad teeth showed. She never wondered what they laughed about, just like now she didn't think to wonder where they were. The men outside her window existed whether they were in plain view or eating at home with their improbable families, and either way she was stuck at the top of the stairs. She believed she'd know when it was time to descend and that if it wasn't her husband who was to deliver her from this purgatory, she'd know her savior straightaway.

Baby Henriette had licorice eyes; two slick bits in a confectioner's window, dark and shiny and impossible to turn from. She fixed those eyes on Eva and grabbed hold of her finger with expressive hands, as if she might deliver a proclamation, an instruction of how to proceed. Her nose was long, not just a baby's blob, and her lips were usually open as if she was in mid-thought, not unlike how Eva remembered Heinrich's lips as he painted. This should have been a disturbing comparison, but it didn't seem so much disturbing as expected; she could be so repetitive even in her imagination, especially there—her thoughts in a loop like the turning wheels of a stagecoach, an image and sound she still managed to see on nights when she closed her eyes. She imagined the wheels and also the soaked hides of those poor, sweating horses whose worth, not unlike her own, was always measured minute to minute to minute to minute by nothing but forward motion. Sometimes, though she was utterly exhausted, she couldn't sleep and she stared for hours at the baby beside her, never fully comprehending her existence, her *rightness,* and was overcome with such selfishness, such greed it bordered on hunger. Henriette slept with her arms above her head, as if she was falling and didn't mind. Eva didn't want to share her with the rest of the world; even though she waited each day and night for Abraham to return, the expectation was tinged with a stingy resentment that he would claim her as his own.

And now here she was doing nothing but waiting at the top of the stairs as Beatrice and Luz cleaned. She hadn't the heart to tell them there was no point in cleaning, that this house, these stairs, they were no longer hers. It was a matter of days until those men barged through the door. Her husband was no longer hers either. He was never coming for her. He would let those men have her first. *I am my beloved and my beloved is mine;* she'd trusted this sentiment not only when she was a girl but also when she circled her husband seven times and the rabbi proclaimed the familiar words in a high nasal voice, so entirely unromantic. She knew she would learn to love Abraham and she had loved him, if in the way a shipwrecked sailor loves the sea. He was everything in her world and now her world was empty of everything but her body—miraculously full of milk—and her child alive at her breast. She had nothing but a commonplace book, a squawking bird, and yes, the sapphires, the rubies, and emeralds, the diamond necklace that she'd only known as hanging low against Mother's *décolletage.*

"Come down, dear!" Beatrice said for a final time, approaching the bottom of the stairs. "You must see this house. I insist you see it! Really, it isn't all that bad."

"Do you imagine I am sitting here because I am afraid to clean?" She laughed then, and it felt like a clean breeze. She couldn't remember the last laugh she'd had.

"You would only feel so much better if you did." Beatrice gave Eva a weary smile, as if she had been attempting a certain role and had decided to finally abandon it. "Eva," she said, "I wish . . ." But she put a clear stop to that sentiment. "My husband thinks you are mad."

"He thinks *I* am mad? It is my husband who is the madman! What is mad is that he has a contract to uphold, *a government contract,* and he has left town. What is mad is that he is running from a duo of dangerous men, men to whom he is obviously in debt."

"Which men?"

"This is why I will not come down the stairs! Do you understand? It is because I am afraid of these men. They will turn us out soon, you know. I only wonder why they haven't done it yet. I tell you, Beatrice, it is my husband who is mad. You can tell *your* husband I said so. I am only being cautious."

"Oh heavens," Bea said, leaning on the beginnings of a banister that Eva knew she would never see completed, "Shein Brothers' lost that contract. Dear, I was sure you knew. They lost it months ago."

Eva snickered involuntarily. "What do you mean *months ago*? How do you know this?"

Beatrice looked down at her hands and said nothing as Luz mopped the floor behind her.

"Beatrice?"

"I know this because the contract was awarded to my husband and his brother."

"But that contract—that belonged to Shein Brothers'."

Beatrice, to Eva's surprise, sat down on the bottom stair. "Abraham lost that contract due to no fault of my husband or my brother-in-law. You know this, Eva." Beatrice looked up at Eva briefly, before turning away again. "Surely you know this."

She wanted to argue, to defend Abraham, but there was nothing left to defend. "I do," she said. She held onto her daughter tightly, maybe too tightly. She didn't want to cry.

"Please, dear. Please come down." Bea's cheerfulness had faltered, and Eva was suddenly panicked that even Bea would abandon her, that she had finally tired out the most indefatigable of all the people she knew.

"Do you want me to?" she asked.

"Please, dear, just take a step at a time. I promise you can do it."

"I prefer it up here," she said, gripping the heavy wood banister. "I like it here at the top of the stairs. I can call out instructions to the servants this way. I can oversee the house without really being a part of it."

"Why don't you come down and hand the baby to me?"

"Do you think I'm mad? Bea?"

"Eva, there are no servants."

She felt herself laughing but no sound came out. "Well of course there aren't."

When a knock came at the door, Eva shouted, "Do not answer it!" The baby cried terribly as Eva suddenly rose to her feet and ran to the bedroom window, and Henriette's cries incited Schwefel the bird, but she heard nothing of the squawking and shrieking as she pushed the sheet aside and saw Abraham right below her, pounding at the door—not unlike the men who watched the house—as if by sheer persistence, he might eventually break it down. It was truly Abraham and she was ashamed she didn't feel worse for him, that she saw his desperation as his due. Overwhelming the slight sense of joy upon seeing him was the very real sensation of terror. He was suddenly no more than a stranger here. "Go!" she called out to Bea and Luz, and she let the sheet fall closed, running with her sobbing baby not only to the top of the stairs but now down the stairs as well. "Please," she insisted, "go on!"

"Eva!" Beatrice cried, but her relief at seeing Eva on the parlor floor quickly faded into confusion.

"It's Abraham," Eva said breathlessly. "He's returned. Now when I say so, I want you to let him in, but then I want you to go immediately. Do not let him near you, do you hear me? You and Luz run as fast as you can away from here." She wasn't sure what she imagined Abraham might do to Beatrice, but she was, after all, a woman of means. She was wearing an ivory brooch that was probably worth a card game or two.

Beatrice took Eva by the shoulders. "What are you talking like this for?" she asked, with a pleading smile. "He may have made mistakes, even terrible mistakes, but—well he is your husband."

And Eva realized with a sudden pang, that for all of her strength and positivism, for all of her keen intelligence, Beatrice Spiegelman was really an innocent. She had an urge to take her hand, and she did so. It was dry and cool; she held it tightly as she spoke.

"You're right," she said. "He is my husband. So please," she implored, "let us be." She forced a smile while bouncing Henriette up and down. She bounced her baby; she swayed and prayed. She prayed for her san-ity, for the clarity that she was afraid to believe was in fact intensifying as her child grew heavier in her arms. She prayed that she might cast off any tendencies to resemble her own mother, who had miraculously not pruned to death while taking all those baths. "You must promise me you'll go."

The pounding continued relentlessly and Beatrice finally had the look that Eva had expected before first making her acquaintance: like a young woman who was far from home, who had only just realized that this life was not a holiday and there was no going back. "But—Eva, what is happening?"

"Poor Beatrice," she replied, as the baby cried and cried. "Thank you. Thank you for everything." She embraced her friend clumsily with her one free arm. Bea smelled to Eva what a woman should smell like: a fresh box of powder, sweet protected shade. She kissed her friend on both cheeks before offering up her breast to her wailing baby in exchange for troubled silence. Then she hurried through the parlor (where the smell of ammonia was now stifling) and back up the stairs as Henriette sucked all the while. *"Now,"* she yelled, and when Henriette detatched from her nipple and Eva heard Abraham's footsteps and muddled shouting, calling out *Eva, Eva*—when she heard him pacing in the parlor, waiting for his wife to come to him, she was sure Beatrice had listened to her and that she'd been correct in asking Bea to leave.

She tore into the bedroom and, before she had a moment to think on it, picked up the stick she kept for protection. When he came into the room, he didn't even look surprised to see her in a corner, holding her baby with one hand and brandishing a stick in the other. Neither of them said anything for a moment. He was virtually unrecognizable, having lost so much weight and having gained an unkempt beard. His eyes were wild and his skin was mottled. The smell of whiskey hardly overpowered his own revolting odor. For a moment she had failed to notice that he was holding her jewelry box by its gilt-painted top; it swung from side to side, empty.

"I need the jewelry," he finally managed. And she realized why he had returned. "Where is it?" He paced the room, never taking her eyes off

Eva. "Good God! You never say anything! How do you do that? You're like a stone!"

"How could you?" she said softly. But she wasn't surprised.

"You think I'm an animal but I'm not." He took a breath. "I am not."

"Abraham," she steeled herself, "what can I possibly help you with?"

His skin flushed quickly and he said, "I know you have those jewels."

"What jewels?"

"Don't smile. Don't you dare smile."

Where she had previously seen only confidence in Abraham's expressions, she now saw something else entirely. She saw dread.

"It's all right, really. I will not be angry anymore. Just—please. Where are they?"

"No," she said, softly at first, and when the baby began to cry, she repeated it, louder. "You thought I'd leave them in that box and let you take them with you? You think you're the only one with ideas?"

"Eva, please listen: My life—*our lives*—depend on it."

She rocked the baby but continued to look at him straight on. She knew her eyes were sunken, the skin beneath them darkly violet, and she wondered if he recognized that she was wearing the threadbare blouse of her dead sister; she wondered if he guessed she hadn't changed clothes in days. "And why is that?" she asked, free of harsh tones, as if she was genuinely asking. She wondered, with an almost pure detachment, what he might do. What he did do was move toward her and she tried not to flinch; she stood clutching baby Henriette with her back against the wall.

"Abraham?" she said, her voice hoarse and questioning. She dropped the stick, and held Henriette close, as he backed away and threw clothes out of the wardrobe, sheets out of the closet; he fingered her vanity—her commonplace book fell to the floor.

"*Abraham?*" she pleaded, and though she knew it was no use: "We have a *child* . . ."

He flinched as if her words were nothing but far-off gunfire, and he got down on his hands and knees. He opened each trunk under the bed, digging through winter woolens, pawing her delicate leather, lace-up boots.

"Where are they?" He said it accusingly—more a statement than a question—as if she'd stolen what was rightfully his.

"We have a child," she cried, feeling nothing like herself. "Those men," Eva said softly. "You must tell me exactly what you owe them."

"What have they done to you?" he asked, as if it had just now occurred to him that he'd put her life at risk.

She stared so deeply into his eyes that she noticed copper shades, onyx flecks, which had, until then, gone unnoticed. She saw herself in his pupils and she didn't blink.

"Just give me the jewels and I will take care of it."

"It is too late for this. They've threatened our child, Abraham. Do you understand? And it is only you who has caused this!" she finally yelled. "You have made it happen."

It was as if she was reeling him in—slowly at first and then with a tug—and he lunged forward from the movement. His hands were on her shoulders. She knew he could crush her and their child, who was obviously faceless and fatherless as far as he was concerned. She felt how his hands gripped her shoulders and moved in toward her neck, everything tight and no air in the room and she was screaming now, screaming and sobbing along with the baby and when he finally let go, he cradled his own arms. She ran into the closet, clutching Henriette to her, shutting and locking the door. He hollered, "Open this door," but as he begged her, she knew he was still looking—under the mattress, under the pillows—and when she heard him progress to the other rooms (which were, of course, empty of everything but dust and rising sunlight) she ran from the closet, down the stairs, and out into the morning.

She knew he'd heard the baby screaming and she was glad of it. Even Abraham would not be able to shut out the horrible sound. He wouldn't be able to stop it from echoing, no matter how far away he fled. He would know that she had given birth to a healthy baby after all, a creature she was already unable to imagine having anything to do with him, a girl who already knew how best to announce her misery.

FINISHED

As he searched for the jewels, as he maintained both focus and hope, Abraham heard Eva leave. He heard her fleeing footsteps and the baby's cries (Eva had tried and failed to shush the child) and he imagined that she would run in search of help. He had the vague understanding that his wife was running *from him,* though he still couldn't quite believe it. He hadn't wanted her to see him like this and it gave him some relief to feel so much shame. Because he *was* ashamed, but he'd also never been so afraid. It was this fear that had made him suddenly furious until he was fiddling with the matches in his pockets and thinking lucidly of burning the house to the ground before letting Doña Cuca have it.

Evidently the house—or so Doña Cuca had explained last night, while Antonio held the famous knife to Abraham's throat—was not going to cover what he owed. The jewels were his last chance. When he'd left town he had taken the box, but once he'd opened it (in the middle of the night, on top of a mesa) it became abundantly clear that he had underestimated his wife. She had anticipated his very worst behavior and for this she'd been rewarded.

He had planned on slipping inside the house quietly this

morning; he had planned on finding the jewels and leaving. What he hadn't counted on was that the doors would be bolted, or, even more pointedly, that anyone else would be there. It hadn't occurred to him that there was a baby—his?—that demanded attention or that he'd feel so sick at the sight of it and so goddamn weak he'd thought he would cry like a baby himself. Or that—for Christssakes—Theo's wife and maid would be there, too.

Here was one of his many problems: He never pictured all the elements.

When he'd met his wife, his initial impression was that she was simple, but he knew now just how deeply he was wrong about people. Eva, as it turned out, understood him very well. She had hid those jewels (when had he stopped checking on them?) and they could be anywhere: in Beatrice Spiegelman's own jewelry box, or even buried deep down in the red-brown earth of Bishop Lagrande's famous garden.

There had been an outpost in the Organ Mountains where no one knew his name. There were tents and girls, liquor and silver, and he'd stayed until a Polish merchant came through, until that Pole saw his face and called out *Shein!* and he'd known it was time to go. He'd imagined he still had one last chance to get out of his debts, but as he left his mare tied to a fencepost now and looked toward the house for what he knew was the last time, as he inched his way toward the plaza, sipping the last dregs of whiskey from a skin, as his pants chafed where his muscle and girth had once been, he couldn't put together just what that last chance might be.

He walked the periphery of the plaza. Every man looked familiar, had at least one gun and every gun had a bullet meant for him. This was a small town and he was marked; he'd be surprised if he lived long enough to find out the child's name. He found himself wondering if he might not be strung up to hang from the tallest tree along the *alameda,* where he had stood in years past, a free and arrogant man among free and arrogant men—cheering the vagrant's, the criminal's, the son-of-a-bitch's death along with everyone else. He looked up at the branches, at their sinister curves, and prayed for a bullet instead. When he'd gone into the mountains, he'd pictured working hard, mining silver, and finding a path toward gold, striking out to find real fortune. But there was nothing in these places but a path to the grave.

He had thought of Eva but never for long. He was presumptuous enough to assume that he had ruined her life. Although sometimes he allowed himself the small luxury of thinking that it was she who was bad luck. That she'd married him only to flee some kind of curse and it was this curse that had pursued her clear across the sea, ultimately settling on him.

Women selling corn and berries set their wares on the reddish ground. Abraham glimpsed how they briefly recoiled at the sight of him and he was faced with the fact that he looked exactly that bad; even poor, dark women desperate to sell now shrank from him instinctively. It didn't stop them, however, from calling out to him with their highest prices. Their voices reminded him that this was America and so, early in the day, the possibilities here were wide-open; poor women could highball a desperate foul-smelling man. A brother—any brother—could ask for help.

THE STORE WAS RUNNING SMOOTHLY. LEVI EHRENBERG WAS BARKING orders out front to a team of workers, and Abraham ignored him, progressing quickly inside. A few new items—Oriental rug, carved rosewood bed—immediately caught his eye, and it irritated him that he should notice, that he should be capable of coveting anything other than life itself. As he worked his way toward the storeroom, the workers busied themselves to a suspicious degree; not one of them so much as nodded a greeting or even looked up when he knocked over a stack of crates. When no one stepped forward to offer help, he rearranged the crates, scrambling like the most doomed of stock boys.

"What happened?" called Meyer to his workers, from behind the storeroom door. Abraham was surprised that he hadn't come running in a frenzy, but when Abraham made his way into the back office and saw his brother, he immediately understood why.

Meyer's head was bandaged and both of his eyes were bruised. His nose was so swollen that he was nearly difficult to recognize; there were cuts healing on his cheek and his brow, and his arm was in a muslin sling. "Good Lord," whispered Abraham, "I'll kill whoever did this."

"Please," he said, "save your heroics for somebody else." He turned stiffly toward a stack of papers and began counting under his breath.

"When did this happen?" Abe, ready to strategize, ready to help, pulled over a chair beside him. "Because—"

"Do not think of sitting down, Abraham."

"Oh," he said, taken off guard. "Of course." He stood silently in the shadows of the room for what seemed like minutes as he felt a mounting need to take a piss, but he couldn't excuse himself, not just then, not when Meyer continued to count as if he were counting out the hours left on his brother's life, and as if such counting were simply another chore, another task to perform before locking these doors and going home to his family at sundown. "Who did this?" Abraham couldn't help but repeat.

Hunched over his desk, without turning to face his brother, Meyer finally spoke: "To ask me this question—" Meyer cut himself off, before lowering his voice. "Are you really this stupid, Abraham? Because I didn't think so. I *don't* think so. I don't think stupidity drives you. At this point I can only wish this were the case."

"I only want—"

"Doña Cuca," he said throatily. "Do you remember how I told you not to go there, not to see her, that very first night you were in town?"

"Meyer, I—"

"You fucking idiot!" he exploded, with unprecedented venom, with spit forming in the corners of his swollen mouth; he winced at what had to be chronic pain. "Who else do you think would do this? They seemed to think I could give them your share of the business. *But you have no share of the business.* Do you understand?"

Abraham nodded, but he couldn't let it go. "If you only gave me—"

"Gave you *what*?" he spat. "Time? Money? Faith? I gave you everything."

"I wasn't charity," he couldn't help saying.

"Not always, no."

"I built this business with you."

"Abraham"—his brother looked at him until Abe was forced to see the extent of his injuries, the fact that there was blood in the whites of one eye, that he might never recover his health—"that is simply not true." He started coughing then, wet storms of coughing, so violent a sound that Abe found it difficult to remain in the room. But he did stay; of course he stayed, until nothing was left of the cacophony besides a terrible wheezing. A clock ticked itself into the next terrible hour. A skinny cat slinked around the room, pacing back and forth. "I paid Cuca for you."

"You did *what?*"

"I paid about half of your debts."

And all he could do, all Abraham Shein could do, was shake his head, as if this action in itself might stop it all, stop everything he'd done since he'd brought Eva Shein to America, stop what he knew would be his own tears falling onto his dirty, unbloodied face while Meyer continued speaking.

"And you are dead to me now. Do you understand? I do not ever want to see you again."

"I—" Abraham started, but Meyer stopped him with a flick of his hand. After the room grew warmer, after more voices could be heard in the front of the store as a counterpoint to their silence, Abe began to walk away.

"Abraham," Meyer said softly, and Abe nearly kept walking; it was preferable to having to face him again. But he stopped and turned and Meyer threw him a one-hundred-dollar note.

He kneeled on the floor to pick it up, and, as if his back had seized and he was forced to stay in that position, he stayed there a moment. "Why are you at work in this condition?" he found himself asking, almost in passing, as if now that it was all over, they might just talk as friends.

"I cannot stand to have my family see me. My children are afraid of me. My wife, she does nothing but cry." He lit, with much difficulty, a thin cigar. "I cannot bear to see that woman cry."

Abe stood up and brushed off his filthy trousers. "It will heal," he said. "It will." Because it would, it would, it had to.

Meyer blew smoke away from both of them; even now, even as he looked like death, his brother was still careful. "Of course it will."

"I am—*please Meyer*—I am wretched—"

"Goodbye," Meyer said softly. And then, louder: "Sell your house."

Abraham Shein imagined that he was already outside, beyond these thick, dark walls. He could picture the sun shining over low-lying clouds, over *piñon* trees, the plaza, and the still-unchanged cathedral, and he understood that he was more familiar with this sight than with the stony street where he was born, where his earliest memories were colored by the piano—such useless, lofty music—waltzing and ponderous and now stuck in his head, as if his mother's preludes and nocturnes were haunting him back through the years, back and back and long before his brother said, *Sell your house,* and he answered: "I already did."

JEWELS

MILK RAN DOWN HER BLOUSE AS HENRIETTE CRIED AND cried, having rejected Eva's breast again and again, yet still obviously twisting with hunger. Eva walked as quickly as possible from inside the walls of the convent, trembling. When she'd fled her home with Abraham still inside it, she had looked back only once. There was the house, the home she had so desperately wanted, and suddenly it had looked like a toy house, built for no more than children's play, a gift which would ultimately be packed away if it wasn't first violently destroyed. As she walked away from the convent now, where she had spent the past hour visiting the charity girls, acting as if she had nothing else in mind besides introducing her baby and doing a bit of good, she turned around again and again, but all she saw were ordinary homes, dogs lying belly-up in the sunlight, and—as she came closer to the plaza—wagons of goods heading out on the trail, out toward neighboring pueblos.

Here was business. Despite life's wild exterior here—its remoteness, its lawlessness—here was a sturdy and hard-won routine; how had she ever believed that Abraham could remain a part of it? He was a gambler and he would keep on gambling with both of their lives until there was nothing left of either of them besides their rumored beginnings. A wagon blocked the Shein Brothers' store and she clutched Henriette as she wove her way forward through the flies and burros and oxen, terrified of seeing those two wretched men, moving too quickly to be afraid of anything but stopping, and there in the doorway, calling out in stilted Spanish, supervising the crates being loaded onto wagons, was not Meyer, as she had expected, but Levi Ehrenberg.

She stopped suddenly and realized that because of where she was standing, if she didn't take another step, he wouldn't be able to see her. She allowed herself the sight of him and was silenced by the way he moved; she had never really seen him move before. And she found that not only was she silenced but that Henriette was as well. They breathed together, Eva and her daughter, taking in the scent of animals and men at work, taking in the view. He of course still had a limp, and he seemed to compensate by gesturing wildly with his hands. He was a hard worker, she knew, but it was still somehow surprising. She found herself moving forward without having made the decision to do so, but still he didn't see her. He didn't see her until she was right there in front of him and Henriette let out a cry.

They stood in the shade between the sweating animals and the overheated store, between the workers hurrying back and forth, shouting in German and Spanish. She wondered how her daughter, not three months old, could weigh so heavily on her arms.

"Mrs. Shein," he said, and if she didn't notice his ears turn red, she wouldn't have known he was surprised. "I see you've had a healthy baby. You must be very happy."

"Happy," she said. "Oh yes."

"Is it a girl, then?"

She nodded excessively. "I am impressed that you can tell. When they're this young it's almost impossible."

"I must confess that I'd heard."

"Did you?" The idea that anyone knew she was still here in town, let alone about her baby girl—it struck her as somehow amazing. She had felt so invisible, as if she'd been buried alive after all.

"And what do you call her?"

Nine o'clock in the morning, and the heat of the day was already creeping up her aching spine and onto her baby's fair skin. Nine o'clock, and her husband had returned as a hunted, angry animal, the most dangerous kind, and still, Eva Shein found herself unable to convey a true sense of panic. She wondered if it was in fact this perverse calm that, despite everything, had thus far enabled her to survive.

She pictured stepping off a steamship in Bremen and falling into her parents' arms. She could feel Mother's pliant skin, Father's worsted wool; she could see their measured strides as they guided her toward the carriage. They would tuck her into an unchanged feather bed. Days of familiar meals and new conversation would ease the past, the pain.

That is not how it would go.

There was nothing for her there besides a small, sharp gravestone, her own craven silence between broken smiles. Years of waking and knowing that nothing about her sister's life and death could ever be forgotten.

"I was about to do a foolish thing," she heard herself say aloud.

"Is that right?"

"Do you know what I was just about to do?"

He shook his head—ignoring, for a moment, the workers' slowed pace.

"I was about to take myself to the post and send word to my family that I would like to come home. I was thinking of asking them to help me. Isn't that foolish?"

He said only, "But this is your home."

She shook her head and it was as if, with that single movement, a lock had turned inside of her. "It can't be." Tears fell quietly, landing on Henriette's wispy hair.

"I see," he said, and then he gasped, as if he'd nearly forgotten something. It seemed such a foreign sound for him, so skittish and alarmed. "I have something," he said. "A crate arrived for you."

"A crate? But—when?"

"I apologize—it seemed too important to send with someone to the house, and I just—I couldn't bring it myself yet, you see I—"

"Please," she said almost sternly, "I understand why you haven't come yourself."

"It's from home," he said, "the postmark," as if admitting a quiet truth: that home would never be here after all. He waved her closer to the store, but she would not go inside. "Wait here," he said, and she stood under the awning, in a square of shade. "I'll be quick."

She hadn't stopped looking out for those two men, but even if she didn't see those particular men, it seemed that every face on the street was a veiled threat. She hummed to Henriette until Levi returned with a small crate in addition to a letter bearing Alfred's familiar and careful penmanship. She tucked the letter into the waistband as he pushed the crate up against the adobe bricks of the building. They both looked at it for a moment as if they were waiting for it to speak.

"Thank you," she said.

He blurted: "You aren't going to open it? But how can you resist opening the letter at the very least? I would tear open anything I received from abroad."

"You would do no such thing," she said, trying not to sound as terrified as she felt, because she suspected what was wrapped so carefully, what had traversed the mighty sea and land and had finally arrived for her. She knew that if she so much as opened the letter, she might sink into the ground and never leave this square of shade. And more than anything, even more than wanting to pry open the crate, to pull the wooden planks aside—what she wanted, what she needed, was to move. "There isn't time," she said.

"Are you actually leaving?"

For a moment she thought he might draw her close, and she nodded as if to give him permission.

"Well," he said, "I don't think you should."

She knew at once that he did not mean it and that—though he did look pained and she could feel him leaning into her, just a shade away from touch—something had significantly changed.

"Please," she said, "please. We're not in a sickroom anymore."

"No," he said, "we're not. You're right."

"We must say only what we mean."

"That," he said, "I'm afraid I cannot do."

A cloud shifted and the sun was suddenly in her eyes; she shaded her face and retreated from it and further toward him, until she could breathe in the very sweat from his neck, the early morning coffee on his breath. "Who is your betrothed?" she whispered.

Like the moment when she'd given him the berries, she saw he was genuinely surprised. "Who told you?" he asked.

"Nobody told me anything." And she was happy this was the truth. She realized she would not have wanted to know. "I can tell," she admitted. "I can see you've changed. You see," she began, and—even though they were close enough to touch—she had to look away, "I don't think you know how well I understand you."

"Yes," he said. "I do."

He bit his lip and she wanted to reach out and place her shaking fingers on either side of his face. "Please just tell me."

"Sarah," he said. "Her name is Sarah."

"Not Julie?"

Levi looked at her as if remembering, for one brief moment, exactly how far he had come. And then he shook his head with a look she had never seen on his remarkable face, an expression between bashfulness and pride. "She is coming from Las Cruces and, before that, Frankfurt."

"You are engaged?"

He nodded, and she swallowed, tasting the dust in the air. *Do you love her?* she asked, but only with her eyes. She knew he couldn't answer even if he'd heard. It was an impossible question if only because, in all likelihood, this was an arranged marriage and he probably didn't know. *Come with me,* she wanted to say. *I want you to.*

She let herself stare openly, both because she could not look away and because she was, frankly, desperate. She inched closer to her crate, touched it, just barely, with the tip of her boot. He returned her look but just barely. He cleared his throat before glancing around, determined

that no one should see them standing so close together. She gave Henriette a tiny squeeze. "So," she said softly, "you have found a German
bride." She knew that he was a man of his word and he'd given that word
to a girl named Sarah. He wouldn't be coming with her, and it was only
then, when she understood that this engagement was absolute, that she
could admit to herself just how much she wished he would. And, much
in the way that she knew that he was yet another person she would never
see again, she realized that if she looked at him long enough, he would
somehow understand the urgency of her situation.

A full minute seemed to pass before he finally asked, "Have you spoken to Meyer?" She saw then that he had heard all the rumors about
Abraham and now he knew they were true.

She shook her head. "I can't," she said. "As I stand here, as I'm talking
to you, I realize that I can't."

"Your husband left here not an hour ago. They had words. Meyer
hasn't come out of his office since then; the last thing he needed was any
further disturbance. He has just returned from a doctor in Las Cruces."

"You speak as if he is ill."

Levi Ehrenberg shook his head for a moment, as a hostile smile played
on his lips. "Didn't you know? They beat him. The men your husband
owes." When he registered Eva's obvious confusion, he looked around
before placing his hand on her back, ushering her quickly inside. "Where
does he think you are now?" he asked. "Your husband?"

"I don't know," Eva said, suddenly flustered, her eyes on her crate just
outside the door. "I don't know."

"Where does he think you are?" he repeated, and her heart beat bru-
tally. She was actually going to do this. She was doing it.

"I'm afraid I need your help," she said. And then she told him everything.

He didn't ask if she thought she might reconsider. He didn't question
her at all. He went outside for a good long while and when he came back
he looked regretful. "Come," he said. "Let's be quick."

He picked up her crate and carefully loaded it onto a freight wagon, without asking her a single question. He pointed to a broad-faced Mexican who was sitting still in the driver's seat, loosely holding the reins. "Feliz will get you as far as Mesilla. You'll join a coach west from there." He reached into his coat and produced a piece of torn paper scribbled with a name and address. "This family," he said, pointing to the paper. "I've heard they are generous, that they employ fellow countrymen. They own a large store." She realized that he had been waiting for this moment, for a time when she might come to him asking for his help; he had, in fact, prepared. "They say San Francisco is beautiful," he said. And then he placed the paper in her palm; he did not let go of her hand. "You'll live in a city by the sea." He looked apologetic for a moment, shaking his head, as if he knew better than to ignore the harsher realities with someone as astute as she. "That is," he admitted, "if you can bear the journey that long." He let her hand go and asked if she had money, as if he was afraid to find out.

She looked around, and, out of necessity, handed Levi Ehrenberg her daughter. He took her in his arms with extreme caution; it was clear he had never held a baby. And between the wagon and the storeroom, which, for the moment, was empty of workers, she lifted up her heavy skirt, which she had not taken off for weeks because she'd feared needing to do what she was doing right now—escaping with nothing but the clothes on her body. She had hoped Abraham would return a new and better man, but she had also stitched the dark fabric carefully with jewels, her jewels, her only chance at freedom.

"Eva," he said, and she heard him say her name for the very first time. It was difficult to guess which he found more shocking—the fact of the jewels or the fact that she was lifting her skirts for him in the open air, that nothing stood between him and her flesh besides a worn-thin, yellow petticoat.

"I need to make a sale," she said, letting the fabric fall.

"No," he said heatedly. "No." He took Eva's shoulders in his hands; he even let his hands travel down the length of her arms, as if she was cold and he was warming her. But then he looked down at Henriette, lodged between them, a keen reminder of where Eva Shein ended and Levi Ehrenberg began. "Don't give them up so easily."

"I would hardly call this easy."

He handed her an envelope thick with cash.

"I can't," she said, but she didn't mean it. She reached out for the money and his hand and for one precise moment she had both.

ABRAHAM'S AMERICA

AS HE'D LEFT HIS BROTHER SITTING IN THE DARK STORE-room that morning, he'd shoved the one-hundred-dollar note deep into his pocket, taking care not to rip it. Had he made it back to the house that morning, he surely would have packed up his wife and his child (of course it was his child) and made for the bishop's land. He would have pleaded with Bishop Lagrande to help them leave this town, and he was thinking of this when he rounded a corner and Cuca's men blocked his path. He was thinking of this when, after they took him down by the dun-colored river, after they threw him to the ground and he swallowed dirt and sour blood, after one man kicked him three times in the gut, the other put a gun to his head. "Here," Abraham said, digging out the bill that Meyer had thrown at his feet. "Take this. And . . . there's more."

The man with the gun laughed out loud. "We have waited for you. We did not throw your wife and child out into the street. Are you grateful?"

He nodded; he swallowed a small, sharp stone.

"Why not say it then?"

"I am grateful," he said. He looked up the hill and could swear he saw Doña Cuca's carriage with her damning silhouette inside. Beyond the carriage was the sky. He knew that in moments the sun would start beaming its brightest lights, and he would have no need to shield his face. He closed his bloodshot eyes, felt the cool metal gun like certainty itself, pushing gently into his skull. He pictured Eva and he pictured his child, who he only now realized was a little girl, a girl who looked strikingly like his mother who was thankfully no longer alive to receive this kind of news. "I am grateful."

WEST

THERE WERE NINE PASSENGERS IN THE STAGECOACH
from Apache Pass. They'd all managed to eat the by-now-
expected station grub of bacon, beans, potatoes, hardtack,
and coffee, and were set to head off once more into the dry
heat. Outside it was springtime, but inside the coach, with
eight other warm bodies (plus Henriette), it was summer.
Since she'd come on board in Mesilla (with her name re-
stored to Eva Frank—who knew how far Abraham's debts
ran?), this coach had stopped at a number of stations, ex-
changing old faces for new ones, and usually, as the stage
left the station, she was too tired and uncomfortable to feel
much more than the immediate and frustrated desires for
sleep and clean air, but this time she had an onset of panic
and guilt as the carriage jolted from side to side in its efforts
to move forward. She was also tempted (as she was during
countless times in the day) to open the letter and the crate.

Every now and then, their existence introduced the kind
of silvery thrill she had thought these past months would
have surely put an end to. Unopened, unexamined, the content went unproven, and in this secreted state could continue to exude sheer promise. The crate was a plain-clothes
deity, capable of transmogrification: Inside could be bottles

of French champagne; a valise full of money; detailed, concerned in-structions from Abraham; or perhaps a novel-length missive from Hein-rich the painter, evoking a revision of the past. And, furthermore, none of these options was as sad and amazing as what she knew, with fair cer-tainty, to be the truth.

She pictured tearing open the crate while she heard the foot stomping of boisterous young men up above. She held Henriette tightly and strug-gled to see out the small windows as if, like some other passengers, she too had someone waving on the ground in one last frantic goodbye.

While she was more than grateful to Levi Ehrenberg and to Feliz the freight-wagon driver, to the freight-wagon burros as well as her daughter who hardly ever screamed, she also chided herself for such a rushed and ill-conceived escape. She had left her husband; she had taken their child. She had nothing more than this letter and crate, the clothes on her body, and the jewels she had sewn as snugly as she could, soon after Henriette was born. What had Abraham done when he'd discovered not only the jewels but also she and Henriette were missing? This she had tried to imagine since leaving town hidden in the covered freight wagon, and what she kept coming up with was this: He would be far too busy trying to save his own life to care what had happened to theirs. Most likely—and it gave her no relief to think it—the loss of the jewels would far outshine the loss of a wife and child.

Her breath was heavy and scant in her chest as it always was when she was battling the poisonous cocktail of competing anger and fear, un-til she imagined Levi Ehrenberg standing with the other well-wishers at the depot, his weight resting on his good leg, his crumpled hat in his hand. She pictured how he'd smile briefly while offering a wave, how he'd squint with the evening sun in his eyes, never taking his gaze from the stagecoach or shielding his forehead with his hands. As the wheels gathered momentum, she could see him walking, following alongside them, and if he could have run she was sure he would have run; he would have run until there was nothing left of the coach in the distance, not even a ghostly after-image. She could see him. He stopped and stared into the distance and kicked at nothing but reddish dirt, and at the hopelessness of this sight (in addition to the fact that she knew it was, after all, imagined), she began to cry; no dignified set of tears but a heaving, weeping mess. Henriette watched her with those curious, candy-black eyes, eyes that seemed unafraid of her mother's unhappiness, which, in fact, as her mother cried, looked positively delighted. But even this did not stop Eva from crying, and she only managed to stop when she saw that the black woman was watching her.

Eva had seen her come on at this station stop (alone—which Eva couldn't help but think was a bad sign) and the sight of the black woman reminded her to be constantly alert instead of consumed with a flimsy fantasy. "Excuse me," Eva stuttered, and without much thought, wiped her eyes on the faded sleeve of what she still thought of as her sister's blouse.

The new face looked back blankly—this young dark woman, the first she'd ever spoken to. She had seen Negroes before—just a few—in New York and Kansas City, but she'd never heard one speak, and though she was downright afraid, she thought it was important to pretend otherwise.

The black woman said nothing, but Eva didn't like being the object of her gaze. Leaning against the hard leather curtain, she was very conscious of being watched but as Henriette fell asleep in her arms, Eva— despite her best efforts—felt her eyes closing.

She woke in a panic with her arms not weighted but flailing and she nearly screamed when she heard a loud "Shhh."

There was the black woman, rocking her daughter. She had taken Henriette.

"How dare you?" cried Eva.

The black woman put her finger to her mouth, shushing Eva again, and then she came closer on the bench. "You fell asleep," she whispered unapologetically. Then she returned Henriette with what even Eva had to acknowledge was remarkable care. Her daughter stirred, seemingly perturbed to have left such a comfortable spot. The black woman sat back and gave Eva another appraising look.

"I wasn't asleep," Eva said.

"Shh."

In spite of herself, she adhered to the woman's instruction and took her voice to a whisper. "I wasn't asleep."

"Oh yes you were. You were dead asleep, too. I thought you were going to drop the poor creature."

"I was not asleep."

"Dear, you were snoring. You were dead asleep. You understand?"

Eva stubbornly shook her head and rocked Henriette, but her daughter was fussing now and Eva suddenly felt as if she were doing it all wrong. She glanced at the black woman who was fanning herself with a leaflet from the station. Eva felt as if she should be shocked by the chocolate hue of her skin, but it was as if, unexpectedly, there were no more shocks to be had. Maybe people were no longer capable of being all that strange, no matter what they looked like, because she was no longer able to be so removed. She supposed that her conception of herself was fading, just as she supposed a soul faded slowly from this world to the next. Being different, she now realized, was a luxury as well as a curse, and though she could tell herself that plenty distinguished her from any other poor soul on this journey, she also knew she belonged exactly nowhere, and she increasingly submitted to the meaning of this as she allowed herself to be carried forward and forward and forward by the swaying rumps of horses.

"That was the first time she's been out of my arms in days," she explained, as Henriette continued to squirm. "I may have reacted excessively."

The black woman nodded. "You want me to take her for a while?"

It was hard to believe, even as she was doing it, but she handed Henriette back to the woman and all at once she felt a tremendous and weightless relief.

"There's a good baby," the woman cooed.

Eva breathed deeply into a nervous sigh. Her arms and shoulders were more cramped than she'd realized. "She *is* a good baby, isn't she?"

"Don't you seem surprised!"

"I am surprised," Eva said, reminding herself to breathe. "I'm surprised by nearly everything."

"Well I don't see how that's possible—a lady traveling with her baby alone. You must have some fine story." She shook her head, clucked her tongue. "Some *fine* story to be riding this coach right now." Eva couldn't tell if there was hostility in her voice or if it was simply her usual tone. The black woman kept her gaze on Henriette, bounced her gracefully on one of her knees while keeping Henriette's chin upright.

Eva wanted to thank her but she only wrapped her arms around herself, staring first at the strange sight of Henriette in this woman's plump arms, but then, for a moment, out at the horizon. They were never going to make it. The ubiquitous thought invaded completely almost every hour or so. But if it was impossible to imagine that she and her daughter would actually make it as far as San Francisco, more accessible was the notion of heading west. *West.* She said it to the ticket master and to anyone who asked. She said it so often in her head that it sounded meaningless.

"You must have seen aplenty already," the dark woman continued. "Lord knows I have. I must confess that I like it, traveling alone. Everything's too strange to be lonesome."

"I suppose," Eva conceded, although she would have said she was often lonesome, traveling or no.

"Where you coming from? What's that accent?"

"German," she said, "I am German." She decided against saying more. Where had she been coming from? Surely not Santa Fe, not when she'd left not only a husband (who might very well have set out looking for her) but a husband whose life was now measured by debt, a debt that his creditors would surely be happy to collect from anyone, if, after they'd squeezed the very life out of him, Abraham proved truly insolvent.

"Well, that's quite a ways, isn't it? Me, I'm coming from New Jersey. And believe me, that's plenty far."

Eva nodded politely, having never heard of it. "This is a Yankee place?"

The woman laughed again in that edgy way. "You tryin' to figure out if I was ever a slave? No, ma'am. My daddy's a minister." Henriette started whimpering, and with one sudden motion the woman flipped Eva's baby sideways.

"What are you doing?" Eva gasped.

The woman ignored her and shushed Henriette.

"Whatever are you doing? Please," Eva cried—crazed with how stupid she'd been to give her baby over to a stranger—"give her to me right now."

But Henriette had already stopped fussing and was now looking terribly pleased.

"Ma'am," she said, once again returning Henriette to Eva, "I am a nurse by trade. A nurse. You understand? You believe me?"

"I only—"

But she waved Eva off, made a click of her tongue.

"Is that why you're headed west?" Eva asked, irritated by how awkward she sounded. "For employment?"

She shrugged. "I have an uncle who's real sick and he's got an extra room. Says he'll help pay for more schooling." Her voice quieted as Henriette continued to smile, and the woman continued, almost as if speaking to Henriette alone. "My sister promises she'll send along my chemistry books as soon as I'm settled. I was in school in New York though. And I've seen an operation performed. The patient was a lady and her womb was injured and in two hours time, a piece of flesh was cut off and the injured parts were sewn up and I tell you I enjoyed it. Everything was so scientific, and you wouldn't think it, with all the blood and whatnot, but everything was so neat. I assisted the other nurses with holding her vagina open. The only problem was the smell of ether; it made me awfully sick. I'll have to get over that though, won't I?"

"That's astonishing," Eva said, not knowing to what exactly she was referring—to the fact that here was a woman (a black woman with over-plucked brows, full lips, and fuzzy, pinned-up hair) who was a nurse, who, as the stagecoach rocked its nauseating rhythms, and as mosquitoes buzzed steadily in and out of dust clouds, was seemingly unperturbed about much, or to the fact that this woman had just said *vagina*.

"It isn't really. What's astonishing is just how difficult it is to be independent." She looked out the dust-flooded window.

In that moment Eva saw her frustration and thought: *Nobody is ever satisfied.*

"I had a husband," the woman offered, as if she knew that Eva was wondering. "He died."

"I am sorry."

"No," she said, "you needn't be. I never want to get myself married again. And I don't want to be anyone's domestic. That's what makes it so difficult, you know, getting out on my own. I'm so tired of being dependent. Always worrying over how much food I'm eating, how big a helping of beans, how fat a piece of pie . . ."

"My husband died too," Eva found herself saying. She wouldn't let herself think of him dead though, couldn't bear the idea of Abraham cold and lifeless, without his ever-infuriating drive, however gravely misguided. Despite his terrible choices, the cheating and the lies, she could never wholly hate him, no matter how she tried.

"Is that right?"

It occurred to Eva that this woman might have assumed that little Henriette was fatherless, that Eva was unmarried, and she felt her face flush at the thought. "He was a wonderful man." And then, without thinking about it: "He was an artist."

"Well now that must have been something."

Eva told herself she was one of so many women traveling alone, that really she was nothing unusual. Here she was riding overland into yet another different world, but it was different mainly because she had no protector. She could be anyone; her daughter could be anyone's daughter. Out the window: red rocks like enormous edifices set against streaming skies. Out the window the vision was dramatic but building inside her was nothing but a whispering dread—a dust-coated, plummeting sensation, too persuasive to be considered a mere mood. The feeling was familiar, like the journey from the east five years ago, except now—though she was more alone than ever, still unquestionably running from something and getting farther from any life she had ever envisioned for herself—she knew she was strangely less afraid.

• • •

"MRS. PAULINE HARBER," THE WOMAN SAID THE NEXT DAY AFTER breakfast, touching a hand to her chest.

Eva nodded and introduced herself, embarrassed that they had waited so long to know each other's names.

"Mrs. Frank, do you think you'd mind looking after my bag? Those ruffians up top, they"—and here she interrupted herself—"if they come inside . . . I . . . I'd just like to take a little rest."

"They're just boys," Eva said, dismissively. She was so used to young American men now; there were so many of them and so little of anyone else.

"They're white boys," Pauline said, with sudden meaning. "And bored out of their skulls like the rest of us. And like I said, you seem like a real lady, a lovely one, but I'm sure you know all too well what some white folks have to say about someone like me."

"I—" said Eva dumbly. "Of course I'll mind your bag." What else could she possibly say? Something else, surely. Something kind and noble and good. Beatrice Spiegelman, she imagined, would have engaged this Pauline on the topic of oppression and injustice, perhaps leading into the controversial topic of the Red Man's better qualities. All Eva came up with was: "Go on and close your eyes," and, quite happily, that is what Pauline did, as Henriette stared at the greenish light coming in through the windows.

She wasn't sure how much time had passed before both Pauline and Henriette were asleep, but all she knew was that she couldn't imagine ever sleeping again. She shifted Henriette gently and reached for the letter and Levi Ehrenberg's piece of paper, both tucked into her waistband. She looked at them the way she might any kind of treasures: as surrogates for those she loved, and she realized she'd memorized not only the name and address on Levi's paper but the exact amber color of the ink, the smudge of dirt in the upper, left-hand corner. She tried to picture this family and wondered if Levi Ehrenberg had carried a similar piece of paper on his own overland journey from the east, paper scribbled with the Shein name. She closed her eyes and tried to imagine what a store in San Francisco might look like. As often as she reminded herself to check her expectations, she saw rows of gloves, strings of pearls, soft-spoken Germans behind a counter. And in the family home: evenings around a lively table, a perfectly tuned piano, a comfortable guestroom where she and Henriette would be invited to stay.

But then she pictured Schwefel the bird flying out of his cage and out of the house, into the clear blue distance. She wondered who would find her commonplace book and if anyone would even glance through its tender pages before using them to feed a fire.

DEAR ALFRED, SHE COMPOSED IN A LETTER IN HER HEAD AS THE days went by. *I am writing to let you know that Santa Fe is no longer my home. Abraham Shein is no longer my husband. I have a baby girl and we are headed west. She is a good girl, Alfred, and I have named her Henriette. We are bound for San Francisco.*

A fellow traveler told me that a cottonwood tree grows along the banks of the Mississippi River, and when the river swells with spring rains, it sometimes carries away part of its riverbank and a tall tree falls into its current. The spirit of this tree can be heard crying and crying as its roots cling to the soil and its trunk floats on the water. I feel like that floating trunk, Uncle Alfred, those clinging roots—nothing but a watery and divided ghost.

She would not include in this letter how that same traveler (a young engineer from Hannibal, Missouri, who had grown tired of riding overhead) had later announced, after a good deal of whiskey, that he "wouldn't sit next to no nigger lady," and how his formerly sensitive voice turned hard and mean, especially after Eva had responded without hesitation that perhaps he should return to riding up top, that Pauline was her dear friend. She fiddled with a shard of glass she'd found at the last depot, watching her face appear and disappear, both compelled and repelled by her reflection: . . . *Uncle Alfred, I wonder if you would recognize me. I am freckled, yes, and I am both thinner and fuller on account of my recent pregnancy, but there is something else that I wonder if you'd see, something subtle and dark, like a patch of earth after so many fires, ruined but also primed.*

Out the window the light grew molten as the heat wrapped its cloak around the day. Once in a while Eva heard the boots of those young men overhead, and she couldn't help but listen differently now, as she watched Nurse Pauline. They gave some whoops once in a while, but mostly it was horse hooves and squeaking leather straps and the driver's whip, silver-quick through mosquito-heavy air.

NIGHTS WERE DIFFERENT, AS MOST PASSENGERS WERE ALL CROWDED inside, pressed up against one another. Eva had never before traveled in such close quarters with strangers and was reminded only of the steamship from Bremen, when the weather turned and she had mistakenly joined the third-class passengers. One night the sky crackled with lightning and even the most boastful and reckless of young men had claimed a seat inside upon the upholstered leather cushions, which somehow felt harder than the benches themselves. The canvas curtains were pulled shut and as the passengers dozed off into sleep, strangers had leaned into strangers with their mouths agape or their chins pinned primly to their chests; winged ants and mosquitoes swarmed inside the stage; folks slapped each other with an aim toward murdering the dreaded bugs and soon there were no more strangers. Once, in the middle of the night, she saw the engineer from Missouri sound asleep, his head resting comfortably on Pauline.

Once a fight broke out between two men over something which neither Eva nor Pauline could understand. Henriette screamed—wailing and writhing until a man named Will with a down-turned mouth fashioned her a *rebozo* from a piece of burlap he'd been saving so that Henriette could stay snug against her mother's chest without having to be held. Then, with Eva's tense permission, he blew tobacco smoke into her daughter's ear until either the pain lessened or she had cried herself out, but either way it seemed no less than a miracle. It seemed impossible that they could ever make it through each night but morning came again and again like a faded sepia likeness of itself, exploding into whatever the new day uncovered.

Pauline rarely spoke when the "boys" were inside the coach, but one evening, as rain came down in torrents, Will listed other sworn remedies besides tobacco smoke for an earache: Sore throats could be cured by wrapping a dirty sock around the neck, the dirtier the sock the better; scraped buffalo horn in a drunk's whiskey bottle would cure him of the habit; dried chicken gizzard mixed with clean sand from a river would grind ulcers right off of any stomach; a cold door key dropped down a shirt without warning would stop a nose bleed immediately. Poor Pauline couldn't hold her tongue any longer and argued against all of them. She was so proud of science, so sure of its authority, and to her great shock (and to Eva's) Will was a sudden and patient listener, interested in her rebuttals. Awkward silence followed the surprisingly elevated discussion, and this silence led Eva to real sleep for the first time in days, while Henriette lay suspended, wrapped up tightly in her brand-new burlap sling.

When she awoke, coughing from the ever-present dust and steamy heat, Eva saw that it was not only dawn, but that they were at another station stop—as crumbly-adobe grim as the last one—with only a few empty corrals as potential places to rest. After eating a miserable bowl of half-cooked, over-spiced kidney beans, she entered one of these corrals and lay her daughter down atop a fairly fresh pile of hay. Then she placed her crate safely against one patchwork lumber wall before leaning back against the opposite one, not much minding the knotty wood kneading into her spine. After staring and staring at the unopened crate (one hinge had come a bit loose), she took Levi's torn piece of paper from her waistband and rubbed its edge like a magic lamp, while she placed Alfred's letter on her lap, lingering on his penmanship as if it were sacred text inscribed on an ancient shard. *Mrs. Abraham Shein.*

The very name had grown strange.

It was getting more difficult to imagine that those men would ever let Abraham live, and she dreaded hearing news of his death as much as she feared being chased and found. She imagined a foggy day in San Francisco—a faceless man approaching her, hat in hand, outside a synagogue or in a park—*Are you Mrs. Abraham Shein?*

But she couldn't picture a life beyond the station stops, beyond the terrible hardtack that tasted like bark, beyond the beans which sent her into a fit of cramps each time she risked a mouthful. She saw San Francisco in her dreams and she knew it was conjured from outdated issues of *Godey's* and *Harpers,* or from Beatrice, who'd relayed a secondhand tale or two about the city, as her cousins had traveled there when she was a young girl for a family member's wedding. Also, Pauline had read aloud letters from her uncle, which mentioned planked streets equipped to resist the iron shoes of city horses, the temperate climate invaded by foggy afternoons, and how the wind often brought showers of sand from dunes so close by. She envisioned a cartoon version of a vast metropolis— a circus of South Seas sailors, turbaned Arabs, Australian con men, and street foods hot off vendors' burners, tasting like nothing she knew. All of this in addition to fashion—she had gone so long without—the puffed-out bustles and swansdown boas, elaborate gigot sleeves. She knew enough to know that different worlds existed—worlds of French restaurants and theater, of Chinese laundries and Polish butchers, and yet she had trouble believing that she might some day find herself in the middle of any of them.

Dearest Eva.

"Uncle Alfred," she said out loud, as if he had come, right then, out of the sun and into the corral—as if he'd bent down and picked up a piece of hay and was running it elegantly between his fingers like a rolled cigarette—wondering what tone to strike, instead of having already struck it in the letter, the letter she now held in her hands—*Dearest Eva.*

She read on and felt her stomach cramping and twisting with such perversity she was immediately reminded of giving birth and her hand instinctively went to her daughter, as if for immediate assurance that her labor had not been for naught.

After reading the first two sentences, she let the letter—dated months ago—fall to the straw-covered ground.

At the time Alfred had written the letter, her father had passed away and her mother hadn't been expected to live out the week. *No,* was her first thought, followed by the realization that, despite Mother's elusive health and Father's stern despondence, there was a part of her that had believed absolutely that upon her leaving Germany, her parents would have another chance at life with each other, if only because they had lost so much. There had to have been some kind of fruitful result born from her retreat, and she'd imagined their reunion was it. That they might die this soon after she'd left them had not played a part in her imaginings. In fact, though it was unbelievably childish and she wouldn't have admitted it to anyone, it had not occurred to her in any significant way that her parents would *ever* die.

She sat upright, and—never taking her hand from Henriette's narrow belly—she vomited over the side of the stall every last frijole she had fought so hard to keep down. And only when she was all cleaned out and gagging on nothing but dusty air could she finally take her hand away from Henriette and let her baby sleep, let herself cry for her parents as she hadn't done since she was young and blameless and they alone could ease her fears.

She had no mirrors to cover and her sister's sleeves were already torn and had she a gun at that moment she'd have shot it off, if only to create disturbance. When her sister had died she had sewn and sewn, solely for the needle's comforting prick and sting. No one in these states or outlying territories knew her father's patience or her mother's arch smile and as distressing as this was, she wept because what stirred her the most— more than any of the lessons her parents had taught her—was the single image of her father's bald and shiny head.

She picked up the letter and read on.

Alfred intended to move his family back to Germany and continue Father's business, to travel all over Europe and enjoy the social aspects of the banking trade rather differently than Father ever had, using business dinners as opportunities to further his politics, even if it meant losing a client or two along the way. As far as Eva could gather, he was oddly cheered by these potential financial losses; they seemed to give him solace in the face of so much death and to signify, at least to him, that he would not be changing too greatly.

She read of Bismarck's successful war, and how although the liberal publisher Sonnemann predicted that such unity would come at the all-too-dear price of lost freedom, Germany would, in fact, unite under one black and red and white flag, and be far better equipped to protect its Jews than France, Austria, or England. Assimilation, he declared, was a real prospect. Leave it to Alfred, she thought in a moment of fierce and unfamiliar irritation, to scribble on about his career and politics—no matter how important the policies!—in the very same letter that contained the news of her parents' deaths.

And there were endless paragraphs about Auguste, his elegant wife, how she liked nothing better than cheese and chocolate and yet she was as trim as her pretty daughter and rowdy son, how she spoke four languages fluently, how she baked a cake on Fridays. And how it had been her idea to return to Germany, how it was Auguste's firm belief that Alfred too dearly missed his country.

Uncle Alfred, she realized, was a man who—despite his obsessive and political tendencies—deeply loved family life.

Eva was jealous. She was jealous of his family. She was jealous that his children would grow up in the same lovely house where she had spent her childhood, while her own daughter was lucky, at such a tender age, to sleep on a pile of hay. She was jealous that they had all lived in Paris, that they had met Heinrich Heine, that they could return to Berlin and change their lives dramatically without in fact traveling very far. She was jealous that she had not married a man like Uncle Alfred.

But her jealousy gave way to a more expansive emotion at the close of the letter, for at the end of many pages (which she knew she'd reread until they were as familiar as the Sabbath prayers that, if she didn't recite for twenty years' time, she'd forever have at the ready) this is what Uncle Alfred had written:

Auguste and I have spoken about it at length and at the risk of insulting you with such an offer, we would like for you to come live with us. I do hope that you understand, dear Eva, that I put this offer to you with the best of intentions and wishes for your happiness. I have taken from our correspondence the perhaps misguided impression that, even though by now you— G-d willing—have a child to consider, you may not have entirely reconciled living out your life in America alongside your husband, and, though such an offer is at worst offensive and at best decidedly unorthodox, I have never

*been one for orthodoxy and I would like to offer you—and G-d willing your
blessed child—a passage home.*

*For now, I do hope the crate has reached you unscathed. Although Au-
guste promises that I am being terribly impractical, I have shipped these to
you just as soon as I could. I knew you would want to have them.*

And then, as if her uncle couldn't quite help himself, and (she
couldn't help thinking) as if he knew everything about Heinrich after all:
Father—bless his soul—never did have the most sophisticated taste.

Sitting in the corral, she let the scrappy wood dig into her back and
her skin—right through her sister's deeply threadbare shirt. She stopped
crying. She looked at the crate but did not touch it.

Wherever she slept—in a corral, upright in the coach, in the rare
shade of a tree—she woke to the sound of Henriette's hungry cries, even
when Henriette was sound asleep and emitting nothing more than
breath. Her daughter—her miracle—sucked diligently at her breast as
the days and nights blended together into one solid state of survival. She
thanked God that regardless of how little she ate and how poor the food's
quality was, her milk continued to come.

"Folks don't come this way to die." Will told her whenever she was fret-
ting. "They come to live. Mark my words: This baby will see California."

The problem with California was that she couldn't envision anything
besides a child's rendering in which everything was golden, everything
was rich, and if she knew anything she knew this: Those words applied
to jewels and food alone. And so she stayed current, starting small—
picturing merely this stagecoach from a hawk's vantage, going outside and
beyond her scope without going very far. There it was: a painted green
box rolling over the trail, slowly moving on. There it was, there they
were—she and this group of eight other souls she'd likely never see after
they disembarked. She hoped Pauline would find work as a nurse, just as
she hoped to walk with her on those difficult-to-picture San Francisco
streets, but even Eva knew that it was far more likely that Pauline would
be working as a domestic in two years' time, or opening the door for a
better brothel, smiling a bitter-pretty smile. It was impossible to specu-

late on her own frightening fate; she imagined herself in that same dreaded brothel but quickly banished the thought.

Or she could return to Berlin. She and Henriette could gaze at birch trees while walking in the Tiergarten—the very same Tiergarten that was frozen in her mind, as was the entire city, in an icy world where time had stopped entirely. And as the stagecoach traveled west at its colossally slow pace and the trail offered no new distractions, Eva thought of her pristine, frozen world as she held Alfred's letter. As she mouthed the word: *home.*

E D G E

A HALF HOUR OR FOUR HOURS MIGHT HAVE PASSED—
Eva hadn't any idea—but she realized she'd dozed off and
that for the first time, when she awoke to the sound of the
whistling wind and rain, to the dwindling twilight, she was
not only uncertain where she was, but for a moment she
thought she was on the trail with Abraham, that it was years
ago and she had yet to see a town called Santa Fe. "It's rain-
ing?" she wondered aloud. It was so dark inside the stage
she could barely make out anyone's faces; she didn't know
who was awake let alone who was inside. "Where are we?"

"Driver says it's a shortcut. Arroyo's certain to be dried up
this time of year so's it's worth goin' out of the way for." One
of two long-faced brothers relayed this information as if it
was his job. "Driver says we'll cross in no time."

"He's a right idiot," said the other brother. "That ain't no
rain out there," he said, insistent. "Y'all realize that, don-
cha?"

"Mother of God," someone whispered. "It sure is dark as
Egypt in here." The wagon came to an abrupt halt.

Pauline hummed a gospel, which she did when she was
nervous. Henriette pulled at Eva's loose hairs. When the

sound of flowing water was unmistakable, everyone, as if it were a con-
test, clamored to look outside, and it was immediately clear that the
driver was mistaken and the arroyo was anything but dry. "We'll make
camp here," Will said, and though of course there was at least one voice
of dissent—a sound argument that Indians could be near—within an
hour the driver unharnessed and fed the horses as the sunburnt young
men built a fire and Pauline spread blankets over the cool, hard ground.
Eva offered to make the coffee but Will said, "You kidding me? You can't
do anything but talk. I don't trust your coffee, no ma'am." And he refused
to let her do anything besides attend to Henriette. When Pauline found
a spot on the river hidden by sage brush, she and Eva stole sips from
medicinal whiskey they'd found hidden in the boot of the stagecoach before stealing away with Henriette, giggling as if they were a couple of
girls who never knew the meaning of sorrow. Eva hadn't washed since
well before leaving Santa Fe, and she took her turn first, carefully stepping out of her jewel-lined skirt and shedding her sister's shirt like one of
those molted snakes Abraham had pointed out on their journey years
ago. She was almost shocked to find she was flesh and blood and that
her own pale skin glowed brightly.

She waded, stiff and frightened, into the achingly cold river, but as she
lowered down into the glassy deep, as her toes gripped fiercely onto
nothing but mud, she heard Pauline singing to her daughter on shore,
and she felt as if she were drowning and flying all at once. She dunked
her sister's shirt in the river, making sure not to scrub it clean for fear
that it would disintegrate right there. But as she took such care she also
realized that the shirt would fall apart soon, there was no way to stop it,
no matter how careful she was. She was thinking about how she oughtn't
to have washed it, how she must be supremely careful not to wring it dry,
when she felt herself gradually loosen her grip and the fabric moved like
the Orient's most delicate silk, like strands of Henriette's hair. As she appreciated her sister's shirt more and more—a touch so soft it was
painful—she let it go, and away it slipped, slowly and as quietly as fishes
wriggling through reeds.

"If I don't get in that water soon"—she heard Pauline cry out—"you know I'm gonna lose my nerve." Pauline sang something to Henriette about a fat old man, about a dog.

"It's gone," Eva said, but she knew Pauline couldn't hear her.

Pauline hollered, "You come on now. You'll catch your death and who do you think is gonna end up takin' care?"

"Shein!" she cried out, although she wasn't sure why.

"What?"

"My name."

"I can't hear you right, but I know you're talking nonsense again. Get on out now!"

Henriette squealed, and she might have even been crying, but Eva wasn't worried. Who was going to collect Abraham's debts from her here? In such a barren place where a river wasn't even a river for much of the year and there were parts of wagon wheels and axles strewn about, skulls littering the trails like buffalo chips, fated to be as much a part of the landscape as sage bush and brier? How many people, she wondered, had ended their journey in this spot instead of farther west or east as they'd planned? How many bathed in this very place, only to die just a shade farther to the right or the left, their hair still wet from the river? As she realized she had handed over her sister's shirt—not only her prized possession but her *only shirt*—as if the river had asked for it in exchange for a chance at traveling safely, the water threw her off balance, but she gasped and caught herself on a group of rocks, caught her fast and jagged breath. Bent at the waist, holding on to slippery stone, she listened for her own breathing the way she might listen for the sound of a coyote in the distance or any of her daughter's new sounds.

"You comin' out now?" cried Pauline, maybe worried, maybe entertained, and Eva waited just a moment longer before she regained her balance and stepped out of the water.

After wrapping herself in a musty blanket, she was still breathing heavily. She took her daughter from Pauline. "My name is Eva Shein," she said, with no immediate explanation. "I was—I am married to a man named Abraham Shein. He isn't an artist. He's a debtor. He's a cheat."

And even though Pauline looked at her as if she was foolish and might have even temporarily lost her mind, she also didn't seem too bothered. Eva had an unwelcome flash of Abraham by candlelight, undoing the tiny buttons of her blouse, his gruff hands suddenly tender. "I used him first," Eva continued, unbidden. "I used him to escape and I wonder if he knew—no, I think he did know."

"Fine," Pauline said, before undressing down to her bloomers and removing a thin gold necklace with the smallest of small gold charms. "You think I got no secrets? We ain't got time for that kind of talk right now." She made a dismissive sound with her tongue. "Hold this," she said, and she put the chain around Eva's neck, making doubly sure it was fastened. "Mrs. Eva Shein, Mrs. Eva Frank, Mrs. Billy the Kid—I'm goin' in."

AS DARKNESS FELL, EVA'S ONE THIN SHIRT, HER DEAR SISTER'S shirt, did not lie carefully over the rocks, drying out in front of a fire that Will had built just for her and Pauline, but instead it was somewhere at the bottom of the raging arroyo. What a fool she was. After she'd thanked Will for the fire, he looked at Eva—with her wet hair, in Pauline's unflattering calico blouse—and waited a moment before saying: *Nobody wants ladies' disapproving glances ruinin' a good and liquored-up campfire.* Maybe it was because Pauline's blouse was many sizes too large, or maybe it was simply the unusually humid air but she was reminded of the one other time she wore another woman's clothing besides her sister's or her own. The dress that Heinrich had insisted she wear—the dress he'd claimed belonged to *his* sister—where was it now? How many had worn it since? The thoughts disappeared as quickly as they'd arrived, and her skin felt tight and clean as if the years had vanished, and after Will walked off toward the men's larger fire, bowlegged as any illustrated cowboy in the pages of *Harpers Illustrated,* Pauline divided up a portion of ham and slightly wormy crackers over a stone that seemed created for eating on, and while baby Henriette lay awake but content in the snug, burlap *rebozo,* Eva realized it was strange but for at least one moment—one sudden flash—she felt she'd never enjoyed herself quite so much. Not only Eva but the night sky, the world—they'd all been stripped like springtime beds of summerhouses—the summerhouses of her youth—overturned and beaten out into being if not brand-new then honestly revived.

A violin half-played and half-screeched by the men's raging campfire, as voices sang songs she had come to—if not enjoy—then at least recognize: "The Red, White, and Blue" and the strangely specific "Hang Jeff Davis in a Sour Apple Tree." At first it was difficult not to sing along—at least in her head—but then the voices tapered off into speech, and the sound rose and fell far enough away so that the drunken talk became a blanket of sound, a kind of cheerful bonhomie to cushion the fact that they were, in fact, a good day away from getting back on the trail.

But that was for tomorrow.

The ham was not too salty and the crackers not too wormy, and the women spoke of peaches and potatoes, currants and turnips, hens and black-tailed deer. Within minutes it became a kind of game—to name a potential ingredient found along the trail and compare the preparation. She felt certain that Pauline won each time, although Eva had come out ahead on the game hens, having not only tweaked her recipe for goose with blackberries but also told Pauline about the time she'd cooked the goose, how she'd worked so hard to make it her way, how she'd wanted so desperately to impress the bishop. And as she described these moments, these recent small struggles, she was surprised to find that Pauline was laughing. "It's funny," Pauline admitted, and Eva was certain she must have looked surprised. The humor in these humiliations hadn't ever crossed her mind. "Oh Lord," Pauline said, laughing still. "Sometimes I wonder how I'll have any strength left in me once we finally do arrive."

"I wonder if we will," Eva mused in a more earnest voice, as she lay her daughter gently down atop a pile of blankets, this fine night's accommodation.

"Oh we'll arrive," Pauline said, nodding.

Eva's fingers rose to her throat as if in response to all the reasons why they wouldn't, and she felt Pauline's thin, gold chain. "Oh," Eva said, unclasping it. "I almost forgot."

Pauline nodded, and for a moment Eva was surprised at how she didn't seem to want it back. Pauline ignored Eva's outstretched hand, and glanced down at Henriette before touching the top of her tiny head so slightly and with a touch so tender that Eva understood at once. "Oh Pauline."

"It belonged to my girl," she said simply. "Can you see the little charm? It's a pansy, I think. I always thought it was a pansy. That was her name. Pansy Elizabeth Harber. Do you see it?"

"I do," Eva said, with both blinding guilt and a crude, fierce urge to keep Henriette awake. "It's lovely," Eva said, shaking, as she leaned over and fastened the clasp easily behind her friend's long neck. She smelled the silty river, faint salt, and oil from the ham and crackers, along with something like eucalyptus. Eva noticed that Pauline had not washed her hair, and she found herself reaching out for it with a curious if cautious touch; it was springy and softer than she had expected. "There," she said, "there."

The stars: They were bright, close, and endless. The Big Dipper, Cassiopeia, Orion's Belt—it seemed difficult to believe they wouldn't all come tumbling down.

She finally noticed Pauline's uncompromising gaze land first on Eva's crate and then on neither the fire nor Henriette but on her, and Eva didn't even wait for the question.

The hinges were loose now, and it didn't take much to pry the crate open with the knife Pauline had used for the ham. Inside the crate there were so many layers of stiff, brown paper and her fingers didn't shake as she peeled them back. She heard Pauline say, "My my my," when she first glimpsed the gilded frame. It looked wildly out of place in this untamed landscape, and Eva was briefly embarrassed, as if she'd come to a party wearing too much rouge. She unwrapped both packages, ignoring a cut on her thumb from the paper's sharp edge. As the paper piled up beside the fire, it looked like a strange, important object in itself.

There they were. Not on a library wall, not lining a gallery of a warm and familiar home, but here, under Pauline's gaze, under a western sky, *the* western sky, with a moon that she could no longer distinguish from the one she'd always known. Here, by the light of a quietly raging fire, she let herself look. Their frames were thinner than she recalled, not quite as heavy or as elegant outside the context of her father's library. As she remembered, the palette was moody—foggy grays and cobalt blues—but she also identified not a button exactly but black and green and white paint that comprised a familiar circle. She saw not hair nor lips immediately, but chestnut butter, pink candy. Light and shadow, shadow and light; color like spices in a market stall. Nothing accumulated, not right away, certainly not into two whole girls. She needed a moment or two of seeing only paint to stave off pure recognition. But she looked at the portraits until she finally saw them. She noticed that the paint itself was thin, almost as if the painter had been trying to conserve his resources. They were the work of a romantic, slightly overwrought. They were not, by any stretch, great.

"Who is that?" asked Pauline, as casually as if she were asking the time of day.

Eva realized Pauline was pointing not to her sister's image but to her own.

Heinrich the painter had captured her exact likeness. Everyone had said so. And so it seemed that she had, after all, achieved what she'd set out to do when she left Bremen on a steamship, when she left Santa Fe only weeks ago, hiding under a blanket in a freight wagon with Levi Ehrenberg's money between her corset and beating heart.

She was unrecognizable.

Eva pointed to the other painting, to Henriette dressed smartly in blue, and—tasting the river in her mouth, in her throat, her chest, her lungs—she said proudly: "That's my sister."

"And the other?" asked Pauline stubbornly. "Who's she?"

"The other?" Eva asked, looking directly into her own dark-painted eyes. She had come all this way so that she'd never need to tell this story. There was certainly no reason to do so now.

"Yes," said Pauline, "the other," with a touch of impatience. "She also your sister?"

Two portraits of two sisters—her two bonny sisters—both alive and well in Berlin. Two sisters with husbands and children and gardens—blissfully ignorant of what two charming though unexceptional paintings could set into motion. Eva's two lucky sisters. And why not?

"No," Eva said, and once she said that one word, she knew the rest would follow. She knew she would start at the very beginning and that it would take some time. After tonight she would choose more carefully. After tonight she would choose which stories to tell and which would be forgotten.

The dresses she and Henriette had worn while sitting for the paintings, Heinrich's tins of paint, the cups used for drinking Father's strong coffee, Mother's linens, Alfred's shoes, the bottle of violet perfume, Abraham's cigars, and even Levi Ehrenberg's elegant handwriting—inked on a piece of paper placed carefully in her shoe—it would all be ground down to nothing but dust, and eventually even the dust would be gone. But something essential would always remain, and she would make sure of it. For although memory had always been such a tireless source of haunting, it was also some kind of paradise: the only place she understood and from which she could never be exiled.

Henriette was sleeping already; her head was thrown back like an opera diva hitting her highest note, and the warmth of the fire had softened her breathing. The air was dry, good for burning. They were somewhere in the Sonoran Desert, but this meant little to her. She didn't know where the Sonoran Desert was, and it didn't matter because wherever she was at any given moment was only a place on a map she knew she wouldn't study for years. She would look back on this journey as a necessary one, but she also knew she wouldn't describe it. She felt certain of this and, with the same odd certainty, she knew that should this stagecoach arrive at its hallowed destination,

California was where she would stay. Her daughter would be an American.

Thank you, she would write to Uncle Alfred, upon settling into their first—and likely terrible—San Francisco lodging, *you couldn't have any idea of how dearly I appreciate your offer.*

Eva lay down and Pauline did too. They were no longer looking at the paintings. "The other," she said, "is me."

ACKNOWLEDGMENTS

Profound gratitude to George Wallace for his enthusiastic storytelling and to his father, Tom Wallace, for thoughtful elaboration. Early thanks to Dan Smetanka for being my first and remarkable editor and for seeing the potential in this book, Elisabeth Dyssegard for her fine contributions, and to my fantastic agent and dear friend Elizabeth Sheinkman for every step of the way. Early help from Helen Schulman, Merrill Feitell, Halle Eaton, and Tanya Larkin was much appreciated. Thanks to Robert Ach for his generous assistance and his interest in this pocket of history. Thanks to Candy Schweder for her family memoirs, and Suzanne Weisman for her interest. In Santa Fe: the impressive Betty Mae Hartman, Thomas Jaehn at the History Archives, Amy Verheide at the Photo Archives, Cynthia Leespring for her tour and conversations, Marilyn McCray at La Posada, Nicholas Potter Books, Collected Works Bookstore, and to Catherine Levy, Walker Barnard, Alexandra Eldridge, and Peter Drake for making Santa Fe not only fascinating but welcoming. I'm grateful to my father, Stuart Hershon, for his appreciation of history and my mother, Judy Hershon, for introducing me to the American Jewish Historical Society and The Leo Baeck Institute, where I had the good fortune to meet Michael Simonson and Anke Kalkbrenner, whose expertise, humor, and patience were invaluable. John Voigtmann, *grazie,* you are the best kind of gambler. I am indebted to Ellen Umansky, Jenn Epstein, Caroline Wallace, Jen Albano, and Ondine Cohane for their imaginative contributions after reading drafts of this book so carefully, and to my gifted editor Susanna Porter. Thanks also to Jillian Quint, Patricia Nico-lescu, and everyone at Random House. Thanks to Clark Buckner for sending books about San Francisco and to every member of the expand-ing Hershon-Buckner-Smith-McConnell family, as well as Inez Ve-lasquez Guzman. Finally I want to thank my husband, Derek Buckner, for his inspired suggestions and more than I can possibly say.

A NOTE ON SOURCES

Although this is a work of fiction, I depended on information and de-rived inspiration from a variety of sources, most prominently: *The Pity of It All* by Amos Elon; *Land of Enchantment* by Marian Russell; *We Lived There Too* by Kenneth Libo and Irving Howe; *Pioneer Jews* by Harriet and Fred Rochlin; *At the End of the Santa Fe Trail* by Sister Blandina Segale; *Santa Fe, the Autobiography of a Western Town* by Oliver La Farge; *Lamy of Santa Fe* by Paul Horgan; *The Wind Leaves No Shadow* by Ruth Laughlin; *Rachel Calof's Story* edited by J. Sanford Rikoon; *Women of the West* by Cathy Luchetti in collaboration with Carol Olwell; *Covered Wagon Women, Diaries and Letters from the Western Trails, 1862–1865* edited and compiled by Kenneth L. Holmes; and finally *The Centuries of Santa Fe* by Paul Horgan, where I am grateful to have found my title. Thank you to all.

ABOUT THE AUTHOR

JOANNA HERSHON is the author of *Swimming* and *The Outside of August*. Her short fiction has appeared in *One Story* and *The Virginia Quarterly Review* and was shortlisted for the 2007 O. Henry Prize Stories. She teaches at Columbia University and lives in Brooklyn with her husband, the painter Derek Buckner, and their twin sons.

This book was set in Fairfield, the first typeface from the hand of the distinguished American artist and engraver Rudolph Ruzicka (1883–1978). Ruzicka was born in Bohemia and came to America in 1894. He set up his own shop, devoted to wood engraving and printing, in New York in 1913 after a varied career working as a wood engraver, in photoengraving and banknote printing plants, and as an art director and freelance artist. He designed and illustrated many books, and was the creator of a considerable list of individual prints—wood engravings, line engravings on copper, and aquatints.